AMBERLOUGH

A TOM DOHERTY ASSOCIATES BOOK · NEW YORK

LARA ELENA DONNELLY

AMBERLOUGH

WITHDRAWN

AMBERLOUGH

Copyright © 2017 by Lara Elena Donnelly

Designed by Greg Collins

Map by Rhys Davies

A Tor Book
Published by Tom Doherty Associates
175 Fifth Avenue
New York, NY 10010

www.tor-forge.com

Tor® is a registered trademark of Macmillan Publishing Group, LLC.

The Library of Congress Cataloging-in-Publication Data is available upon request.

ISBN 978-0-7653-8381-5 (hardcover)
ISBN 978-1-4668-9341-2 (e-book)

Our books may be purchased in bulk for promotional, educational, or business use. Please contact your local bookseller or the Macmillan Corporate and Premium Sales Department at 1-800-221-7945, extension 5442, or by e-mail at MacmillanSpecialMarkets@macmillan.com.

First Edition: February 2017

Printed in the United States of America

0 9 8 7 6 5 4 3 2 1

To my parents, who read to me.

ACKNOWLEDGMENTS

You wouldn't be holding this book in your hands if not for my editor, Diana M. Pho, and my agent Connor Goldsmith. They believed in *Amberlough* enough to turn it into something beautifully corporeal. Thanks, Max Gladstone, for being in the right hot tub at the right time to provide the right entree to the right editor. And thanks to Victo Ngai, for such a luscious cover.

I owe gratitude to a whole swarm of Sarahs (Sarah Brand, Sarah Mack, Sarah Gulick), along with Olivia Sailor, Ken Schneyer, and Kendra Leigh Speedling. They helped me mold the clay of this world and these characters into something coherent. My dad's reaction to my novel pitch told me the book was ready to shop around. My mom was the one who turned it into a novel at all.

Amberlough began its life as a short story, mercilessly but lovingly critiqued by wonderful alumni of the Alpha SF/F/H Workshop for Young Writers. That short story got me into Clarion and later became my first fiction sale. After some growing pains, my incomparable Clarion class helped me hone the novel. Thank you, Awkward Robots, for your time and insight and unconditional love.

Seth Dickinson and Rich Larson, whose novels I critiqued while writing this one, inspired me. Their intricate plots and sparkling prose made me fiercer with my own revisions, more demanding in my drafts. Sam J. Miller swooped in while I was just about sick of this book and led me astray to work on a wonderful collaboration, giving my brain some much-needed resting space. Leah Zander—literary and literal savior, actual angel, and fellow mischief-maker—saw me through some major life upheavals and the bitter tail end of copy editing. Brayton Joseph Phair provided me with Microsoft Word when I needed it most.

Gwenda Bond and Christopher Rowe sheltered me during a blizzard and gave me excellent advice about the publishing industry. Pat Donnelly and Marty Raff put me up in their strange and beautiful house while I wrote most of this book. The whole Raff-Donnelly-Von Roenn clan made a place for me at their table and made Louisville feel like home.

And my thanks to Sunshine Flagg, co-kween of the Pickle Palace, who fed and watered me with pasta and gin, and who made up some marvelously off-color jokes for Ari's act. She kicked me in the seat of the pants so hard I ended up in New York City, the magical land that spawned her.

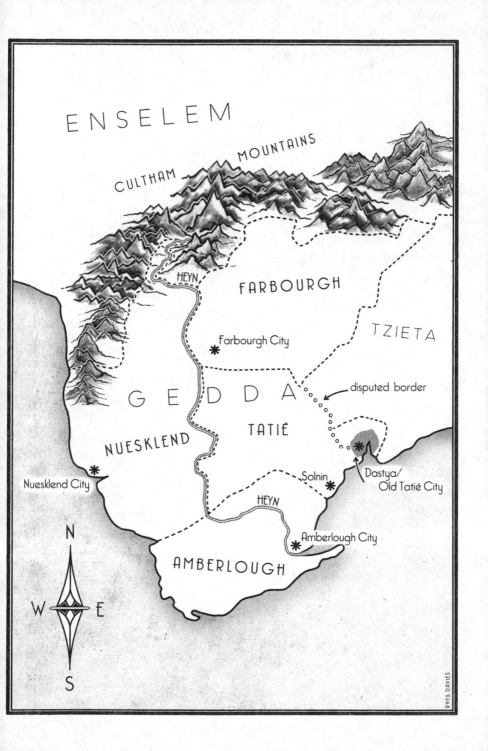

He wondered whether there was any love between human beings that did not rest upon some sort of self-delusion. . . .

—John Le Carré, *Tinker, Tailor, Soldier, Spy*

Does it really matter so long as you're having fun?

—Sally Bowles, *Cabaret*

PART

CHAPTER
ONE

At the beginning of the workweek, most of Amberlough's salary-folk crawled reluctantly from their bed—or someone else's—and let the trolleys tow them, hungover and half asleep, to the office. Amberlough City, eponymous capital of the larger state, was not home to many early risers.

In a second-story flat on the fashionable part of Baldwin Street—close enough to the river that the scent of money still perfumed the air, and close enough to the wharves for good street food and radical conversation—Cyril DePaul pulled himself from beneath a heavy duvet of moiré silk. The smell of coffee was strong outside his nest of blankets. An early spring storm freckled the bedroom windows with rain.

Though this was not his flat, Cyril slipped from bed and went directly to the washroom without hesitation. He ran a wet comb through his hair, brushed his teeth with cloying, violet-flavored toothpaste, and borrowed the dressing gown hanging on the bath rail. Despite Aristide's penchant for over-warming his rooms, the last of winter lingered in the tiled floor. Cyril left the cold mosaic of the washroom behind and gratefully took to the plush carpet running the length of the hallway. Its tasseled end debouched onto the parlor, where he met the maid balancing an empty tray.

"He's at the little table, Mr. DePaul," she said, without so much as a blush.

"Thank you, Ilse." She had charming dimples when she smiled.

At the far end of the parlor, where it joined with the dining room, the corridor belled outward into a breakfast nook bracketed by windows. An elegant, ochre-skinned man sat at his ease in one of the gilded chairs. Reading spectacles rested halfway down his dramatic nose—narrow at the top, wide at the base, deeply curved: as if a sculptor had put her thumb between his eyes and pulled firmly down. His thin lips were arranged in a pout practiced so often in the mirror it had become habitual.

He held the society pages of the Amberlough *Clarion* against one knee. The rest of the paper—all the crosswords done, and still damp from the storm—was scattered among a silver coffee service set out for two, and dainty plates of almond pastry. As Cyril sat down at the unattended coffee cup, Aristide snapped his paper and said, without looking up, "Finally. I was beginning to wonder if you'd d-d-died in your sleep."

"And miss the pleasure of your company at breakfast? Never." Cyril poured for himself, luxuriating in Aristide's affected stutter, and the soundless slip of coffee against the shining glaze of his cup. "Are you finished with the front page?"

"*Ages* ago."

Cyril reached for the paper and grimaced when the wet ink left streaks on his palm. "Been up long?" He asked the question casually, but over splotchy headlines he catalogued Aristide's appearance with strict attention: satin pyjamas under a quilted dressing gown, the same set he'd—almost—worn to bed. His tumble of dark curls had been swept casually over one shoulder, but they still showed traces of damp. A flush lingered across his cheeks. He'd left the flat already this morning, but changed back out of his clothes. Something illicit, then, and Cyril was not supposed to notice. Obediently, he ignored it, just as Aristide ignored his scrutiny, and his question.

"Eat." Aristide pushed one of the pastries across the table. "Or you'll be late to work. I shiver to imagine C-C-Culpepper in a fury. She's frightful enough as it is."

"Ari—"

"I know, I know. I'm not supposed to know." He reached two bony fingers into the breast pocket of his dressing gown and removed a slip of paper, folded in half. "And neither should she, right?" Without looking at Cyril, he handed over the cheque. "Discretion, as they say, is p-p-priceless."

Cyril made the payoff disappear up his sleeve. "You don't have to remind me." The money was a symbolic gesture, allowing for plausible deniability. "But I'm glad when you do." Ignoring the pastry, he drained his coffee cup and stood. "Clothes?"

"Ilse p-p-pressed them. They're hanging in the wardrobe."

Cyril dipped down to kiss Aristide on the top of his head. His hair smelled of rain, salt, and smoke. Somewhere on the wharves, then. Probably the southern end, near the Spits. Bad part of town— smugglers docked there, in the wee hours.

Aristide grabbed a fistful of Cyril's fox fur lapel and pulled, forcing him to bend deeper, until they were face-to-face. "Cyril," he purred, and there was menace behind it. "You haven't got the t-t-time."

"Ah," said Cyril, "but don't you wish I did?" He kissed Aristide again, on his pursed, displeased mouth. After half a moment's resistance, Ari gave in and smiled.

The rain was done by the time the Baldwin Street trolley stopped at Talbert Row. Cyril disembarked and joined a bedraggled wave of late commuters all headed for the same transfer.

Wedged at the front end of the trolley car, between the driver's partition and a dozing woman in a loud plaid suit, Cyril took the *Clarion* out from under his arm—he'd bought his own copy at the Heynsgate trolley stop—and propped it against his leg. The headliner was a story about a train station bombing in Totrajov, a disputed settlement on the border of Tatié.

Of the four nation-states in Gedda's loose federation, Tatié was the most fractious. The only state to maintain a standing army, it had been locked in a bitter territorial conflict with the neighboring republic of Tzieta for generations. Lucky for the rest of the country, federal funds and energy only went to mutually beneficial projects— infrastructure and foreign policy and, particularly relevant to Cyril, national security—so the decades-long skirmishing hadn't drained the national treasury, just nearly bankrupted an economically precarious Tatié.

By and large, Amberlinians ignored their eastern sibling except as the subject of satire, and an occasional creeping nervousness vis-à-vis Tatien firepower. Though it wasn't strictly good form, Amberlough's covert operatives kept a close eye on Tatié. The best of navies was no good against a landlocked, militarized state, and they weren't the most cordial of neighbors.

Tucked neatly under the gruesome account of the bombing was a smaller headline on the upcoming western election. Parliamentary elections were all offset by two years, and this year it was Nuesklend's turn. In the accompanying picture, outgoing primary representative Annike Staetler stood next to a young woman with marcelled hair and deep-set eyes. The caption read *Staetler endorses Secondary Kit Riedlions, South Gestraacht.* Below that, another picture, of a pale, flat-faced man in rimless spectacles, looking down from a podium swagged with bunting. *Caleb Acherby stands for the One State Party in Nuesklend.*

Poor Staetler. She'd been good to her constituents, and they would have had her for another eight years if she'd let the state assembly dissolve Nuesklend's term limits. Cyril hadn't been at the luncheon where Director Culpepper and Amberlough's primary parliamentary representative, Josiah Hebrides, went to work on her, but Culpepper had come back in a foul humor, filled with apocalyptic premonitions. Staetler was a staunch ally against encroaching Ospie influence in parliament. As long as regionalist Amberlough and Nuesklend stood against unionist Farbourgh and Tatié, things stayed at a deadlock. If Acherby took the primary's seat . . . well, he'd always been the brains behind the Ospie cause. He'd had to wait through two election cycles, unable to run for office outside his birth state. Now it was his turn, and he'd have a long to-do list.

He'd probably calm things down in the east, and feed the starving orphans in Farbourgh, but at a crippling cost to Gedda as a whole. Acherby's aim was unification: the loose federation into one tightly controlled entity. The manifold diversity of Gedda's people into one homogenous culture.

Sighing, Cyril opened the paper to the center and folded it back on itself, hiding Acherby's severe expression under layers of cheap newsprint.

He was deep in a conservative opinion piece in favor of further increasing domestic border tariffs—the same tariffs Aristide had been neatly avoiding in the small hours of the morning—when the trolley cables caught and the gripman bawled out "Station Way!"

Cyril disembarked to walk what was left of his commute. The gutters ran fast; bicyclists and motorcars splashed oily water across the footpath as they passed. Behind the marble edifice of the capitol, masts and smokestacks striped the sky above the harbor. Seabirds wheeled and shrieked, peppering the green copper dome of government with their droppings.

Amberlough's branch of the Federal Office of Central Intelligence Services hid on the top three floors of an unassuming office building, just across Station Way from the capitol's sloping gardens. Like everything in the FOCIS, the office had its own facetious nickname: the Foxhole.

"Morning, Mr. DePaul," said Foyles, from behind his racing form. Foyles had presided over the lobby as long as Cyril had been working in the Foxhole, and probably twice again as long as that. Deep wrinkles creased his face, and the tight spirals of his hair stood out in striking white against his slate-dark skin.

Cyril half-waved at him and stepped into the lift, standing back while the attendant shut the grate. He didn't need to tell her his floor.

The lift paused once, at three, where the clerks and auditors held court amidst the clamor of ringing lacquer telephones, heads bent over pencils and adding machines. Floors four and five were sleight of hand—espionage to ensure the security of the Federated States of Gedda—but three was where the true sorcery happened. The bursar's team made eye-popping embezzlements into minor calculating errors. Bribes and payoffs disappeared into endless columns of numbers and names. Agents were paid in secretive exchanges, the intricacies of which could escape even authorizing division heads. The accountants were, to a person, discreet, clean-cut, and scrupulously polite. They terrified the rest of Central.

The attendant scissored the lift grate open and stepped back for a new passenger. A young man in a shabby suit got on, ducking his head of bright copper hair. He smiled at Cyril without making eye contact. Against his chest, he held a sheaf of papers under a fat leather datebook, arms crossed tightly over it all like a shield. Cyril ticked through his mental files, checking names against faces, stories against facts.

Low-level auditor. Been in the office two years. Uncommonly straight, for an Amberlinian: He'd never tried his hand at extortion. Painfully fair, with a winning tendency to blush when embarrassed. Embarrassed very easily. What was his name, again? Lourdes. That was it. Finn Lourdes.

They'd only spoken once or twice—Finn had visited Cyril, just out of hospital, to express Central's sympathies, and deliver by hand a comfortable bonus and promise of promotion: Culpepper's blood money.

They ran into each other sometimes in the halls, now that Cyril was settled behind a desk. And anyway, Cyril wouldn't be working on the fifth floor if he didn't have a mind for details.

CHAPTER

TWO

Across town, near the train yards, a few thin rays of morning sun burned through the clouds and fell through an open window, warming the freckled arms of Cordelia Lehane.

She pushed her hands through Malcolm's hair. He normally kept it slicked back in a ducktail, but now it stuck up at all angles. Last night's pomade greased her already-sticky fingers. He turned his face, swarthy against her winter-pale skin, and his stubble rubbed her belly. Sunlight struck threads of gray at his temple. Cordelia traced one strand, her finger sliding through the sweat gathered at his hairline.

"You're the best thing that's happened to me in an age," he said.

She half-smiled and shoved his face away. "Go on," she said. "I ain't."

He pressed his face into the softness of her, between hip bone and navel. The pressure made her bladder ache, but she didn't tell him to stop. The pain mingled with the tingling comedown of sex.

"I'll prove it," he said, and pushed her thighs apart.

"Mal."

He didn't lift his head. She grabbed his hair and pulled his face up. "I'm dying for the toilet," she said. "Give me half a minute."

He laughed and let her go, rolling over onto his back to fill the space she'd left. "You're a treasure," he said.

"Even treasures gotta piss sometimes."

When she went to flush, the pipes groaned and shuddered. "Queen's sake. Ring round a plumber once in a while, why don't you?" She rinsed her hands in water that came out reddish brown with rust.

"Can't afford to. The washrooms at the theatre've got to be done over this month."

"Maybe you ought to move in there." She came back to bed and flung herself across the sheets. A breeze, fresh with high tide brine, rolled through the room. Cordelia shivered and moved into the warm curve of Malcolm's body.

"You don't take care of yourself," she said, but she didn't put much into it. Half a shake of the head, a rueful smile. "You'd sell your own ma if it'd bring in a bigger crowd."

Malcolm cuffed her gently on the side of the head. "My old man, maybe. But never Ma. She was—"

"The jewel of the peninsula, I know." She rested her face on the hard curve of his bicep, staring up at his seamed, stubbled face. "The finest dancer in Hyrosia."

"She would've loved to see you," he said, drawing a calloused hand through her hair. It caught, but she didn't complain. Malcolm's eyes changed when he talked about his mother: The flint went out of them. "My mother would've loved you," was as close as he ever got to "I love you."

But everybody knew—especially Cordelia—that Malcolm only loved the Bee.

His mother had given up her stage career to come north and marry. And it had gotten her nothing but accounting books and two sons dead at sea, killed by Lisoan pirates somewhere south of her home country. Her youngest, Malcolm, she'd kept at home despite her husband's squalling. Malcolm heard all her stories, saw all her tintypes and mementos. Promised her she'd have a stage to walk again.

When she died of fever, he took what she'd left him and abandoned his father's shipping company for the boards. All his love for Inita Sailer went into making a go of the Bumble Bee Cabaret and Night Club.

"How's the new routine?" he asked. "Speaking of dancing."

She shook her head. "I got it all down, but the orchestra's having trouble."

Malcolm sat up and threw his legs over the edge of the bed. "I'll ask Liesl about it." He picked his watch up from the bedside and flipped it open. "Better be getting over there. Got a delivery coming in for the bar."

"Ytzak can take care of it," said Cordelia, wrapping her arms around Malcolm and tangling her fingers in the dark hair across his chest. She tried to pull him back into bed, but he resisted.

"No, he has the morning off—said his ma's sick, but you know he's courting that razor who plays bass in Canty's band, and he was a little too eager to run out last night."

"So drag him in," said Cordelia, hooking one leg over Malcolm's thigh.

He laughed and pinched her, but stood nonetheless. She let him go and collapsed against the bedspread, giving him her best pout.

"You learned that one from Makricosta," he said. "You know it won't work on me." Pulling a threadbare cotton undershirt over his head, he added, "You're welcome to hang around here, if you like. But I won't be back before curtain, almost sure."

Cordelia sighed. "You gonna ask me to run to the cleaners for your swags again?"

"Be a swan?" He swooped in and kissed her cheek. "Tell Kieran to put it on the account."

"You owe him half a fortune this month already."

"He knows I'm good for it. Especially once this new show's up and running." Malcolm slipped his braces over one shoulder then the other, and hooked his jacket and hat down from the back of the bedroom door. "Later, spicecake."

"Remember to talk to Liesl!" she shouted after him. The downstairs door slammed, rattling the bottles of hair tonic and cheap cologne on Malcolm's nightstand.

Cordelia fluffed a ratty pillow and leaned back, staring at the cracked plaster ceiling. The Bee did a swift trade. Malcolm only lived in such a shambles because whatever he made running the theatre went right back into it.

Not that she was complaining. Every stage-strutter in Amberlough wanted a spot on the Bee's pine boards. Malcolm paid his performers better than any place in the city—still a pittance compared to salaryfolk, but Cordelia padded her pockets out with dealing a little bit of tar on the side. It wasn't pretty work, but it was steady and it turned a profit.

Speaking of, she was due to make a pickup from her man on the docks this afternoon. Malcolm didn't clock she had a sideline, and wouldn't approve. But he wouldn't have to know, as long as she got him his swags on time, in fine condition.

Malcolm's evening clothes hung from the luggage rail, swaying with the motion of the trolley. Rain struck the windows. Everything smelled woolly and damp. Cordelia was running late, but the commute was so cozy, she didn't mind. It had been a good afternoon—the pickup went smooth, and after, she'd swung by Tory's.

He was tucked against her side now, warm and noisy, chatting on about . . . oh, who knew what. He talked all the rotten time. Half of it she didn't clock, but the sound was pretty. He tried to keep his Currin burr tamped down, but it always came out when he got pinned about something or—and she'd been pleased to find this out—when he was in bed.

Tory tugged her coat sleeve. "Our stop." Passengers were standing in the aisle, taking down packages and purses, tying their scarves tighter and flipping their collars up against the rain. "Come on," he said, jumping down from his seat. His head was on a level with the other passengers' bellies, but the way they made space for him, you'd never know.

They both stepped in the gutter, and Cordelia shrieked at the cold water soaking through her shoes. Tory waved her over the curb, toward a pair of wet metal chairs under the awning of a cafe. On the corner, a Hearther evangelist had set up a soapbox for his street sermon. He'd been a regular feature of Temple Street for going on two years now, trying to convert fallen stagefolk and the punters who came to cheer for them. Lately he'd taken to wearing a gray-and-white Ospie sash. Most of the Hearther congregations in town were backing the Ospies. Cordelia was fine with that. Keep the prissy people together and let them entertain themselves, however they proposed to. Folk in the theatre district had better things to do.

Across the street from the preacher, the Bee stood tall between a wine bar and a casino, brighter than any other theatre on Baldwin Street. Brilliant swirls of white bulbs, lit against the gray afternoon, made the golden moulding of the marquee shine twice as bright. Richly illustrated posters glowed in their illuminated frames across the front of the building—Cordelia spied herself just to the left of the entrance, all red ringlets and black roses, her lips stung puffy by the swarm of gilt bees that spiraled around the poster border.

"Check me," said Cordelia, hauling down the collar of her dress. "No marks?"

Tory looked over each shoulder, conspiratorial, and then buried his face in her chest. "No marks." His voice was muffled.

The preacher saw them, lifted an accusing finger, and started hammering hard on modesty and decency and good, upstanding citizens.

Cordelia made a rude gesture at him, then grabbed Tory's ears and hauled him out of her tits. "Stop it! Be serious."

"No marks," he said again, brushing his thumb down her breastbone. "I know Malcolm does his damnedest to keep from splotching this bonny fair skin—"

"Sometimes even his damnedest ain't damned enough."

"—and I wouldn't want to spoil it either. Besides, he might recognize the teeth marks." Tory grinned like a nutcracker. "And jealous old Sailer wouldn't stand for that."

Cordelia smoothed the damp garment bag over Malcolm's tailcoat. "Let's go in. Before we're any later."

Tory stood on his tiptoes to kiss her, quickly, and then set off across the street with the preacher howling behind him. He caught her eye from beneath the marquee. Standing just under the illustrated

Cordelia in her ring of black roses, he reached up and mimed pinching her nipples, where they would be beneath the garland of flowers. She made the same rude gesture at him she'd thrown at the Hearther. He laughed, then hauled open the heavy black-and-gold doors and disappeared, stumbling over the threshold.

They weren't supposed to go in through the front, but Malcolm held Tory pretty dear and let all sorts of his mischief slide. Cordelia didn't feature him giving a pass for ducking under her skirt, but what he didn't clock wouldn't bruise him.

She waited a moment longer, picking absently at the soggy edge of the garment bag. The rain slacked off, but a sudden wind off the harbor shook droplets from the budding plum trees, spattering the restaurant awning. Gathering up her purse and Malcolm's swags, she waited for the street to clear, then dashed across between the puddles and slipped down the alley that ran along one side of the Bee.

The stage door was propped open with a chair to let a breeze into the stuffy backstage corridors. Stella, one half of the twin acrobat and contortion act, sat in the chair smoking a hand-rolled cigarette. Cordelia caught a sweet whiff of hash. Stella got bad butterflies—her sister Garlande was the showy one.

"Sorry," mumbled the acrobat, and stood aside to let Cordelia through. The corridor was mostly bare beams, a bit of plaster here and there, stairs leading up to the costume loft. A stagehand sat on the edge of the staircase, retaping Garlande's trapeze and flirting with a seamstress making last-minute repairs. Someone was listening to a record; the shoddy walls muffled and distorted the strains of a smooth-voiced crooner. Sawdust and greasepaint musk hung in the air.

She had to pass Malcolm's office to get to her dressing room, and as she neared the open door, she braced herself for a hiding. But he was already shouting at somebody, and it wasn't her. The new tit singer, Thea Marlow, stood in front of Malcolm's great scarred slab of a desk, hunched up like a naughty schoolchild waiting for the switch. So, Malcolm must have talked to Liesl, and the conductor had put the blame for the shoddy number on Thea. All things fair, she did have awful trouble with the key changes. Tit singer was a hard sort of job if you had half an interest in naked girls, and judging from Thea's saucer-eyes whenever Cordelia went up onstage, she wasn't cut out for the task.

Cordelia hooked Malcolm's swags onto the doorknob and tried to slip away, but he caught her. Instead of scolding her, he just said, "Delia, Antinou's tonight? Tory's treat—he owes me."

She didn't want to think of all the dirty jokes the dwarf comedian would make of that. Instead she nodded, and blew Mal a kiss.

As Cyril was getting ready to leave for the day, his telephone brayed, startling him from his latest report out of the train yards.

It was one of the switchboard kids, a girl with a little bit of a lisp. "Mr. DePaul? The skull wants to see you."

"Thanks, Switcher." By tradition, all the kids crammed in the exchange room were called Switcher. Cyril tipped the pages of the report into his briefcase and locked it up, then put his coat over his arm and went down the hall.

Culpepper's personal secretary, Vasily Memmediv, was in his late forties or early fifties, but his thick, dark hair was only barely touched with gray. The lines that marked his hawkish face cut hard and full of character at the edge of his nose and beneath his deeply set eyes. Cyril had briefly nursed a terrible passion for Memmediv, but rumors put him firmly loyal to Culpepper, in more ways than one.

Cyril rested an elbow on the edge of Memmediv's desk. "Switcher said the Skull wants to see me."

"Director Culpepper," he said, "asked to see you, yes, before you left." His Tatien accent had faded with time in the south, but still colored his speech with overemphasized vowels and swallowed, liquid consonants.

As if speaking her name had summoned her, Culpepper's voice rang out from the half-open door to her office. "Is that DePaul?"

Before Memmediv could answer, Cyril cut in with, "Last time I checked." He skirted the scowling secretary and crossed into Culpepper's lair.

She didn't look up when he entered. "Don't be flippant, DePaul. It's unbecoming."

"Really?" He flung himself into the chair opposite hers. The vast, cluttered expanse of her desk stretched between them. "Usually people are charmed. Maybe you should get your head checked."

The Foxhole folk called her "the Skull" because she kept her hair shaved close. Bones and muscles showed sharply under the dark skin of her scalp. When she ground her teeth, as she was doing now, the grim movement of her jaw rippled beneath the faint shadow of razored curls. That was what they called her type, in the city: razors. Women in well-cut suits with their hair shorn close, posing and snarling at one another like big cats, their sparks tucked snug under their arms. He didn't envy Vasily—razors tended to be as sharp in temperament as their namesake was in function.

"You'll need your head checked if you don't shut up and pay attention," said Culpepper. "I'll put the dents in it personally."

Case in point. "Oh, Ada. I love it when you're cruel."

She crossed her arms. "Less carrot, more stick? Is that the secret I've been missing all these years?"

"I'm ruined for a soft hand, since early days. My first was whipper-in with the Carmody hunt."

"Spare me," she said, falling against the high back of her chair. The leather upholstery creaked. "You're saying if I slapped you around a little, your ragtaggers would finally get it together to burn Makricosta's network?"

"Don't be ridiculous. With the border tariffs so high, people like him are the only thing keeping us out of a civil war." Besides, Aristide's smuggling crews had taken on a little extra work ferrying refugees into the city. Ospie supporters—blackboots—roamed the streets in Farbourgh and Tatié, making life hard for immigrants, writers, radicals, wind worshippers, cultists of the Wandering Queen . . . The blackboots had their own little streets in Amberlough, too, but the ACPD didn't like them, and they knew it.

"I want to think," said Culpepper, fingers at her temples, "that the stability of Gedda hinges on more than illegal commerce."

"Ada, if the northeast couldn't sell through smugglers, they'd—"

"Throw their lot in with the Ospies? Perhaps you haven't noticed, DePaul, with your face between Makricosta's thighs, but we're past that point. Pinegrove and Moritz were both elected by overwhelming majorities, and the Ospies have been taking secondary seats left and right."

He let the sexual snipe slide by unaddressed. "I was going to say they might secede. Or worse, collude to overthrow the parliament."

"Secede? They need our docks. Until Moritz reaches some kind of agreement with the Tzietans, the harbor at Dastya is a war zone. Forget exporting overland. You saw today's headlines: Westbound trains are targets for Tzietan terrorism. And Farbourgh is just a tragic novel in three volumes. Mountains, rocks, and blighted sheep. What would they do without federal aid? No, secession isn't in the cards."

"So that leaves a coup." He wanted her to laugh. She didn't.

"You're right, you know." She sighed. "I'd love to tear you up and down over Makricosta—don't give me that look. How much does he pay you to keep his business out of your reports? Or is it just the sex? Or—mother and sons, don't tell me you're in love."

Cyril snorted. "Ada."

"He's bent stronger rods, don't doubt it."

"You should really think about things like that before you say them."

"You weren't even supposed to have contact with him—Cyril, I'm serious, stop laughing. Division heads *run* agents, they don't pretend to *be* them."

"I was! I—I am. Ada, nobody knew how deep he had his hooks into the market, and we wouldn't have found out if . . . His name kept coming up in dispatches, all right? And none of my foxes could get close to him. Or he made it worth their while not to."

"But you've gotten very close indeed. Good job."

"What happened to tearing me up and down?"

"Oh, I'm pinned about it; don't think I'm not. But it proves you still know your way around fieldwork."

Cyril's hand jumped. He covered by reaching for his cigarette case. Culpepper pretended not to notice, but she couldn't fool him. They knew each other too well. Before she was the Skull, implacable Queen of the Foxhole, Culpepper had been Cyril's case officer. Good work saw her promoted to assistant director, and then director, of the Amberlough chapter of the FOCIS while he was still out running under a work name.

"Look, Cyril." Culpepper sighed and put her hand over her eyes. "With the job you've been doing lately—or haven't been doing, more like—we both know you're not cut out to play division head; you don't have the right temperament. I want to send you back into the field."

He was going to be sick. He could feel the bile creeping up the back of his throat.

"You're what, thirty-five?" Culpepper, who was herself perhaps twenty years older, looked him up and down. "You're too young to be behind a desk. You should be out earning your position, not rotting in it. You know Yeffa, over in personnel? We ran her until she was in her sixties."

Cyril put a straight to his lips but didn't light it, not trusting his traitorous hands. His current title—Master of the Hounds, Central slang for the division head who played police puppeteer—was guilt-reeking restitution, a courtesy Culpepper had paid him when his last action went sour.

"Besides," she said, still talking, in that too-casual way that flagged all her serious conversations, "you're probably bored to tears."

Bored. Once, it would have been true. Boredom was Cyril's chief failing. He'd been bored as a child, and it had made him mischievous. He'd been bored at university, and it had nearly gotten him expelled; only the timely intervention of one of Culpepper's talent spotters had saved him from being sent down in ignominy. And he had been bored behind the desk, a disinterested operator directing the moves and countermoves of domestic espionage. Smugglers and tax dodges, money laundering and corruption. Old hat to any Amberlinian. Bored, but afraid, wretched with cowardly self-loathing and the pain of convalescence. Bored, until Ari had made things interesting.

"Cyril."

His attention whipped back to Culpepper, who hadn't stopped talking. "Sorry. What?"

"Bascombe's gone."

"Ira? How?"

She locked eyes with him. "Tatié was your purview once. How do you think?"

"Dead?"

She shook her head: half rue, half negation. "Just . . . gone. Tatié's Foxhole is getting smart. They know we aren't keen on the whole *Dastya for Tatié* gambit; think how much tax revenue

Amberlough would lose if Tatié didn't rely on shipping down the Heyn."

"Shake with the right, shoot with the left?"

"And use a good suppressor, exactly. They learned from . . . last time. No trace. No messy politicking. But they know we know. And that we'll feel the squeeze."

Mother's tits, he would defect to Liso if she tried to send him back. Taking over for Bascombe, he'd be running a network, rather than doing the work direct. But barely safer, for that. It was unofficial cover, spying on the other states within Gedda; if they caught you, you were on your own.

His throat already felt thick with the dust of no-man's-land: those blasted, burnt steppes between the orchards and the sea. He was back amongst the tattered khaki ranks of Tatié's armed forces, in the stuffy chambers of cigarillo-smoking officers. Dry earth and endless sky, the smell of blood and cordite . . .

"But you're not headed east," said Culpepper, snapping the thread of his memories. From the ill-concealed pity on her face, she knew what he'd been thinking. "We're promoting one of our Hellican operatives—"

"Poor fox."

"Be honest, Cyril. You would take Tatié over the Hellican Islands. Even now."

He wouldn't. He had learned: Better bored than dead.

"Anyway. He'd been building an action for us, but the whole thing's easily moved to a new agent."

"So you're handing it to me."

A shallow nod. "The work name is Sebastian Landseer. A wool merchant. Bit of a playboy—never at home. Skiing in Ibet, snowbirding in the Porachin Gulf. Polo, yachting. You know."

"I begin to see your logic."

"In choosing you? Yes. It's hard to teach someone that kind of privilege. I know what your parents settled on you in their will; very generous, given Lillian was the heir outright. You won't have to pretend on this action. Not much, anyway."

"All right, all right." She was going to make him ask. "Tell me, then. What's going on?"

"The election."

Cyril reached for the table lighter, finally remembering his cigarette. "Acherby won't win."

"He will if he throws it."

"He won't. Ada, he's got a pry bar for a spine. He doesn't bend for anything. Just bulls at it straight and hard until it breaks."

"He'll bend for this. Three primary reps, and a majority in the lower assembly? Do you know what he could do with that?"

"I have some idea."

"Be serious, DePaul. The Ospies want Amberlough knocked down—they think we're impeding trade, sacrificing Gedda for the sake of state interest. Pinegrove and Moritz have already endorsed Acherby, and intelligence out of both capitals says they won't stop there. They want to impeach Josiah."

Cyril froze with the lighter wick halfway to his mouth. The flame wavered in his caught breath. "Ada. There hasn't been a primary impeached in forty years."

"You don't need to give me a history lesson. I'm out of the schoolroom."

"Sorry." He lit his cigarette and exhaled a thin, artful column of white. Josiah Hebrides had been Amberlough's primary representative for six years, two-thirds of his allotted term, and the mayor of Amberlough City for eight years before that. He was crooked as a kinked zipper, but charming, and his equally unscrupulous constituents adored him. If he wanted an unprecedented second term as primary, he had only to reach out his hand and take it; none of Staetler's nobility for him. "Stones, Ada. This is what you throw at me, first thing back?"

"You're a sharp fox, or you were. I'm confident. So don't let me down."

"Thank you. That helps me relax." Tension between his shoulder blades crept up the back of his neck, coiling into a headache.

"I don't want you to relax." She tapped a column of ash into her empty coffee cup. "Do you know Konrad Van der Joost?"

"Acherby's assistant campaign manager."

"Courtesy title. He runs their intelligence operation."

Cyril rested his chin on the back of his hand. A small kiss of heat bloomed on his cheek near the tip of his cigarette. "Engage with him?"

"You'll have to." She flipped her watch open and blanched. "Sacred arches, is it really? Look, I've got to dash."

"We haven't finished." But Cyril's protest was halfhearted. The longer he put off his full briefing, the longer he could maintain his denial.

"Come back tomorrow morning. Say half eight? I'll have Hebrides in and all three of us can go over it. In the meantime, the Landseer letters." She took a thick dossier from her desk drawer and flung it down. It hit the red leather with a smack and slid within Cyril's reach. "Take a good look, when you get home. Now, if you'll excuse me, Cross is back from Liso and I want to sit in on her debriefing."

"Get a few scraps of news from the old country?" It was a joke, in poor taste. Culpepper had never been to her ancestral homeland. Her parents were political dissidents who had fled from Liso long before the Spice War wrenched the north out of the king's strangling grasp. Her surname had always been Culpepper, never

Kuleppah—changed to avoid retribution, even so far from home. Cyril had seen the file.

"I'll scrap you," she said. "Get out of here and do your job."

He should have gone back to his flat and cracked the Landseer dossier, but thinking of it made him faintly ill. Instead, he stopped at a basement wine bar in Harbor Terrace and got pleasantly drunk on overpriced sherry, until the dinner rush pushed him up the narrow stairwell and into the wet dusk.

He really ought to go home and see to his post. Might even be able to trick himself into reading the Landseer letters, if he stuck them at the bottom of the pile. Swinging onto the next trolley headed up the Harbor line, he hung onto the railing until he could transfer north at Armament.

Near the edge of Loendler Park, a shudder of awareness ran along the rows. Heads turned; people murmured. The woman in front of Cyril cranked her window open, and he heard chanting. Whistles. Hundreds of human voices raised, dissonant. The trolley rounded a shallow bend in the road and shuddered to a halt.

The streetcars of Amberlough did not stop in the middle of their routes. Cyril was not alone when he got up from his seat to peer down the aisle.

He couldn't see much, not around his fellow passengers, and so he sat back down and turned the hand crank to open his own window. The sound of voices was much louder now, and when he removed his trilby and put his head outside, he saw dozens of people standing in the street, bent close to one another, turned black and yellow by the streetlights. Farther up, the crowd thickened, packing Armament Avenue from footpath to footpath, pressed against shopfronts and night-locked market gateways. Residents crowded the balconies above, and hung over their windowsills. Lit cigarettes spangled the dusk.

The trolley driver stood and addressed his passengers. "Can't go further, I'm afraid. You can either get off and walk, or ride back to Station Way."

"What's happening?" asked a woman near the front of the car. She held her straw hat to her chest, glass cherries bright against her white shirtfront.

The driver shrugged. "Probably just some of those artists causing mischief in the park again."

A group of students had staged a rather tasteless piece of performance art in the bandstand last month, but the crowd hadn't been nearly so big.

"What'll it be?" the driver asked. "Walk or ride?"

Most of the passengers remained sitting, content to catch the Station Way transfer, but Cyril's flat was only a few blocks away. He settled his hat back on his head, gathered his overcoat and briefcase, and pushed to the rear doors.

After the close, damp warmth of the streetcar, his first breath of outside air was refreshing. Then he shivered and paused to replace his overcoat and pull on his gloves, slotting his fingers together to push the leather into place. By the time he finished, the trolley was disappearing around the curve of the road.

He slipped into the gossiping crowd and tapped a young razor on the shoulder. She turned, spat a mouthful of tobacco, and cased him with an appraising eye. "Yeah?"

"What's all this?" He waved vaguely at the people around them.

She shrugged. "Heard there was a march in the park. Some kind of political thing."

"In aid of what?"

"How am I supposed to know?" she snapped. "Just trying to get to my old auntie's flat, aren't I? And now I'm stuck in this mess."

Cyril tipped his hat and gave her his apologies, then pushed on, doling out "pardon me"s and dodging dirty looks as he maneuvered up the block toward Blossom Street.

"Can't get through up there!" someone called after him. He ignored them and shouldered on until he found himself at the edge of the park, and face-to-chest with an imposing police officer—one in a long, unbroken line across the pavement.

"Sorry sir," said the officer, through an impressive array of bristling facial hair. "Can't let anyone past."

"Why not?"

"Been an accident." He had to raise his voice over a sudden swell of chanting from the park.

"Accident? Someone told me there was a demonstration."

The officer's neck went stiff. "Suppose you could call it that."

"Listen," said Cyril, "I live just up the street. You can see my building from here." He pointed over the officer's epaulet.

"I'm afraid I'm under orders, sir."

Though he was Master of the Hounds, Cyril couldn't pull rank on an officer; the federal position wasn't technically a part of the force. Shifting his briefcase from one hand to the next, he reached for his billfold. "And how much are those orders worth? Let's say, thirty-five?" The officer turned red, but said nothing. "Fifty?"

"Please, sir. I really can't."

"Well," said Cyril, irked to have found the one honest hound in all of Amberlough, "perhaps your friend here can." He turned to the next officer in line. "This is ridiculous. I live right there. What's going on that's so damned important?" He slipped the woman a folded bill.

This officer, younger and slighter than her stubborn colleague, was also more susceptible to bribery. She made the money disappear.

"OSP demonstration," she said. "Got a bit nasty. Some hecklers broke in and beat one of the unionists bad. Turned into a brawl, and now we've got orders to keep everyone out who's not a party member."

"For fifty, will you pretend I'm an Ospie?" Cyril gave the woman a smile that should've been charming, but probably came off more like a teeth-baring grimace. His face felt stiff with frustration.

The younger officer looked sideways at her neighbor, who was silently projecting a air of deep disapproval.

"I really can't, sir," she said, shaking her head. "I'm sorry."

Cyril let his shoulders slump forward. "Fine. Good luck with this wreck." He turned away and moved back through the crowd.

Halfway down the block, he body-checked a man in a heavy overcoat who was paying more attention to the police blockade ahead than he was to the two feet in front of him. Cyril staggered back, and the man caught him and set him straight.

"So sorry," he said. "Careless of me. Are you all right?"

"Fine, fine." Cyril smoothed the front of his coat. "You're in an awful hurry for nothing, I'm afraid. They're not letting anyone through."

"Not anyone?"

"See that?" Cyril pointed. "I live just there."

"Awful. And they wouldn't budge for anything?"

"Not for fifty crisp slices."

The stranger sighed. "Well, I suppose it's all to the good. I'd rather an upstanding hound any day of the week."

Cyril laughed. "You can't be serious."

"Deadly so. You'd prefer the agents of justice roll over for a little bit of pin money?"

"If it would get me home with my feet up." Cyril squinted at the man in front of him. "Where did you say you were headed, exactly?"

"The rally, of course." He flipped open his coat to show a gray-and-white cockade pinned in his buttonhole. "Election's coming up. We've got to support our people in Nuesklend. Acherby's fighting for all of us, not just the western constituency. For honest, upright folk who are sick of the way things are. Sick of the graft and embezzlement and the coastal blockade. People ought to know we've got a vocal presence, even in Amberlough."

"Vocal, certainly. Caterwauling, even." Cyril snapped up the collar of his coat and turned away. "Excuse me."

"That's right, walk away." The man's shout followed him down the street. "Afraid of a little civil discourse? Afraid we might be right?"

He knew he shouldn't, but he turned and shouted back. "If you want to scare me, do a little better in the polls."

The man turned red, and blustered, and Cyril left him there before he could come up with a response. Bitterly, he reflected that the polls didn't matter anyway, if what Culpepper had told him was true. It gave him a modicum of pleasure to realize he had misled the man; the hounds had said they would let Ospies through, but this fellow would probably turn around and go home.

Unfortunately, Cyril didn't have that option. Without the prospect of a change of clothes and a tumbler of rye with his landlord's excellent supper, exhaustion and disgust threatened to break over him like a gray wave. Nothing for it but to keep moving. His post would have to wait. He made his slow way back to the edge of the crowd and followed the streetcar tracks to Buttermarket.

The sky lowered, threatening more rain. He sat on a bench under the meager shelter of a budding pear tree, briefcase on his knees, waiting for the southbound trolley that would take him to the Harbor line, to Temple Street, and the Bumble Bee Cabaret.

CHAPTER

THREE

From the stage, Aristide couldn't see much of the audience. Not with the spotlight in his eyes, striking sparkles off his jeweled false lashes. But he could hear their thunderous applause. Pleasure curled through his middle, and he took a bow.

The curtains, heavy swathes of black velvet, fell between him and his admirers. He blinked, still dazzled by the spot, and waited for the lights to come up onstage. Before he could quite see again, he heard Malcolm snarl at one of the chorus dancers, then her despairing wail as she burst into tears. Well, she'd tripped up her half of the kick line. What did she expect?

He let his hands uncurl from the warm metal of the microphone stand and took a deep breath.

"Almost makes you wish we weren't switching up the shows."

Malcolm was next to him suddenly, standing with his weight on one leg, arms crossed. His biceps, strong from hauling ropes and set pieces during strike and rehearsals, were cleanly outlined by the black wool of his tailcoat. He reeked of aftershave and whiskey.

"You don't think the p-p-punters would get tired of the same show all year round?" Aristide ducked his head and lifted away the towering powdered wig he wore for the last half of the first act. His emcee was a languid fop with a dry, pointed sense of humor and a tendency toward glamour that bordered on carnivalesque. Really, he was playing himself, in gilded heels and face paint.

"I think they wouldn't," said Malcolm, "but Lady knows we would."

Aristide picked an invisible bit of fluff from Malcolm's lapel. "If you insist," he said, and floated off to his dressing room on the echoes of applause.

The Bee employed a card boy to circulate during the first act, collecting names in labeled boxes for each star performer. At the interval, cast members made rounds among their admirers. It was a way to collect tips, free drinks, and goodwill. Malcolm harped on them every night to flirt like blush boys, though he was comically jealous and turned an alarming shade of red if he caught Cordelia sitting in anybody's lap.

Before Aristide could address the formidable stack of cards on his makeup table tonight, he had to get through the woman waiting on his chaise longue.

"Merrilee," he said. "Back from Liso already?"

"It's been two years." Her heart-shaped face was deeply tanned, and the equatorial sun had bleached her salt-and-pepper hair white at the tips. "Or hadn't you noticed all those pretty profits rolling in?"

Merrilee Cross represented Aristide's interests in southern Liso, where Gedda had very little influence since the disaster of the Spice

War. Twenty-some years ago, in an ill-conceived bid for influence in a resource-wealthy nation crippled by repressive monarchy, Gedda had put an army on the ground in Liso to shore up a nascent revolution. Like quicksand, or a pit of tar, the situation had grown deadlier and more difficult the longer Gedda was involved.

The federal government sank money and soldiers into the mess in alarming quantity. Most of the money came from the national treasury's tax revenue—all four states poured their income into the enterprise, which put a squeeze on the southwest but positively crippled the northeast—and most of the soldiers were Tatien. They had the training, unlike the rest of the nation. But it was Amberlinian strategist General Margaretta DePaul who wrangled a somewhat . . . hollow victory for Gedda. Related to Cyril somehow, no doubt, and a divisive public figure to put it mildly.

Her solution to the military crisis left Farbourgh bankrupt and Tatié furious, contributing to the nation's current troubles with the Ospies. The army pulled out of Liso, leaving a partition in its wake. Northern Liso still traded and politicked with Gedda, but the south was where the poppies grew.

Luckily, smuggling could be a lucrative sideline for a secret agent, as long as Ada Culpepper didn't pick up on it.

"Is this just a social call?" asked Aristide. He set his wig on its stand and pulled the stocking cap from his pin curls. "I'm sorry to say my evening is already sp-p-poken for."

Cross picked up the stack of cards. "Impressive. Taormino's little contribution would outfit a few of her larger divisions. You must have important things to talk about."

"Merrilee, I'm wounded. You know I am imp-p-possibly incorruptible." He took the police commissioner's card from her hand. It was pinned to a thick wad of folded bills.

"What's this?" She slipped the second card from the pile—this one in heavyweight satin cream. As she turned it, Aristide caught a glimpse of blue-black copperplate, deeply embossed. He knew that card.

Cross *tch*ed. "Speaking of incorruptible. How is Culpepper's golden boy? And what is his card doing in *your* dressing room?"

Aristide knew his smile looked lecherous, and didn't care a fig. "Mr. DePaul is . . . somewhat t-t-tarnished since you last encountered him, shall we say?"

"Wrong precious metal," she said. "Gold don't tarnish."

"I'm a t-t-terribly bad influence."

She laughed like a dog: wide mouthed and panting, more exhalation than sound. One hand in the air, she said, "I'll testify in court. Tell me, is he a hard knock? Always thought he was fine, but I couldn't get him to look twice."

He took Cyril's card from her. "Did you *need* something, Miss Cross?"

She reached into her jacket and pulled out a velvet bag—the kind jewelers used to store diamonds. Aristide took it, and tipped it out into his palm. Three sticky squares of poppy tar tumbled free. Aristide rubbed his thumb across one of them—it left a streak dark and tacky as pitch.

"Uncut," she said. "Strongest stuff you ever smoked. My man can get it by the brick."

"And I, sweetest girl, will buy." He kissed her cheek.

"Better be off," said Cross, standing from the chaise. "Have fun with Cy, but don't turn him too rotten. I don't want him moving in on my market."

"Don't fret. He's got no ambition beyond keeping c-c-comfortable." Aristide stripped his sweaty costume from his skin and reached for the brocade dressing gown flung across the chaise. "You've been away. I think some sort of Foxhole mischief has d-d-dinged his p-p-pretty plating."

"Well, you know what they say."

"'A chipped pot still holds soup'?"

"I was going to go with 'one-legged whore's still got holes.'"

"How . . . colorful. Now, if you don't mind."

She laughed her dog-laugh, and left him to his business.

Aristide slipped between the patrons, narrowly avoiding the languid swipes of expressive hands and cigarette holders. A blush boy snaked out jewel-heavy fingers to pinch Aristide's bottom and got a sharp look for his trouble, but nothing worse. There were bouncers for that sort of thing.

In the beginning of their association, when Cyril was just curious, he'd been at the Bee nearly every night. He'd dropped off coming when he caught on to the fact that Aristide didn't just have a finger in the pie, but that he'd stolen it from the windowsill as well. After that, Cyril couldn't be reasonably seen paying court to a black market kingpin, so his attendance at the Bee slacked off in favor of more private meeting places.

Still, when he did come, he had a preferred table—slightly house left of center, second row back—and he paid well to make sure he got it.

Perched on a high iron chair, he had one heel hooked on the rail, one foot dangling. He wore the same dark suit he'd left in that morning. Yesterday's suit. Ilse had done a good job on it, but it was undeniably past its prime. Patchy stubble gilded his jaw. Surrounded by the sparkling evening crowd, he looked wilted. Though he'd checked his overcoat at the door, he still had his briefcase. Curious. Aristide filed the observation away.

Opposite Cyril, a gin cocktail sweated onto the mosaic table. Aristide sat, sipped it, and insinuated a toe between Cyril's cuff and ankle.

He jumped, then smiled. The expression was weary. "I have had a *beast* of an evening."

"Gracious." Aristide dipped his finger into Cyril's drink, and licked it. "What is this, t-t-tonic and lime?" Either he was off his feed, or he had secrets to keep. "Ask Ytzak for something stronger. T-T-Tell him it's on me." Aristide settled his bare feet on Cyril's chair, between his thighs. "Why on earth didn't you stop at home to ch-ch-change?"

Cyril shook his head. His hands lit on the tops of Aristide's arches, and he dug his thumbs into the cables of muscle that stretched from heels to toes. It sent a shock of feeling up Aristide's legs, into his groin and belly. He let his head fall back and groaned.

"Ari, that's obscene." Tory passed them, poking Aristide in the hip. "If you've got to shuck a quick oyster at the interval, will you do it in your dressing room at least?"

Cyril pulled his hands up and cupped his drink.

"Why don't you come down to Antinou's with us after the show?" asked Tory. "Malcolm's buying, for once. Cordelia's going to come. Aren't you Delly?" He reached out one short arm, and Cordelia wove through the crowd like the Wandering Queen coming down from the mountains, shot-away chin held high and her hair streaming out behind her. The whole cast knew she dyed it—going gray early, poor thing, but did it have to be quite so *scarlet?*

"That's not how Mal tells it," she said. "Says you owe him and you're picking up the tab."

Tory put his arm around the backs of her thighs, and something about the proprietary gesture, and the sharp look Cordelia dropped on Tory, piqued Aristide's curiosity. Were they sleeping together?

"How about it?" asked the comedian. "Antinou's, I mean. You can bring your pretty friend." Tory shot Cyril with the imaginary pistol of his finger and thumb.

Cyril sagged over his drink, playing along, but there was real exhaustion in it. Aristide pushed one foot deeper into the crease of Cyril's hip and curled his toes. "Not tonight, I think."

Tory raised one eyebrow and squeezed Cordelia's legs close. "Lucky man, you," he said. "Eh, Delly?"

"What?" She was looking warily over one shoulder, back to Malcolm chatting up punters at the bar. She was definitely sleeping with Tory. When Malcolm found out . . . well, that would be an interesting week at the Bee.

"Maybe next time." Aristide inclined his head graciously, letting the weight of his pin curls pull it forward.

Tory shrugged. "Suit yourself. We all know you can find your own fun."

The chandelier dimmed and the footlights flared, illuminating the gold tassels hanging below the proscenium.

"That's us," said Tory. "See you up on the planks, lad." He disappeared between the hips of the audience. Cordelia turned to follow, but Aristide caught her wrist.

"Cordelia," he said, "must you really?"

"Ah, go yank yourself." She shook free of his grip and slunk away, the red glass beads of her costume shimmering.

Aristide stood, smoothing the folds of his dressing gown. "Will you last through the second act?" he asked Cyril. "It's Ilse's night off, but I can get you my k-k-key."

"Oh, I'll be all right. I need some cheering up, and you look good under the lights."

Aristide pushed his gin across the table, toward Cyril. "What happened today?"

"I'll tell you later." To Aristide's satisfaction, Cyril came to some agreement with himself and tossed back the larger portion of the cocktail. "Go play up there. You're killing them."

"Stop flattering me. It will make my head swell."

Cyril gave him a significant, downward-sweeping glance. "I'm counting on it. Now, go."

Aristide went.

When the heavy black curtains pulled up and away, he was blind again, to everything but the spangles of his own glitter and gems. Still, he knew where Cyril was and he smiled brighter to stage right, flirted crooked, canted his hips.

He wasn't an idiot; he knew Cyril didn't love him and, stones, he was sharp enough not to fall for Cyril. But if Cyril was in a better mood, he'd open up. Aristide might get a few more drinks in him, might find out what had put that charming worried wrinkle between his eyes. And it might be useful.

Oh, perdition, but he was handsome, too. And if Aristide had to have the foxes on his tail, at least he'd ended up with an agent he didn't mind stuck to it.

Several hours later, in a dark niche of Amberlough's best absinthe bar, they were both well into a green-tinged haze and Aristide had related his observations about Cordelia and Tory.

Cyril howled with laughter, burying his face in Aristide's neck. "Never," he said, his mouth against Aristide's skin. "I know you: You're a perfect liar."

Aristide grabbed Cyril's shoulders and propped him straight against the leather upholstery of the booth. He had nearly six inches and a few dozen pounds on Cyril, but he was still dizzy enough that he overbalanced and fell half into Cyril's lap. When he tried to sit up, Cyril tangled his hands in Aristide's curls and held him close.

"I'm glad you find it so amusing." Aristide's cheek pressed against Cyril's waistcoat buttons. "You're much p-p-prettier when you smile. Much easier to put up with. Now let me go." He plucked at Cyril's fingers where they tangled his hair. "Cyril. *Cyril.*" He sat up, pulling free. "Why are you in such a foul temper?"

"Oh," he said, all his laughter fleeing in a violent sigh. "The Ospies had a march in Loendler Park today."

"*What?*"

Cyril ran a fingertip around the edge of his glass, then licked it clean of sugar. "I'm sure it'll be all over the *Clarion* tomorrow," he said. "There weren't so many of them, but a fair number of police. And hecklers. Turned into a brawl. Someone ended up in hospital. The streets were jammed up all around, and they had to shut down the trolleys. I couldn't walk through it to get home."

Aristide pulled a face. "Well, have another drink. You need it."

"I really shouldn't," said Cyril. "I should try to get back to my flat. I still have work to do, before tomorrow. And an early appointment." He reached for his watch, but Aristide put a hand on his wrist, curling his fingers around the protruding bones. Cyril's pulse stuttered under Aristide's fingertips, and quickened. Smiling with the corner of his mouth, Aristide raised Cyril's hand and brushed a kiss across his knuckles. He left a smudge of dark red lipstick behind, coloring the skin like a burn.

"Come home with me," he said.

"Ari, I know I said . . ." He stopped, and shut his eyes. "But I really can't. Not tonight."

Turning Cyril's hand, Aristide kissed the center of his palm, then let his tongue trace the crease of Cyril's life line.

"Ari—"

Aristide opened his mouth, pressed his teeth into the swell of muscle at the base of Cyril's thumb. Cyril drew a sharp breath. On the table his free hand jumped, fingers flexing, scratching at the satin finish on the wood.

"Let me—" he said, but Aristide didn't. He followed the sweep of skin at the inside edge of Cyril's hand, to the tip of his pointer finger, and slipped it into his mouth. It was still sweet from the crushed sugar, faintly flavored with anise.

Cyril choked on a lewd sound, pressing his free fingertips against Aristide's jaw. "Mother and sons," he said, his voice rough. "Someone's going to see you."

Aristide pulled away from Cyril's finger, slowly, drawing his tongue along the soft flesh between the joints. "And they'll be rabid with jealousy." He moved around the curve of their booth. Slipping both hands beneath Cyril's jacket, he pulled him close. "Come home with me."

The shuddering, inward rush of Cyril's breath hissed in Aristide's ear. "All right."

Aristide left enough for their tab and tip beneath the foot of his glass. When he slid out of the booth he held a hand out for Cyril— to steady him; to make sure he followed.

Cyril lurched drunkenly at every trolley stop, holding the leather strap with an aching fist. The press of bodies put Aristide at his back, curved over him, sharing his handhold. Aristide's breath caught in the fine hairs at Cyril's neck.

It was not late enough that they had the streetcar to themselves— in fact, it was the time of night when most of the city started to head up Temple Street to the red light district on Princes Road.

Cyril held his briefcase tight, cursing himself. Surely he could have gone around a back way, earlier. He could have come to his flat through the alley, or up the fire escape. At least he should have stayed sober. He'd been out of the field too long. What was Culpepper thinking, sending him back? He hadn't even left Amberlough yet, and he was already bungling the action.

They crested a small rise and the trolley jumped. Aristide's weight shifted. He was hard with wanting, and Cyril felt it in the dimple of his lower back. Aristide laughed and pushed, this time with purpose.

Queen's sake, what a mess. Cyril leaned into the crook of Aristide's body and shut his eyes. His thoughts wandered from fantasy to self-flagellation, until Aristide whispered against his ear.

"Our stop," he said, "unless you want to ride it all the way to the P-P-Prince and Temple." The famous brothel was a seething offspring of sex and theatre. It stood at the corner of the two bawdiest streets in Amberlough, from which it took its name.

"I think you're about all I can handle, tonight." Cyril let the leather strap free and put his hand to Aristide's shoulder, steadying himself. "Come on."

Revelers thronged the Heynsgate trolley stop, packing Baldwin Street Bridge. Aristide had changed his costume for street clothes that were only slightly less gaudy, and he fit right in. Cyril, dizzy and exhausted, wanted to close his eyes again. The river shone with reflected lights, cigarette butts flecking the ripples.

He lit his own, fumbling with the matches, then tripped on a paving stone. Aristide caught him, but not before he'd dropped his straight. He cursed and reached for another one, but Ari stopped him.

"It can wait," he said. "Come on."

It was a matter of four city blocks, and then the doorman was waving them in. Ari's large, bony hand splayed at the center of Cyril's back, warm even through his overcoat.

The sleepy lift attendant scissored the grate closed behind them. She very professionally did not notice when Aristide pressed Cyril into the corner of the lift and pulled his tie from its knot. Cyril's briefcase knocked the wall, and he set it down, bracing it with his heel to keep it from falling.

As the dial wound past the first floor, Cyril grasped the back of Ari's neck, pulling him down into a kiss.

"Second floor," said the attendant, staring at a spot on the tile. Ari tugged Cyril's arm, drawing him across the threshold of the lift. At the last moment before the grate shut, Cyril dove back, tripping on the edge of the carpet, and grabbed his briefcase from the corner. He didn't have time to tell if Ari looked disappointed, because Ari grabbed his coat and pushed him face-first against the wall. Adrenaline jumped like electricity through Cyril's veins, laced with desire.

"Is your evening getting better?" Ari asked, closing his teeth on a tender divot of skin at the back of Cyril's neck.

"Even better—" Cyril's breath was harsh, his speech slurred. He tried again. "Even better once I sit down."

"Sitting?" Ari snarled, mouth against Cyril's ear. "Try flat on your back."

Ari's rooms were dark, but neither of them moved to turn on the lights. Cyril dropped his briefcase on the sofa and covered it with his overcoat—painfully casual, but did his drunkenness make it obvious?—then tossed his hat aside.

Ari twirled Cyril's wrinkled tie in lazy arcs. "Shoes," he said.

Feeling petty, Cyril fumbled with one of his cufflinks.

"I said *shoes*," snapped Ari, pulling the tie tight between his hands. When they were off, it was "Socks. Waistcoat. Braces. Trousers." Then, "Shorts," and, with satisfaction, "Now your c-c-cufflinks."

Cyril set them on the end table with a clatter, hands shaking. "Shirt."

He flung it away and shivered at the cool air on his naked arms.

In the yellow light drifting up from the street, the scar across his belly shone platinum.

"Your wrists, please," said Aristide. Cyril held them together and let Ari loop the necktie taut. He could feel heat gathering between his cupped palms. Ari tugged, not gently, and Cyril staggered after him.

In the bedroom, he let Ari fling him across the silk expanse of the duvet. The woolen necktie scratched his wrists as Ari drew the loop apart. Cyril reached for the gilded buttons of Ari's waistcoat, but Ari struck his hands away. "No," he said, like iron. Then, more softly, "I'll do it."

Cyril lay back, grateful and furious, and let him do it—let him do everything—until Ari was leaning over him, slippery with sweat and gasping for breath. One of his hands was pressed deep into a pillow, the muscles of his arm corded with the effort of holding his weight. With the other, he was pulling himself off. He was close; Cyril knew from the cant of his head, from his crooked mouth. He was biting the inside of his cheek. Sometimes he made himself bleed, like that.

Unable to resist, Cyril grabbed two handfuls of those sinful curls and yanked Ari's head back, stretching his skin over the sharp ridge of his larynx. Cyril drew the flat of his tongue up the deep groove of Aristide's throat, where the tendon was thrown into sharp relief. The chemical bitterness of cold cream coated his mouth, and the alcohol base of Aristide's cologne. Ari cried out, his supporting arm buckling. Cyril pressed his hips up. Ari's buttocks gave against the ridges of his hipbones. Cyril's jaw ached around his clenched teeth.

"No," said Ari again, ripping free of Cyril's grasp. "No!" He pinned Cyril's wrists over his head with one hand and slapped his face, hard.

Hissing through clenched teeth, Cyril spent himself, crumpling the fine linen of the pillowcase in his grasping hands. He closed his eyes, exhausted, but Ari put a fist in his hair and hauled him up.

"Finish it." His dark eyes were wide and mad, curls snarled and springing around his head like the mane of a big cat. "Perdition take you, bastard son of a whore, you *finish it*."

Reeling with fatigue, Cyril still felt a twist of desire, and he marveled at it. He lay on his side, cheek pressed in the crease of Aristide's thigh, and said, "Come on, then." Ari twisted, and Cyril took him into his mouth, pressing the pads of his thumbs into the hollow of Ari's hips.

When Ari finished, he let his grip on Cyril's hair go loose. His hands ghosted past Cyril's ears, slipped through the sweat beneath his arms. They pulled him higher, so his head rested on Ari's chest. Light from the street caught stray flecks of glitter still stuck to his skin.

Cyril squinted and yawned, painfully wide. There was something he needed to do. But what was . . .

Oh. His briefcase. Mother's tits.

"Ari," he said, and even to him it was nearly unintelligible. "Ari. I need to clean up."

Ari's arm tightened around his shoulder. "In the morning."

Cyril squirmed. "No. Really. Just quick."

A sigh, and Cyril's head rose and fell with Ari's breath. "Fine."

Leaning against the wall, he tried to make himself move fast. Aristide would realize what he was up to, if he was gone too long. But the lingering effects of the absinthe conspired with his own traitorous, postcoital body. He had only just made it back to the washroom, briefcase in hand, when Aristide called his name.

"Half a minute." Cyril climbed unsteadily up on the lid of the toilet and reached above his head to lift the top off of the decorative tank. The case was oiled leather, and if he angled it just right—

yes, like that—it would stay mostly out of the water. He replaced the lid and stepped down.

For appearance's sake, he wiped clean with a towel and threw it into the tub, then splashed a little water on his face. A headache was creeping in beneath his dizziness. With luck, he'd get to sleep before he witnessed the squalling birth of his hangover.

Shuffling back into the bedroom, Cyril shivered. Goosebumps came out across his damp skin. Ari held the blankets back and Cyril fell in, pressing against the warmth of the body beside him.

Close to the spillway on South Seagate Road, a narrow alley dove off the street into a deep brick courtyard. The arches of old tenements sheltered crisscrossed laundry lines and a mossy fountain. Antinou's took up the northern edge of the yard, tables and chairs crowded under the striped awning and scattered more thinly right up to the edge of the water.

This late, the place was still jammed full of students, actors, and whores. Tory stood on a chair, running through some new material. He'd been working on a routine for the election, and now he was doing his impression of Caleb Acherby, the Ospie candidate running for Nuesklend's primary seat. He was so good at it, the crowd was hissing. Cordelia wondered how it would play with their punters, though. It wasn't hard-scrabble types the Ospies pandered to.

Malcolm laughed at Tory's jokes, jabbing with his cigarette and calling out suggestions. One of his hands rested on Cordelia's neck, his thumb rubbing absent circles at the base of her skull. He was in his shirtsleeves, not bothered by the chill.

When their waiter brought the food out, Tory gave his audience of drunken night owls some peace and slipped back into his seat. Snatching one of the sticky pumpernickel buns, he took a bite and said, through a mouthful of nuts, "Delly, sit up and have a cup of something hot. You've had a big day."

Huddled in the raised collar of Malcolm's khaki overcoat, she glared at him. Was he trying to show his hand?

"Big?" Malcolm tangled his fingers in Cordelia's hair and shook her head back and forth. "Last I saw you before rehearsal you were flat on your back and half asleep."

"What I get up to ain't your business. Now leave off." She slapped his arm. "I'm perishin' for some coffee."

The stuff was gritty, thick as oil, and potent. Within a few minutes of her first cup, she was awake and sitting straight, holding a red-checked piece of waxed paper piled high with charred and dripping lamb. Still pinned about both of her companions, she hunched over the kebab and used her fingers to eat—no one with half their senses trusted the silverware at Antinou's.

"Commissioner was at the show tonight," said Malcolm, tearing chicken from a skewer. He stopped to chew and swallow before he continued. "Makricosta was supposed to talk to her. I asked Tito to tell him at the interval."

"That boy's too poor to take any orders that don't come well-padded with cash." Tory poured himself another cup of coffee.

"I rotten pay him," said Malcolm. "He works for me."

"But you don't pay him much," said Tory. "That piece our Ari was flirting with looked like a sheep past due for shearing, but I know a fine suit when I see one. Even two days worn. Tito's passed out drunk somewhere with a whore on his prick. Taormino never had a chance."

"Talk to the commissioner?" Cordelia set down her kebab and licked her fingers. Malcolm grabbed her hands and tried to finish the job for her, but she yanked away and wiped them on his coat instead. "About what? The ballast?" Ballast liquor was tax-free, smuggled in the bilges of ships coming into Amberlough's harbor by river and sea. "Every place in town has a sailor or two brings 'em cheap hooch."

"Not every place is the Bee," said Malcolm. "We're a rotten example now. And it's pay off the hounds or hang in the snare."

"Why didn't you ask me?" Cordelia picked at her food.

"Makricosta knows the market," said Malcolm. "And Taormino's a fool for a pretty face."

Cordelia pursed her lips. "And what am I? A sow? I'd've had her here." She cupped her palm.

"And how were you going to convince Taormino to blind-eye our ballast? Stimulatin' conversation?"

She sneered. "Oh, that's flattering. I'm just two pears and a peach, is that it?" She grabbed her crotch.

"Aw, Delia, put away your fangs. Far as I've heard, Taormino don't go in for tits anyhow. She likes her squeezes with a big prick and too much paint. Halfway won't sway her."

Cordelia knew her makeup was probably smudged beneath her eyes by now, her lipstick blurring at the edges. She shoved Malcolm, and not gently.

"Hoggies! Hoggies! Stand down." Tory held his hands up as if he could push the two of them apart. "You're just hungry and it's making you snap. We were having a nice little supper before *somebody* started talking business." He leveled a baleful glance at Malcolm. "Now. Let's all be civil and finish our kebab. Agreed?"

They went back to eating, and it wasn't long before Malcolm and Tory were lobbing friendly insults back and forth. Tory was a bowlegged ladychaser who came out so short on account of his ma taking too many men while she carried him. Malcolm was a lecherous old cur who couldn't please a lover 'cause he'd spent too long pleasing creditors. Cordelia was cold, disgusted, and ready to go to bed.

CHAPTER

FOUR

Cyril peeled himself out of bed hideously early the next morning and briefly considered the merits of vomiting. Perhaps on Aristide. The other man stretched like a sensual fresco across more than his share of the mattress, lustrous tangles of hair fanned out against the linens. He looked peaceful, sated, and not at all like he'd been up in the night searching through Cyril's things. Drunk, Cyril was a fitful sleeper, and he hadn't missed Aristide's nocturnal reconnaissance.

Swiping his billfold from the nightstand—Ilse must be back in, and already pressing his abandoned trousers—Cyril staggered to the washroom. He looked like a tragic melodrama: shadowed, bloodshot eyes, his neck and chest mottled with bruises . . . One particularly livid splotch colored his jaw. He desperately needed a shave.

What he got instead was a face full of cold water, and his brief-case. It was exactly as he had left it, untroubled by Aristide's nosi-ness. The leather was beaded with moisture on one side, but the lock was dry. He held out hope for the contents.

Wrapped in one of Ari's ridiculous robes—poisonous green velvet that did nothing for his complexion—Cyril hauled himself to the parlor and collapsed into the wingback chair by the bookcase. Ilse came when he rang, her cheeks still rosy from a cold commute.

"Get me a pot of coffee," Cyril said. His stomach lurched. "And maybe a wastebasket."

She nodded and disappeared, returning a few moments later with the basket. "Coffee in a minute or two, Mr. DePaul."

She was true to her word. He was still contemplating the clean bottom of the wastebasket when he heard the faint whistle of a kettle somewhere in the flat. The smell of brewing coffee sent rich tendrils through the stillness of the parlor. Cyril released his grip on the basket and put it on the floor, within easy reach.

Ilse returned bearing a tray and a folding table, which she set up at Cyril's right elbow. In addition to coffee, she'd brought him a tumbler of . . . something.

"Ilse," he said, tipping the brownish orange concoction to catch the light from the table lamp. "What is this?"

"Mr. Makricosta's proven hangover remedy," she said. "An egg with tomato juice, a healthy dash of fish sauce, and three spoonfuls of hot chili paste. Oh, and a little bit of black pepper bounce. The liquor takes the edge off."

He closed his eyes and breathed shallowly through his mouth against the briny, bitter smell of the potion. "Thank you," he said, trying to sound like he meant it.

She snorted and made herself scarce.

Taken all at once, it wasn't as bad as he'd feared, though he was briefly blinded by the spice. He poured a cup of coffee against his exhaustion and splitting headache. With the key from his billfold, he unlocked his briefcase.

It was stupid to read this here. But Ari wouldn't be up for another hour or so—the sky outside the arching parlor windows remained deep purple in the west, the barest flush of gray light creeping over the gabled roofs and chimney pots across the river.

He flipped the cover of the file. Focusing on the words made his eyes ache, but he was a professional, for queen's sake, and a hangover was not going to dull his edge.

As if to chastise him for his confidence, his stomach contracted unexpectedly. He lurched for the wastebasket, but nothing came up. Setting the basket aside, he picked up the file and straightened the ruffled papers.

According to a one-page biography of the fictitious Sebastian Landseer, Cyril's new working identity was an obscenely wealthy landowner in the Hellican Islands who had contacted the owner of a Nuesklend textile mill some five years back with a proposition: He could source wool from farmers on the islands and facilitate shipping to the Nuesklend mills. Taxes on international shipping were only nominally higher than interstate, and the quality was better. Nobody bought wool from Farbourgh anymore. Landseer had hit the timing perfectly: His offer coincided with the worst year of ovine skin blight Farbourgere farmers had seen in a decade.

The typeset on Landseer's outgoing letters matched Central's standard-issue typewriters, copies of the originals. The replies were of varied appearance, from different people typing and writing on different paper, with different ink. Cyril paged through and took note of the names: Rotherhite, Keeler, Berhooven, Pollerdam . . . Mill owners, Landseer's colleagues in the textile industry, all prominent Ospies. Because Landseer's occupation and lifestyle kept him far from Gedda, and a stranger to his peers, it was possible now for Cyril to take over and leave these people none the wiser.

The letters revealed that Landseer's interest in Geddan textiles had been piqued by the upcoming election. Mills and dealers would reap higher profits if domestic tariffs were abolished. Landseer's one compunction with unionist ideology was sourcing from within Gedda's borders. His friends and contacts made veiled allusions to a black market, promised his wool would still sell to Geddan mills. After all, fabric couldn't be made without raw materials, and a change in regime wouldn't cure Farbourgh's sheep. Money made hypocrites of most people, in the end. It was how Aristide earned a living.

Landseer's last letters, postmarked from Ibet in northern Tatié, where he was enjoying heaps of fresh powder on the slopes, showed he was still holding out, still hesitating. But he promised his correspondents he would be in town during campaign season, "just to keep an eye on you," he said, to Berhooven. "Rumor has it you're a rager when there's free champagne."

"Lady's name," said Aristide, "what a *hideous* hour to be awake."

Cyril was too well-trained and too hungover to snap the file shut with any speed. Anyway, Ari's voice came from somewhere behind him, probably the hallway. Cyril could picture him, half-wrapped in his dressing gown, leaning forward on his toes at the edge of the fringed runner.

Carefully, Cyril folded up his research and switched it out for a set of innocuous memos.

"Do you realize what t-t-time it is?" asked Aristide. Cyril heard, just barely, footsteps on the plush carpeting. Cool, bony hands slipped over his shoulders, settling on the planes of his chest.

"I can't lie in when I'm hungover." Cyril shuffled the memos into a tidy stack and set his briefcase aside, unsteady enough that he didn't have to worry about looking casual.

"Poor, p-p-pitiful Cyril." Aristide settled on the arm of the chair, his robe falling away from a lean thigh, waxed smooth. He picked up the yellow-filmed tumbler from Cyril's coffee tray. "Did Ilse bring you an egg tonic?"

"If you mean that vile mix-up you call a remedy, she did." Cyril set a hand on Ari's leg, stroked it. His skin was golden-brown, smooth but delicate with the first faint signs of age—Cyril placed Ari in his early forties, but would never dream of asking. He let his head fall into the curve of Aristide's ribs and stomach, still warm from bed, and listened to his heartbeat and the waking growls of his hungry stomach.

"Ilse was going to do herring rollmops," said Ari, finger-combing Cyril's pomade-sticky bed head, "but you look like you mightn't want any."

Cyril swallowed against a rush of bile. "How is it," he demanded, "that you're awake and in good health while you drank at least as much as I did—"

"P-P-Practice—" started Aristide, but Cyril ran over him.

"—and spent half the night going through my things? I heard you rummaging around. Did you find anything interesting?"

The sly good humor vanished from Aristide's expression. "Cyril."

Cyril sighed and straightened. "No. Never mind. Let's not get into it." But he'd crossed a line. Their conflict of interest was not something they discussed. Ari stood from the arm of the chair and straightened his dressing gown.

"I'll go see about some breakfast, shall I." It was not a question. He stalked off in search of Ilse, leaving Cyril scowling over a third cup of coffee, his stomach not entirely convinced of the wisdom of a decent meal.

His hangover had passed into new and undreamt-of agonies by the time he arrived at the Foxhole, briefcase clutched in one white-knuckled hand and an unread copy of the *Clarion* wedged into his armpit. He'd been too sick on the trolley to do much but sip the cold, wet air and pray.

Foyles, whose powers of observation matched those of Central's brightest, smiled with one side of his mouth. "Feeling woozy, sir?" he asked. "You won't like what's happening upstairs. I ain't supposed to know it, but the Gentleman's in with Culpepper and they're both waiting for you."

If Culpepper was "the Skull," to the Foxhole, "the Gentleman" was Josiah Hebrides, Amberlough's primary representative to the upper assembly of Gedda's parliament. Cyril's stomach sank further into turmoil.

On the fifth floor, Memmediv gave Cyril a sour look over the tops of his reading spectacles.

"Morning, Memmediv." Cyril had discovered on the ride over that he'd lost his cigarette case during last night's activities. "Don't suppose you've got a straight?"

The secretary made a small noise through his impressive nose. "Honestly." But he pulled a black leather case from his pocket and flipped it open. His hooded glare followed Cyril, who took time picking. The row of crisp white tubes had a tendency to blur together, and the smell of tobacco made him dizzy with craving and sickness in equal measure.

Memmediv was saved from giving up his cigarettes by Culpepper, who chose that moment to stick her head out the door.

"DePaul," she said, and nothing else. But it was enough that Cyril groaned and straightened up. "Vaz," Culpepper went on, and she must have been distracted, because usually she was scrupulously professional with Memmediv. "Be a swan and fetch us some coffee?"

"Yes, Vasily," said Cyril. "Do."

Culpepper leveled a thin finger at Cyril. "You. In here." The finger curled.

Gathering himself, Cyril sighed and followed her.

"Don't embarrass me in front of Hebrides," she said, close to his ear. "If you hurl on the carpet, you're cleaning it up."

"Ada." He put his hand between her mouth and his ear. "After coffee. Please. "

She was about to snap at him—he could feel the sharp intake of her breath against his cheek—but she didn't get the words out.

"DePaul!"

"Mr. Hebrides." Cyril let his hand be drawn into a vigorous shake. Hebrides's grip was dry and warm, his palm meaty. He was shorter than Cyril, but probably weighed half again as much: a solid man with flushed features and black, receding hair. Gray gleamed under the dye.

"How are you keeping?" He stopped pumping Cyril's arm, but kept his hand and drew him close to slap his back. In mint condition, Cyril would've borne this jovial greeting with better spirits. But while his liver worked to exorcise half a bottle of the city's best absinthe, all he could do was nod and try, wanly, to smile.

"A little worse for wear, eh?" Hebrides pulled out Culpepper's plush leather chair. "Have a seat. Need a straight?"

Cyril settled into the soft, creaking cushions. "Gasping for one."

"I'm glad a few of Ada's foxes still know how to have fun." Hebrides flipped open his cigarette case and slipped out two gold-banded straights. "She's come down hard on her pups. When old Aurelio was in charge of the 'hole . . . well. There were more than a few of his agents who stumbled in late reeking of gin. Always got their jobs done, though." Hebrides spoke with a thick urban drone, the hallmark of a city-born Amberlinian.

"DePaul's methods have become . . . unorthodox in the last year." Culpepper set her stack of files down and favored Cyril with a sneer. "But I'm confident he'll clean up well."

"And quickly too, I hope." Hebrides lit his cigarette, then tossed the matchbook to Cyril. "Your ticket's booked for next week."

"Precipitous."

"Efficient." Culpepper drew up the guest chair and sat across from Cyril. "You've read the letters. Do you have any questions?"

"A few. Landseer's wormed his way into this cohort very smoothly. But what for? I mean, it looks like they want his money, but why? To buy votes? What's the point of sending me?"

"Not buying votes, no," said Culpepper. "The Ospies need financial support. Their constituency is made up of people hurt by shipping tariffs; money's tight by default."

"So I'm tempting them to . . ."

"Tell us all their dirty secrets." Hebrides rubbed his hands together. "Make them convince you. Landseer won't get a return on his investment unless the Ospies win the election. So make them tell you how they'll do it. The reports coming out of Nuesklend say the Ospies have the results sewn up. But no one's talking; we don't have proof enough to scuttle Acherby's plans."

"Ah," said Cyril. "So I'm bait. A honeypot."

"A moneypot, more like." Hebrides laughed at his own joke. "Hold out, DePaul, like a blush boy playing for his rent. Hold out."

"And Staetler. She's given the all-clear?" Tatié had been unofficial. White work, they called it, for the paper between the lines. Unconstitutional, and dangerous. But with the permission of Staetler, Nuesklend's governing primary . . .

"She's promised to endorse our action during the endgame." From the look on Culpepper's face, she knew it wasn't what Cyril wanted to hear. "But you understand, she can't issue any official permissions. We aren't sure who in her office or the Nuesklend Foxhole is on the Ospie payroll."

The door swung inward and Memmediv entered, hip first, bearing a tray of cups, sugar, and a salver of cream. He set it down in the midst of a stiff silence, under the weight of a secret conversation obviously suspended. But working in Central, Cyril supposed, he must be used to that sort of thing. He managed it with grace.

"Thank you, Memmediv," said Culpepper, her professional manner reassembled.

"No trouble." He retreated and shut the heavy door behind him.

Hebrides settled onto a corner of Culpepper's desk and dashed cream into one of the cups. "Doctor says to take it black," he confided. "But when half the nation stands against you, I say take it however you damn well please."

Cyril curled his hands around his own cup, breathing the dark scent deep down into his queasy center. "So," he said. "I dangle a blank check in front of their noses and make them convince me. And you're hoping to shut it down before things come to a head?"

"Ideally. You get the evidence; we bring an accusation. The regionalists mount a fraud suit against Acherby, destroy his political career, and get him thrown in the trap."

"And what if I can't get you anything until after the election?"

"Same story. Just riskier. Possession is nine-tenths, et cetera." Culpepper hitched an ankle over her knee. Her trouser leg pulled up, showing a length of muted argyle sock.

"Can't you just get Nuesklend's Master of the Hounds on this? It sounds like a police matter to me. Or maybe ask parliament for election monitors?"

"Election monitors are out," said Hebrides. "Tensions too high with the Ospie states."

"Shake with the right, shoot with the left." Cyril massaged his forehead, pressing on his tender sinuses. "And the police?"

"We strongly suspect the unionists have bought Nuesklend's force," Culpepper said. "It's part of why they're hurting for money. And party members aren't afraid to wield a cudgel in service of the cause. They have intimidation down to an art form. Finding witnesses to testify will be a problem."

"But I'm not allowed to be intimidated, am I?"

"Why?" asked Culpepper. "Are you?"

Cyril set down his coffee cup and took a deep drag on Josiah's very fine cigarette. The smooth tobacco tasted of malt sugar. Closing his eyes, he pretended to savor it.

Fieldwork. The scar that split his belly itched. He fought to calm his heart rate, to put the terror of his last action out of his mind. This was a simple job, set up by someone else, already half-done. An easy entrée, for an experienced agent stepping back into harness. He'd been very good at this sort of thing, once. He realized he was still holding his breath, and forced himself to let it go slowly.

Mid-exhale, he opened his eyes, and met Culpepper's gaze through the smoke. "Who's my case officer?"

She finally smiled, barely, and there was an edge to it. "You'll report to me. It's a little bit beneath my purview, but I thought you'd appreciate the familiarity."

"For old times' sake?" Cyril ground out his straight. "You're a treasure."

It got him one of her rare smiles. He tried to match it and knew he hadn't. Shaking hands with Hebrides, he excused himself, then retreated to the washroom. As soon as the door was closed and bolted, he stripped his jacket and loosened his tie, then collapsed against the toilet bowl and vomited.

Culpepper gave him samples of Landseer's handwriting to copy, and he spent a few hours covering pages and pages with the back-slanting script. His eyes hurt and his wrist was cramped, and he wasn't getting any better at it. Besides, the sun was out at last, shining on the spires and naked treetops of the university. He didn't want his back to the window. He wanted the sun and clear air.

The lift shuddered to a halt at the third floor. That redheaded boy—Finn Lourdes, wasn't it?—got on with hat in hand, shapeless greatcoat unbuttoned at the front to reveal his shabby suit, worn to a shine. He nodded at Cyril, politely, but seemed to catch halfway through the gesture, like a faulty piece of clockwork.

"Here, now." He leaned forward in concern, and his forelock flopped into his eyes. They were slate gray, generously ringed in blue. "Are you all right? You look bashed."

Sacred arches, Cyril must look dire, if the accountants were catching him out. "Late night," he said. "And a little too much of the green witch."

"Ah, that explains it." He pushed his hair back. It was unstyled and wanted a cut, though its copper brilliance distracted from its disarray. "You look like you're about to drop."

"I am," said Cyril, and Finn laughed.

"Finn Lourdes," said the younger man, holding out a hand. "I don't believe we've ever met, not properly. You were pretty far gone with the morphine, last time." He had the soft, rolling accent of an urban Farbourgere. Pleasant to listen to.

Cyril shifted greatcoat and briefcase. Finn's handshake was good. Cyril held it a moment longer than necessary. Finn had soft palms, but for a scrivener's callous on his pointer finger, black with an ink stain. As their shake lengthened, a flush started across the bridge of Finn's nose, rising up his cheeks.

"Cyril DePaul." He broke the handshake and eye contact and took his card case from his breast pocket.

"A pleasure." Finn took a card, scanned the front, then slid it into the battered leather folio he held under one arm. Spiraling a finger to indicate the building around them, he asked, "Making a break from this tomb?"

"Hah." Cyril let himself half-smile. "I suppose you could say that. You?"

"Actually . . ." Finn looked over his shoulder, as if he suspected eavesdroppers. "Yes. I've told them I've got a doctor's appointment. Don't let on. It's just, it's been raining for ages, and the sun's finally out . . ." He cocked his head, watching Cyril from beneath strong brows like gulls' wings. "I was thinking I might go down to the harbor for lunch, watch the boats come in. Say, you wouldn't join me, would you?"

Cyril must not have kept the dubious expression from his face, because Finn blanched and stammered and said, "Only, if you've got somewhere else to be, or if you're too tired, I under-stand—"

Finn seemed sweet, but Cyril didn't do sweet. "Is this a pickup?" he asked, more sharply than he meant to. Exhaustion made him blunt.

Finn went from sick white to burning redhead blush in less than a space of a breath. "Oh! Oh, no, I—it's just it's nice out, and you seem so . . . well." He checked himself. "I'm sorry. Please, don't pay me any mind."

The hectic color in Finn's cheeks shamed Cyril, and suddenly he felt small and mean. The lift doors opened onto the ground floor. Before Finn could rush off in embarrassment, Cyril stopped him with a hand on his arm. "Where to?"

Finn started, then smiled. "Nowhere special. There's a little place I like near the spillway. Cheap oysters, but they won't kill you."

It wasn't quite a dive, but it wasn't what Cyril was accustomed to, either. Finn advised against the establishment's liquor, so Cyril had beer, which was surprisingly good.

Finn's shabby suit and shiny elbows fit snugly into the ambiance, and when Cyril caught a glimpse of himself in the mirror behind the bar, he admitted they probably wouldn't have let him through the door at Sola's. Bags under his eyes, patchy stubble, rumpled suit. No wonder Finn had worried about him on the lift.

"You're fifth floor, right?" Finn spooned horseradish into another fan-shaped shell. These were big, earthy Amberlough Phrynes— cheap local oysters, not the sweet, small, dearly expensive west coasters.

Cyril nodded. "A paper pusher. Rather like you, I expect. A lot of budgets."

"I thought fifth floor was supposed to be thrilling," said Finn. "Espionage and cloak-and-dagger and things like that. Like in the novels."

Cyril laughed into his beer, tried not to think about the packet of Landseer's false papers locked in his desk. Exhaustion sank its claws into his back, pushed his shoulders forward. "I hate to disappoint you."

"No glamour at all, then?"

"Well. I wouldn't say that." Cyril spread butter across a slice of brown bread, but saw white greasepaint shining on the angles of Aristide's face, light through the rising effervescence of champagne. Damnation. What was he going to tell Aristide?

"Anything would be more exciting than the old adding machine," said Finn. "Believe me, I'm good at what I do, but mercy! It's unbelievably dull."

"Even with all the Foxhole's little secrets passing under your nose?"

"Secrets turn tiresome faster than you'd think."

"Pithy," said Cyril.

"I didn't mean it as an epigram." Finn tipped the last oyster down his throat, then wiped his fingers and face with a cheap brown paper napkin. He signaled the bartender, and Cyril reached for his billfold.

"Oh, my treat," said Finn.

"No," said Cyril, "really."

Finn shook his head, once, decisively. "I said the oysters were cheap. I made the invitation, and I'm paying. You make an invitation, you can pay."

Cyril raised the last of his beer. "Until the next time, then."

Finn smiled, and tipped his empty pint glass in acknowledgment of the toast.

CHAPTER

FIVE

———————————

"Queen's sake, Tory, not here!" Cordelia shoved Tory away, looking over her shoulder to make sure no one had seen him reach up her skirt.

"Why not?" He leaned against the bannister of the backstage stairway. "You've got ten minutes and an empty dressing room."

"I can't," she said. "I don't got my cap with me, and I ain't having your kids."

"I've got a mouth and two hands, Delly." He wiggled his fingers. "Quit makin' excuses."

"Tory, Malcolm ain't stupid. I know he looks it, and Mother knows he acts it half the time, but he's not gonna—Tory!" She slapped his hands away.

"Ach, he'll be caught up flaying Thea alive. If that girl's job lasts out the day, call me a trout and salt me." He lowered his eyelashes and the pitch of his voice, walking his fingers up her thigh. "Come on. Let's give old Sailer good reason to be jealous."

She sighed. "Oh, damnation. All right. Come on." She took his hand and pulled him down the hall, toward her dressing room. Backstage was quiet—it was still early in the day, and Malcolm had only called a rehearsal for the orchestra, with Thea and Cordelia, to work on their one iffy number. Cordelia had a ten-minute break while Liesl drilled Thea on her key changes. Tory was here because he wanted to be, and Malcolm wasn't pinned about it.

As soon as she closed the door of her dressing room, Tory grabbed her waistband and hauled her close, pressing his nose into the groove of her spine and taking a deep breath. She could feel the air move on her skin, through the cheap wool. His hands swept up the fronts of her legs, catching on her skirt, slipping beneath it.

"Tory," she said, and he murmured into her blouse. "Tory, you don't mind me doing what I do. Right?"

"Stripping?" He drew away and pushed at her hips until she turned to face him. "There's far worse you could do. You haven't ever killed anybody with it. And if you have, you can't hold yourself responsible for them that's got weak hearts."

"No," she said, tracing his chin with a thoughtful finger. "I meant with Malcolm. And any others that come along." She made herself laugh, a little. "And they do tend to."

He chuckled and grabbed her rear. Bending down, he pressed his face into the divot of her groin. "Delly," he said, "you're a big girl, and you like your fun." The pressure of his weight pushed her back, and she fell into her makeup chair. It started to spin, but he stopped it. "If I minded—" He flipped up the edge of her skirt, and ducked under. "—I'd already be gone."

His fingers crept to the tops of her stockings, found the edge of her panties, and pushed them aside. She dug her varnished nails deep into the scarred leather of the upholstery. Tory's breath warmed her skin. She felt a flush rise up her neck, across her chest, and lifted a hand to touch her breast. She crossed her ankles across Tory's back, sliding down in her seat into the slippery heat of his mouth.

Five minutes later, she had her blouse unbuttoned, and one shoe half-hanging from her big toe. Tory was pulling himself off with his face still pressed between her thighs. Her breath was dry and ragged, her hands curled into fists. Tossing her head back, she caught a flash of her own red face in the mirror. And then Malcolm opened the door without knocking, already halfway through whatever sentence he meant for her to hear.

"—she was a man I'd cut the oysters off her, and then she might hit those high no—Queen's cunt, Delia!"

Tory startled beneath her skirt, then froze. Cordelia blinked once, twice, watching the color drain from Malcolm's face.

"I thought you were rehearsing," she said, stupidly.

"Delia," he said again, and his voice was dangerously even. Then, he looked down and lost his composure completely. "Tory MacIntyre, you son of a half-price whore! Get out of there!"

Tory flipped back Cordelia's skirt like it was a curtain and he was making a casual entrance onto the stage. "Sailer," he said. "Didn't expect you to finish with that poor girl so soon. From what Delly's said, I hadn't got you pegged as a sprinter."

Malcolm's pallor evaporated in the heat of a sudden, furious flush. He reached out, unseeing, towards the shelf where Cordelia kept her wigs and headdresses. There was a fifth of gin there, and an empty tumbler. Malcolm's hand closed around the glass, and he hurled it at the wall. It shattered, and Cordelia took a moment to be grateful he hadn't thrown the bottle.

"What, I ain't enough for you?" Malcolm threw himself into his chair. She'd cajoled him into his own office, where at least anything he broke would belong to him.

"We're friends, Mal. Tory and I are good friends."

"You're knockin' him."

"Why do you care? We ain't married."

He crushed an invoice in his fist. "Is that what you want?"

"Oh for pity's sake." She rolled her eyes. "No one in their right mind would take you home."

"You can turn that one around," said Malcolm, sneering.

Cordelia opened her mouth to reply, but the door to Malcolm's office swung open and Aristide Makricosta looked in, flicking a damp ringlet from his face. "I heard you sacked the tit singer," he said. "I'll fill in, but I expect a b-b-bonus." He pulled the door to, and his footsteps echoed down the hallway.

Malcolm swept the ruined paper into the wastebasket. "Like he needs it."

"Why do you put up with him at all?" Cordelia flicked her fingers, as if cleaning them of dirt. "He's a certified prick."

Malcolm reached into his breast pocket and pulled out a battered cigarette. He made her wait while he lit it, took a deep drag, and blew the smoke straight up at the ceiling. Stubble shadowed the column of his throat. "Because he brings in the punters with the deep pockets."

"Oh, and me?"

"You just reach in and make 'em pay."

"Get hanged." Slamming the door, she stalked back to her dressing room. It was one scrap too many. On top of being interrupted with Tory, on top of the fight with Malcolm, she was behind on rent. Tips had been harder to come by, with all the punters on edge. The number of sour faces she'd seen, the number of whispers about the election . . . It ought to be illegal to sell newspapers on Temple Street. Ruined business for the entertainment trade.

She borrowed a broom from Lucia, the old caretaker, and swept up the shattered glass in her dressing room. Two bits she couldn't afford sent Tito scrambling down toward the boardwalk for a bite of whatever the food carts were selling.

Backstage started to fill up with cast and stagehands. Cordelia stripped off her street clothes and hung them on the coat hooks behind the door. Goosebumps broke out on her bare skin—Malcolm must have axed the boiler for the season. Pinch-pocket miser.

She was gluing on her pasties over nipples stiff with cold when Tito returned holding a greasy paper bag.

"Barley fritters all right?" he asked. "Stuffed with eel."

"Suits like a tailor," she said. "Take one yourself."

He reached a hand in the bag, took his due, and handed it over. She had to put down her second pasty to take it.

Tito didn't look away, and she wouldn't have minded, except he said, "Heard you had a scrap with Mr. Sailer."

"And if I did, I did." She held the bag of fritters in front of her chest. "Now get away and do what you're paid to."

When she had her pasties and merkin fixed tight, she scarfed the fritters and knotted herself into her dressing gown. Settled in her makeup chair, she tried to put Malcolm and Tory and Tito out of mind. Men. Mother's tits! She scowled in the mirror, then smoothed her expression and started layering on the powder.

CHAPTER

SIX

_____

When Aristide came down the stairs into the long, low dining room of the Crabtree House, he saw Cyril waiting at the bar. Unaware of Aristide's scrutiny, Cyril curled one hand around his signature rye and soda and made the other a fisted column for the bowed weight of his head. His crisp navy suit and the high shine of his brogues might have fooled a casual observer, but Aristide knew the curve of those shoulders intimately, and all the pride had been beaten from them.

He didn't brighten up over dinner. By the time the server took away the cheese plate, Aristide had had enough.

"You're awfully quiet," he said, stirring a lump of muscovado into his coffee. When Aristide had last seen Cyril, five days ago, he'd been hungover and peevish, gray with fatigue. Now, the flickering candle on the tabletop cast warm light onto the planes of his face, disguising the dark shadows under his eyes. He had shaved— no, *been* shaved—and the clean line of his newly starched collar made a bright stripe against his smooth skin.

"Am I?" Despite his fresh appearance, lingering exhaustion colored his speech and movements. He stared into a cordial glass, turning it on its base so the liqueur hung in veils on the crystal. "Sorry."

"Hard d-d-day at the office, dear?" Aristide flirted over the rim of his cup, waiting for Cyril's riposte. It didn't come. Instead, Cyril snorted, and sipped his digestif.

The susurrus of other tables' conversation, the quiet nip of silver against china, rose into the silence as their repartee faltered. Aristide sighed, loudly enough that Cyril looked up from his drink with weary eyes.

"Go on," Cyril said. "I know you want to ask."

"What is *wrong* with you?" Aristide set his spoon down harder than he meant to, spattering the tablecloth with coffee. "You haven't said four words together all evening, and you look like a whipped spaniel."

Cyril covered the coffee stains with his fingertips. "I have to leave Amberlough."

"Trouble with the lower element?" asked Aristide, only half joking. "Who did you murder? I can p-p-probably smooth it out."

"No, it's just work. But thank you for the offer." He was silent for a moment, then added, "I'll be gone a while. A month or two."

"So, Central's finally realized you're wasted on the d-d-demimonde." Aristide slid his palm across the linen and took up Cyril's resting hand. "Where are they sending you that required such a *sublime* manicure?" Cyril's nails shone, freshly buffed, filed to white-tipped crescents. "I hear that fieldwork can be quite . . . *strenuous*. Won't you only ruin it?" He didn't have a clear picture of Cyril's career, but that scar . . . it marred his skin with a memory of violence. Without thinking, Aristide tightened his grip.

"Not this time," Cyril said, extricating himself. "At least, I hope not."

"Are they sending you to woo foreign nobility?" asked Aristide. "Or imp-p-personate a concert pianist, perhaps?"

Cyril flexed his hands self-consciously, curling them into fists to hide his fingernails. "No," he said, crisp with finality.

Aristide ignored Cyril's irritation and kept up the banter. "True, I don't suppose you know how to p-p-play. But you could learn. You're clever. Culpepper wouldn't p-p-put up with you, otherwise. And, let's be honest: neither would I."

"Ari—"

"So what is it? Or were you just suddenly struck by the *shameful* state of your cuticles"—here his diction turned sharp, accusatory—"and thought you'd have a shave and haircut at Padgett and Sons while somebody buffed your nails?"

Cyril's face went slack in surprise, and he looked ten years older.

"Give me some credit," purred Aristide, low and smooth with malice. "Not that you don't keep in fine trim on your own, but even a common b-b-*bootblack* would notice the difference. And anyway, the scent of the pomade is unmistakable. You *reek* of sage and ambergris." This last comment he kept light, tossed onto the table like a thoughtless tip.

It earned him a scowl. "Maybe I just decided to treat myself."

"Cyril, p-p-please. From one professional liar to another, d-d-don't work tired. Your t-t-t-technique suffers." He finished his coffee. He'd been hoping for the gratification of Cyril's trust, but settled for his shock instead. "Now. Why don't we retire somewhere more p-p-private, and you can tell me all about Nuesklend." Because of course it was Nuesklend. Aristide paid enough attention to politics to know what was at stake there.

Cyril's expression settled between fury and affection. "Why do I consistently underestimate you?"

Aristide pushed his chair away from the table and stood. "A p-p-pretty face will do that. You, of all p-p-people, ought to know."

Aristide had always been an insomniac. Usually, it didn't bother him—he lived in a good city for wakeful people. But now he stared dry-eyed into the cavern of drapery above his bed. Beside him, Cyril's sleep was fitful, more so than usual. Aristide was used to the twitches, the soft dream mutterings, but tonight Cyril was sweating, his face drawn into a deep frown.

It wasn't unwarranted. Besides Cyril's obvious misgivings about his upcoming trip, they'd sniped and hissed at each other on the walk back from the Crabtree House. Cyril accused Aristide of interrogation. Aristide acted grossly offended, but they both knew it was true. The upshot was that Cyril hadn't told Aristide much about where he was going, or why.

They'd put fighting aside at the door to the flat. No use in wasting what time they had left.

Low against the column of Aristide's spine, a tight muscle that had been threatening all evening finally curled into a spasm. He bit back a curse. Careful not to disturb Cyril, he eased himself up against the headboard and reached for the drawer of his bedside table. The chemist on Barley Street had mixed him a tincture of morphine and valerian to help with sleeplessness and back pain. He rarely used it for the former, but had needed it more and more for the latter.

Ten drops later, he set the bottle aside and closed his eyes, waiting impatiently for relief. He was just drifting off when Cyril jerked and came awake with a strangled yelp. Aristide startled, undoing all the good the drugs had wrought on his recalcitrant muscles.

"Sorry." Cyril's voice was hoarse and thick. A bar of light coming between the curtains showed his cheeks were wet.

He seemed to realize it too, and slashed at his face with the heel of his palm. "Damnation." He took a deep, uneven breath, and went limp against the pillows. After a long moment spent considering the canopy above, he ran a shaky hand through his hair and looked at Aristide, and the bottle on the nightstand. "Trouble sleeping?"

Aristide nodded, his neck stiff. "My back."

"Turn over."

He complied, folding his arms and tucking his face into the crook of his elbow. Cyril lifted the covers away, exposing the aching length of Aristide's back to the cold. Aristide felt the movement of air over his spine, and then the pad of Cyril's thumb pushed into the center of the spasm. Aristide groaned. "Perdition."

Cyril dug in harder, and Aristide could only exhale and blink against the pain. Tense muscles uncoiled like a knot of angry snakes teased apart. "They'd better count those ballots quickly. I'll pay Culpepper very well to make sure you're reassigned to—oof—my beat." A tingling jolt ran down Aristide's leg, and his foot twitched. "Cyril," he said. Then, *Cyril.*

The pressure on his back let up, fast. "Too hard?"

"No. You're just quiet."

"Sorry." Cyril's hands settled into a rhythm again. After a moment, he said, "I haven't had one of those in a while. Not since—well."

Aristide turned his head so his cheek rested on his forearm, and he could see Cyril's face. "Nightmares?"

One corner of his mouth quirked up. "Oh, no. I've had plenty of those. Just . . . I haven't woken myself up screaming."

"More of a squeak."

Cyril's smile was haunted, and he didn't meet Aristide's eyes. Abruptly, he patted the curve of Aristide's hip and lay back down, turning his face away.

From their first meeting—outside the theatre, in the rain, after weeks of cat and mouse through various informants—Aristide had never asked questions. He didn't want to hear Cyril's answers. What he knew was secondhand, through reliable sources, and that was enough. It let him separate his own Cyril from the Foxhole's.

He suspected Cyril practiced the same delicate art of compartmentalization. There was the Aristide lying beside him in bed—the charming performer and monarch of the demimonde—and there was the other Aristide, the one he was supposed to arrest and interrogate. The one whose life and livelihood he was meant to raze.

They both knew where the boundaries lay. It was impossible to love someone when you spent your time digging at their secrets in the hopes of undermining their career. And vice versa. But suddenly this Cyril, *his* Cyril, was crying out in his sleep because the other Cyril was afraid.

Aristide swallowed another ten drops of opiate, and considered his scruples.

When the tension began to drain from his limbs, he slid back beneath the covers. Wrapping himself around the fetal curve of Cyril's spine, Aristide slipped an arm into the divot of his waist, pulling him close.

"Did you know." Cyril choked, swallowed, and tried again. "Did you know, it's even odds on your life when they pull your belly open and find your guts torn apart?"

Aristide did not let his hand stray down to the tough length of scarring that bisected Cyril's middle, but some small movement must have telegraphed his curiosity. Cyril exhaled: not quite laughter, but not a sigh.

"They told me they had to pull everything out into a bucket and scrub my insides clean with salt water. My belly was filled with shit. If I had gone another day like that, I would have died."

Aristide wondered what, or who, had come so close to ending Cyril's life. The scar had been fresh when they met, but they were more careful with their mysteries then. "Darling," he said, "I'm sure this time—"

"I never used to think about it." Cyril's interjection came fast, like he had to speak before he could stop to think about it. "Dying. I suppose I didn't think I would. And then I almost did, and I realized I . . . Ari, I'm not sure I want to do it anymore."

Uncomfortable with this sudden breakdown in their careful protocol, and trying for levity, Aristide said, "I rather think it's the sort of thing you can only do once."

"That wasn't what I . . ." Cyril shook his head. "No. Never mind."

Ashamed, Aristide pulled Cyril closer; close enough to feel the edges of his shoulder blades when he breathed. "I'm sorry. Facetious remarks are a nasty habit to break." He buried his nose in Cyril's hair, breathing in the scents of cigarettes and sage. "It will be fine, I'm sure. Nobody's going to kill you. It's just a little bit of politics: flirtation and double-talk."

"Maybe they ought to send you."

"Cheeky." Aristide's lips brushed the fine stubble at the base of Cyril's skull, snipped short by the barber. "This is politics. I *loathe* politics." It got him a laugh, at least. "You'll handle it beautifully, whatever it is. The Ospies haven't got a chance."

CHAPTER
SEVEN

Cyril's rooms in Nuesklend were freezing. Ocean currents kept the west coast temperate during the winter, but did nothing for the damp cold that pervaded every stone. And the capital was practically made of the stuff. Quarried from the Cultham Mountains, the gray slabs breathed mineral chill. Cyril tipped the bellhop who brought up his luggage, but didn't let the man take his hat or overcoat.

He drew a chair up to the radiator and set his feet on the metal only to find it cold. Cursing, he searched for the valve, already fed up with Nuesklend.

On the long train ride from Amberlough City, where the false trail of Landseer's journey left off and Cyril's real one began, he'd composed a set of letters letting his correspondents know he had arrived in Nuesklend. When the train stopped at the state line in the village of Büllen, Cyril asked about good hotels in the capital, and had them wire ahead to the best one they could find.

On arrival, he'd posted the letters at the desk, collected his keys, and asked for a bath before bed. Outside his window, the last shreds of sunset colored the horizon. The sea was a dark plane, and seemed still until Cyril closed his eyes and listened. Waves struck the gravel shore and receded, rhythmic as breath.

The attendant who came to run his bath left a letter on the card table. Before Cyril abandoned himself to soap and steam, he slit the seal on the envelope and read his correspondence. From Rotherhite: an invitation to lunch at his club tomorrow. He'd got that one off fast. They really were slavering after Landseer's money. Well, if they'd bought the whole of Nuesklend's police force, or even just the capital hounds, they'd be nearly skint.

Cyril left his response for the morning, dropped his traveling clothes in a heap on the washroom floor, and sank into the deep brass tub.

Rotherhite's club, the Klipsee, was farther up from the hotel on the steep cliff road that wound around the capital's heart. Cyril, his legs still cramped from traveling, chose to walk it. A changeable sky spat brief showers, but the wind precluded an umbrella. He turned up his collar and tried to keep to sheltered side streets. Still, every now and then his route afforded him an ocean vista of frothing waves and gray rocks like broken teeth. Across the widemouthed harbor, where the wharves clung to a crimp of stone, dozens of ships rocked at their berths.

Ospie propaganda painted Nuesklend and Amberlough as wicked twins, exclusive economic gatekeepers; but in this colorless limpet of a city, Cyril saw nothing that reminded him of home.

He arrived at the Klipsee raw-cheeked but refreshed, in body if not in spirit, and gave his name. It wasn't the first time he'd called himself Landseer—he'd been using it with every ticket taker and customs clerk on his journey west—but it felt different now, and it got a different reaction. Obsequious staff showed him to a quiet, dark-paneled room, offering him coffee, brandy, and some sort of absurdly red local liqueur.

Two men arrived shortly after Cyril's coffee. A tall, underweight character with a severe mustache—"Willem Rotherhite. It's good to meet you at last, Mr. Landseer!"—and a doughy man with a bland round face and thinning hair. Cyril recognized him, from the photograph in his file, but let himself be introduced.

"This is Konrad Van der Joost," said Rotherhite. "An associate of mine."

"Textiles?" asked Cyril.

"If only," said Van der Joost, casting his pale eyes around the richness of the room. "No, we're in the same chapter of the One State Party."

"Oh, Konrad, let's not get into it just yet. We've got a month or so to get our friend to open up his wallet. Have a brandy first, Seb, and let's hear about Ibet. I'll wager the slopes were fine, this time of year, and the schoolgirls finer. They all go up to the mountains for mid-quarter break, from the university. I studied for a few years there, back in my halcyon days."

Cyril admitted the skiing had been excellent, but kept mum on the condition of the students. He'd read the letters; Landseer was cautious at first, socially. Even with a few years' worth of correspondence, this was his first meeting with Rotherhite in person, and he'd never spoken to Van der Joost. Crass remarks could wait until Landseer was more comfortable.

They chatted for an hour or so, and lunched on bass and plovers' eggs. Cyril let himself be talked into a glass of the scarlet digestif, which turned out to be tart cherry bounce—a Nuesklend specialty. Conversation was trivial. When Rotherhite checked his watch over brandy and declared it was time for his next appointment, Cyril shook his hand and accepted an invitation to dine at his home later in the week.

"I'll have some of the others round," he said, "Keeler and her girls, and maybe old Berhooven. I'm sure they'd love to see you in the flesh. The young misses Keeler especially." His wink was theatrical, almost flirtatious, but not in the way Aristide's would have been. Cyril had a pang, and ignored it.

Van der Joost lingered after Rotherhite had gone. Cyril smoked and swirled his brandy, waiting for the other man to make some conversation. When it came, it made him catch his breath.

"You know, you're not at all what I expected." Van der Joost was busy slicing the end of a cigar, and didn't see Cyril flinch. "From Rotherhite's description of your letters."

"Really?" He steadied himself with a sip of brandy. Not blown, not yet. "You thought I'd be . . . what? Older? Less charming?"

Van der Joost smiled around his cigar, puffing against the wick of an elaborate table lighter. "I can't say I'm sorry you defied my expectations."

"Well, Mr. Van der Joost," said Cyril, grinding out his straight, "I'll endeavor to go on defying them. Good day."

Van der Joost's handshake was cold and a little clammy. When Cyril was safely out of the room, he wiped his palm clean on his jacket. The fine dark wool wouldn't show the sweat.

Cyril's walk in the rain caught up with him; he contracted a nasty head cold for the next few days, rereading the Landseer letters and quizzing himself on his four main correspondents. Rotherhite he'd met—a widower, but a bit of a man about town. Then there was Pollerdam, a sober man with keen business skills, not apt to stray far from his factories. Berhooven was full of stories of rowdy weekends and big losses at the gambling table, but he could probably afford to lose.

Keeler was the most interesting. A widow, and Rotherhite said she had children, though she'd never mentioned them in her letters. Acherby hadn't been too shy when it came to his opinions on working women—he was a raving Hearther evangelist—so Keeler must be supporting the unionists for purely financial reasons. Nuesklend's mills would profit from lower shipping tariffs.

The night of Rotherhite's dinner, Cyril's cab switchbacked up the cliffs, crested the rise, and began a descent toward the interior. The houses lining the road drew farther and farther back until the driver pulled into a cul-de-sac surrounded by low stone walls and iron fences. Warm lamps lit the pavement, but not the sweep of gardens that separated each grand house from its neighbors and the street. The neighborhood was far enough from the edge of the sea cliffs that wind stirred the trees but didn't threaten Cyril's hat. He paid his fare and the cabbie left him standing at the apex of the cul-de-sac, staring down a long front walk lined in privet.

When the footman opened the door, light from the foyer spread in a golden fan across the path and the hedges. Cyril blinked in the sudden brightness.

"Mr. Landseer?" The footman bowed him in and took his coat. "The others are in the drawing room."

Upstairs, Rotherhite held court at an upright piano, singing some sort of rowdy folk song. A fat man with a wide nose and wind-burned cheeks sang along. Berhooven, most likely. Van der Joost leaned on the side of the upright, holding a glass and half-smiling.

A young woman in a green silk bolero sat on the sofa. She had a strong jaw and straight nose. Her hair, cropped into a wavy shingle, shone the warm maple-brown of buckwheat honey. She tapped thin fingers on her knee, mostly matching the beat of the music.

A patrician older lady—by appearance, the mother of the seated girl—welcomed Cyril from her place at the sideboard. She had the same long neck as her daughter, and the same set jaw. Citrine earrings threw spots of gold onto the papery skin of her throat. "You must be the long-awaited Mr. Landseer." She poured two aperitifs and brought them to where he stood. "I don't suppose I have to tell you, but we're all inordinately pleased you could finally make it to Gedda." She offered him a glass. "I'm Minna Keeler. Please, have a seat."

He took the chair at a right angle to the sofa, but not before shaking the hand of the striking woman seated there.

"Sofie," said Keeler. "My eldest."

Sofie's handshake was firm and dry, and she met his gaze. Her eyes were bright hazel, more green than brown, flecked with spots of orange. "Mr. Landseer," she said. "Mother's told us so much about you."

"All of it good, I hope."

"I'm afraid Loelia was struck with a cold," said Keeler, "and couldn't come. Shame, she's such a charming girl. And my youngest, Jane, is still in school."

"My sincerest well-wishes for the invalid," said Cyril. "I've only just recovered, myself."

"Keeler!" Berhooven waved her over to the piano. "Come tell Van der Joost he's talking rot."

"Do excuse me." She swept away in a ripple of navy skirts.

"Poor Mummy," said Sofie Keeler. "Always called on to defend the ladies when Konrad hares off on one of his screeds."

"And is that very often?"

She rolled her eyes. "You wouldn't believe it. And the absurd thing is, *she* was raised by a lot of hair-shirted Holy Hearth missionaries at a cloister school in Enselem." Sofie's speech was rapid but smooth, rolling in the careless rhythm of privileged gossip: Each word ran into the next as if she expected he already knew what she was going to say. "Half the time, I think she's quite nearly on his side. Only, if she gave in too easily, you can be sure he'd use it against her. He's got a lot of clout." Smirking, she lowered her voice and added, "Even if he does look like a lamprey."

Their conspiratorial laughter was interrupted by the arrival of the butler, with the dinner announcement. Cyril, to his great delight, was seated with Sofie.

"Newcomer's privilege," said Rotherhite. He took the chair at the head of the table, with Van der Joost to his right and Keeler to his left. Berhooven sat at the foot, like a jester.

Rotherhite steered conversation—mostly sports, and his own exotic travels. Berhooven nodded along, occasionally interjecting with his own opinion, which invariably made him, and sometimes the rest of them, laugh. Cyril could tell Berhooven didn't quite fit here. Even his appearance made him a stranger. He was shorter than his peers, and fatter, with a swarthy complexion and floppy dark curls.

Keeler talked with Van der Joost about business, business, business. Rotherhite picked on her and called her a killjoy, but her icy stare sent him into retreat.

With regret, Cyril saw that his attention to the group dynamics had cost him Sofie's initial fondness. She toyed with her guinea fowl, pushing a bit of crouton through the raisin sauce. She was thoroughly out of the conversation by the time it swung around to the absent Mijkel Pollerdam, and Cyril asked, "Yes, where is Pollerdam? I was hoping I'd meet him tonight."

"You'll very rarely find Pollerdam venturing south of Morray." Rotherhite dipped his fingers in the pewter bowl offered by a footman. "He spends nearly all his time at his factories." Morray was a mill town tucked into the foothills of the Culthams, on the border with Farbourgh.

"He prefers more rustic entertainments," said Berhooven, and Cyril wondered if it was supposed to be a double entendre. No one laughed. "But he's promised to come down in time for the election."

"Well, I think it's admirable."

The whole table turned to look at Sofie, whose silence had rendered her invisible until then.

"What is, dear?" Van der Joost's pale eyes stuck to Sofie like barnacles.

"His staying in the north. If he doesn't enjoy society, why force him? He's keeping a sharp eye on his means of production, which is more than the rest of us can say."

"You've got a clever daughter, Keeler." Cyril favored Sofie with a smile at last. She returned it gratefully. "You're lucky she'll be here to inherit the family business."

"Oh, no." Sofie twirled her fork against her plate, scratching at the china. "I'm afraid it all goes to Steben. Mother thought I might be . . . overwhelmed."

"Sofie." Keeler cast a sharp glance down the table.

Cyril ignored the matron's censure. "Steben?"

"Loelia's going to be married in the summer," said Sofie. "Steben is her intended."

"And he has a fine head on his shoulders," said her mother. "He's just come down from the university at Farbourgh City, with a degree in economics. He'll be a credit to the Keeler mills."

"Will he keep the name, do you think?" The venom in Sofie's voice told Cyril this was an old argument. "Loelia isn't."

"Sofie, that's enough."

Sofie opened her mouth, but Berhooven cut her off.

"What a spirited young woman," he said. "Keeler, your supper table must be a lively place. Why don't you have us all around some time?"

The conversation turned towards memorable past parties. Cyril invented some anecdote about the dreary social scene in the Hellican

Islands: "Really," he said, "I try never to be at home." Sofie retreated into silence, and maintained it through dessert and coffee.

The party broke up earlier than Cyril was used to. He had already resigned himself to retiring when Berhooven cornered him in the drawing room.

"You're not thinking of heading back to your hotel?" He kept his voice low and watched Cyril from under thick eyebrows. "You've come all the way from the Islands and you're just going to go to bed? I had you pegged as a bit of a playboy. 'I try never to be at home' and all that."

"I'm still a little under the weather," said Cyril, but he let it sound like he could be convinced. Berhooven he knew the least about, from Landseer's correspondence.

The man jumped on his hesitancy. "Come on, you've got to let me show you a little Nuesklan hospitality. Nothing for a complaint of the throat like a little tipple."

"Don't let Ives lead you down a path of dissipation." Sofie threaded her arms into her coat, held open by a footman, then cast an appraising glance down Cyril's figure. "I've seen him lay stronger men low."

"You're afraid for my morals?"

"I'm afraid for your liver," she said, and followed her mother out the door.

Berhooven's car was surprisingly shabby, dinged in small collisions and left unrepaired. And he drove it himself, whereas the Keeler women both got into the back of a sleek blue affair with ebony running boards. Van der Joost stayed behind for cigars and, presumably, political talk, but there was a man waiting for him in the driver's seat of a black car with a long bonnet.

"I thought we'd start at the top and work our way down," said Berhooven. "Does that sound all right by you?"

Cyril assured Berhooven he would defer to a local's judgment.

Their first stop was an upscale club decorated in tacky bucolic fashion. Farther down the cliffs they sat through a tame burlesque. Cyril tried to figure out if Berhooven was testing him, or truly thought that these were titillating venues.

He got his answer over thin, sour wine in an empty hotel bar. They sat by the window, looking over the boardwalk. Few people were out enjoying the seaside—the night had turned icy with sleet. Cyril was tired and bored, and had so far got nothing worth knowing out of Berhooven.

"You don't seem to be enjoying yourself," said his host.

"My head," said Cyril. "I don't think drinking is helping my cold after all."

But Berhooven caught him in his lie. "I think you're just a hard man to impress," he said. "It's time we went around the bay."

Cyril realized it *had* been a test, and his apathy had helped him pass. "Around the bay?" he asked.

"If you want real entertainment," said Berhooven, putting down a few bills for their tally, "you've got to head down to the wharves. I hope you don't mind beer in the evening."

"I don't mind beer at all," said Cyril, "provided it's good."

"This is Nuesklend," said Berhooven. "Bad beer is a hanging offense."

On the other side of the bay, Cyril felt at home immediately. Here, among the low buildings and towering rock, people braved the slippery pavement. They scurried in between bars and restaurants, flashing warm light and sound into the street each time they opened a door. In anticipation of the election, blue-and-yellow bunting hung from second-story windows: the colors of the regionalist party.

"Up on the cliffs it's all industrialists," said Berhooven, shouting over the roar of wind-driven surf. "A lot of them Ospies, like our friends at dinner."

"But not like you?" Cyril followed him as he ducked into an alley. A door was propped open onto the narrow cobbled walkway, and Berhooven waved him inside. The crowd forced them to maneuver slowly.

"Oh," said Berhooven, guiding Cyril to a table, "I move with the tide. And I could use a tax break or two. You saw the state of my poor buggy. Here, you first. Mind your step—the floor's wet." They slid into a booth, under an orange-paned lantern on a looped gold chain. The shallow arch of the ceiling was painted deep blue, spangled with mirrored tiles to imitate stars. Heat rose from the mass of bodies and warmed the room. On a low stage, a duo of accordion and double-reeded pipe wailed away at a syncopated reel. Smoke hung in a ragged veil over the heads of patrons and dancers.

"Put up your feet," said Berhooven. "I'll see about drinks."

The band brought their reel to a staggering, stuttering, breakneck finale, and the dancers applauded. In the general rush for the bar, Cyril lost Berhooven. Scanning the press, he saw sailors from Liso, Hyrosia, and coastal Enselem. Three young women in Nuesklan police cadet uniforms drank in the corner, seemingly oblivious to the gaggle of prostitutes cruising the establishment. Cyril wondered if they knew yet, these laughing girls so smart in their jodhpurs and epaulets, that their force was on the Ospie payroll.

A flash of green drew his attention to the bandstand, where the piper and accordionist were arranging their instruments for the set break. A woman in a black dress and a green silk bolero had just brought them each a tall glass of cloudy beer. A familiar woman, with hair the color of buckwheat honey.

Sofie handed one glass to the piper, a willowy young man in a patchwork jacket. She kissed him, and Cyril smiled at what Sofie's mother would no doubt consider an unsuitable attachment. Then, the accordionist set aside her squeezebox and opened her arms. Sofie sat on the woman's broad lap and kissed her too, barely saving her beer from a spill.

Berhooven returned with a plate of smoked salmon and two glasses. He noticed Cyril watching the trio on the bandstand, now talking animatedly over their drinks. The accordionist, eldest of the three, had a weathered brown face and broad nose. She kept pushing back her dark curls, which threatened to cover her eyes like the shaggy fur of a sheepdog.

"Ah, so you spotted Sofie." Berhooven laid a wafer of lurid pink fish across a cracker. "I wondered if we might see her here tonight."

"Does she make a habit out of slumming with musicians?" But the familiarity between the three people on the bandstand told Cyril it went beyond that.

"Oh, our Sofie's been keeping it up with those two since last summer. She's asked them both to marry her, but her mother put a stop to it."

"Both of them? One right after the other?"

"No," said Berhooven. "Together. The ancient temples in Gedda allow for bigamy."

"The Queen's Cult?" asked Cyril, who knew already but wasn't himself, and had to pretend.

"Yes. Keeler's family are all Hearthers, just like most of your Ospies. The husband didn't subscribe to anything, except maybe a religious interest in the stock markets. From what I've heard, the eldest Miss Keeler converted to the old religion as soon as she was of age."

"I can't imagine her mother was pleased."

"As far from it as you can think. But the real scrapping came with the marriage proposal. Minna threatened to disinherit her."

"But she's already losing the business to her brother-in-law."

"Well, yes. But she still has a comfortable allowance and a share in the mill." He shook his head. "If you ask me, Minna's more afraid for Sofie than anything else. If the banns are posted for her wedding, they go into the public record. You've probably heard what Acherby has to say about the temples. And with the Ospies on the make, Minna doesn't want her daughter down as a cultist in a bigamous marriage. Let alone a bigamous marriage with a Chuli."

"Chuli?" Cyril asked. Again, he knew, but Landseer wouldn't.

"Nomadic shepherds, in the Cultham Mountains. Not Enselmese, not Farbourgere. They've always had a hard time, and if the Ospies get their way, well . . . it's not just the states they want to unify. Society, religion, culture . . . the Chuli are scrapped. Nobody wants 'em and they don't want nobody." A rueful twist to Berhooven's mouth hinted at his next admission. "I should know. My granny was one. Not such a fine accordionist, though." He cupped his hands around his mouth and called out, "Play 'Feer Miri'!"

The accordionist looked over Sofie's shoulder and saw him. She nodded and picked up the squeezebox, settling it across Sofie's knees, her arms around Sofie's waist. Sofie caught Cyril's eye, and nodded a greeting.

Cyril looked away, back at Berhooven. "Why are you telling me all this?"

"Because I know why you're here."

Cyril's stomach dropped to the floor, but Berhooven went on. "Konrad's been after all of us to bring you round. Woo you like a courtesan after favors from the queen. The Ospies have the people's support in the north and the east, but the people don't have money.

The mill owners here can give a little, but not enough—if they could give, they wouldn't need Acherby in office."

"And this is how you're going to convince me?" asked Cyril, raising his voice over the first yelping minor chords of Berhooven's requested Chuli jig. "A few pints of beer in a regionalist pub, and a tragic love story?"

"Nonsense," said Berhooven. "I just want to make sure you have a good time."

"So you're not advocating for the regionalist cause?"

Berhooven's offended scoff was just this side of farcical. "Mr. Landseer. Only think how that would look to our friends uptown. I'd be drummed out of business."

The use of his work name threw Cyril for a moment. In the din of the pub, under the glittering swathes of mirrored stars, he had almost forgotten who he was supposed to be.

His reports to Culpepper started out optimistic, but took a turn for the frustrated as the unionists continued to dance around. They were solicitous, but wouldn't confide; Pollerdam came up in conversation repeatedly. Cyril began to understand that the absent mill owner was Landseer's opposite number, another set of deep pockets whose compunctions might not keep him from contributing. If he gave, and took the edge off of the Ospie's hunger, Cyril might lose leverage. So far, he'd stayed in the north and kept to himself, but as the weeks dragged on without development, Cyril's anxiety intensified. He wanted this done. He wanted to incriminate the lot of them and get back home.

He was dressing for a fundraiser gala when he got the telegram. The party was a last-minute affair, ostensibly pooling money for a big publicity push in the final week of election season. Rumor had it Pollerdam was finally due down, and there were hints he might be generous.

One of the hotel staff knocked on his door as he was tugging his cuffs into place. When he answered, she handed him an onionskin paper, folded and sealed.

"Wire for you, sir," she said, and clicked her heels. He tipped her and waved her off.

Hotel bar Stop fifteen minutes Stop Rye Soda End

To an ignorant reader, "Rye soda" might have read as a drink order, but in truth it was one of Cyril's call signs. He hurried to fit his cufflinks into place, checked his bow tie in the mirror, and went downstairs.

At the bar he ordered—what else?—a rye and soda, and waited for his contact to find him. It must be important; they'd never met in person. Usually he dropped his reports for the other agent—man or woman, he didn't know—to pick up and relay.

"Well, you are a fine one." The voice was low and rough with smoke. "Their descriptions didn't do you justice."

He turned and found a woman of generous proportions on the stool beside him. She was girdled into a perfect hourglass, the brown expanse of her bosom marked with a single beauty spot.

"Hello," he said. "Buy you a drink?" There was a slim chance she wasn't the person he was waiting for, but after so many years, you got a feeling for it. Even rusty from his time out of the field, Cyril was close to certain.

"A gin fizz will do all right."

Cyril put the order in.

"Listen," she said, while the rattle of the cocktail shaker drowned her out. "Pollerdam's not going to give you any trouble now. His money's staying in his pocket. They wanted me to tell you." The bartender deposited her cocktail on a folded napkin and moved on.

"Is he . . . ?"

She shook her head and sipped her drink.

"Look," he said. "I'm not exactly free all night."

"Culpepper put the squeeze on him," she said. "Got a couple big buyers in Amberlough threatening to cut their orders. He's not going to give the Ospies anything. Got me?"

"I do indeed." He toasted her, and drained his glass. "Now, if you'll excuse me, I have a party to attend."

Cyril didn't have much luck at the fundraiser. Not until Van der Joost caught him in the foyer, near the doors. "Mr. Landseer. Off so soon? You'll miss supper."

Cyril forced a smile. "Headache coming on," he said, tapping his forehead. "Thought I'd go out for a little air."

Van der Joost linked arms with him, without asking. "Let's you and I abandon ship. What do you say? Ms. Linsky's spread of hors d'oeuvres wasn't anything to fuss over, and I don't imagine the meal will do much to redeem her."

Trying not to let his sudden interest show, Cyril gave in to the gentle pressure on his arm and went with Van der Joost into the street.

The weather had grown markedly milder since Cyril's arrival, but the night air still had a nip to it. He turned up the collar of his coat and resettled the white silk of his scarf against his neck. "Where are we headed?"

"I thought we'd have a nightcap in my local," said Van der Joost. "Quiet place. Lots of tradesmen. Good for conversation."

Conversation. He hoped it meant what it ought to. It was the right time—a week until the election, and Pollerdam had fallen through. So tonight, Van der Joost was going to put his cards face up and tell Cyril what he was here to find out.

They took a winding path through damp brick streets, under the leaning shadows of increasingly old and dingy buildings. The sign above the pub door showed a leering kobold. Van der Joost held the door for Cyril, letting him onto the landing of a narrow staircase. The back of Cyril's neck prickled as they descended. Ridiculous—Van der Joost shouldn't mean him harm—but it was an instinct, and Cyril gave it credence, sharpening his attention to the other man's proximity.

The pub was dark, with a low ceiling, and smelled of water and dirt. Cyril felt as if he'd stepped five hundred years or more back in time, except for the white-and-gray pennants hanging over the bar, marked with the Ospies' quartered circle within a circle.

"The corner table," said Van der Joost. "I'll be back in a moment."

Cyril went where he was bid and tucked himself into a chair against the sweating stones of the wall, his back covered and his eyes on the room. Van der Joost returned with two tiny glasses of Nuesklend's ubiquitous cherry bounce. The liquor was viscous and bright in the gloom.

Cyril toasted him and drained his glass. The sour-sweet tang of last spring's cherries coated his tongue. It was powerfully alcoholic. He wished he hadn't been drinking at the fundraiser—on top of champagne, the bounce wasn't going to clear his head. But it would look odd to be the only man without a glass at a party, and at least Van der Joost had matched him in raising and downing the scarlet liquor.

When their glasses were empty, Van der Joost leaned across the table and said, without preamble, "We're not polling well."

Cyril affected tipsy camaraderie. "Oh, come on Konrad. You've still got a week. You'll turn things around."

"Are you offering your help?"

"Ah." He looked down to avoid answering.

"It costs nothing to encourage, does it?" Van der Joost tipped his empty glass so the dregs pooled in the tiny hollow at the top of the stem. "But you want to be sure of a victory before you back the party."

"Where's the benefit in writing the unionists a check if you don't win the majority?" Cyril could feel tension piling on between them, teetering dangerously, ready to fall. "With your party in power, I'd earn my contribution back within the first quarter. But that doesn't look likely right now."

"And what if I told you we don't need your help to win this election?"

Cyril kept admirably calm, though he was a whisker away from victory. He leaned back in his chair and crossed his arms. "If that's the case," he said, pinning Van der Joost with a disapproving stare, "I'd be interested to know what we're doing across this table."

"We're finally having a truthful conversation." Van der Joost's smile was lipless and self-satisfied. "It's time to drop the charade, DePaul."

Acid burned the back of Cyril's throat. Deadpan, he said, "But I'm so fond of party games." There was no point in denying his identity, if he was blown. "How long have you known?"

Van der Joost steepled his fingers. "Since before you got on the train."

"You have a mole in the Foxhole."

Van der Joost's steepled fingers flexed, hyperextending. Around his short nails, the skin went white with pressure. He said nothing.

"I'm only a replacement," said Cyril. "Were you going to turn the first agent they assigned?"

"We already had. But you're a better catch—what's that quaint little nickname your branch of the FOCIS gave you? Oh, yes: Master of the Hounds."

It clicked for him, then. Why Van der Joost had let him run free like a pet mouse for more than a month, before jerking the string that held him. "My assignment caught you off guard," he said. "Just like it did me. You've been busy with your research, trying to predict my reaction to whatever offer you're about to make."

"Very good," said Van der Joost.

"And what was your conclusion?"

"I think," he said, polishing his spectacles on his tie, "that you will do what I'm going to ask of you. But even if you don't, the outcome is the same: the One State Party triumphs."

"Then why even bother asking?"

"It would be good to keep Culpepper complacent," said Van der Joost. "If you disappear, she'll scent trouble and start scheming. If you arrive home safe, our plans come to fruition unchallenged. And"—he smiled, almost flirtatiously—"because despite the somewhat . . . unsavory things I've turned up in my research, I believe you might be useful to the party. It would be a shame to waste your potential."

Cold fear filled the groove of his spine. "What?"

"It wasn't supposed to come to threats." Van der Joost sounded almost apologetic. "But you have no choice, DePaul. Not really. We have the police force here, and mercenary ships on the mill owners' payrolls"—he spread one hand on the table to represent Nuesklend—"and the army in Tatié." He put the other hand down, and drew them both together, matching thumbs and index fingers.

The spade-shaped hollow between Van der Joost's palms showed Cyril his city, hemmed in. "And if I'm not keen on the idea of treason?"

There was a weighty pause. Then, instead of an ultimatum, Van der Joost said something unexpected and banal, but all the more chilling for that.

"You don't want to be here, do you?"

"You mean Nuesklend in general, or sitting here, across from you?"

"I mean on this action. In the field. My sources say Culpepper pulled you out from behind a desk to do this job. But I've read your personnel file. I know about Tatié."

Cyril curled his hand into a fist, breaking the crease at the front of his trousers.

"You were stationed within the army, reporting on their training and their capabilities. Amberlough likes to keep a close eye on her neighbors. Especially her well-armed ones. A navy and volunteer militias are no use against a landlocked military power."

And Tatié was rabidly unionist. Though the ongoing border conflict with Tzieta occupied most of the army's attention, things were changing under Moritz's regime, probably at Acherby's behest.

"Blown, tortured, nearly killed. And Culpepper hushed it up, to keep Amberlough out of a civil war. She used to be your case officer, didn't she? That must have stung."

"It was good policy," said Cyril, through gritted teeth. "You said yourself: We couldn't fight them. As it was, the reparations Amberlough paid were brutal." It was illegal for a state to use FOCIS agents in domestic rivalries, especially given the military aspect of the action. Cyril's presence implied mistrust. "It was more than I should have expected."

"But not as much as you wanted." Van der Joost sat back in his chair. "I have it on good authority you were reluctant to return to active service."

"Purely speculation." True, nonetheless.

"Do this for the party, and you have my word you'll never be put in the field again."

"And if I don't do this, I'll die in it?"

He didn't get an answer, but Van der Joost's silence had an affirmative heft.

"I'll be honest with you," said Cyril. "I'm not thrilled."

Van der Joost's chuckle felt jarring, though in retrospect Cyril's gross understatement had struck an almost humorous note.

"You've read my file," he continued. "You know who I am. Well, I've read up on Acherby and the blackboots too. I know your platform. I won't condemn myself to a life of celibacy, or risky assignations in the shadows. If I die now, I'm dead, fine." His hands felt like ice, but he made himself say it. He might be a coward, but he was also a hedonist. "If I help you, I destroy the city that lets me live my life, and I end up a pariah, or in prison."

"Are you saying you'd rather die now?"

"Of course not," said Cyril. He wanted it to come out smooth, but it just sounded desperate. "I want you to make treachery worth my while."

"You're not in a bargaining position."

"Yes," said Cyril. "I am. First off: You're right. I'm the Master of the Hounds. I already have the police in my hands. Second, my death puts the foxes' ears up. You don't want that. So here's my proposal: I'll help you tear down the four-state system. I'll tie the ACPD up with a bow and hand them over. But when it's all said and done, you get me—and my assets—out of the country."

Van der Joost's expression shifted from blank shock to sly approval. "I think that could be arranged. We could procure you a residential visa, for Porachis, say. You have family there, don't you? A sister, a nephew?"

There was a subtle threat in that. Cyril logged it, but said nothing. His sister was a diplomat, and smarter than him, besides. She would be safe even if he ended up scratched. Probably.

"There is a certain elegance in it." Van der Joost's smile was flat and slow, reptilian. "You help us consolidate our power, and we help you escape it."

Cyril thought of the vise that would tighten around the citizens of Amberlough, the lives he would destroy. And suddenly he remembered Aristide calling the whole fiasco "just a little bit of politics." He was overconfident; he would never expect this, never see it coming. "There's one more thing."

Van der Joost raised an eyebrow.

"A second visa. For a friend." He knew he was testing the limits of his precarious position, but fortune's wind never filled timid sails. He wasn't hugely surprised when Van der Joost shook his head.

"That I cannot do. Not yet."

The last phrase caught Cyril's attention. "But maybe?"

"I suspect this is the sort of 'friend' you would be unwilling to sacrifice under Mr. Acherby's governance. Therefore, I cannot promise anything. It would be risky for me to facilitate such an . . . elopement. But I might consider taking that risk if your work—and behavior—prove satisfactory."

"My behavior?"

"You may do what you wish when you are in Porachis," said Van der Joost. "But while you are in Gedda, working under the auspices of Caleb Acherby, you will adhere to the party line. I cannot help you if you make me look too lenient."

PART

2

CHAPTER

EIGHT

Cordelia woke up late on the morning after the election with a roaring headache. Her hair was tangled in a glittering paste tiara; face paint stained her pillow regionalist gold and blue. Amberlinians couldn't vote in the western elections, but that didn't mean they couldn't celebrate.

A naked Lisoan boy sprawled upside down in the bed, one foot propped on the headboard. His broad chest rose and fell with whistling snores. Cordelia stretched and rubbed the crusted makeup from her eyes, then reached for her alarm clock, which she had not set the night before.

"Oh, queen's cunt." She kicked free of the snarled sheets and hit the cold floor. "Get up, you!" She grabbed a handful of the boy's woolly dreadlocks and shook his head. "I need to get to work."

Still torched from whatever he'd been taking the night before, he only smiled and reached out for her. She sneered and shook free. "I gotta get to work. Ten minutes before I throw you out, clothes or none."

He staggered into his trousers, gathered everything else, and made a hasty exit.

The taps downstairs ran icy cold, so Cordelia washed up fast. Shivering but clean, she sprinted back upstairs to throw on culottes and one of Malcolm's old sweaters she still had lying around.

She had to make the next trolley if she didn't want a hiding from him. He'd stayed surly with her, after the Tory scrap, and while they'd had a few good nights, on the whole he was thornier with her than anyone else at the club.

But she didn't worry long about it. By the time she got on the trolley, she'd seen the papers.

Surprise Acherby victory sweeps Nuesklend. Acherby takes western seat.

It was all any of the passengers were talking about. She turned to the man next to her, who had a copy of the *Clarion* spread across his knees.

"What's it say?" she asked. "It can't be true, can it? Everybody said Riedlions was a shoo-in."

"She shoulda been." His impressive white mustaches rose and fell as he sighed. "There's more than a few crying false. 'Allegations of fraud,' is what the paperfolk are saying."

"And no wonder!" Cordelia didn't hold back her reedy whine; no need to play fine and fancy at this end of Station Way. "Ain't no Nuskie with half a bit of sense would cast a ballot for that dredged-up dog prick."

"And we all know it, don't we?" He folded up his paper. "This'll get sorted out fast, see if it don't." As the trolley drew to a stop, he handed it to her. "Here," he said. "I'm through with it. Got enough troubles hangin' on my tie."

At the theatre, most everybody was gathered in the house. Seated around the mosaic tables, the cast and crew smoked and talked and passed the afternoon papers between them.

"Delly!" Tory stood on his chair and waved for her to come over. She went, reluctantly. She'd tried to avoid him, the last month, just to keep out of the pot with Malcolm. But the tight cliques and couples of the theatre were unraveling right now. Hearsay flew between the tables about Acherby, and Nuesklend. The air was electric with nervous laughter and cocky assurances that Staetler would put the old Ospies in the corner quick enough.

"How's it turning?" she asked, sliding into a seat.

"How's it look like?" Tory stubbed out the butt of a twist and let his hands rest on the table for a moment. Then, unable to stop fidgeting, he got out his tobacco and rolling papers and made up another one. "Plague and pesteration, but what must've happened last night in Nuesklend?"

"They counted their cards," she said. "Paperfolk are all saying it. No matter if the fat fish were backing the Ospies, everybody knew Riedlions was going to win the seat."

"You seem fair confident. Not worried about the Ospies taking over and shutting down all Amberlough's tit shows?" He licked the edge of his rolling paper and twisted it into a neat tube, pinched at each end. "I s'pose you've always been a day-to-day type."

She didn't think he meant it as an insult. Not Tory. "It's better than sitting on my ass, smoking all my shag." She flicked the end of his freshly rolled cigarette. "It's a heavyweight kinda battle. Nothing any of us welters can do about it."

"No?"

"Not unless you're packing a snubby and planning to cozy up to Acherby some night soon."

"I can poke a hole in a man without a gun, Delly."

"Oh yeah, I forgot. The firepower of a good joke." She rolled her eyes. "Killing him with comedy."

"And why not?" He struck a match and lifted it to his face. The firelight shadowed the frown lines in his forehead. They ran deep, for such a funny man. "I've known a good, hard laugh to bring on apoplexy."

Cordelia was going to tell him she'd known a couple other things to bring on apoplexy too, but Malcolm came barreling onto the stage with a fistful of wrinkled sheet music and the morning's stubble darkening his jaw.

"Am I paying you all to sit around and bark at one another?" His voice carried across the space, turning heads. "I didn't think so."

That projection was wasted off the stage. Then again, Cordelia couldn't think what kind of act would fit him. Maybe strong man. Or a lion tamer.

"Curtain goes up same time tonight as every night." He strafed his employees with narrow black eyes like machine gun barrels. People cringed, but he held his fire till he struck on Tory and Cordelia. "You all better be on your toes," he said. Though he meant it for the company, Cordelia knew it was aimed at her. "I ain't above sackin' anybody who lets this election get in the way of their performance."

It would've been a solid threat, but it didn't hold up long. The double doors at the back of the house swung open like a set piece, revealing Aristide Makricosta like the climax of a campy drama. The entrance was perfectly timed; Cordelia didn't think he was above listening at the keyhole for the right cue.

"*Awfully* sorry I'm late," he drawled, stripping off a pair of claret kid gloves. With theatrical surprise, he took note of them all gathered in front of the stage, half in street clothes still. "My, my. What *is* happening here? Haven't we got a *show* to put on?"

Malcolm turned a dangerous shade of red, not too different from Ari's gloves. "Makricosta." He leveled his crumpled sheet music like a baton and thrust it at the target of his rage. "What kept you?"

Aristide's smile was thin and sharp as the blade of a Market Street fish knife, and he broke out the central city stutter. "Apologies, Malcolm. It was a t-t-trifling matter, and *obviously* it could have waited. I didn't realize what a *state* the place would b-b-be in when I arrived."

Malcolm let his fistful of music fall to his side. "You and me both."

"It's 'neither,'" said Aristide, and flounced off to change. His departure seemed to signal the rest of the cast, who rose from their chairs. Cordelia followed in the general rush, hoping to avoid a scene. For once, she was grateful to that overgrown, overrated blush boy. He'd drawn enough of Malcolm's ire that she might make it out unnoticed. But just before she gained the downstage entrance, Malcolm grabbed her by the arm. The overlarge sweater made him miss her flesh, and he ended up with a handful of knitted wool. Still, it was enough to yank her from her path.

He scanned her face without meeting her eyes. "You don't even have your paint on yet."

"Trolley was running late," she said, thrusting her chin in the air.

"Swineshit."

She huffed. "Look, Mal, the whole city's hung right over, or still asleep, or they've got their noses in their rears over the headlines out of Nuesklend." She grabbed her sleeve and tugged it from his grip. "What do you want from us? We ain't no different from the rest of 'em."

"Oh, you are," he said, "and *you're* a damn sight worse." Then he did a double-take, half reaching toward her arm again. His face went soft, then crumpled back into a frown. "Delia, what are you wearing? You look like a rag lady."

She gathered the folds of his oversized sweater more tightly around herself and marched for the stage door. Over her shoulder, she offered, "At least I don't look like an asshole."

CHAPTER

NINE

Culpepper paced the debriefing room like a zoo animal, shoulders hunched around her ears. "Mother and sons, DePaul, what happened over there? Where's my evidence? What am I supposed to tell Hebrides?"

"Tell him I was blown before I could get anything." It was the story he'd cooked up, bolstered by an artfully hectic exit from Nuesklend and a week lying low amid the dust sheets at the DePaul estate in Carmody, waiting for the election drama to play out. "They're sharper than you thought, and they didn't buy Landseer. Or maybe you've got a mole at home. I don't know."

"A mole?" she snarled.

"How do you think they clocked me? Somebody told them, and I'd wager it's someone in the Foxhole. Who else would know?"

He'd been wondering too, though his few inquiries had amounted to nothing.

Culpepper stopped in front of his chair and jabbed at him with her cigarette—her fourth during the debriefing. "Why don't *you* tell *me*? I know *I* don't slip FOCIS secrets to any old blush boy with a generous pocketbook."

"Oh, very flattering. He's got *nothing* to do with this."

"You're telling me he didn't know where you were headed?"

"I'm a professional, Ada, not a gossiping grandparent."

"I hope that's true. You've run honeypots before, but that doesn't mean you won't fall for one if it smells sweet enough."

Unbidden, Cyril thought of the crease of Aristide's neck, where it met his jaw: the musky remnants of his everyday cologne mixing with the softer, darker smell of sweat. "Ada, I'm insulted."

"Don't be. It's not personal; I've seen it happen to far better agents than you." She smiled sourly. "There, you can be insulted about that one, if you want."

"Thank you." He stood, gathering his coat and hat. "No, really: thank you. You're extremely generous."

"And *you* are extremely useless."

He stiffened. "Director, you are out of line. I have served this organization faithfully"—indignation made the lie easy—"for the last ten years of my life and more. *Useless?*"

His excoriation seemed to strike her like a blow. She sagged and sank into the chair he had just vacated. "I apologize. You're right. But you have to understand . . . This is extremely upsetting."

"I do," he said. "Believe me, I do."

"Go home," she said.

"And what? Wait for orders? What's the next step?"

"We have some contingencies, but I want to meet with Josiah. I'll ring you up. For now, just get some rest. You look like somebody peeled you off their shoe."

Slinking out of her office, he passed beneath Memmediv's appraising eyes and had a sudden, creeping suspicion. Before he turned the corner, Cyril looked up and met the secretary's gaze. Insight struck him in the gut like a boot, and he turned to flee.

He stood in the corner of the trolley stop, pressing one shoulder each against the cold walls. He was weary with travel, verging on ill. Pity, too. The evening was beautiful: sun low over the western edge of the harbor, fruit trees ready to burst into blossom. Yet all he wanted to do was go home, drink something strong, and sleep until he died.

He needed to see Aristide, or send him a message, but couldn't scrape together enough acuity to address the problem of *how*. Van der Joost had made it clear he couldn't see Ari anymore, not and hope to keep his skin. It had to be roundabout, however he dropped the news. He already knew he wouldn't tell the truth. No, he'd just jettison Ari and let him figure it out on his own. Because of course he would. He was many things, but never a fool.

"Mr. DePaul?"

Cyril didn't jump, but he must have moved, or made a face, because Finn apologized immediately.

"I didn't mean to startle you," he said, stepping under the overhang of the trolley stop. When he drew closer, his brows knit together in concern. "Queen and cairn, do you always look so rough?"

Cyril shrugged one shoulder. "Came in on the sleeper. Didn't sleep much."

"Ah, yes. I never do either. Where were you coming from? Or shouldn't I ask?"

"You can ask," said Cyril, and made a point to say nothing else. Silence hung in the air, explanatory.

Finn laughed, though the joke was weak. "I don't suppose you'd join me for a pint, then. You ought to go home and turn in."

"Oh, damn. I owe you one, don't I?"

"It can wait, really." Finn waved him away, a blush rising on his broad cheeks. "Anyway, I didn't mean to call in the favor. I only—"

"No, no," said Cyril, because despite his exhaustion, he suddenly saw an opportunity opening in front of him. Maybe his methods didn't have to be so roundabout, after all. He just needed a patsy, and a boring colleague would work perfectly. "Listen, I do need to drop by my flat and freshen up, but how would you feel about dinner and a show?"

Finn made a sweet, sly face, like a naughty child. "Is this a pickup?"

It took Cyril half a second to realize he was being mocked, and when it hit him, he surprised himself with laughing. "I deserved that."

"Aye, you did. What sort of show?"

"The only sort," Cyril said. "The best. Have you been to the Bumble Bee Cabaret?"

They'd rolled things over while Cyril was gone, put up a new revue. It was like coming home to find all his neighbors had changed.

Spotlights swirled across the boards and the drape of the velvet curtains, sparkling on the jeweled costumes of the nymphs in the tableau. It glanced off the buckles of Aristide's shoes, and the gold leaf glued around his dark eyes like dazzling freckles.

The applause for the opening number went on so long, Aristide had to hold up his hands and pat the air. "Children, children," he said, "p-p-*please*."

Gradually, they quieted. Aristide fanned himself with a languid hand, theatrically overcome. "You do know how to make a fellow blush." Someone shouted a lewd remark from the rear of the theatre, to which he responded, "And I'm sure *you* know how to do a bit more."

Three separate wolf whistles blended in sharp harmony. Aristide simpered, flicking dismissive fingers at his fans.

"Stop it," he said. "You'll give him a big head. And that's *my* job." He executed an obscene gesture involving a closed fist and the clever application of his tongue to the inside of his cheek. The audience went crazy.

Despite himself, Cyril grinned. That was *his* line, from weeks ago. His laughter died in his throat when he glanced over and saw Finn, and remembered why he was here. If the boy drooled any harder, he would need a nanny to wipe his chin.

"Don't get too excited, darling," said Aristide, eyeing his admirer at the back of the room. "They call it 't-t-tongue-in-cheek' for a reason."

The show only grew more raucous from there.

Just before the interval, as Aristide was introducing each member of the chorus with brief, tantalizing biographies rich in sexual euphemism, the card boy began to make his rounds. It was good there were so many dancers in the kick line; every table had at least one card for Tito, and a wad of cash. He made slow progress toward their seats.

It gave Cyril time to make his move. "You've got a look in your eye, Mr. Lourdes."

"Hm?" Finn turned. The dancing stage lights flashed through his hair and eyelashes.

"Why don't you send your card back?" Cyril tipped his chin toward the stage, ignoring the small, sharp pain of jealousy where it dug beneath his ribs. "Makricosta can be very friendly with his clientele." He let insinuations slide into it, and saw Finn's eyes dart away.

"You know him?"

"Finn, I'm fifth floor. I know everyone."

Finn bought it like a gullible mark, eager to believe. "He's not going to come out here for an accountant." To Cyril's satisfaction, he belied himself reaching for his card case.

Tito strolled past their table and recognized Cyril. He opened his mouth, but before he could extend an incriminating greeting, Cyril stopped him with a hand on his arm. "This gentleman has a card for Mr. Makricosta."

Tito took Finn's proffered scrap of paper, slipping it into one of the divided sections of his tray. "That it?" His gaze lingered on Cyril for a weighty moment, but Cyril gave him nothing. When Finn turned his blushing face back to the stage and Tito started to walk away, Cyril snagged the gold-piped edge of his livery and tugged him back.

"Make sure he comes to our table," he said, offering several folded bills of an impressive denomination. "But not for me, understand?"

"Yes sir." Tito made the cash disappear in the cup of his small palm, then retrieved Finn's card from the rear of the stack and dropped it at the front. It gave Cyril sick satisfaction to see him do it—a sour, noble feeling between masochism and confidence.

When the curtain dropped on the final tableau, Finn swiveled on his stool to face Cyril. "Do you really think he'll come by?"

"Only one way to tell," said Cyril. He raised his glass. "To taking chances."

Finn tipped his drink in rueful return. When he lifted it to his mouth, Cyril grinned through shame.

"I don't care *who* he is," Aristide snarled, "*or* how much he p-p-paid you. Madame Fa is a friend and c-c-client, and what's more, a very wealthy patron of the theatre." She'd married rich the first time, and well the second, and was prone to dropping big cheques on artistic—and illicit—enterprises. "Do you want to explain to Mr. Sailer why I was ch-ch-chatting up an accountant while an Asunan b-b-baroness sat unattended in the front row?"

Tito's fists spasmed, then opened into beseeching palms. "Mr. Makricosta," he said. "Please. Just see him for a moment."

"No." Aristide slashed the air with an open hand. "For the last time—"

"It's Mr. DePaul," said Tito. "I weren't supposed to say, but . . . well, he's given me a hefty wad to make sure you see the young gentleman."

Cyril was back? Aristide's negating hand curled around the cuff of his dressing gown, drawing it close. "Is that so?" He squeezed his genuine smile into a foxy, acquisitive expression. "Give me twenty percent of your cut and I'll see to it."

"Ten," said Tito, crossing his arms.

"Fifteen or he goes home disappointed."

They shook on it, and Aristide took his cash and stack of cards from Tito's tray. What was Cyril up to? He had twenty minutes to figure it out, before the interval ended—Malcolm ran them long, to give his stars more mingling time.

Habit helped him locate Cyril's immaculate head, bent over his usual table in conversation with some copper-haired schoolboy in an ill-cut jacket. Business sense and good manners bade him stop front and center first to pay his respects to the Honorable Baroness I Fa.

"I'm awfully sorry I can't stay." He kissed her bird-boned knuckles. "Something's come up."

"How much did they bid?" she asked, her smile teasing. She was gray-haired, but still an incorrigible flirt.

"My dear, I'm afraid this is a p-p-pillow matter, rather than a pocket one. I simply *cannot* be swayed."

"Oh, my iris. It is a wonder you ever escape your boudoir."

He dimpled at her endearment. Traditionally, comparison to the flower implied elaborate beauty without artifice, and was clearly meant in irony. "May I ask you to luncheon tomorrow, instead? Caviar and brown butter sole will *hardly* remedy my t-t-treachery, but . . ."

"No, tomorrow is not good for me." She took a small diary from her beaded reticule. "In fact, I am hemmed in for ages. But I am giving a little soiree in a few weeks. Shall I send you an invitation?"

"Oh, my d-d-darling, that would be simply *splendid*." He kissed her hand again, rose from the table, and bowed. "Until then."

With her bright black eyes following him, he made his way between the tables, approaching Cyril from behind. The shabby young man was shredding the carnation from his boutonniere. When he looked up from its bruised petals, he saw Aristide and turned the same appealing pink as the bloody inside of a steak.

Aristide couldn't help it—he licked his lips. The boy's eyes went wide, and wider still when Aristide settled his hands on Cyril's shoulders. His long, lacquered nails put dimples in the wool of Cyril's jacket.

"The p-p-prodigal," said Aristide, his lips touching the edge of Cyril's ear. "You smell like foreign parts. How *thrilling*."

Cyril cringed beneath Aristide's grip. "Mr. Lourdes," he said, the tone of his voice chill with warning. "I'd like you to meet Aristide Makricosta."

Cyril ground his teeth. This moment was the most delicate piece of his plan, and Aristide was threatening to derail it.

"Ch-ch-charmed," said Ari, slipping into the seat between Cyril and Finn. "Charmed, I'm sure." He took Finn's hand—offered for a shake—and brushed painted lips over the backs of his fingers. While Finn was busy stammering and trying to look anywhere but Aristide's face, Aristide shot Cyril a glance from beneath feathered, gem-studded lashes.

"I meant to get to the bar before the mob," said Cyril, light and conversational. "But I didn't, quite. Mr. Makricosta, if you'd be so kind as to use your celebrity to jump the line, I'll gladly pay and carry." Before Finn could volunteer his services, Cyril put a hand on his arm. "What can I get you, Mr. Lourdes?"

"Oh, just—" He looked between them, surprise plain on his face. "Gin and celery bitters? With a little soda."

"Excellent choice." Cyril slipped his palm beneath Aristide's elbow and drew him out of his seat, away from Finn and into the interval hubbub.

As soon as they were away from the table, Aristide pulled his arm free. "Cyril," he said, in his most affected accent, "if this is supposed to be some kind of a *sting*, you're making a c-c-complete *hash* of it."

"Shut up," said Cyril. He didn't let his façade slip—anyone watching would see him smiling over the crowd, following Aristide to the bar.

But Ari obviously heard the change in his tone, and paused to look back. "Then what is that c-c-copper top *schoolchild* doing at your t-t-table?"

"Keep moving," said Cyril. "And don't ask questions." He could tell Aristide wanted to demand an explanation—the tension showed in the line of his shoulders, in his fingers curled around the cuffs of his dressing gown. But he flashed a rhinestone smile, as if Cyril had told an excellent joke.

As they approached their destination, Aristide dialed up the charm. "Pardon me," he said, to a woman in blue-dyed fox fur. "I'm p-p-parched, and in a t-t-terrible rush. Interval only lasts so long, you know."

She gave way, thrilled and tittering at his touch on her arm. Cyril slipped into Aristide's wake. Crushed by giddy patrons, he had no choice but to press against Aristide's side. Ari radiated heat, smelled of greasepaint and cologne.

"Ytzak, *darling*." Varnish flashed at the tips of his fingers. "One celery snap, an absinthe on fire, and a d-d-double rye and soda."

"Make it a single," said Cyril. "Nice try."

When Ytzak's back was turned, Aristide took something from the pocket of his dressing gown and slid it across the bar beneath the pads of his fingers. Light skimmed over monogrammed silver.

"You left this," said Aristide. "I thought about smoking them, but frankly, d-d-darling, you've got *abysmal* taste in tobacco. I can b-b-barely stand to k-k-kiss you sometimes."

Well *that* was a lie. Cyril palmed the cigarette case. "Thanks."

"You're welcome, I'm sure. Now. What *is* the reason for all this . . . *subterfuge*?" He drew the word out with central city sibilance, feigning interest in his nails as he spoke, one hand spread in front of him like a decorative fan. Cyril couldn't tell if he was just playing along with the intrigue, or if he was genuinely offended. It didn't matter, anyway.

"Listen," said Cyril, without preamble. "I have to stop seeing you."

"What?" The whites of Aristide's eyes flashed as he cut his gaze toward Cyril.

"We're done. I just . . . we're done."

There was a long pause. When Aristide did speak, he had damped down his sparkling affectation. "Something happened in Nuesklend."

"I can't talk about it."

"Of course you can't."

"Ari, don't be sour—"

"Who's the boy?"

The question brought him up short. It was not what he had been expecting. "A colleague. An excuse. I owed him a drink. I couldn't be seen coming to the Bee on my own. Not now."

"I won't ask why not." Aristide pushed away from the bar. His words were clipped. "Because I know: You can't talk about it."

"Don't—" But Ari was gone. Cyril slumped against the bar, angry with himself for breaking character. Had he thought Aristide would just nod and smile? He should have been ready for what he got. He wanted, desperately, to explain. To tell Ari that the deception was for his own benefit. That the ends would justify it. But Van der Joost's hesitancy made him hold back. No good promising what he couldn't deliver.

"Your order, sir." Ytzak set the tray of glasses down. "Should I put it on Mr. Makricosta's account?"

"No, no." Cyril took his money clip from the pocket of his jacket and put down a bill. "Keep the rest," he said, and Ytzak nodded his thanks.

By the time he got back to their table, the sugar cube over Aristide's absinthe was burning low and poisonously blue, dripping molten threads through the slots of the silver spoon. Aristide had drawn his chair close to Finn's, and was flirting like a Princes Road harlot. Well, Finn couldn't possibly be suspicious now. He wouldn't remember his own name by the time Ari was through with him. Cyril set the glasses down.

Aristide barely acknowledged him, which was childish, but deserved. There were probably better ways to have done this. But Cyril had panicked, and taken the first route that presented itself. Bad technique. Culpepper would have switched him raw. But

Culpepper would never know he'd thrown Ari over, would she? Or if she found out, he hoped she wouldn't pin the reason.

He caught Finn's gaze over the top of his drink. The accountant's eyes were wide, blissful and disbelieving. In that moment, Cyril hated Aristide more than he had ever hated anyone.

Then, with excruciating elegance, Aristide upended a shot glass of cold water over the last embers of his sugar cube. Like alchemy, the liquid in the absinthe bulb turned milky green. Aristide touched the tip of his tongue to the intricate twists of the flat absinthe spoon, though it still must have been hot, tracing and tasting the remnants of burnt sugar.

It was an ostentatious metaphor for spite, but Cyril could not look away. The house lights dimmed and rose, then dimmed again, signaling the end of the interval. Aristide turned away from Finn, at last, and lifted his glass to Cyril.

"Thank you for the d-d-drink, and a d-d-divine introduction." He was curling his words against the roof of his mouth again, his speech peppered with that false, delicious stutter. "Mr. Lourdes is quite the charmer."

"My pleasure," said Cyril, matching his toast and his empty smile.

Aristide tilted back his head and drained the last of the absinthe. The edges of his white greasepaint were blurred where they met his brown skin; brown as the burnt sugar on the spoon. And, Cyril knew from experience, as scorched and sweet.

The whiskey, when he drank it, tasted like nothing at all.

CHAPTER

TEN

After the last curtain call, Aristide went straight to his dressing room, ignoring Cordelia's snappish "Well you assed that one bad enough, didn't you?" The striptease had been a disaster, but by the end of the second half, the audience was inevitably drunk, and as long as they saw flesh, they didn't care how.

He showed most of what he had to stage right, which snarled the choreography and put Cordelia in a snit. But Cyril's machinations had cost Aristide a pleasant chat with an influential heiress, and then—without any explanation—the man had dropped him like a burned-down cigarette. Now Aristide was seething mad, and revenge was worth a little improvisation onstage.

During the interval, Aristide hadn't slipped Finn a card, or made any lewd suggestions. If he couldn't find the boy right after the show, still stuck to Cyril's side, there'd be no point in picking him up. So Aristide had to hurry.

Peeling off what little was left of his costume, he replaced it with the tight black jersey he wore during rehearsals. The buttons of his dress shirt and waistcoat were too much hassle. His hair was already down—most of the pins came out while Stella and Garlande did their contortion act, so that during the striptease, Cordelia could pull the few that were left and let loose his curls.

He tore his false eyelashes away and slashed cold cream across his face. A quick dash of plum lipstick, and he was out the stage door with his coat still unbuttoned. A few admirers waited with programs and flowers, but he slipped between them, turning up his collar before they realized who he was.

His anger had cooled by the time he made the front of the theatre. Taxis queued against the curb, ready for the audience streaming across the pavement; their doors popped open and slammed shut. Aristide briefly considered blending in with the punters and going home to a book and a stiff drink. Then again, Central had been known to pick up people of interest in cabs, and Aristide didn't want to risk that, thank you. Rumor had it you couldn't bribe the Foxhole cabbies if you shat solid gold.

Still, there was always the trolley, or a hack if he could find one. Maybe it was better to leave things lie. But then he spotted Cyril and Finn coming through the gilded doors, and he made his choice.

They headed for the trolley stop at the end of the block. Aristide followed. The northbound would be along in—he checked his watch—two minutes, headed for the transfer at Heynsgate. The transfer that Cyril would take to get back to Armament. Who knew where Finn was headed? Unless they were going out. Or Cyril was taking him home. Or . . . oh, none of it mattered, because Aristide was about to dash whatever plans they had.

Cyril cracked his cigarette case and put a straight between his lips. When he offered the case to Finn, the younger man fumbled and dropped it. Drunk? Good. Aristide took three quick steps, knelt, and offered the case to Finn.

"Yours?" he purred, though the monogrammed *DP* was clearly visible to both of them.

"No, sorry." Then, Finn recognized him. "Oh my."

"That would be mine." Cyril's hand closed on the case. "Thank you."

Aristide stood and leaned against the trolley schedule, taking a cigarette from his own cache. He made a great show of searching for matches. "I d-d-don't suppose you've got a light?" he asked, looking at Finn.

"I don't smoke," said Finn, helpless.

"Ah! Never mind." Aristide "found" his matchbook and struck one, drawing deep as he lit up. "D-D-Don't smoke? You're a rare gemstone, Mr. Lourdes. A veritable cabochon of virtue."

Cyril made a small sound that might have been a snort. Aristide ignored it. He could see the light of the trolley coming up Temple Street. "Come here," he said to Finn, curling the hand that held his cigarette.

Finn looked back at Cyril, who gave a nearly imperceptible shrug.

Aristide reached for the lapel of Finn's greatcoat and tugged him forward. "You're a grown man, Mr. Lourdes. You d-d-don't need a chaperone."

The trolley bell rang out, and the car slid to a stop on its cables. Outbound passengers poured onto the Temple Street footpath. Aristide took another drag, and the flare of his straight lit Finn's face crimson. He wrapped a hand around the back of Finn's neck— soft-prickly with the stubble of an old haircut—and kissed him. Rich, dark tobacco smoke twisted between their mouths.

Over Finn's shoulder, Aristide saw Cyril look back, once, as he boarded the northbound trolley. Under the brim of his hat, his face was blank. The trolley began to pull away. Finn broke the kiss.

"I'll miss the tram," he said, putting a protesting hand against Aristide's chest.

"But I'll hire a cab." He could call a hack from the theatre.

"A cab?" Finn's heavy eyebrows drew together. "But how will I—oh." Then, as Aristide pushed a knee between his thighs and slipped a hand beneath his coat, he said it again, like another breath of smoke. "*Oh.*"

Sleep didn't come. An hour passed, and then another, and then Aristide's bad back wouldn't let him lie still anymore and he had to get up. Finn stirred. His bright, shaggy hair flopped across his forehead as he turned in his sleep. Unthinking, Aristide reached out and brushed it back, then cringed away lest Finn wake. But he didn't.

The bedside clock read quarter to four. Aristide wrapped himself in a dressing gown and padded to the front parlor. He poured a schooner of port and stood in front of the tall windows, watching a few determined revelers weave across the footpath below. Thin clouds blurred the moon, hanging over the river.

Something was wrong with Cyril. Now that his fury had abated, Aristide could acknowledge that. If it had just been Culpepper forcing Cyril to break it off, none of tonight's chicanery would have been necessary. Then, there was the election to consider. The unexpected result stirred things up for many Amberlinians—Aristide had spent the afternoon reassuring contacts, delaying or expediting certain clandestine shipments, speculating in back rooms, variously calming hysterical tempers and leveling stern warnings at anyone who didn't take the upheaval seriously. Everyone knew the outcome had been thrown. It was the only way to explain an Ospie victory in Nuesklend. And Cyril had been there, sent on Central's bidding.

Or had it been official, after all? Cyril had never said "Culpepper's sending me." Only, "I have to go."

Aristide set down his drink and put his palms together, pressing his index fingers against his lips. After a moment of contemplation, he slipped back to the bedroom.

He dressed quickly, trying not to make noise. Finn slept like a sated child. At least he wasn't a snorer. Oh, plague take it, he was all right, in his own meek way. Aristide felt almost guilty about using him as an instrument of revenge. Almost, but not enough to stay by his side through the night.

He wrapped his hair into a knot and pulled a broad-brimmed felt hat low over his face, checking the picks secreted in the band. In a plain, dark overcoat with a scarf across his face, he was unidentifiable. If Cyril couldn't be seen with him, he would disappear.

Amberlough's trolleys ran all night, so Aristide took the eastbound Baldwin line. Without a press of bodies around him, the wind was bitter. At Armament, he transferred south and rode to Blossom Street, where he disembarked and walked back along the high iron fence of Loendler Park. Strange quiet, the hush of a concert hall, filled the street. Aristide was used to the constant clamor of life in the southwest quarter, and it was rare for business or pleasure to bring him east of Talbert Row.

Cyril's block of flats was dark. All respectable Amberlinians, gone to bed early. Or, still out on the town. Aristide crossed the street, glad his memory had served him. He hadn't been sure he'd know the building when he saw it. To avoid the lift attendant, he slipped up two flights of stairs. At Cyril's door, he knocked but got no answer. Five minutes later, the lock sprang under the ministrations of his pick and wrench, and the door swung open with a long, low creak.

Clever, that. Oil the hinges and anyone could sneak in.

The entryway was dark. Aristide paused on the threshold. He had only rarely come to Cyril's flat—unwise to bring an enemy home. Unlike his own rooms on Baldwin Street, here, Cyril was very much Central's fox and Aristide his adversary. The few times Aristide had visited, he'd never gone further than the entranceway. Cyril had ushered him out too quickly to take stock. He didn't pretend he could navigate it in the dark.

But when he stepped out of the tiled alcove, a stripe of light crossed his path. He traced its length across the parquet, to a slice of window visible between the heavy curtains of the drawing room. Cyril had pulled an armchair close to the sash. A lamp in the street below shone through the crack in the curtains, illuminating the sharp line of his jaw.

"Evening," he said, and lifted a glass. The streetlight glanced off dark liquor as it moved. Cyril drank and lowered the glass, but did not turn.

"I thought you'd be in bed," said Aristide, though he hadn't.

"I slept a little. Not very well."

Aristide snorted. "I wonder why."

"Damnation, Ari. Don't go all jilted lover on me." His words were slurred. He bent his head. Aristide heard the bite of glass on glass, and the three liquid pulses as Cyril poured.

"How much have you had?"

A short, hoarse laugh. "Too much."

"Well, share the burden then." Aristide took a few steps, but Cyril flinched, and he stopped. He settled one hip onto the back of the sofa and unwrapped his scarf from his face. "Cyril," he said, but Cyril didn't look at him. "Why don't you tell me what happened in Nuesklend."

"Where'd the stutter go, Ari? I always liked the stutter. Thought it was ch-ch-charming."

Cyril only picked at Aristide's dictional affectations when he was angry, or trying to avoid whatever serious conversation had occasioned their disappearance. "Nuesklend, Cyril."

"I really can't say, Ari. Not a word."

"And if I guess?"

"I won't tell you if you're right or wrong." He moved in the arm-chair, and Aristide could see enough to know he had a blanket wrapped around his shoulders, and was drawing it closer. It was cold in the drawing room—the radiators must have gone off hours ago.

"You went on orders from the Ospies." He made it half a question.

There was a sharp silence, a pause that said too much, and then Cyril threw his head back and laughed. He shook with it, splashing liquor on his lap. "Oh, Ari," he gasped. "You're giving me too much credit."

Relief washed down the muscles of Aristide's back. But Cyril's pause had been significant. "Then what?" he asked. "Why now?" It couldn't be coincidence, his coming back and breaking things off right away.

"What does it matter?" The words came out between his teeth, harsh and poisonous. "You can't be jealous, not the way you snatched up the first pretty thing that stumbled across your path."

"Me, jealous? You can turn that one around." A Kipler's Mew expression, one he'd picked up bickering with Cordelia. *Arrogant, vain, jealous: You can turn that one right around.*

It made Cyril smile. "You sound like a blush boy out of Eel Town." He reached back, his hand unsteady, and offered his glass to Aristide, who did not take it. "Honestly, I don't blame you. Lourdes is just your type."

"Government employee?" He meant it to sound flirtatious, but it came out snide.

Cyril missed the jab and shook his head. "Blue eyes. Bright hair. Young and pale." He jerked his chin at the mirror hung opposite the gramophone, where their two dark reflections were visible only as slight movements. "Sober dresser, and a little bit . . . conservative. You like a foil, Ari." He hiccupped. "I should know."

Though the mirror was useless in the gloom, Aristide could see them in his mind's eye. A striking couple: himself, tall and dark and not quite handsome; Cyril smaller, trim and golden-haired, with leading-man good looks. "You're not exactly fresh with morning dew, Cyril. Not like Mr. Lourdes."

"No," said Cyril. "But the best vintages age superbly." He looked around, like he expected Aristide to have brought his guest along. "Where is Finn, anyhow?"

"Sleeping, at mine. I wore him out."

"Very trusting," said Cyril, letting his head loll against the back of the chair. "But I suppose he's just an accountant." He closed his eyes, and for a long moment, didn't say anything. Then, sounding on the verge of tears, "Oh, Ari, where's the thrill in that?"

"It's not obvious?" But revenge felt hollow, now that he was here. He closed the distance between them and sat on the arm of Cyril's chair. "What happened?" he asked again.

Cyril shook his head, finished his drink. The bottle of rye at his feet was two-thirds empty. Aristide wondered how much of that had gone in the last few hours. When he looked back up, Cyril was still shaking his head—a hypnotized movement, like a snake watching a piper. "I'm so sorry," he said. "I'm so, so sorry. I've ruined everything."

"For queen's sake, Cyril, don't . . . oh, perdition." Tears spiked Cyril's lashes. "You're being maudlin."

"I just . . ." Cyril's face crumpled. "Ari, I'm all tied up this time."

Aristide put his hand on the back of Cyril's neck, pushing his fingers into the fine short hair at the base of his skull. "Good," he said. "That's how I like you."

Cyril stood so quickly Aristide didn't have time to startle. He whirled around, swaying, a dark shape against the bright slash of windowpane. "You don't understand," he hissed. "You've got to get out of here. Leave. I mean it—I can't see you anymore."

"Culpepper's not tearing you up about me, is she?"

"Rot Culpepper!" He slung his glass into the depths of the armchair. It bounced and struck the floor but didn't break. "This isn't about her."

All the tension that had drained from Aristide at Cyril's laughing dismissal of Ospie collusion . . . it came roiling back to the surface. He was almost surprised at the level tone of his own voice. "Then who is it about?"

Cyril turned away and stared out the window. Aristide saw his breath cloud on the pane as he spoke. "I'm such a coward."

Aristide rose from the arm of the chair and came to stand behind him, not quite touching, but close enough he could feel the heat of Cyril's body. "So what if you are?" he said. "What did you *do*, Cyril?"

Lines of pain creased the edges of his eyes. Without warning, he turned and thrust his hands out, striking Aristide in the chest. "Go on," he said, "truss them up. The strings'll come in handy for Acherby, or whoever." He jerked his arms in a grotesque parody of a marionette.

Aristide retreated, until the backs of his knees struck the chair and he was forced to sit. But Cyril shadowed him, staggering, then tripped on his abandoned glass and fell. The tumbler rolled beneath the sofa, rattling over the herringbone inlay.

"Go on," he said, putting his wrists on Aristide's knees, opening his palms so the yellow light from the street fell across them. "Are you going to tell her?"

"Culpepper?" Aristide shook his head. "If I did, you could deny it. What sort of credit do I have with her? Anyway, you haven't told me what you—Ah!" Aristide put his fingertips over Cyril's open mouth. He felt a sudden weight of responsibility, and the sharp intake of Cyril's breath. "No. Don't. I have no desire to see you executed for treason."

Cyril's damp cheek pressed against Aristide's knee. He started to speak, several times, his lips moving against the pads of Aristide's fingers, but only at the third attempt did he manage, "Sweet of you."

Aristide wondered what he had tried to say, the first two times, but thought it better not to ask.

"If you're going to work with them," said Aristide, when Cyril had finished weeping, "you can't keep on like you're accustomed to."

"Thanks." Cyril slumped with one arm folded across his face, his nose in the crook of his elbow. "I wouldn't have thought."

They sat next to each other on the cold linen damask of the sofa. A draft slithered along the edge of the threadbare heirloom rug— old money never bothered with luxury, or proper insulation. Aristide drew his feet up.

Hard on the heels of Cyril's revelation, he'd started scheming. If Cyril had thrown in with the Ospies, it meant he thought—he knew—that Acherby would keep his seat, whether he'd earned it or not. There were things Aristide had to do now, people he had to see, and soon. But first . . . "Cyril, I'm in earnest. It's not as if your tastes are any secret. If you're collaborating with the Ospies—"

Cyril made a small sound of protest, but said nothing.

"—you need to look the part."

"I know, I know. Celibacy."

"More than that. You need a girl."

Cyril let his arm fall, and stared bleakly across the drawing room. "Ari, it's too late for that. They already know everything about me."

"This isn't an issue of disguising your past," said Aristide. "It's a gesture of good faith. This shows them you'll play along."

Cyril's pout made him look so much like a sulking child, Aristide's heart almost softened. "You *are* playing along, aren't you?"

His assent was a bare incline of the chin.

Aristide made his voice cold and final. "So look like it." Relenting a little, he added, "I know one. A girl. She'd be a bit of a handful. A little scandalous. But the right kind of scandal, for the Ospies."

The putt-putt-putt of a single motor echoed in the street. It switched to an idle, and Aristide, who had sharp ears, heard the clank and jostle of a milk delivery headed down the alley to the service entrance.

"I've got to be going," he said. "There's an accountant on Baldwin Street who'll want his breakfast."

"Of course." Cyril scrubbed at his face. "And the girl?"

"You'll bump into her," said Aristide. "At Bellamy's."

"When?"

"I'll let you know."

"Ari, I told you, I can't—"

"I'm not stupid, Cyril. How long did it take Central to clock me? And even then, it was only because of one stubborn rule-breaker." He had to swallow against a tight throat, dry with sudden emotion. "I can send you a date and time without drawing anyone's suspicion."

He made to rise, but Cyril stretched out an unsteady hand. His sleeve was rolled past his elbow; the fine hair on his forearm stood up over gooseflesh. "Wait."

"No." Aristide lifted Cyril's hand from his knee. "It's time for me to leave."

Cyril, who was still very drunk, struggled admirably to keep his composure, and failed.

Aristide stood and tugged on his hat. He let one gloved hand brush the back of Cyril's bowed head, and then he left.

CHAPTER

ELEVEN

Cordelia hunched in front of her mirror, chewing on the end of her hair. Things had not gone well this week.

After the western vote went crooked, it was like the whole city had a pin in its ass. Fights and riots and demonstrations on both sides—blue and yellow scrapping with gray and white. And the ACPD acting like just about anybody might be out to get themselves in trouble. The hounds were snapping folk up left and right, trying to look tough.

Including her man on the docks. Ricardo hadn't brought in her allotment on account of being locked in the trap, his whole shipment confiscated by the police. Acting for the good of the community, righteous as a temple full of Hearther virgins. Like they wouldn't turn around and sell it. And she'd wager high they'd undercut those who'd earned a right to the market. Wasn't like the hounds had to make a living off the stuff.

She, on the other hand, had rent to pay. And customers who'd help her pay it, if she could rustle up a wholesaler. She'd have to go down the pier and start shopping around. Or . . . no, she couldn't endure his scorn.

But she knew he wouldn't sell her tar cut with ink, or rubber, or whatever trash the scullers were mixing up these days. She'd get better stock, and faster, if she could put up with Ari's attitude.

His dressing room was two down from hers, and the door was three-quarters closed. After the show, he usually had a highbrow punter or two back for drinks and who knew what. Everybody figured Ari was in on things besides a little bit of tar. He made more money than sheep made shit. Malcolm hadn't clocked Cordelia's sideline yet, but he kept the books and he knew he wasn't paying his emcee so much. He didn't dare complain. Really, what had he got to harp on? Ari had his fingers in the pockets of people Malcolm needed, and Malcolm was more than happy to put up with his airs and snobbery if it meant Taormino turned a blind eye when ballast washed up under the bar.

Cordelia tried not to get tied up with him. They worked together up on stage, all right, but off the boards he drove her screaming mad. Besides, near as she'd gathered, Ricardo was his competition. She didn't know if Ari had clocked she was selling tar, but if he had, he couldn't be happy about who she was running it for.

She listened carefully at the threshold of his dressing room, but didn't hear any chatter. One more moment to assemble herself, and she slipped in and shut the door behind her. Didn't bother knocking. Like as not he'd say no without asking who had called.

His dressing room wasn't much larger than hers, but he'd brought in enough trinkets and plush-shabby furniture that it looked like a thieves' den out of a folktale. Silk scarves softened the corners. Business cards and kiss-stained love notes were stuck to the walls with jeweled hat pins and brooches that might or might not have been paste. A string of glass bells looped above the door chimed softly, still swaying from Cordelia's entrance.

She sat on the arm of the battered settee. "How's it turning?"

"Smooth enough." He didn't seem surprised to see her, but he was a stage man: Of course he wouldn't show it. He peeled his false eyelashes away and rubbed pellets of glue from his skin, blinking glitter out of his eyes. "Is there something you need?"

In the mirror, she met his gaze. "Maybe."

"I'd rather you didn't d-d-dance around it, whatever it is. Must rush—I've got a dinner engagement."

Well, he'd asked for it. "I'm looking for some work."

"You *have* work. Or doesn't Malcolm p-p-pay you anymore?"

"Come on, Aristide." She could hear the wheedling cant of Kipler's Mew creep into her voice. "I'm looking for a little tar, and everybody knows you can get the good stuff."

"Maybe. But I only sell it wholesale." In the mirror, he pursed his lips into an appraising moue. "And I d-d-doubt you could afford it by the k-k-kilo."

She bit back a snipe. "Who says I need it for myself?"

He paused, holding a piece of cotton wool above his cold cream. When he spoke, the words came out precarious, as if he were afraid of being caught in ignorance. "Don't you?"

A sneer caught her upper lip and she stood, pulling her robe tight.

He sighed. "Cordelia."

"No." She reached for the door handle, pulling it half open. "I see how it is."

"Wait." He set the cotton on his vanity and turned in his chair. "Come back. Close the door."

She paused, considering. It was put up with him or put up with an empty belly. "All right," she said, lowering herself on the settee proper. "What do you got to say?"

"First," he said, putting a finger to his chin, "that I'm favorably impressed."

"What, just 'cause I ain't a junkie? Flattering."

"Hmm. I suppose I did deserve that one." He finger-combed his hair, from scalp to tips. "Who've you been running for, till now?"

"Ricardo Ty."

"Ah." Drawing the springy mass of his hair over one shoulder, he began to braid it with deft, bony fingers. "That explains it. You're the third of his I've had this week. I said no to the other two."

She cursed. "Guess I'll take myself down the pier, since you're not picking up new help." She made to get up again. Hang it all, her legs were getting tired.

Aristide waved her down. "Oh, Cordelia. Don't be b-b-*beastly*. Just sit for a moment and let me *finish*." His curling central city accent soared into stage parody, tripping over itself in his hurry.

She matched him with a crude gesture and a higher, nasal take on her native whine. "Bet it won't take long."

"Very funny." Leaning back in his chair, he lit a cigarette. He did not offer one to her. "As it happens, I need a favor. And I'd be quite willing to do you one in return."

"What sort of favor are we talking?"

"I have a friend," he said, "who needs some . . . female company."

She shook her head. "I'm outta that game, Ari. Have been since I started on the stage."

"I am not a p-p-pimp, Miss Lehane. You misunderstand me. What you do with this gentleman, once you meet him, is your affair entirely. Though, I should mention that if the t-t-two of you continue your association, I could be p-p-persuaded to continue ours."

"So all I gotta do is chat up some swell, and you'll stock me? What do you get out of it?"

"Philanthropic satisfaction."

"Swineshit."

He sighed, nostrils flaring, and stood from his chair. "Will you meet my friend or not, Cordelia?"

She thought of her empty larder, and her landlady. "Yeah, I'll meet him."

"Excellent." Aristide arranged a velvet scarf around his neck. "He'll be at B-B-Bellamy's, three days from now, at half past two. And don't worry," he added. "He'll be paying."

She bared her teeth at him, and slammed the door on the way out.

Madame Bellamy's was on the swell end of Baldwin, too refined for catcalling. When Cordelia let her wrap slide down so she could sun her bare shoulders, she didn't get any whistles, but she did catch a few passersby smiling at her from beneath the brims of their hats.

The front of the place was decorated with wrought iron in fancy spirals and flowers. Tiny colored panes made up the windows, above and below two larger, plainer stretches of glass printed with "Tea" and "Coffee." Between the curlicue letters, Cordelia saw the bent heads of diners, and black-jacketed waitstaff drifting from table to table.

Cordelia had never been to Bellamy's—couldn't afford it, for queen's sake. But she'd chatted up enough of the punters to walk and talk like a swell. No one would realize where she came from if she didn't want 'em to.

"Ma'am." The maitre d' gave her a courteous half bow. "Do you have a reservation?"

"I'm afraid not," said Cordelia, holding her voice carefully even. "Will that be any trouble?

The maitre d' maintained a mask of bland indifference. "No trouble at all."

He led her to a table near the center of the room. A waiter took her order and returned with coffee. Oh, she liked this. She liked it very much. As she was stirring cream and sugar into her cup, she heard the distant chime of the bell hanging above Bellamy's door and looked up, wondering how she was supposed to know Ari's friend if she saw him, or if he was supposed to come to her.

The man who entered was a pinch shorter than average, but he had charm enough it made up for the extra inches. Turned out in a white tennis sweater and pleated flannel trousers rolled at the ankle, he was a little too dressed down for the scene, but he looked at his ease. The maitre d', who she would've pegged as a starched proper, gave him zero grief about his rags. If Cordelia knew anything, that meant money.

The maitre d' made to show the newcomer to a table, but the man stopped him and shook his head. He was looking straight at Cordelia, a wolfish half-smile curling the corner of his mouth.

Trouble. She'd have to turn him down fast, before her date got here. Unless . . .

He produced a thin, glossy billfold from his trouser pocket and tipped the maitre d' with the casual graciousness of someone used to burning cash. For a brief, hot second she despised him. He said something that made the dour maitre d' laugh. The way both their eyes flashed in her direction, she knew he'd made some kind of dirty joke.

"Come on over then," she said softly, cupping her coffee with both hands and raising it to her lips. "Come on over and make me laugh."

But he didn't. He watched her all the way as he walked to the bar, then smiled, and turned his back.

Cyril didn't go straight to the woman's table. He was supposed to be meeting a stranger and taking a liking to her, and that required a little bit of patience. It wouldn't do to march up and introduce himself like they'd both been sent here for that purpose. So instead, he made a tasteless joke to the maitre d'—*Isn't that the stripper from the Bumble Bee? Looks different with her clothes on*—and went to the bar that curved against the western wall of the tearoom. The brass espresso machine hissed steam. Cyril followed the vapor's progress to the ceiling, watching it dissipate amongst the frescoes of nymphs and half-clad hunters, snag on the antlers of gold stags' heads and the crystals of the twin chandeliers.

When he looked back down, the woman was watching him, her head tipped quizzically over her coffee cup. A ringlet had escaped from the twist at the nape of her neck. It fell across her shoulder, into her décolletage, so perfectly placed he suspected she had let it free on purpose.

Cyril called the bartender over. "A glass of champagne, for the lady at that table. Green label, the forty-two."

The bartender inclined her head. "An excellent choice, sir."

He couldn't tell if she meant the wine, or the woman.

When he'd come through the door and seen that scarlet hair, he'd wanted so badly to turn around and walk away. She was pretty, yes, and yes, Aristide was right: She'd make the perfect mistress for a hypocritical politician. But she was also Aristide's colleague, and she'd keep Cyril close to the Bee. She'd cover for him, but she'd keep him within Ari's orbit.

Champagne dispatched, the bartender brought Cyril a rye and soda dashed with house bitters. A twist of orange peel rested on the rough edge of the ice. He thought of complaining—he liked his drinks clean and simple—but before he could draw the bartender's attention, a waiter leaned in beside him.

"The lady asks if you'd join her at her table."

He took his cocktail and strolled between the remnants of the lunch crowd. The woman—he remembered Aristide saying her name, but what was it?—watched his approach with narrow eyes like chips of imperial topaz. He paused beside her and offered his hand.

"Cyril DePaul," he said. "How's the plonk?"

She put the tips of her fingers across his palm. "Sublime." The barest hint of a nasal drone hung around the "i": the signature sound of Kipler's Mew. She'd worked hard to leave it behind, and he could tell.

He raised her knuckles to his lips. She didn't break eye contact, and neither did he.

"Cordelia Lehane," she said, when he'd straightened. "Go on, bend your knees."

Cordelia. Yes, that was it.

"Are you lunching late?" he asked, sliding into the chair opposite hers. "Or are you only here for an afternoon tipple?"

"This is breakfast." Cordelia tapped the side of the champagne coupe. "So far."

"A late riser. I have to admit, I'm envious." It was almost too easy to play this part. The words and actions flowed like oil over the top of water, leaving him untouched beneath the veneer of his character.

"I get about as little sleep as you. Nights run late in my line of work." Cyril raised an eyebrow, and she scoffed. "Please. If I was, you couldn't afford me."

He smiled at her grammatical slip-up—she might have climbed out of the Mew, but bits of it clung to her shoes. "You don't know that."

"True." She dragged her gaze up his front, and he could almost feel her fingers catching on the cables of his sweater. "I don't. What is it you do, Mr. DePaul? Ari didn't say."

He fought the urge to look around, make sure no one had heard her use Aristide's name. "I can't exactly talk about it."

"A man of mystery," she said. "I'm intrigued."

"Intrigued enough for a second drink?"

"You don't have to intrigue me for that."

"Ah, but I'd like to. Even if it isn't, strictly speaking, necessary." He waved a waiter over. "Another glass for the lady—actually, leave the bottle. And . . . oh, hang it. Two of the stuffed lobster tails. And asparagus tips, with white truffle butter." There was no menu, and if there had been, he wouldn't have needed it. Bellamy's was one of Ari's favorite haunts.

"I was happy with just the fizz," said Cordelia, as the waiter poured her a second glass.

"To tell the truth, I haven't eaten yet either. And that's from a man who was up and out with the sun." He pulled his napkin from the table and spread it across his lap. "If you can't do justice to your lobster, please know it won't go to waste."

He hadn't been up early by necessity; he just hadn't been sleeping well. So far, Culpepper wasn't asking for anything beyond his initial debriefing. She'd sent him a note telling him to sit on his hands until Hebrides asked to see him. That summons had not been forthcoming.

His other task kept him hopping. Van der Joost had left his base of operations in Nuesklend under the watchful eye of a deputy and had relocated to Amberlough City under the assumed name of Karl Haven.

Cyril didn't know where he was staying. They'd met a few times in public places, and he had been sending instructions daily and arranging rendezvous as if Cyril was a sponging younger son who needed to be married off. Cyril, who was used to a more lenient approach, ground his teeth and put up with it. The kitty was big in this game, and he had to bring it home.

Time was short, too. Van der Joost wanted things wrapped up by midsummer. Cyril thought it was ambitious, and told him as much. That conversation had been uncomfortable, and ended badly. Like it or not, Cyril was operating under a deadline.

Before lunching with Cordelia, he'd spent a cramped and smoky hour in a private room at the back of a down-market club, listening as the deputy chief of police for the fourth precinct—Eel Town included, poor man—listed his grievances against Taormino and haggled for the price of his service to the unionist cause.

Cyril knew the ACPD intimately: who was susceptible to bribery, who was not. Who had long-standing grudges, and who could be torn apart with a well-placed word. The fourth district would be easy to snatch, from the top. Getting the hounds on the beat to crack down on unlicensed pros . . . harder, especially when they made it so profitable for the force to turn blind eyes.

He realized he'd let his conversation stutter to a halt. When he looked up from smoothing the spotless napkin over his knees, Cordelia was watching him. She had her fingers pressed against rouged lips, her free hand hooked into the crook of the opposite elbow.

"You look sort of familiar," she said.

"Would you believe I hear that all the time?"

"Must be you look like somebody in the pictures," she said, so preoccupied her syntax slipped. "Come to think of it, you're a dead ringer for Solomon Flyte. You know him? Murdered by his girl a few years back."

"Are you trying to insinuate something, Miss Lehane?"

She smiled a cat's smile, her carmine lips pulling into a shallow vee. "Don't worry, Mr. DePaul. I ain't *that* dangerous."

A few hours and a second bottle of champagne later, they parted ways. Cyril left Cordelia with a promise to ring her up soon. She didn't have a card, so she wrote her number and exchange on the back of one of Bellamy's matchbooks and tucked it into his pocket. When she got close, he smelled cheap perfume and the faint chemical scent of her freshly dyed curls. She had a wrap around her arms, but it left her freckled shoulders bare.

"Will you be warm enough on the ride home?" he asked. "I like this suit, but I'd part with my jacket if your need was greater. As long as you promised to return it sometime."

"Keep it, Mr. DePaul. I'll be just fine."

"It's Cyril," he said.

The trolley slipped by, speeding up as it headed west from the Armament transfer down the road. With the ease of a born Amberlinian, Cordelia stepped off the curb and reached for the handrail. In one smooth motion, she was up on the rear steps. She blew him a kiss as the trolley crested Seagate Hill. He waved back, but she had already disappeared over the rise.

He strolled home through Loendler Park, in the opposite of a hurry. Wandering led him to the famous lilac walk that lined each approach to the park's central fountain. Decades of careful tending had produced four straight allées of uniform lilac trees. Their canopies burst like champagne from the necks of slender bottles. Fragrance from the drooping bunches of flowers lingered in the air, soft and sugary sweet. He tossed a coin into the rippling water of the fountain's pool, checked his watch, and sighed.

Dusk had gathered by the time he arrived at home. He put down his post and poured two fingers of rye against the chill spring evening. The glass beckoned from the sideboard while he shucked off wet socks and outerwear in exchange for slippers and a smoking jacket. The post sat beside his drink, less inviting, but more important.

He turned the radiator valve, raising the heat in the drawing room, and put a record on the gramophone. With Aster Amappah's clarinet crooning along above her big band, Cyril settled across his sofa. He propped his head up on a throw pillow, envelopes and telegrams piled on his chest. Bills and business correspondence he discarded for later perusal. There was a letter from his sister in Porachis, where she was stationed with the diplomatic corps. Her son had added a postscript in blocky child's writing: a crooked heart in blue crayon, "Uncle Cy" cramped within its lobed confines. He smiled and almost laid the letter aside on the coffee table. But he saw what was behind it first.

The thick, plain envelope was addressed by typewriter. All his unionist communiques came like this—unidentifiable, in cheap but sturdy packets, with no hint about what lay within. No postage, either. Likely they came by courier, to avoid Foxhole interference.

The fine grain of Lillian's letterhead lay against the Ospie envelope like silk against rough skin. He ran his thumb over the lines of his nephew's drawing, fighting sudden apprehension.

They would be fine. They were far away. Lillian was high-ranking and very, very good at what she did. They wouldn't approach her. And if they dared, she would maneuver neatly out of the trap. She had never gotten in trouble when they were children, even when she was naughty. It was always Cyril who ended up locked in his room without his supper, depending on Lillian to sneak him some.

Sighing, he set aside her letter and picked up his whiskey. After a drink, he tore the Ospie envelope open: fast, like removing a sticking plaster from a healing wound.

Another envelope fell out, this one soft and cream-colored, sealed with a gold stamp. It was wrapped in a piece of onionskin paper, spidery with writing. Cyril unfolded the note and read it through, then opened the second envelope.

It contained a heavy piece of card stock, velvety smooth and embossed with more gold. The Honorable Baroness I Fa requested the honor of his presence at a musical evening featuring the acclaimed Asunan contralto Ms. Srai Sin.

The party was in three days. The instructions said Cyril's reply had gone out last week; of course he would attend. Deputy Police Commissioner Alex Müller's wife was an intimate friend of the baroness. Müller would likely be accompanying her to the soiree.

Van der Joost's people were good at what they did; there was no denying. Cyril didn't have anyone on Maxine Müller. He was trying to run a network without a stable of agents, and he couldn't be everywhere all the time. But it still grated that the Ospies had scooped him on this one.

There was bad blood between Müller and Commissioner Taormino—the latter had gone from deputy chief of police in the third precinct straight to her current position, crushing Müller in the citywide election; there were rumblings of graft and underhanded favors. More importantly, Müller's wife was a close friend to expatriate nobility. The Ospies were nationalist to an ugly fault; connections to foreigners would not behoove anyone once Acherby took power. In addition, the baroness was a known associate of one Aristide Makricosta.

Müller was a straitlaced policeman, so bribery was out. But if he could be won over to the Ospie cause, by persuasive argument or some less pleasant means, he could be controlled through his wife's close friendship with an undesirable alien.

The record finished playing. Cyril set aside his correspondence and covered his face with his hand, listening to the hiss of the gramophone needle on ungrooved shellac.

CHAPTER

TWELVE

Cordelia had just arrived in her dressing room and sat down to supper when Malcolm barged in without knocking. She ought to put a lock on the door if he was going to keep this up.

Spinning around in her makeup chair, she faced him and demanded, "What do you want?"

"Smells like an Asunan flophouse in here."

Cordelia reached back for one of her spicy pork skewers and bit off a mouthful of juicy meat, grilled crispy on the outside and rubbed with garlic and hot peppers. She chewed slowly, waiting for him to lay out whatever was bruising him.

"Telephone call for you," he said. "In my office."

She swallowed the pork and got up, licking her fingers clean. Malcolm followed her down the hall, needling her like a Market

Street heckler. "What makes you think you can give out my office line to your johns?"

"Who said he was a john? When have you known me to hire out?"

"I know you done it."

"And you know I ain't doin' it now." She shoved him aside.

"How am I supposed to?" he demanded. "How am I supposed to know you ain't been taking three bits a jockey ever since I picked you up?"

"You didn't pick me up," she spat, bracing herself across the entrance to his office. "You begged for me." And then she slammed the door in his face and shot the bolt home. Because of course *he* had a lock.

"Delia!" His fist came down against the wood and made it rattle. "Delia, damnation! Open the rotten door!"

She sat in his chair: a rolling, swiveling throne of ripped leather that stank of old civet cologne and stale cigarettes. Drawing her feet underneath her rear, she picked up the earpiece of the telephone and leaned in to speak.

"Hello?"

"Miss Lehane?"

"Cyril," she crooned, drawing out the "l" with her tongue against the roof of her mouth. "I didn't expect to hear from you so soon."

"Who was that character that picked up the 'phone? I couldn't tell if he was your husband, or a tight-fisted landlord."

"Neither," she said. "You're lucky he didn't hang up on you."

"He did; I called back. Twice."

She laughed into the mouthpiece, glad he couldn't smell the garlic on her breath. "Sorry about that. He's my boss."

"This is your work exchange? I'm sorry. I didn't mean to—"

"No, no," she said, "it's all right. I gave it to you." Then, pulling a face, she admitted, "I ain't got a telephone at home." Now he knew that, she might as well slip back into the cant.

"I'll send a telegram next time," he said, "if you'll give me your address."

She gritted her teeth. Her flat was in a bad part of town. Not as bad as her childhood Mew, or Eel Town, but not exactly Harbor Terrace, either. "What's the occasion?" she asked, trying to put him off. "For the call, I mean."

"I was wondering if you'd like to meet me tomorrow afternoon for the cherry blossoms."

She hadn't been to see the famous cherry trees of the central city in . . . well, not since she was a kid. She'd noted them in passing—they were hard to rotten miss, once they got going—but it had been a long time since she took a good stroll under the branches. And never with such a fine gentleman on her arm. "Sounds like a treat."

"Around noon?" he asked. "Or is that too early?"

"Better make it half one. I'll meet you at the Van der See Arch. Sound good?" Malcolm hammered on the door again.

"Perfect," said DePaul. "What is that racket?"

"Workmen," she replied. "Sorry. See you tomorrow, then?"

"Time will drag."

She snorted at his smarm, and hung up. Was all this some kind of scam? What was Ari getting out of it? What did Cyril expect?

Whatever the two of them were hoping for, she had money in her pocket. And if things kept up like this, she and Ari might work out a tidy arrangement. Ongoing. Lucrative.

"Are you good and done yet?" shouted Malcolm. "Get your worthless ass out of my office and go put it in some tasseled panties—we got punters coming in."

Now she was off the 'phone, she let her voice rise sharply. "Mother's tits, anyone'd think you're about to wet yourself and this was the only washroom." She opened the door. "Though mind you, the way it smells . . . Lucia must have a time scrubbing it. Probably worse than changing the sheets at Mama Filetti's."

"At least she's not liable to get the clap cleaning up after me." Malcolm pushed past her and prowled around his desk, as if he was trying to figure out what she'd stolen or soiled. "Your little warren, though . . . I hope she wears her thickest gloves."

"Go yank yourself," she said, and turned tail.

She remembered to set her alarm clock when she got home, and sure enough, it rang her out of sleep at noon. She broke off some stale bread from the loaf on the mantel and coated it with butter, going off but still edible.

Once she'd splashed her hands clean in the basin on the dry sink, she went to pick through the pile of clothes on the foot of her bed. She needed something that said *good girl*, but not *too* good. Whatever Ari had told this punter, she didn't want to come off like a racehorse, but she didn't want to look too buttoned up, either. Let him think he might get a squeeze or two. Oh, hang it, he was easy on the eyes; she might let him.

When she'd finally painted up her face and put herself in harness, it was going on one and she looked likely to be late. Well, she'd never met a man who didn't like to be kept waiting. They squealed about it like bit-pinching fishwives, but they loved thinking she'd put in all that work for them.

On Talbert Street, the trolley whisked beneath the hanging branches of the cherry trees, stirring up a wake of petals. When Cordelia stepped off the trolley, the heels of her shoes sank a quarter inch in fallen flowers.

She let her scarf slip down around her neck, baring her loosely gathered hair. She knew it was garish, but it was also a calling card. Nobody forgot that shade of red. Sure enough, not half a minute passed before Cyril spotted her from the park gate and waved her over.

"I thought we'd go down to Blossom Street," he said, "and walk to the Ionidous Arch. Then we can cut through the park and come back to Talbert Row for a late lunch."

"Suits like a tailor." She'd find out what he was after, but she'd try and wait till after they ate. No sense marring a free meal with business.

"Good." He offered her his arm, and they started down the street through a soft snow of petals.

In the park, they took a footpath along the side of a wooded riding trail. Naked oaks stood tall between the tender green of smaller trees. A horse whinnied from the trails in the ramble, and the thin sound reached them through the forest. The air was still nippy in the shade, and Cordelia buttoned up her coat. Cyril surprised her with an arm around her shoulders. A woman on a glossy hunter cantered past, spraying mulch as she sped toward a jump.

"Do you ride?" Cyril asked, and she couldn't help snorting. "Me neither," he said. "Not for years, anyway."

Swells. You had to laugh or you'd want to slug 'em.

They came out of the woods into a sea of tulips. A breeze made the flowers sway, top-heavy and bright. Cordelia caught her breath.

"Spring's my favorite time to walk here," said Cyril.

Cordelia turned a full circle, taking in the view. "And no wonder."

A wide gravel path divided the flower beds, following a gentle slope down to the shores of the lake. The water lilies weren't blooming yet, but the drooping branches of the willows dusted the currents with pollen. A pair of russet swans floated across the open water. Ripples spread where their wakes crossed.

"You know the swans were a gift from a Niori ambassador?" he asked. "They're protected by a state endowment. The gamekeepers take them indoors before the first frost. There's a special outbuilding hidden in the ramble."

As if they'd been listening, the pale copper-pink birds drifted closer. Probably looking for breadcrumbs, the greedy things.

Cyril led her along the shore until they reached a small, curved bench of painted iron. He gestured for her to sit, then lowered himself into the space beside her. The side of his thigh touched hers, warm and solid. The metal was cold on her rear.

"Cordelia," he said.

"Hm?" She looked away from the swans, who had figured out there was no bread in this for them and were back to dipping their dark beaks between the lily pads.

"I need to ask you an important question."

This would be something about discretion. About his family, or her lover. Or maybe Ari had let slip about the tar, hang him, and now Cyril had some kind of opinion about her running, some kind of bargain he wanted to strike. She waited, one eyebrow arched.

But all he said was, "Musk, or vetiver?"

"Sorry?"

He took a flat, white box from the pocket of his greatcoat. "I guessed the latter, but if you don't like it, I'm sure we can find you something suitable."

She pulled the ribbon out of its knot and opened the box, revealing a wide bottle of pale perfume. The glass was unmarked except for a thin gold band at the base. Etched into the metal, she read the perfumer's name: *Alain de Nils*.

"It's an odd fragrance," said Cyril, "but it reminded me of you.

May I?" He held out a hand, and Cordelia surrendered the bottle, flattered but suspicious, thinking of the twelve-bit bottle of attar of roses she wore near-daily. She'd left it off this morning, in her hurry, and was suddenly glad.

"It's not as sweet as what you wore the other day," he said, confirming her fear. She pressed her lips together, ready to sling a bit of sass—who'd he think she was, a Harbor Terrace lady?—but he already had the bottle open.

When he waved the ground glass stopper under her nose, she jerked back, surprised. "Smells like a diesel engine."

"Give it a moment," he said, lifting her wrist to stripe the scent across her veins. "Let it settle for a while."

"So," she said, "why the perfume?" Oh, Ari was going to get a hiding tonight. What exactly did this swell expect from her?

"I can't give a beautiful woman a beautiful present?"

She twisted her wrist, letting the shrinking wet streak catch the light. "You didn't like what I usually wear."

"Any woman can wear roses," he said. "But I want you to stand out a little. And I think you wouldn't mind it, either."

She let her lashes drop and watched him through narrowed eyes. "Stand out where?"

He took a folded piece of card stock from his billfold. She opened it, read the name and the address, and barely kept her mouth from flapping open. "But this is . . . this is tomorrow."

"The timing's awful. I apologize." Leaning close, he took a deep breath of the air above her raised hand. "There. Smell it again, now."

Curious rather than obedient, she sniffed her wrist. "A little less like the shipyards," she admitted. "More like . . . like burnt wood, and lemons."

"Very good," he said, looking genuinely surprised.

Pleased with herself, though she suspected she ought to feel insulted, she smelled the perfume again. "It's nice," she said. "Odd. But nice."

"It gets odder," he said, "and nicer." He handed the bottle back to her. She held it in the cup of her hands. It was heavy, with all the weight of quality and cash.

"I got work," she told him. "And I got nothing to wear. Not to a party like this. We get some pretty swell punters in the Bee, but even their tips ain't gonna put me in an evening gown by tomorrow night."

"However," he said, "the generosity of a grateful friend just might."

"I ain't wild about charity, Mr. DePaul."

"And I'm not wild about society musicales." He stood, and offered his arm. "But I'm sure we can make the best of both."

CHAPTER
THIRTEEN

The Bee put on a show every night of the week but one, and that one did not coincide with I Fa's party. It didn't help the matter that Cyril asked Cordelia to accompany him on such short notice. In the end, she couldn't get away much before one. Cyril was supposed to pick her up in a taxi at the front of the theatre. The cabbie let the meter run while they sat, for a quarter of an hour.

"Sorry," she said, when she finally slid in beside him. "I was having some words with the boss."

"Only cordial ones, I hope," said Cyril, thinking of the gruff voice he'd heard on the other end of the telephone.

Cordelia snorted. He could smell the Alain de Nils perfume hanging around her like smoke, mixed with the musk of her sweat. Of course, she hadn't had time to bathe after the show. Well, no one would notice; by the time they got to the party, the guests would be so steeped in hock they wouldn't notice a dead wharf rat stuffed down their shirt.

"Busy night?" he asked. "Will you be up to much mingling?"

"Please." She pulled a foot into her lap. "In these shoes? Point me to the sofa and put a drink in my hand."

The pumps were turquoise suede, beaded in jet, and they had a fearsome heel. Cyril didn't remember buying them—had no idea where one might go about buying them—and so concluded they must be something Cordelia had already owned.

"Careful," he said, lifting her foot delicately from her knee, "or you'll put a run in your stocking."

"Sweetness," she said, hiking her black satin dress up to her thigh. "I ain't wearing stockings."

Nor was she wearing a garter belt, or a slip. Just her own freckles. "Suppose it saves you time."

"Boy," she said, snorting. "Does it ever."

He wondered what she thought he knew, or if she thought he'd just used Aristide as a pimp, a procurer. Actually, he had no idea what Aristide had told her, what he'd said, what he'd traded for her services. Or what she thought those services included.

The car let them off at the curb outside the Fischer Building, an edifice of white marble above the Harbor Terrace boardwalk. Floodlights shone across the dazzling façade.

"Sort of makes you wanna squint," said Cordelia, screwing up her face.

There was a private lift to the penthouse, emblazoned with I Fa's family crest. Cyril gave his card to the attendant, who nodded crisply and ratcheted the lever into place. The cage of the lift began to rise.

When they arrived, Cordelia swept the train of her gown across the copper lintel, careful not to catch her heel in the gap. The movement was surprisingly elegant, at odds with her brassy talk and demeanor. But she was a dancer; he shouldn't be surprised.

Once he'd tipped the lift attendant, he caught up with Cordelia and folded her hand over his arm. Her new, white glove was startling against his navy sleeve. He laid his own gloved hand over it.

"You look quite at home," he murmured. "Are you sure you're not secretly a lady of quality?"

"Quality? Nah." She nudged him with her elbow. "Just a keen observer."

Tulip lamps cast gold reflections on the highly waxed parquet, flanking a runner from the lift to a set of double doors, open onto I Fa's parlor. Laughter sparkled over the murmur of conversation, punctuated by the snap of glasses biting each other in a toast. A footman bowed them across the threshold.

I Fa's parlor was all white and gold and tones of peach, long and wide with a low ceiling. It ended in a row of windows looking over the bay. Against the brilliance of the room, the view of the nighttime harbor was breathtaking, spangled with ship's lights and blinking buoys.

Most of the guests were gathered at the windows. I Fa had placed the tables of food there, where the platters of fruit and caviar were lit to best advantage against the dark vista. A caterer in a bright silk suit poured champagne over a tower of glasses. Cyril scanned the crowd and saw Deputy Commissioner Müller deep in conversation with an intent group of harriers.

The center of the parlor was sunk a few feet deeper than the rest of the room. I Fa held court there, seated on a pouf at the center of a circular couch upholstered in velvet. A long-boned man had his dark head in her lap, his face turned into her belly. Müller's wife, Maxine, sat beside the baroness, gesticulating with a champagne coupe. Each sweep of her hand threatened to splash her companions. Abandoned lovers and spouses lay across the cushions, no doubt discussing social intrigues as vicious and vital as those of their politically minded companions circulating by the windows.

"Well," Cyril said to Cordelia, gesturing toward the jeweled tableau of gossips. "There's the sofa. Shall I get you a drink?"

When she laughed, she sparkled. "You're a treasure."

He handed her down the steps. "I won't be long," he said. "I promise."

She settled onto a cushion and stripped off her gloves. A girl in livery offered her a tray of chocolates. Lifting the candy to her lips, she said, "Pigeon pie, you can take as long as you need."

At the bar, Cyril dispensed with his own white kidskins, tucking them into his tail pocket and then lifting a coupe of champagne from the tower. The stem was faintly sticky, owing to the extravagant manner in which the wine had been poured. Transferring it to his other hand, he flexed his fingers, disconcerted.

Müller's group of hangers-on had thinned, leaving him pinned down by one tenacious gentleman. The deputy commissioner looked drawn and gray, his expression sour. Every few seconds, he would glance over his companion's shoulder, staring anxiously toward his wife. Cyril knew that look. *Can we leave yet?*

He lingered by the window, watching Müller's reflection. Finally, the stubborn petitioner wandered off. Müller winced at his handshake and made for Maxine with the singular focus of a stalking cat. Cyril peeled off from the bank of windows and pursued.

He caught Müller's arm before the other man made it halfway across the room. "Deputy Commissioner," he said, offering his hand.

The intense concentration on Müller's face collapsed into annoyance. Cyril braced himself for a rude reception, but he was pleasantly surprised. Müller reassembled himself and shook hands, a consummate professional.

"DePaul." Müller looked over the rims of his narrow eyeglasses. He had deep, yellow-brown eyes, like a bird of prey, and a nose to match. Crow's-feet cracked the skin at his temples. Well into middle age, he was at least ten years older than Commissioner Taormino, which must have put an extra sting in the tail of his thwarted career. "Are you here for work or pleasure tonight?"

"I'm talking to you, aren't I?" Cyril tempered the insult with a crooked smile.

"I'd hope we could exchange a few civil words, outside all that," said Müller, "if it came to it. Did you enjoy Miss Sin's performance?"

"I'm afraid we missed it. My companion had a prior engagement, and it made us late." He nodded in Cordelia's direction. She leaned in close to Maxine, and as Cyril watched, both women burst into laughter.

"Fetching," said Müller. "That's . . . quite a head of hair. She looks familiar."

"I can't think why," said Cyril. "Surely the deputy commissioner of the ACPD doesn't frequent Temple Street nightclubs."

Müller's eyes drew into a squint, then widened. "Lady's name, she's the stripper at the Bee."

"Yes. Lovely woman. Actually, I'm meant to be fetching her a drink."

"Well, then I won't keep you," said Müller, stepping aside. Relief was plain on his face.

Cyril took his card case from his pocket and flipped it open, sliding one card free with his thumb. "Ring me up sometime. This is no place to talk business, but I've got a few things I'd like to chat about."

"I've got your office line," said Müller.

"Maybe I want to exchange a few civil words," said Cyril. "Outside all that."

"This isn't about what happened last week on the wharves, is it?" An edge of apprehension came into Müller's voice. "Chief Sturinopoli's barely out of the academy. Taormino seemed confident enough about her promotion, but . . ." His pause meant several things. He doubted Taormino's faith, or perhaps her ethics. Maybe he even suspected Sturinopoli and Taormino of purposefully skewering their own raid. Cyril had caught the tail end of it in the papers, after his return from Nuesklend. Acting on an anonymous tip, the police went looking for smugglers docking at the southern wharves in the early hours. They'd ended up scaring the piss out of the crew of a fishing vessel. One woman fell overboard and drowned.

"Oh no," said Cyril. "It's nothing to do with that, believe me. In fact, it might be welcome news. Call when you get a chance."

Müller scanned Cyril's card and put it away. "I very well may." They shook hands again. "But for now, I think I'll collect Maxine and go home to bed."

"Goodnight, then. Safe travels."

From behind the long spread of pâté and ice sculptures, Cyril watched Müller approach his wife. She looked up at him, then around at the party. Her shoulders slumped, but she rose and took his arm. Together, they disappeared out the door.

When Cyril returned to the sofa where he'd left Cordelia, bearing two glasses of champagne, he was concentrating hard to keep from spilling. "I'm sorry it took me so long," he said, watching his feet on the steps. "I was waylaid—"

"Well, this *is* a surprise. Hello, Mr. DePaul."

Aristide's hauteur froze Cyril in place. He looked up from the precarious coupes and met umber eyes, ringed in kohl. Aristide was sitting straight now, but that long-boned man on I Fa's lap . . .

Cyril should have recognized him earlier, even with his sumptuous hair drawn into a tightly plaited coronet, and his relatively sober evening dress.

His paint was limited to lipstick the color of dewy mulberries, and the thin, dark stripe around his eyes. The satin facings of his lapels shone under the low-hanging chandelier.

"Mr. Makricosta." Cyril tried to keep his greeting bright, surprised, but even he could hear how sharp it landed. A decorative letter opener used as a knife. "I didn't realize you were going to be here."

"Likewise." Aristide turned to Baroness Fa. "D-D-Dumpling, I didn't know you and Mr. DePaul were acquainted."

The baroness looked Cyril up and down, and suddenly he wondered just how Van der Joost had wrangled this invitation.

Cordelia saved him. "He's here with me."

"Ah, that explains it." I Fa patted Cordelia's knee. "An orchid needs an elegant stem to lift it toward the sun. And you are a shrewd little orchid, darling. You picked a very nice one."

Well, Cordelia had obviously charmed her way into their hostess's good graces far faster than Cyril had managed to squirm into Müller's. Which meant he could leave her here while he dealt with Aristide.

"Madam, Ms. Lehane," said Cyril, nodding to them each in turn. "May I borrow Mr. Makricosta for a moment?"

"Oh, but won't you sit with us instead?" I Fa gestured to an empty space on the sofa. "You would make a lovely addition to the general tableau."

"I'm afraid we would bore you," said Cyril. "It's just business."

"Darling," said Aristide to their hostess, "I p-p-promise I'll be simply *celeritous*. You'll hardly even notice I'm g-g-gone."

She pursed her lips. "Incorrigible little liar. Do not lay the blame at my slippers when you return and all the sweets are eaten."

Bestowing an indulgent smile on her disapproval, he rose and straightened his jacket. Cyril transferred both glasses to one hand and put the other in the center of Aristide's back, maneuvering him out of the crowd.

In the quiet of the foyer, Cyril handed the two coupes of champagne to Aristide and took his money clip from his pocket. He slipped several bills from the center of the fold and handed them to the footman.

"Find somewhere else to be," he suggested.

"Elegant," said Aristide, as the footman disappeared into the party. "Are we supposed to k-k-keep out the gate-crashers, too?"

Cyril took back one of the glasses and drained it, then scowled at Aristide over the rim. "What were you and Cordelia talking about?"

"We work together, Cyril. I was surprised to run into her, especially since she wasn't invited." He flicked his fingers in a dismissive gesture. "Anyway, we were just having a ch-ch-chat."

"Excuse my skepticism."

Aristide *tch*ed. "Mr. DePaul, so *suspicious*. It's a p-p-party. At least try to enjoy it." He crossed his arms, hanging his wineglass above his elbow with elegant fingers. "How did you manage to get in, anyhow? As I said, I happen to know Cordelia was not invited; whether the b-b-baroness remembers it is another story entirely."

"How much does she know, Aristide?"

"The baroness?"

"Don't be obtuse. What have you told Cordelia?"

"That you need some *female company*." He made it sound like a disease.

"Queen's sake, Ari, I'm not a john."

"P-P-Preferable to an Ospie."

Cyril's fingers tightened on the stem of the coupe. "Aristide."

"Are you going to t-t-take her home?"

"I don't want to talk about this with you."

"It would serve me right, if you did."

"I'm not going to knock her to put a pin in your ass, Ari. That's your style, not mine."

Aristide rolled his eyes, his disdain caricaturesque. "I haven't told her anything," he said, "if that will p-p-put your hackles down. You needed a girl; I found you one. Obviously you like her well enough; she'd never b-b-buy that p-p-perfume for herself. Alain de Nils, isn't it? *Very* nice."

"Well my *mistress* couldn't exactly wear attar of roses to a party like this, could she?" Cyril put his free hand to his face, fingers pressing into his forehead. "You could have told me it was going to be her, Aristide."

"You t-t-trusted my judgment. I'm t-t-trying to help you."

"By *spying* on me?" He checked himself, bringing his volume down. "Do you think you can get my secrets out of her? Why would you suppose she knows them? I've always done an excellent job of hiding what needs to be hidden. It's my rotten job."

The second champagne coupe smashed against the dark parquet. Aristide shoved Cyril against the wall, using the height and strength he usually downplayed in favor of effete elegance. "*Not from me.*"

"Yes," said Cyril, hating how hungry he sounded. "Even from you." It was a patent lie, and they both knew it. But it was a lie that went both ways.

The wainscoting scraped Cyril's scalp. He looked up into Aristide's face, watched his hard-lined snarl collapse into desire. Aristide slipped his knee between Cyril's thighs. He let Cyril's jacket free from his grasping fists and put a hand on the wall to either side of Cyril's head.

"Ari," said Cyril, nerves strung taut. "Ari, not here." But his voice was weak, breathless, and belied his words. He opened his mouth. Aristide's face was very close; Cyril could feel the warmth of him, smell his sweat. Like Cordelia, he hadn't bathed between the stage and drawing room, though he'd touched cologne to his throat: a Padgett and Sons vanilla musk, redolent with cinnamon and ambergris, leather and white flowers. Cyril took a ragged breath, inhaling as Aristide exhaled, drawing the other man into his lungs.

He closed his eyes against a sudden scent-memory: Aristide's big hands unstoppering the bottle, the sheen of drying perfume on each pulse point, his nakedness in front of an open window. It was his special scent, for occasions and indulgence.

Aristide's tongue traced the burning skin of Cyril's ear.

"Not *here*, Ari." His voice broke.

Aristide laughed, quietly, against Cyril's temple. The sound made his knees buckle.

"This is I Fa's house." Aristide dropped his pitch to an animal growl. "Who will care?"

Cyril gathered his wits, shoved Aristide back, and wiped his ear. The cuff of his shirt came away stained with lipstick. He pulled his jacket down to hide the purple smudge. "You know as well as I do that someone will. I'm here on business, and there are Ospies in that crowd. The baroness may not realize, but you and I both do." Shaking himself, he settled back into his clothes, then touched the back of his head. His fingers came away slick with blood. "Damnation."

Aristide shook out his pocket square and gestured for Cyril to turn around. He pressed the linen to Cyril's bleeding scalp. "Hold it there," he said, and Cyril did.

Toeing the broken glass, Aristide drew an arc of spilled champagne across the floor. "Shall we get someone to clean this up?"

"This is I Fa's house," said Cyril, bitterly. "Who will care?"

CHAPTER

FOURTEEN

Standing on the boardwalk in front of the Fischer Building, Cordelia squinted against the wind. Her hair snaked around her face, lashing her cheeks. It was nearly four in the morning, and the harbor spread out before them, cold and black.

A crowd of party guests spilled into the street, looking for cabs. One of them wolf-whistled, and the others looked where he pointed—toward Cyril and Cordelia.

Feeling showy, she gathered him closer. "Wanna go to yours?" she ventured.

He was still staring at the group that had followed them out of the party. His pale eyes narrowed, sharp as the steely edge of a razor. The skin at their corners puckered into faint, nervous wrinkles.

"Someone over there prettier than me?" she asked, jostling his elbow. "Come on. Take me to your place."

The edge of a smile flirted with his mouth, and then was gone. "All right. Sure."

They took a cab. She could get used to late-night car rides. The trolleys were fine, when the weather was. But on a windy night like this, the breeze cut something wicked.

Leaving the harbor behind, the hired car took them north, up Armament. They drove past the spires of the university, black against the city-lit night haze. Cordelia wondered what sort of place Cyril called home. She was guessing just west of Talbert Row, maybe somewhere south of Seagate Hill, when the cab drew up at the corner of Mespaugh—not quite as swell as she'd been thinking, but Mespaugh ran straight into the Sergia Vailescu Arch, the eastern entrance to Loendler Park. No wonder Cyril knew his way around the place.

He handed her out of the cab and paid the driver. "I'm afraid my landlord only offers hot coffee until midnight," he said. "But I can rustle up a glass of something, if you like."

"Don't you have a domestic?" asked Cordelia. "Somebody to dress you, and do your breakfast?"

He shook his head. "No. I live alone. No servants."

"You're a curious swell," she said, and took his arm.

Cyril lived up on the third floor. The sleepy lift attendant had to be told twice. When Cyril opened the door, the drawing room was dark. Cordelia reached for the light switch, but he stopped her.

"Wait," he said. "It'll ruin the view."

He led her across the sitting room. The curtains were drawn, but he pulled one set back to reveal Loendler Park and, far away across the dark expanse of green space, the cherry trees of Talbert Row. Streetlamps lit them from below, so they glowed like rosy eggs candled with a torch.

"Gorgeous," she said.

"I had them make it up, just for you."

She snorted. "They fall for that one?"

"You'd be surprised."

"Bet I wouldn't. My line of work, I seen people do some dumb stuff when they're dazzled."

"Are you calling me dazzling?"

"You're smooth as an elver, I'll give you that."

"And just as long and slippery." He winked. "What can I get you?"

"A little gin'll never go amiss."

He disappeared into another room—library? Study? She heard the hollow whoop of a cork withdrawn from the bottle. He called out, "Tonic?"

"Hang it. Why not?"

In the quiet after the hiss of the siphon, she tried to pick out the sound of his returning footsteps but only heard the scratch of a needle on a record. The gramophone whirred to life behind her, soft trumpet and a crooning tenor. With no warning, cold glass pressed against her back where her dress dipped low. She gasped, and rounded on Cyril.

"I'm sorry," he said. "I took off my shoes. Did I frighten you?"

"Gave me a chill, is all." She took the glass from him and knocked it back.

Cyril was a little shyer with his whiskey, tipping the glass so the rye caught the light from the streetlamps. He took a small sip and set it aside, staring after it. He didn't come closer to her, though she saw his eyes move and knew he was watching.

Mother's tits, but she was tired of waiting on him. He was a fine piece and knew it, but the way he danced around . . . If he was angling for a ride, well: the poor jockey didn't have the first notion how to mount up. She set her glass down and stepped forward. When he lifted his face, startled by the movement, she kissed him.

He froze, and she drew back.

"Oh, for queen's sake, DePaul." She slipped her hands beneath his jacket and pulled him closer. "I ain't made of glass."

He nearly laughed. Encouraged, she drew his face down and kissed him again, running fingers beneath the straps of his backless waistcoat. His shirt was warm and damp with sweat where the linen tape trapped it against his skin. She tugged his jacket away and finessed the buttons at the top of the vest, pulling the tape through his collar loop. The waistcoat fell from his chest, hanging awkwardly until she opened it at his back and unhooked the trouser tab. The piqué crumpled on the floor.

He pulled back, eyes wide. "You're fast at that."

She pushed his braces down the curve of his shoulders, relishing his embarrassed flush when she asked, "What is that supposed to mean?"

He didn't answer: just tugged his bow tie loose, smiling ruefully.

She pushed his collar stud from its hole and his collar sprang away. Slipping one button free, and then the next, she pulled the fabric of his undershirt down at the neck to rest her lips on his collarbone. His breath caught. He seemed to like the water all right, now she'd pushed him in. She finished unbuttoning his shirt and dropped it to the floor with his jacket and waistcoat.

"My dry cleaner will be furious."

She tugged his undershirt over his head and sent it after the rest. "More like grateful; after all, I'm keeping them in business." Turning her back, she said, "Unzip me."

He did, in one smooth motion. The dress came loose around her waist and she let it fall. Kicking her feet free of the puddle of black satin, she looked over her shoulder at Cyril.

Oh, but he was easy on the eyes. Hazy light from the street picked out the gold patch of curls in the shadow of his lean chest, the fine stripe of hair below his navel. His belly was sliced clean down the center by a neat silver scar, but Cordelia liked a man who'd been marked a little by life. Blue shadows lay across his face, and a piece of hair had fallen in a curve over his forehead. His lips were swollen from kissing.

He didn't scold her for staring. Instead, he backed away, snatched up his glass, and drained it.

"If that's what it takes," she said. She meant it as a joke, but he sighed into his chest and then, so quick it made her jump, snapped his empty glass back onto the table. The impact made the record skip.

"All right," she said, crossing her arms. "What's wrong?"

Something about the slump that came into his shoulders—she knew where she'd clocked him before. "You and Ari was together at the Bee one night."

Streetlight shivered across the sharp movement of his eyes. "I suppose it's possible."

"Swineshit. I know it. I seen you both, cozy as kippers."

"What's your point?"

She took him in, from his downcast face to the flat front of his trousers. "You don't go in for tits, do you?"

"Don't be ridiculous." But it came out lackluster.

When she laughed, he looked genuinely surprised. "Queen's sake," she said, "I ain't pinned about it. Just curious how come you got Ari to pick you up a peach. I mean, I know what's in this scheme for me, but I can't clock your why-sos."

He stared at her for a long moment, his face slack with wonder. Or horror. She couldn't tell which, and not knowing pinched her sharp. "What?"

"It's just . . . I'd realized you were from the Mew. But it certainly comes out, doesn't it?"

"I cover up pretty good," she said, though she wasn't bothering now. "We're alike that way." She offered him her empty glass. "Now be a swan and top us up, and we'll have a nice jaw over all the little gems our Ari didn't tell us."

He laughed again, this time with genuine humor, and caught the rim of her tumbler between two fingers. "You could make a whole necklace out of mine."

"How long you two been sparkin'?" she asked, a while later. They were sitting on Cyril's sofa—fine linen damask, soft as lily petals—with the better part of his liquor cabinet in their bellies. Sometime in the last hour, the radiators had gone off. Cyril had fetched a flannel dressing gown for her, and draped an afghan around his own bare shoulders.

"A year," he said. "Give or take."

"You oughta get a medal. I can't stand him for more than ten minutes. Say, you got any straights?"

"Liquor cabinet," he said. "In the office." A loose wave of his hand indicated the direction.

She got to her feet, steadying herself on his knee. Through heavy double doors, she found a book-lined room done in dark wood, highly polished. A desk topped in red leather fronted a big bay window. Across from it, under an unlit stained-glass panel, was a three-sided cabinet with a marble-topped wet bar.

"What exactly do you do?" she asked, scanning the labels of his stock. She didn't recognize many of them. What she did clock, she knew she could never afford. "Or don't you work at all?"

"Oh, I work," he said.

But tastes like this didn't come with steady employment. "You're from money though, ain't you?"

"DePaul," he said, his voice pitched loud enough she had no trouble hearing. "You don't know the name?"

She shrugged, then realized he couldn't see her. "Not as I can remember." She started pulling drawers out, searching for his cigarettes. Each one was silent on its casters. There were shakers and shot glasses, sugar and stir sticks. No straights, though.

"Diplomatic service," Cyril went on. "My father was ambassador to the Asunan court, and my sister's in Porachis, now. Grandma was a military genius, a decorated general—you could say she won the Spice War for us, and you wouldn't be exaggerating. Amberlough's done well by the DePauls. And the DePauls—" Here he stopped, and she thought she heard him laugh. "Well, the DePauls have always done well by their state in return."

"You don't have a city accent," she said.

"I spent most of my childhood in the northwest weald. The family has an estate there, near Carmody. Moved south too late to pick up the drone."

She was glad he couldn't see her face, the rueful shake of her head. "Course you did." She opened a shallow drawer beneath the slate-topped counter and found a humidor, stocked with cigars and straights. "You want anything?"

"Whatever you're having."

She put a handful of cigarettes in the pocket of the dressing gown, and one between her lips. There was a table lighter tucked at the back of the bar. She pushed it down and pulled the wick out, burning. Once she'd lit the straight and drawn a breath, she said, "So, you work. Doing what?"

There was a long silence. She went to the doorway and leaned against the frame, watching him. She took another drag on her cigarette. The orange spark flared with her breath.

"Put another record on," he said.

"What's your pleasure?"

He shrugged, and adjusted his blanket. Kneeling behind the sofa, she started to shuffle through the collection stacked beneath the gramophone. He spoke while she was still sorting, so she couldn't see his face.

"Let's just say it's the kind of thing I can't tell you much about," he said. "Unless you like the idea of a quick bullet with your head in a bag."

She was proud she only fumbled with the records, instead of dropping them. Even prouder when she kept her voice steady. "Sounds a treat."

That startled a noise out of him, but she couldn't tell if it was mirth or bitterness. "How about that music?"

Whatever she picked, she didn't read the name. It surprised her when the needle struck the grooves and she recognized the song. Marcel Langhorn's "Don't Let the Sun Rise." She'd worn her own copy clean through.

"Did you bring me a straight?" he asked when she settled on the sofa. In answer, she drew one from her pocket and put it between his lips.

"It was all right at the start," he said, talking around the cigarette. "The work, I mean. Especially when my other option was being sent down. My last year at university, too."

"I'd ask why, but . . . a piece like you?" She leaned in for him to light from her. Their foreheads touched, and he closed his eyes as he inhaled. "I think I know. Caused a little trouble with some teachers, didja?"

He smiled tight, like it hurt him. "A little. Luckily, my father had enough connections that the family could pack me off to serve in a foreign country. The gossip died down. I was gone so long I think people forgot the DePauls had a second child."

Silence settled over him, after that. Ash crept up his cigarette. When he finally tapped it clean, he paused with one hand hanging over the ashtray. A chance flutter of his breath made the scar on his belly flash silver in the gloom. Ghosting her hand down the plane of his stomach, Cordelia asked, "What happened?"

"They barely pulled me home in time for the doctors to help."

"Help what?"

Smoke curled in twin columns from his nose. "Peritonitis. I was beaten so badly I . . . you've never felt anything like it."

Her sister had died like that. Took a solid whack from her man when he had his work boots on. It had taken days for her to go.

"I . . . the work I used to do . . ." Cyril put a hand over his mouth, pressing his thumb into the muscle of his jaw. "Lady's name, Cordelia, I shouldn't be talking about this."

"You don't have to tell me."

"When I was younger," he said, ignoring her, "it seemed so exciting. Everything was a game, and ruthlessness had a kind of . . . romantic appeal." Then, he looked up, and his eyes widened, gleaming like mercury. "I'm sorry. You're from the Mew. I wasn't thinking."

She licked her teeth, tasting good tobacco and clean gin. "Nah. I ain't pinned. We're all idiots when we're kids. Only difference is, I stopped being a kid a lot sooner than you."

The shame was plain on his face, and satisfying.

"You're still in it," she said. "Right? The game. And now you're dragging me along."

"That's the thing: I was wrong. It's not a game. And I don't want to drag you." He pushed a hand through his hair. "I want . . . I want you to work with me."

"Then you oughta tell me what I'm doing," she said. "At least as far as I need to know. I ain't keen on following blind."

He drew in a deep lungful of smoke. It came out in a cloud when he spoke, hiding his expression. "Right now, you know enough."

"And if that changes? If I need to know more?"

"Let's just hope you won't." He waved the screen of smoke from his face. She expected his expression to be calculating, but all she saw was fear.

CHAPTER

FIFTEEN

Cordelia came to Aristide at the beginning of the interval, just after Tito dropped his payload of cards and bribery.

"I got your note," she said, falling across his chaise longue as gracefully as a silk ribbon in a breeze. "Cyril's here; I can't spend long with you."

Aristide's grip tightened on the thick stack of cards Tito had left him. Cyril's was not among them. He bit the inside of his cheek. *That's the way you want it, fool.*

He took his coat from its hook and reached into an inner pocket. Removing a package wrapped in brown paper, he offered it to her. "Take that."

She weighed it in her hand, her expression considering. "There's a lot here."

He said nothing. It was true.

"Something happen to Ellie? I was fine making pickups from her."

"No. Nothing's happened to Ellie. But this came across my path, and I thought you'd d-d-do it credit."

"You trying to ask me a favor?"

"You've already done me several. Consider this a b-b-bonus." He'd taken it, with her in mind, from the lot that had come in this afternoon—delayed after the dummy raid for Taormino.

So far, their arrangement had worked flawlessly. Cordelia had been spotted all over the city with Cyril. He'd even seen her in the background of a photo in the *Clarion* society pages. Cyril, of course, had avoided the camera's gaze. And now, he felt confident enough to come back to the Bee posing as her lover. He must be in good stead with the Ospies, and with Cordelia.

Speaking of . . . Her eyes were suspicious as she tugged one flap of the package open. After a quick inspection of the blocks of tar, she arched one finely plucked eyebrow and pinned him with an accusatory glare. "Damn sight finer'n what you pass on to Ellie." When she rubbed the edge of a brick with the pad of her thumb, her skin came away stained brown.

"Like I said," said Aristide. "I thought of you. You needn't mention it to her when you see her next."

"Quiet as a sleeping eel." She surprised herself by pecking his painted cheek. "You know, you really ain't as bad as all that."

"Oh no," he said. "I prefer to think I'm worse."

In short order, Aristide followed Cordelia out into the house. The jumble of voices poured over him, and the press of bodies and adoration propelled him forward. Everyone reeked of wet fur and smoldering, damp tobacco.

The crowd hadn't changed much in the few weeks since the election—at least, not on the surface. Corks still popped from champagne bottles, and flirtations flew with as little discretion as they ever had. But if one listened carefully—and Aristide always did—conversation around the mosaic tables tended strongly toward politics, and little else. Moritz had moved to impeach Josiah Hebrides in a special session of parliament, and the wheels of the process had begun to turn.

Most of Malcolm's star performers found their stacks of interval invitations diminished. Aristide, on the other hand, stuffed both his pockets and even then ended up putting off some punters until after. Since Acherby's victory, he could count on one hand the nights he'd gone to his bed before the sun rose from hers.

He had people to see tonight—he was especially keen to rendezvous with Zelda Peronides about moving some hot Lisoan ivory. But he lingered near the front of the house, careful to keep hidden in the crowd and stage left of center.

The chance movement of a large group toward the bar gave Aristide a clear line of sight. Cyril was at his regular seat, resting his elbows on the blue and green tiles of the tabletop. As he spoke, he gestured with a cigarette. Cordelia sat beside him, sipping a cocktail. And in the chair across from him . . . Aristide couldn't be sure. He could only make out the back of a head: long-skulled, square-cornered, furred with close-clipped silver hair. When Cyril's guest turned, attending to Cordelia, Aristide saw the flash of spectacles resting on an aquiline nose: Deputy Police Commissioner Alex Müller.

"Mr. DePaul," Aristide murmured, hand over his mouth. "Keeping such *low* company these days." But it made sense. If Hebrides fell, the unionists would move into Amberlough. Without a standing army, the police were the nearest thing the Ospies could touch that might help with a coup, or whatever they had planned.

He thumbed through the business cards Tito had brought him, scanning the crowd, matching names to faces. When the pad of his thumb struck cheap matte paper amidst the creamier textures, he looked down, surprised. His finger hid the given name, but left *Lourdes* visible.

He didn't have time—really, he didn't. But seeing Cyril had stung him more than he cared to admit. And if he didn't have one lover's card in his pocket, at least he had another's. Casting his attention over the crowd, Aristide searched for the bright distraction of the accountant's copper hair.

When the curtain rose on the second half, Cyril indulged in a single, relieved sigh. Watching Müller flirt with Cordelia at the interval was equal parts gratifying and embarrassing. Müller was clearly smitten with her, and she clearly knew it. He'd take them both out after the show. He needed Müller feeling catered-to, expansive. There were a few things Cordelia could contribute that Cyril, though he was willing if it would get him what he wanted, couldn't quite. And they were all on display in the penultimate number of the cabaret's second half.

The show would end with an extravaganza: all the members of the cast onstage, confetti, streamers, swelling orchestra. But the eleven o'clock number was a sultry partner striptease: Cordelia and Ari, sliding around each other like oil and paraffin, just as slippery and just as volatile.

They started on opposite sides of the stage, alone in dramatic spotlights that hit the boards with a crisp beat from the orchestra. Aristide was wrapped to the neck in white fox fur. He had abandoned the powdered wig in favor of his natural curls, gathered in an elaborate coif pierced with two long, gold pins. His hands, clutching the fox at his throat, were gloved in black satin.

Cordelia contrasted in every way. Where Ari was dark, the spotlight turned her fair skin ghostly pale. Her brilliant hair was tucked beneath a silk top hat. Against Aristide's white fox, she wore a black tailcoat, nipped in tight beneath her ribs. High-cut dress trousers made her legs look impossibly long for her short stature, and her spats were blinding. She struck an arrogant pose with a gold-topped cane, smirking over one shoulder at the audience.

There was no introduction. The emcee was otherwise occupied, and really, they didn't need one. The audience sucked in its breath. In the orchestra pit, a slinky vamp skipped between the snare and the cymbal and a soulful clarinetist coaxed an aching note from somewhere below her waist. As the moan of the reed reached its climax, the timpani growled to the brass and Cordelia and Aristide rolled their shoulders in perfect unison. Another growl, another roll. And then the drummer struck a fast one-two and they each turned their heads on a separate beat, skewering the other with a glare.

It should have been slightly farcical, mildly absurd. The emcee dressed like the mistress of a magnate, the sultry stripper done up in glad rags like a concert tenor. But the personalities under the clothes burned through. And soon enough, the clothes started coming off.

Ari dropped the fox fur in one heavy shrug, and it fell like a diva dying on the opera stage. He spun out of the coat's radius in a swirl of red feathers and kicked Cordelia's cane out from under her. Rather than staggering, she swept it in a circle, executing a crisp barrel roll straight out of her jacket. It slid down the cane, hanging inside-out from the trapped sleeve to reveal a red lining that matched her waistcoat. Her skin was bare beneath the brocade.

With a flick of her wrist, she flung the jacket offstage. Aristide grabbed the cane and strutted away, dragging her with him. She pouted spectacularly, appealing to house left as he hauled her along.

Appealing, Cyril realized, straight to him. Or rather, Müller. Under the guise of reaching for his glass, Cyril snuck a glance at his companion. The deputy commissioner had half his mouth tucked up in a secret, satisfied smile, and he stared unwaveringly at the stage. The lights glanced off his spectacles, turning his gaze blank and gleaming.

As if she had seen the white flash of shining glass, Cordelia flung out one beseeching arm toward their table, chasing it with a blown kiss. Müller chuckled and swept a hand over his close-clipped hair.

Cyril sipped his drink, satisfied.

On the far side of the stage, Cordelia pulled the pins from Aristide's hair and dipped him over one knee, hard and fast. His neck snapped back and his curls tumbled free from their knot. Cordelia lowered her head and bit his outstretched fingers with delicate teeth, dragging her mouth down until she caught the tip of his glove.

The slip of satin against his skin played against a raunchy brass arpeggio, a muted trumpet caterwauling over a pulsing backbeat. As soon as the glove came free, Cordelia yanked Aristide up and nearly sent him flying. He took the momentum and slid back, out of his second glove, pulling her into a tight spin so she ended up against him. He swept the top hat from her head and brought it across her breasts, pulling her close so their hips aligned. The trombone howled and they ground down, Cordelia sliding her hands along her thighs to press her knees wider and wider apart. Ari stared over her head with hooded eyes, showing one dogtooth in a foxy smile.

Cyril knew that look. He'd met it countless times, from this very chair. Someone would go home happy tonight. Knowing he didn't want to see, he still turned to scan the crowd.

At first, he couldn't tell for whom the smoldering glance was meant. A giggling clutch of students snatched at each other's hands, their cheeks pink with wine and embarrassment. But Aristide wasn't looking at them.

Alone at his table, Finn Lourdes nursed something he probably couldn't afford. He was redder than the students, with better reason. Cyril's jaw clenched. The faces of the crowd around him went slack in sudden amazement, and they all gasped. A few applauded. Something magnificent had happened onstage. Cyril shut his eyes and turned away from Finn.

Another gasp, another round of applause. Someone whistled, sharp and clean. Cyril took a deep breath and opened his eyes again.

Cordelia's trousers and waistcoat were gone. She wore an elaborate construction of black lace and gold fringe that covered all it needed to and not much more. Aristide was down to rather less than that, and a red feather boa.

Or, no . . . not a boa. He pulled the drape of ostrich plumes from his shoulders and twirled. The feathers snapped open into two huge fans. He kept one and passed the other to Cordelia in an exchange that involved popping the clasp on her top. She slapped a hand across her chest to keep the cups from falling.

They both spun until they stood back to back at three-quarter angles, fans held open across their bodies. The snare and timpani raced against each other, counting heartbeats between trumpet blasts. And then, with a wail of brass and woodwinds, both Aristide and Cordelia pulled off what little they had on behind the shivering feathers and tossed the jangling bits of gilt and tassels into the pit.

The orchestra hit a beat, the fans snapped shut, and for half a moment they both struck a tantalizing pose. Not quite long enough to see exactly what they were or were not showing, but long enough to make everyone in the audience wonder. Then the lights went out and the crowd screamed for more.

CHAPTER

SIXTEEN

Cordelia was half-in, half-out of her street clothes when Malcolm stepped into her dressing room.

"Knocking," she said. "Ain't it a habit some people have?"

"Some more than others." She scoffed, and he ducked his head. "Sorry, Delia." He closed the door behind him. "Next time."

"You're assuming, Sailer."

"Queen's sake. Why you gotta stomp on me before I'm even standing? I came in to ask if you were free for a bite."

"You clocked me at the interval," she said. "You know I ain't."

His shoulders pulled down and back, tugging the starched front of his white dress shirt into strained wrinkles at the buttonholes. "So you got plans with that swell you been seeing." It wasn't a question. It was an accusation. "What about old kite-face Müller? You ain't angling to take on both at once, I hope."

"Don't be a pig, Mal." She turned her back and presented him with her half-done buttons. "Finish me up. You can make sure I'm shut in nice and tight." His fingers were calloused; she could hear them, rough against the fine fabric of her dress. "Careful," she said. "Don't snag my satin."

He let out a frustrated breath. It stirred the fine hair at the back of her neck. "You make me so vexed I'd like to skin you, Delia."

She smiled, then realized he could see her face in the mirror. Too late to drop it, so she looked his reflection in the eyes and made it a tease. He blinked, twice, then scowled and turned his attention back to her buttons. His touch was hot and dry against her bare skin.

"You're so warm all the time," she said. "Bet you gave your ma a fright when you was small; always feverish."

His steady progress up the line of buttons faltered. "Dell . . ."

"What?" She turned her head, tossing hair across his face. "Something wrong?"

The heat of his hands spread as he opened his palms over the taper of her hips. His thumbs met in the small of her back. "How long you gonna keep this up?" He spoke with his face down, forehead resting in the curve of her neck. His sticky pomade smelled of sweet tobacco.

"I ain't the one who got all sour in the first place," she said, leaning into his touch. She shouldn't encourage him, but it felt good to fall back against that solid chest. They'd get on so well if he wasn't such a jealous ass.

"So you'll come on out with me tonight?"

"Mal, I can't."

His grip on her waist tightened briefly, and then he pushed away. "Delia!"

"Look, I would, all right? But Cyril wants me to tag along with him and Müller, and I can't exactly say no."

"And why's that? You selling out 'cause he can treat you like a center city swell? You think you're better than the rest of us?"

"Oh, that's rich. I'm high and mighty *and* a whore. The sense you ain't making would buy a house! Just listen to yourself."

"Nobody else does."

She rolled her eyes and reached back to finish her own buttons. "Stroll off," she said. "I got places to be."

"I ain't strolling anywhere. I'm gonna sit here"—he dropped into her makeup chair with a tremendous squeal of metal and straining leather—"and you're gonna tell me what it is about this welterweight swell that makes him so special."

"Get *out*, Sailer."

Malcolm checked his watch, casual as a man waiting for a train. "Think he'll mind if you keep him waiting?"

She slammed her hairbrush down on the table and rounded on him. "Mother's tits, Mal. Fine. You want to know why Cyril? Because Ari's making me a tidy trade over it."

"Makricosta?" Malcolm looked caught between laughing and rage. "What, he's pimping for you now?"

"Is it always gotta be about whoring with you?" She fixed her hat in place, so fast the combs tore her hair. "Just 'cause I grew up in the bad end of the first precinct doesn't mean I gotta make my living on my back."

"I figured you was more in the side streets line. Standing in an alley, or something like that."

Oh, she nearly slapped him then. "You got no idea what line I'm in." Furious, she dug into her handbag and hauled out Ari's brown paper package. It struck Malcolm's lap with such force that he flinched, probably aiming to protect his tackle. The smack of it against his thighs gave her grim satisfaction.

"Go on," she said. "Open it. See if you like what you find."

He peeled back the edge of the paper and sniffed. "Tar?"

"Real good stuff, too."

"Makricosta's selling to you? Delia, I didn't know—"

"You better shut your mouth before you swallow any more trouble." She took the package back and carefully rewrapped it. "I don't smoke tar. And if I did, I couldn't afford this." It hit the bottom of her handbag with a heavy thump. "I can get enough from that to live on. Better than what you're paying. Ari's not selling to me. I'm running for him."

Malcolm crossed an ankle over his knee. She watched him watch her. "Since how long?" he asked.

"A couple of weeks."

"How'd he hook you? You owe him money?"

"*He* owes *me*."

"What for?"

She flung her hands wide. "For spending my time with Cyril. Queen's sake, use the head your ma pushed out, for once."

"So you are hiring out."

"Only my time, Malcolm. Get outta my chair. You're sitting on my coat."

He snorted, but followed orders. "He's awful pretty, Delia. 'Scuse me if I don't believe it."

"Believe it," she said. "I tried him out, but that bayonet won't fix. Not for this charge, anyhow." Swiping her coat from the back of the makeup chair, she shoved her arms up the sleeves. "He don't go in for peaches and pears. More like big noses and bad attitudes. Come to think of it, you'd be just his type. So if anyone's got cause to be jealous, it's me." She pulled the door wide open and swept her arm to show him the way out.

Aristide didn't say much to Finn at the interval, and didn't get anything done besides drop by people's tables and jot names and dates into his diary. The two of them arranged to meet after the show, in front of the theatre. It took Aristide a long time to spot Finn's bowler through the wreaths of adoration the crowd was laying on. Disengaging from a bevy of admirers, he crept up on Finn and lifted the brim of his hat with one finger. Finn jumped like a cat, then saw who it was. His smile spread, unguarded.

"I'm so sorry it took me such a long time to come back," he said. "I was out of town for a family matter. You were brilliant, of course."

The hint of his Farbourgere lilt made the words musical, and eerily evocative: the sound of Aristide's childhood. To stop him talking, Aristide ducked down and kissed him. "D-D-Don't trouble your pretty copper head about it, darling. You're here now." He shuddered elaborately. "Family matters. How t-t-*tedious*."

"Actually, my mother's been ill. We don't . . . didn't get on, but it was good to see her before . . ."

Oh, perdition. Aristide grabbed his ankle and pulled his foot out of his mouth. "Poor dear." He put an arm around Finn's waist, squeezing him close. He was soft about the middle, and gave pleasantly under the pressure. "You'll want cheering up, then."

The warmth of Finn's exhalation against his collarbone was welcome in the cool, damp night. "Yes, I suppose I do. It's why I came."

"And are you feeling better?"

"Mightily."

"What's your p-p-pleasure? Another show? A quiet drink? Or would you rather just . . . head home?"

He could've scraped Finn's blush from his cheeks and used it for rouge. But before the boy could answer, someone in the crowd checked his shoulder, and he stumbled.

"Pardon me." The accidental assailant reached out to steady Finn, but Aristide had already caught him. Highly polished spectacles flashed in the golden light of the marquee. Aristide froze, assuming an expression of polite disdain.

"D-D-Deputy Commissioner Müller," he said, extending a languid hand. "So p-p-pleased to see you. And how is Maxine? It was d-d-*divine* running into her at the baroness's little party." Müller's grip was lackluster, and he drew away quickly. Aristide was accustomed to having his hand kissed, pressed to cheeks, wrung enthusiastically; he was underwhelmed by the deputy commissioner's performance. "T-T-Tell me, did you enjoy the show?"

From Müller's expression, he hadn't been impressed with Aristide's performance either. Still, he said, "It was all right," and nodded, once.

"Mr. Makricosta," said Cyril, drawing Aristide's attention from Müller's narrow, sunken eyes. He realized Cyril had been watching him this entire time, and wondered if he'd seen Müller take his collision course, seen where it would lead them, and hadn't stopped it. "I didn't realize you and the deputy commissioner were acquainted."

Aristide knew when he was being mocked. But he also knew when he was being given a warning. And Cyril, hang him, had managed both at once.

"Only by reputation," said Aristide. "His, of course, not mine."

"I'm sure I've heard your name before," said Müller.

Aristide graced him with a smile like a rabid dog's.

"Mr. Lourdes," said Cyril, defusing the situation. "I don't believe you've met Alex Müller."

"A pleasure, sir." Finn's earnestness was refreshing.

"Mr. Lourdes and I are coworkers," Cyril explained.

Müller gave Finn an appraising look. "Are you—?"

"Oh no. Office of the Bursar."

Müller let his hand be shaken. "It's always a pleasure to meet another civil servant, Mr. Lourdes."

There was an awkward pause, as conversation scrabbled to find a crack through which it could enter. Aristide looked at Cyril again, and caught him with his guard down. He was searching the crowd with shifting eyes, looking hunted.

Finn saved things by yawning enormously and putting his weight on Aristide's arm. "I'm so sorry," he said, "but I'm utterly bashed. Been traveling."

"You'd better let Mr. Makricosta take you home," said Cyril.

Tastelessly blatant innuendo. Aristide did not engage. "Indeed. Time to put your feet up and have a t-t-toddy." He nodded to Cyril, and to Müller. "Gentlemen."

Even after the crowd had separated them, Aristide felt two pairs of eyes on his back. He pulled the ribbon from his hair and let his curls tumble down, trying to cut the intensity of imagined scrutiny. Finn caught one of the ringlets and wound it around his finger.

"Are you really so t-t-tired?" Aristide tipped his head to the side, tugging his hair free of Finn's grasp.

"Yes," said Finn, leaning his head on Aristide's shoulder. "But I'd rather not go to sleep just yet, if it's all the same to you."

"It's t-t-two quite d-d-different things, in fact, and we're in full agreement. Ah, but we might not be able to slip away just yet." Because he was taller than most of the people on the footpath, Aristide could see a plume of peacock feathers swaying like glamorous semaphore over the crowd. Zelda Peronides had spotted him and was waving her hat to catch his attention. "There's a friend I need to speak with, before I go."

"Ari," said Zelda, as she hove through the press of people. "Oh darling, this is the first I've seen of the new show. It's simply marvelous. Even Mab thought so. Didn't you, Mab?"

Zelda's companion, a leather-faced woman in country clothes, laid a hand on Aristide's free arm. "Pleased to meet you, and it certainly was." Her pursed, immobile lips, the way her words crowded behind her teeth . . . Even more than Finn's soft lilt, her dialect was intensely familiar to Aristide. This woman was mountain-born: the Currin Pass, or somewhere nearby. Her dark skin and darker curls said she was at least part Chuli, too.

"I didn't get the chance to introduce you two during the interval," said Zelda. "But Mab's got a little bit of a problem I hope you might sort out for her. Mab, this is Aristide Makricosta. Ari, meet Mab Cattayim."

"If you sort my problem," said Aristide, shaking Mab's hand but speaking to Zelda, "I would be more than delighted to sort hers." They hadn't got the details of the ivory worked out in the short minutes he'd spent at her table. Zelda's fee was exorbitant, and Aristide was a ferocious haggler by nature. "B-B-By the way, this is Finn Lourdes. You didn't get to meet him at the interval either. Because the silly thing actually waits in the q-q-queue for the washroom."

Zelda shook her head, laughing. Her long earrings jangled against her neck. "Darling," she said, kissing each of Finn's cheeks. "That's what the mime is in the show for. So you have a tidy five minutes to piss and you won't miss anything good."

"I'll bear it in mind," said Finn.

"Now, Ari." Pixie-sized Zelda had to cock her head back to meet his eyes. "When can we have our little sit-down? I suppose a pretty thing like you has all manner of dinner engagements after a show of that caliber. I hear you're dabbling with one of Culpepper's foxes these days." Finn stirred at Aristide's side, but Zelda went on. "Rumor has it he's a roto print of poor old Solomon Flyte."

At that, Finn froze—he knew she wasn't talking about him.

"D-D-Dabbling?" Aristide assembled his strongest quelling glance and aimed it down at Zelda. "I wouldn't say that. Not any-more."

"Oh dear. It always stings to be thrown over. You must be shat-tered. *Do* let us take you out. It would be *such* a treat."

"I'm afraid I'm t-t-tied up," he said. "Might we have a bite of lunch tomorrow? And let's keep it strictly business, please. I prefer not to air my d-d-delicates in public." He squeezed Finn close. The accountant's spine held stiff against his embrace.

"Mab?" Zelda looked at her friend.

"I'll be free." She smiled at Ari like she expected something of him.

"Perfect." Aristide caught Zelda's hand and kissed her knuckles. "Ring me up in the morning, Zelly. But not t-t *too* early, understand?"

"Makricosta, Makricosta . . . why do I know that name?" Müller chewed his lower lip. "Damned familiar."

"The smugglers on the southern wharves owe him most of their success." Cyril lit a cigarette and offered one to Müller, who took it but made no motion to light up. His eyebrows were drawn down against the thin frames of his spectacles, and he watched Aristide with the intensity of a hungry raptor.

"Of course," he said, at last. "Makricosta's his stage name. He goes by a different handle when he's bringing in ships."

"I know."

"Isn't that Zelda Peronides he's talking to?"

Cyril finally let himself look at Aristide, instead of watching Müller look at him. He still had Finn tucked under one arm, and the accountant was suffering himself to be kissed on the face by a slip of a woman in an outrageously feathered hat. "Looks like it."

"The two of them can't be up to any good."

"Relax, Alex. You're off the clock. You can't spend all your time chasing criminals."

"That's the kind of attitude that's got the ACPD into such a shameful state," said Müller, finally lighting his straight. "They don't want to spend any time cleaning the place up. They'd rather play in the filth."

"Well, then it's good I'm not an officer." With relief, he spotted Cordelia coming toward them. He held out an arm to her as she sidled between people queuing for the trolley. "Ms. Lehane! So kind of you to join us."

She dipped gracefully into the circle of his arm. "Had a beast of a time gettin' out," she said. "You wouldn't believe the kind of stuff that goes on behind that curtain."

"Try me," said Cyril, and kissed her. She tasted like fresh lipstick, and kissed back.

"You put on a sterling show," said Müller. "That last part especially. I've never seen somebody get out of a girdle with such panache."

Cyril felt Cordelia smile against his mouth. She broke away, and gave Müller a once-over. "Glad you enjoyed it. It's for the punters, after all."

"Surely you enjoy it, too. Or you wouldn't be doing it."

"Damn right I wouldn't. Pay's piss-poor."

"And all those bits of paper pushed into your garters at the interval?" Müller's flirtation made him grin, showing sharp teeth stained with nicotine. "What were those? Telephone exchanges?"

"You'd be surprised."

"No." He flicked ash into the gutter. "No, I don't think I would. But I'd hope they were written on some hefty bills."

"All right, you two." Cyril pressed the heel of his palm to his mouth, checking for lipstick stains. "I'll just head home now. You seem like you're getting along fine."

"DePaul!" Müller laughed, and Cyril felt a bit of tension ease from his shoulders. He'd been worried Müller would stay stiff all night. "I didn't have you pegged as the jealous type."

"Not jealous," he said. "Sensitive to the needs of my friends. For instance: Next round is on me. Where should we head?"

"You a port drinker?" asked Müller. Cyril wasn't, but nodded anyhow. "The Kelly Club, then."

It was on the other side of town, the northeast quarter, not far from Cyril's flat. However well Müller liked Cordelia, he didn't seem enamored of the theatre district. "I'll get us a cab," said Cyril, and left the two of them together.

Leaning against a streetlight with his arm out—the first rush after curtain had taken most of the nearby taxis—he watched Cordelia work on Müller. She was a sharp one—she'd figured out first thing, at the interval, that Cyril was using her for something, and started laying it on thick. Her flirtation was a seamlessly choreographed dance: She tossed her hair; touched Müller's arms, the back of his hand; threw her face to the sky in exaggerated laughter. All so smoothly it seemed natural. Like he was brilliant and special and must think the same thing about her.

No wonder she couldn't stand Aristide. There was barely room for both their egos on the Bee's broad stage, let alone in conversation. Their clashing tempers and over-the-top personalities were what made that striptease so sizzling.

In the backseat of the cab, he would put her in the middle. Let his weight fall on her in the curves, so she'd fall into Müller in turn. If only he could pass his pocket flask around. But Müller was the deputy police commissioner, and he'd proved himself vigilant even out of uniform.

Headlights made him squint. A black cab drew up beside him, and he waved to Müller and Cordelia. Müller went around to the street side. Cyril stopped Cordelia with a hand on her wrist.

"You're perfect," he told her. It would pass for an endearment, if Müller overheard them, but from the look in her eye, she knew it wasn't flattery; it was fact.

Car doors fluttered along the curb, opening and shutting like the shells of beetles. Before Cyril followed Cordelia and snapped his own door closed, he looked down the taxi rank and saw Aristide arm-in-arm with Finn. Aristide noticed him staring and their eyes locked. Cyril caught his breath and looked away.

"You know Cyril," said Finn, as Aristide ushered him into the back of an illegal hack.

"What's that?" Aristide climbed in and gave the driver his address, hoping his feigned inattentiveness would put Finn off. He wasn't so fortunate.

"You know Cyril DePaul, somehow. The first time he brought me round, I kenned it. Too much frizzing in the air."

"Frizzing?" Aristide pretended incredulity, though he knew the northern slang.

"You know." Finn wiggled his fingers. "Electricity. Even just now, and you two hardly said a word. Still, zap!"

Aristide snorted. "Silly boy. C-C-Come here. I'll show *you* electricity." He lifted his arm and Finn hesitated. "Oh, Finn, p-p-please. We all have p-p-pasts."

Finn relented and slipped across the leather seat into the curve of Aristide's body. "He's an old spark, isn't he? Why was he so keen on introducing us?"

"What Mr. DePaul once was to me is now irrelevant." To prove it to himself, Aristide tipped Finn's face up to his own. The accountant's mouth tasted like gin and tea tree chewing gum. "I'm sure he has his own c-c-curious motives, but in general I try not to question them. He's a very useful friend to me sometimes, and he may be useful to you someday as well. Don't put him off over a t-t-trifling little thing like jealousy."

"It's not that," Finn started, but Aristide stopped him—utterly.

CHAPTER

SEVENTEEN

The Kelly Club was a set of second-story rooms on Orchard Street, just off Ionidous Avenue. The avenue was distinct from the arch; cocooned in the fashionable central city, Loendler Park boasted the patronage of wealth and beauty. Ionidous Avenue ran straight through the heart of the financial district. The Kelly Club had wealth, but lacked elegance.

The club was within walking distance—strenuous walking distance—of Cyril's flat, and he'd gone there a few times in years past. He hadn't been recently. They'd done the place up, polished the brass, et cetera, but Cyril still caught a whiff of old cigar smoke. Probably the same stale stuff he'd wrinkled his nose at the last time he came around.

There was a pack of razors at the bar, talking textile futures.

They ignored Müller's entrance, but when Cyril helped Cordelia out of her coat, they roused a chorus of wolf whistles. Cordelia flicked her skirt at the offenders, and chased it with a vixen's smile.

The high ceilings bounced sound, but the tables were nearly filled. So many people were murmuring to one another, the effect of the echo was more obscuring than revealing.

"Table in the rear," Cyril told the maitre d', and she took them to a booth in the corner. He stood back and let Cordelia slip in. Müller settled beside her—not too close, Cyril noted, but close enough their feet could be doing who knew what under the table.

"What are we having?" Cyril asked, hanging Cordelia's coat from one of the booth's hooks, and hanging his own over it. He topped the column with his trilby, at a jaunty angle.

"They serve a good Maleno vintage," said Müller.

"Hang it," said Cordelia, "I don't know port from nothing. They got gin back there?"

"A dry white'll do for the lady," said Müller.

Cyril, who was inclined to agree with "the lady," resolved to have the same. At the bar, he squeezed past a hefty razor in her shirtsleeves and a backless waistcoat. She cased him and growled appreciatively.

"Sorry," he told her. "I'm here with company."

She cast her eyes whence he had come. "The old eagle or the pretty young jay?"

"And if I said both?"

"You'd put me in a twist," she said. "I couldn't straight envy you, but I wouldn't give you any pity either."

He propped a foot up on the bar rail. "What's good here?"

"Not a port drinker?"

"I prefer whiskey," he said.

"Are you a rye man, or do you like barley?"

"Rye, when I have a choice."

She slid her schooner down the bar. "Try that beauty. Babe turned me on to it." One of her companions saluted. "Thirty-year tawny. You're gonna think it's sweet, but give it a chance."

He lifted it to his nose and barely smelled it, then took a sip to be polite. It *was* too sweet, but he could see where she was coming from. The butterscotch and nutmeg notes were reminiscent of a good, dark rye.

"All right," he said. Then, to the bartender, "One of those. And the Maleno. And . . . oh, whichever dry white you like."

The bartender went to work. By the time Cyril brought their port to the table, Müller was lighting Cordelia's cigarette from his own, their heads bent close. Cyril doled out the glasses.

"Cheers." Müller lifted his and looked at Cordelia. "To pretty things."

She rolled her eyes, but let him drink to her.

Cyril did his best not to taste the syrupy stuff he'd ordered. Conversation wandered. When Müller was distracted by some detail of his story, trying to recall a name or place, Cordelia caught Cyril's gaze and angled her head out of the booth. Presumably toward the washrooms, or the bar. He nodded, barely. When Müller finished up his punchline, she laughed, told him he was a lying show-off, and then excused herself for the toilet.

"Stuff's gone right through me," she said, tapping her nail against the streaky glass. "Ah, don't look so shocked, Mr. DePaul. You know you love a little plain speaking."

He caught her hand as she rose and pulled her down for a kiss—a wordless *thank you*. The dry port lingered on her lips, bright with citrus and a hint of nuts.

When he let her free, she fetched a tube of lipstick from her coat pocket. "Better take a minute and repaint the pucker too, if you're going to keep on like that."

"Hurry back, pigeon pie." Müller's smile was indulgent. "He's going to make me talk business, I'll wager. And I'd rather talk with you."

Cordelia snorted and turned away. As she crossed the room, her hips rolled like a buoy in choppy water. Heads turned, including Müller's.

"You're awful, Alex." Cyril shook his head. "What would Maxine say?"

His smile turned brittle, and fell. "Nothing she hasn't already. I'm a terrible husband."

"But an excellent policeman."

"Am I?" Müller took a drink. The port stained his teeth purple, briefly. "Then why wasn't I made commissioner five years ago?"

"Perhaps," said Cyril, crossing his arms, "that's exactly why. You said it yourself: The ACPD isn't exactly on the up-and-up. Take that raid on the docks, for instance. We both know it was a sham."

"Taormino's under pressure to crack down on the smugglers. You know. You probably put the squeeze on her. It wouldn't surprise me if she cut a deal with somebody so she came out looking good. Makricosta, maybe."

It wouldn't have surprised Cyril, either.

"DePaul," said Müller. "Why are we here? What do you need me for?"

Tapping his fingers against the foot of his schooner, Cyril thought for a moment and finally said, "You know, I really don't like this."

"I can tell."

Pushing the glass away, Cyril looked up at Müller. "What gave me away?"

"You're putting up with an awful lot," said Müller. "You said you're not the jealous type, but a man doesn't let somebody get so close to his mistress unless he wants something, badly."

"I meant the port," said Cyril.

Müller's snort was expressive. "Oh. That was easy." He picked up the glass Cyril had been studiously ignoring and tipped it so the liquor climbed the crystal. "It's a single-year tawny. Cove Oscár, or something like it. Overpriced, overrated, too sweet. You should've told me you didn't 'know port from nothing.' At least Ms. Lehane got a glass of something she enjoyed."

"Next time," said Cyril.

"So there's going to be a next time?" Müller picked up his spectacles from the water-ringed table and polished them with his handkerchief. "How long are you going to keep courting me, DePaul, and what do you want at the end of it?"

Cyril looked past Müller, into the warm, dim expanse of the dining room. The crowd had thinned, but a few of the razors were still gathered in a die-hard clump at the far end of the bar. Cordelia returned from the washroom and put herself in the thick of it, flirting with the woman who'd recommended the port Müller so disdained.

"You're not satisfied with the work the ACPD is doing," said Cyril.

"Damn right I'm not."

"And you despise Marissa Taormino."

"I don't respect how she got where she is." His scowl belied his diplomacy.

"This might be a hard sell, then." At the bar, Cordelia hopped up between the razors and settled herself among empty glasses and smoldering cigar butts. She crossed her ankles with the delicate precision of a society matron, and let her new friend light a straight for her. "But if you buy, you'll be commissioner within the year. Maybe the next six months."

Müller's face went slack, but he caught himself and reassembled it into grim outrage. "Whoever's goods you're shilling, I don't want 'em."

"Even if it means a straitlaced police force? Things done above the board? Promotions based on merit, not on graft?"

"In this city? Tar dream. Never happen."

"It is happening," said Cyril. "Now." This wasn't strictly true, but he could afford to talk an enormous amount of absolute swineshit, as Cordelia would put it, as long as it bagged Müller for the Ospies. "You can either ride the wake, or you can drown."

Müller looked over the tops of his spectacles, his eyes like chips of yellow resin beneath his prominent brow. "Are you *threatening* me, DePaul?"

"No. No, of course not." Cyril adjusted one of his cufflinks, projecting unconcern. "The idea never crossed my mind. I'm merely telling you it's a good time to consider some alternatives. Because later . . . well, no one likes a brown-noser."

"I've lived in this city far too long. I know that isn't true."

Cyril wondered if the entendre was meant for him.

"You think the Ospies really have a chance?" Müller's stare was calculating.

"I know."

"How?"

Cyril switched to the other cufflink, barely sparing a glance for Müller in between. "Who do you think I'm 'shilling' for, Alex? Certainly not the current regime. Hebrides knows where he is with Taormino; she's tucked right into his watch pocket, on the end of a gilded chain. And knowing Josiah, that chain was paid for with dirty money."

"So how exactly are you proposing to buy me? And what un-complimentary metaphors are you going to use to describe our relationship?"

"I don't want to *buy* you, Alex. I want to offer you the appointment you deserve, in a system that works the way it should. And I represent people who can make that happen."

"The Ospies. You're in league with the Ospies. What was *your* price? Just so I can benchmark."

This was not going as well as he'd hoped. Leaning in, he brought a ferocity to his tone that he'd so far let lie dormant. After Müller's snipe, it wasn't hard to find. "Look, I'll be blunt with you—"

Müller cut him off. "Yes, please. I've had enough of your dancing around."

"All right. I'm asking you to compromise your principles, yes. But I'll only ask you once. Look the other way, this time—just for a little bit, while things are ugly—and I promise you'll never have to look away again. We won't want you to."

The "we" nearly stuck in his craw, but he said it nonetheless. His chain wasn't gilded, and it held him by the throat.

Müller finished off his port and fell against the cracked leather of the booth. "Well, I'll give you credit: You know how to tempt an upright officer of the law."

"And are you?"

"What, tempted? Of course." Something caught his attention in the dining room, and Cyril followed his gaze. Cordelia had left the bar holding what looked suspiciously like a gin and tonic. She picked her way between abandoned chairs, watching her shoes. Vermillion waves of hair rippled over one bare shoulder and fell between her breasts. "But a man's got to draw the line somewhere."

"Stones," said Cordelia, after Müller had caught a cab. "What did you say to him while I was gone? He looked like he'd been sucking on a lemon."

They stood on the corner outside the Kelly Club. Two more cabs went by, but Cyril didn't flag them, and other night wanderers climbed in. "I made him a proposition he didn't like."

"Did you now?" Cordelia's eyebrows arched up like drawn bows.

"Ah, go yank yourself," he said, mocking her. She slapped at him, playfully. He deflected it and tucked his arm through her elbow. "Walk me home? It's nice enough outside."

"I'm supposed to keep you safe from muggers, or what?" But she let him draw her along the footpath, dodging between drunken salaryfolk.

"Sure," he said. "If you do a good job, I'll pay for your cab back home."

He wondered where she lived. Somewhere in the southern half of the city, almost certainly. It would be a hefty fare, but he wanted company, and wouldn't force a late trolley ride on her. He didn't like the thought of facing his failure, and entertaining would take his mind off of it. Midsummer wasn't immediately looming, but the mild night reminded him his deadline was much closer than it had been.

Cordelia wasn't going to let him avoid her questions. "You threw me at him pretty hard," she said. "You gonna tell me why?"

"I threw you?" He jostled her arm.

"Hang it, you know what I mean. You needed a little bait for your trap."

"And you were clever enough to figure it out. Thank you." He liked that she was sharp. Smart, beautiful, and disaffected . . . She would have made a good fox, perfect for running honeypots, if only one of Ada's recruiters had cornered her when she was young. Then again, she could be anywhere from eighteen to thirty and he couldn't have guessed her age with the barrel of a gun to his head. Central might still have time to groom her.

Might've, rather. He wondered if the Ospies would be amenable. Maybe he could put in a good word. If he swung the ACPD. If he couldn't do that, he was just the party's instrument, and no one valued the opinions of a tool.

He hoped she could find something to do under the new regime, because he imagined it would be hard going on Temple Street after Acherby rose to power. So much rode on Cyril's treachery.

"You're welcome," said Cordelia, hauling him back into the conversation. "Now what exactly am I in the middle of?"

"Cordelia, I told you, I can't—"

"You said you'd tell me if I needed to know. I think I do."

"It's not exactly your decision."

She halted, in the center of the footpath, and pulled her arm from his. A drunk stumbled past and tried to steady himself on her shoulder. She shoved him away with the unconscious brutality of someone used to dealing with public disorder.

"I can walk," she said, thrusting an arm out, hand extended toward the street. "You want me to walk?"

He stopped too, and turned so they stood face-to-face, about three feet apart. Around them, foot traffic continued, uninterested.

Holding the lapels of his overcoat, he leaned back on his heels and took in her defiance. "Here's the thing," he said. "I don't think you can."

"No?" She flung the trailing end of her scarf over one shoulder. "Watch me."

He let her get a quarter of the way down the block before he realized Aristide would kill him if Cordelia left now. Pushing between pedestrians, he hurried after her. When he caught up, in front of a darkened tobacconist's shop, he pulled her into the doorway. "I'm sorry, all right?"

She shook him off and backed up against the grated window. Behind her, cigars and pipes lay on a fall of red velvet, arranged around bunches of silk cherry blossoms. "Can we get a couple things straight, right now? I don't have to be here. Ari's making it worth my while, but I don't have to hang around with you."

"He's—he's paying you?" Cyril wanted to laugh.

"In a manner of speaking."

"Mother and sons, that's just what he needs. A procurement charge. Unless you're licensed?"

Her glare would have cut diamonds.

"Wonderful. A reason to shove him in the trap and get a good look through all his affairs. Wish he'd done it when I—" He stopped himself, but Cordelia had caught it.

"When you what?"

"Nothing."

She took a step toward him and he gave ground. She stepped forward again, and he backed into the window. Delicately, she slipped his bow tie from its knot. Then, with more force and speed than he would have credited, she wrapped it around her fist, pulling his face close to hers.

"Cyril," she said. "What are you?"

"Let's take this indoors."

She tugged on his tie. "No stalling."

"I'm not stalling," he said, putting his hand over hers and drawing it away from his throat. "I'm just trying to keep things quiet."

Back in his flat, Cyril chain-smoked. He needed something to do with his hands, and his straights were convenient. If he paid excruciating attention to lighting them and flicking away the ash, he didn't have to look up at Cordelia.

They'd ended up hiring a cab—the incident in the street had left him too unnerved to enjoy a walk. And he didn't trust Cordelia not to bring the issue up in public again.

"I can't tell you exactly what I do, or who I work for," he said now. "But know that I need you, or I'm hanged."

"Is that a saying, or actual fact?"

"Bit of both." He sighed. "All right, the thing is, I may be doing some business with the Ospies—" From Cordelia's face, she didn't approve. He hurried to assuage her, before she could cut him off. "I don't like it either, but it's keeping me out of trouble."

"Hanging trouble?"

"More or less. The only problem is, well . . . you know how they feel about . . . well, about everything."

"You mean, the only problem is Ari."

"Well, Ari and a few others."

"More'n a few, I'd wager." He could tell she wanted him to laugh, but all he did was nod and stub out the end of his third cigarette.

"Load of dead fish," she said. "Not an ounce of spark in any of 'em. How'd you end up under their heel?"

"Work," he said. "I was . . . sent on an errand, but they got in the way. And it was go along, or get trampled."

"So now you're running for 'em. Or something." She kicked off her shoes and pulled her feet under her skirts. "And you need a pretty girl on your arm to make you look the part. Did you ask Ari to rustle somebody up?"

"No. No, that was his idea. I—well, I hardly thought about it."

"He's a good friend to you," she said.

"How did he convince you to take me on?" asked Cyril. "What did he tell you?"

"All he said was you needed a girl. Sounded off-color to me and I told him so, but he said it was strictly underthings on, no wandering hands. At least at the outset. Made it sound more like a matchmaker's scheme than any whoring I ever done."

"Oh, so you did used to be in the profession?"

"Sure, after Ma bumped off. For a little while, anyhow. Then I turned to stage life. And a few things on the side I don't like to mention to a gentleman."

"You already told me you hired out. And believe me, I'm beyond shocking, by anything you might say."

"Maybe I won't shock you, but I don't want you hauling me in to the vice squad, either."

"Cordelia," he said, "you've got enough leverage on me I can't haul you anywhere."

"All right. Fine. So I ran some stuff. Catha, hash, morphine, tar. It was good business."

"Ever try any of it?" If she was an addict, he might have a problem. A scandalous mistress was one thing; he didn't want to cover up any nasty habits in case Van der Joost came sniffing.

"I ain't a fool, Cyril. I know a runner ain't supposed to dip out of her own stash. And I don't. Truth is, my ma took to tar pretty hard when I was a kid. Killed her, in the end."

"And you still sold it?"

"Well sure. I said my ma took to it hard. But the runner who was selling to her? You didn't see him hiring out to keep himself fed."

Cyril ran a hand through his hair, pushing it out of its carefully waxed coif. "You've got me there. Where were we?"

"Ari," she said.

"Right. So he asked you—" It struck him then, like a fast-moving cosh to the side of the head. "Holy stones. You're running for *him* now, aren't you?"

"And it's damn good business," she said. "I don't even have to buy the stuff. His girl just hands it over, and I go on my way. No overhead equals pure profit. Pays better than regular running, better than whoring, and birds and above what I get on the stage. But—" And here she leveled a finger at him. The nail was done in varnish dark as sweet cherries. "Remember I can always walk away. I got other ways of making money."

"But you just said this money is better than all of them."

"No money's as good as knowing what you're in for."

"And are you satisfied, now?" asked Cyril.

"No. But I think I'm as close as I'm gonna get. You're closed up like a mussel, and I don't wanna break my nails prying you open. You gave me the gist. It's enough for now."

CHAPTER

EIGHTEEN

To meet with Zelda, Aristide donned summer-weight gray wool with a pashmina shawl and heavy pearl earrings set in platinum. The noodle house on Prattler was a bohemian establishment, right in the heart of the southwest quarter. Businesses on the banks of the Heyn, where it flowed behind the theatre district, were as likely to cater to pirates as to penniless aristocrats. Wealthy courtesans mingled with starving artists. The men wore jewels and the women suits and everyone else a mixture of both. The place was a magpie's den of true gems and counterfeits, impeccable taste and outrageous lack thereof. Aristide liked to strike a balance, and his pearls, at least, were real.

The day was fine—spring was coming on strong now, bringing warm sun and low-tide stink. Aristide stood at the back of the trolley, leaning on the rail. His hair fell over his shoulder and streamed in front of his face, catching the light. No gray in it yet, thanks be. He looked more like his father with every passing summer, as the sun, and smiling for the stage, put lines in his face. He wondered how long the old man had kept a full head of hair, and when it had gone silver, if it had, before he died. He surely had done, by now. Life was hard for a farmer—which was why Aristide was a smuggler and a stage man in the most frivolous city in Gedda, and not wrangling with blighted sheep in a windswept pasture.

He stepped down from the trolley at Prattler Street and Solemnity and walked the last block dodging the dandified lunch crowd. The noodle house didn't have a name—just a beautiful lapis-tiled arch above the door. Thick vines crept up the façade. In the summer, they were laden with corkscrew flowers in shades of white and purple, but this time of year the tender green shoots were unadorned.

Aristide ducked in through a low door. The whole place seemed built for a more petite clientele. Sweeping through garlands of spider plant and sweet-smelling hoya, he searched for Zelda in the maze of folding screens and silk hangings. The deep bay windows were positively stuffed with blooming orchids.

"Ari. Ari, over here."

He turned his head, and realized he'd already overshot. Hard to believe he'd passed her—she was draped in a resplendent silk wrap dyed black and orange, bright as embers. A headache band of fire opals low on her forehead glowed and shifted with her movements.

Still, she was short, and kneeling to boot, and her table was tucked behind an elaborate teak screen to keep conversations private. Her friend Mab sat beside her, feet drawn to one side. In a patchwork waistcoat and a yoked linen shirt thick with smocking, she occupied the decidedly more bohemian end of the southwest quarter's spectrum.

Between the two women, a squat iron kettle balanced on a frame over a burner. When Aristide sat, across from Zelda, she poured for him. Tea pooled in the crystal glass, inky and thick with dark honey. He took it from her with a slight inclination of his head. The brass finger loop was warm, but not uncomfortably so.

"Delightful little p-p-place, as always." He flicked his fingers over one shoulder, to indicate the noodle house. "I don't think I've been since sometime around the new year. Love what they've d-d-done with the orchids." Sipping his tea, he turned to Zelda's companion. "My d-d-dear, how is the city treating you? Usually she's *divine*, but she can be a bit of a b-b-beast if she's feeling ornery."

"Everything's been wonderful, thank you." Mab's accent was thick as fur. She held her diminutive teacup with both broad hands. "Zelda's been an excellent host."

"Shown her all the sights, have you Zelly?"

The fence made a moue over her teacup. Her gaze held him like a jeweler's tongs. "Only the pretty ones."

From the corner of his eye, Aristide saw Mab bite back laughter.

A waiter came around the edge of the screen and bowed. "Good afternoon, sir. Madam, does the tea suit?"

Zelda swirled it in her cup. "Like a tailor."

"Tell me," said Aristide to the waiter, "have you still got those little sesame b-b-buns? The ones that are shaped like rabbits?"

"Of course, sir. And will you require anything more substantial?"

He waved the waiter's attention to Zelda, who ordered for all of them. When he had gone, Aristide turned back to Mab, refreshing her tea.

"So," said Aristide. "I told Zelda a little bit about my problem last night, but nobody gave me any t-t-tidbits about yours. What's the nature of your sticky situation?"

"Interstate immigration," she said.

"That's not exactly d-d-difficult."

"For me, nay. But for my husband, for my wife . . . things get complicated."

"Hmmm. An old marriage. Interesting." He brought out his cigarette case and offered it around. Zelda took one, but Mab turned him down, taking instead a pipe from her vest pocket. It was new, though smoke had already stained the ivory bowl, and beautifully made. Too new and too fine to be a family heirloom. A gift, then. He wondered from whom.

When she'd finished drawing and the scent of tobacco hovered in a cloud over the table, he asked her, "Where from?"

She cocked her head, balancing the bowl of her pipe in one hand.

"Where are you emigrating from?"

"Nuesklend," she said.

"Ah. Unhappy with the results of the election?"

"Acherby isn't kind to the faithful."

The waiter returned, bearing a heavy tray. He set three bowls on the table, one in front of each of them. The noodles were broad and clear, tangled around small shrimp with pinprick eyes. A fried egg sat slightly off center of each portion, floating on the surface of the delicate broth. With each bowl came a selection of smaller salvers filled with cashews, saffron, and puffed barley. Lastly, the waiter set down a platter of small steamed buns shaped like fat rabbits.

When he'd gone again, Aristide took a moment to scatter crushed cashews over his noodles, then a pinch of saffron threads. The dainty, floral filaments made the broth shiver at their impact.

He tossed in a handful of the puffed barley, which began to pop and snap as the liquid seeped into it.

"So," he said, "your family wants to cross the border into Amberlough. Even with the c-c-current political climate, you should be perfectly able to acquire a residency permit."

"Nae together," she said.

Her evasion was piquing his interest. "Why? Unless . . . is it a legal marriage? Saying words in a temple is one thing, but have you signed the p-p-papers?"

She lifted her spoon, not looking at him.

"I see. So you can't apply for a residency permit as a family. Why haven't you formalized your vows?"

"Her mother doesnae approve."

"Is she of age?"

"She is."

"But her mother has some hold over her. Financial, I presume."

Another nod, another sip of soup.

"How . . . *substantial* is this hold?"

"Without her income," said Mab, "we're penniless. Nae that it matters. Taphir and I love her, and she loves us, and we'll starve if we have to. But you understand. Things are much harder . . ." She trailed off, one hand lying flat on the table. With the other, she held her pipe. Her grip was tight enough to stretch the chapped skin across her knuckles. It cracked into thin, red lines. "We're just a couple of pipers, Mr. Makricosta. And she's . . . well, she's used to better than we can provide."

"I must ask," he said, "since it is beginning to seem important: Who exactly *is* your wife?"

She set her spoon down and stared at it. Sucked her teeth. Turned the spoon.

"Mab?"

"Sofie Keeler."

Aristide, who'd done many things to elide his country upbringing, nevertheless let loose a low whistle. "Champagne tastes, indeed."

Mab scowled. "I told you, it's nothing to do with the money."

"I'm sure that's not what he meant, dear." Zelda put her hand on Mab's forearm.

"Not exactly, no." Aristide lifted a spoonful of broth and sipped it. "But I begin to see where your difficulties lie. Minna Keeler supports the Ospies, correct? And must therefore t-t-toe the line."

"If she knew about the marriage," said Mab, through teeth clenched around her pipe stem, "Sofie'd be out the house without a three-cent piece. If she were lucky."

"Indeed. So you hope to . . . what? Transfer her current capital in secret? I imagine she's forfeiting any share in the family business, not to mention her inheritance. Then you'll immigrate, marry legally behind Amberlough's borders . . ." He wasn't really asking her questions, now. Just planning aloud. "And consolidate your assets once the contract is signed."

"Sounds likely," said Mab. "Can you do it?"

"My d-d-dear," he said, finally remembering to stutter. "You were introduced to me by one of the most notorious fences in Amberlough City. If anyone can move a great d-d-deal of money, very quietly, it's one of Zelda's friends." He bit a tiny shrimp in two. It collapsed between his teeth with a satisfying crunch. "I'll want a cut, of course. I d-d-don't run a charity."

"And I'm nae a fool." She took a purse from inside her waistcoat and dropped it on the table. The contents clacked together. "There's for good faith."

Aristide was not shy, nor bound by propriety. He tugged at the drawstrings of the pouch and tipped it into his palm.

"Emeralds," he said. Then, sharply, "Will these be missed?" The elaborate collar had the look of a family heirloom—the cut of the stones was not stylish, but they were of surpassing quality and exceptionally well set.

Mab grinned. "Nae if you work fast."

Insistent ringing clawed Cyril from a deep sleep. In the semi-dark, he flung out a hand and rapped his knuckles on the sharp edge of the telephone base. Dragging the heavy apparatus from his bedside table, he lifted the receiver.

"DePaul," he said. It was too early for niceties.

"Get in here," said Culpepper.

"Do you know what time it is?"

"I don't care. Now kick whoever's in your bed out of it, and get your sorry ass to the office, immediately."

He jammed the receiver into its switch hook and took a moment to lie back against his pillows. The weight of the telephone pressed into his chest. At last, he rolled over and out of bed, cringing in expectation of a cold floor. But spring was turning into summer, and his feet struck temperate wood.

Unfortunately, he hadn't aired his warm-weather clothes. His navy suit was three days worn and crumpled at the joints. The charcoal had a lipstick stain at the lapel. Times like these, he almost wished he did have a valet.

He went with the navy, hoping the wrinkles would inspire a little empathy in Culpepper, and knowing he would only get scorn. Downstairs, his landlord had laid out the early cold spread of cured ham, bread, and preserves. He forewent food in favor of strong black coffee, and was out the door.

A scrap of a girl stood on the corner, cutting the twine on her first stack of papers.

"Copy of the *Clarion*," said Cyril, handing her a crisply folded bill.

"Aw, sir, it's not even half five yet. Ain't you got any change?"

He thrust a hand into his pocket and scrounged up a handful of coins. "Here, have that instead."

She pocketed it, and gave him a paper.

"I'll have the rest back, if you don't mind," he said.

Scowling, she took his bill back out from her pouch and returned it. He admired her pluck—she was young for a quick change artist, and she'd picked a good hour to pull one over. People didn't pay too much attention to their money this early in the morning.

Nor did cabbies venture forth to search for fares. Cyril tucked the paper under his arm and headed for the trolley stop at Mespaugh. Tucking himself into a corner of the shelter, he snapped the *Clarion* open across his knee.

The first time he read the headline, he did it with only passing interest. But a double-take turned his stomach acid.

Keeler heiress kidnapped. And the house burgled too. Jewelry and cash gone. The paper gave pictures of the suspects: an older Chuli woman and a thin young man with messy hair. Mab Cattayim and Taphir Emerson. He recognized them. The musicians from the pub: Sofie's lovers.

He'd lay a heavy sum that this is what had got Culpepper on the 'phone to him. He wondered if she'd known before the papers went to press, or if it had caught her unawares. Must have been the latter. If it had been the former, he'd have been out of bed much earlier, or never got there in the first place.

Foyles was at his desk when Cyril came through the door. Did the man ever go home? Or did he sleep on a bed of racing forms, curled beneath his bank of telephones?

"Morning, Mr. DePaul. Skull's waiting on you."

"Thanks, Foyles. Sleep well?"

"Well as can be expected, sir: not at all."

Though Foyles was in residence, the lift operator was not. Cyril shut himself in and cranked the lever to the fifth floor. The gate opened onto an empty hallway, lit by every third sconce. Rubbing sleep from his eyes, he turned toward Culpepper's office.

Memmediv, of course, was in. Cyril hadn't seen him since being sent away to recover from his failure in Nuesklend. Not since suspicion slid into him like a straight pin slipping beneath a fingernail.

None of his Ospie contacts would confirm or deny—they might not even know. Cyril got the sense the mole inside Central reported straight to Van der Joost. And he couldn't ask Memmediv to his face—he didn't know how much Van der Joost had told him, or how loyal he was to the Ospies, or what he might give up to Culpepper.

Had espionage really seemed like a game to him, once? Now it felt like threads of piano wire tightening across his skin.

Memmediv, unaware of his internal struggle—or fully aware and secretly amused—nodded a silent greeting and depressed the button on his intercom.

"Mr. DePaul is here to see you." His voice was deep and rough with the early hour, and his faint accent lingered over the rounder vowels. Stones, but why did he have to be fetching? It was just salt in the wound.

"Send him in, Vaz." Even over the crackling intercom, Culpepper sounded tired.

Memmediv stood and held the door open for Cyril. Cyril's greatcoat brushed Memmediv's knees with a whisper of wool against wool. Cyril strained toward him as if physical proximity might give him a clue. No luck. The door fell shut behind him with a soft thud.

"It's Sofie Keeler," he said, "isn't it?"

"Her mother's one of Landseer's correspondents, right? You met her, when you went west."

"I did."

"Does this have anything to do with us?"

"No," said Cyril. "Nothing."

"Are you sure?"

"As a keystone. The two kidnappers . . . they're Sofie's lovers. Her mother wasn't in favor of their marriage. If you want my opinion, all three of them made a break for it together and burgled the old lady. Keeler's implicated Cattayim and Emerson but not her daughter. Can you imagine the scandal, if the truth came out?"

"Bless her garters. I was thinking some rogue regionalist cell had pulled a stupid action. We'd look bad, if freelancers started kidnapping prominent citizens."

"No." Cyril dropped into the chair opposite Culpepper. Her desk was even messier than usual. "Sofie got herself into this trouble voluntarily. She's a smart girl, though—she'll probably manage to get herself out of it too."

"Whether she does or not, I'm just glad it's not our concern."

"Was that all you wanted to see me about? You could have said on the telephone."

Culpepper ran a hand over her scalp. Cyril heard the susurrus of millimeter hairs bending beneath her palm. "Safer to do it in person; I know my office isn't wired. Anyway, I need to talk to you about contingencies."

"Contingencies?"

"We might need the hounds to do a little dirty work," she said. "Most of Josiah's foibles are off the record, but have them go through and clean up their files; anything anybody ever said about him, I want it expunged. We can't afford to have him pulled out of office."

He gave her a limp-wristed salute and yawned, hugely.

Culpepper frowned. "I'm glad you take your job so seriously."

Behind a lazy façade, his brain was working. He'd have the off-record offenses restored, and maybe add some too. Müller could help him, if he could nail the man down. The problem would be Taormino's people—the ones who liked where they stood under her governance. Unless Cyril could offer them something better. He'd have to squeeze money from the Ospies, and some promises, if Van der Joost wanted the city by midsummer.

"I do take it seriously," he said. "Much more than you know."

Two sleepless days later, brought up short by an unexpectedly Taormino-loyal faction in the upper echelons of the ACPD, Cyril dragged himself from his flat hoping fresh air and a walk in the park would inspire miracles. In reality, he made it as far as the other side of the street, and got the opposite.

The quick change artist-cum-paper seller was waving her wares at the curb, a breeze slapping at the pages. And there, on the front page, was Taphir Emerson's haunted mug shot.

Cyril snatched the paper out of the girl's hand. She squalled and he threw a crumpled bill at her. He didn't even ask for change. Leaning against the iron bars of the fence that bordered Loendler Park, he scanned the article. Taphir had been caught in customs at Bythesea Station, but Sofie and Mab came up only tangentially; they'd managed to slip through. He felt relief out of proportion to his involvement, followed by sharp anxiety. Sofie and Mab were wanted women, and they were in the city. He wondered if he should reach out—he could probably find them, if he wanted to. He knew enough people.

And half those people, he reminded himself, were now in league with the Ospies—he'd won them over. Finding Sofie and Mab would put the women in danger. Cyril was already a liability to Cordelia, and to Aristide, as much as they were to him. He couldn't bring more people into this mud pit. All he could do was hope, quietly, while he tried to save his own skin, and Ari's.

CHAPTER

NINETEEN

While they were waiting to go on toward the end of the second act, Cordelia asked Aristide for a straight—she was out, and his would be better than hers anyhow. She'd never have dreamed of it, three weeks ago, and he wouldn't have obliged. But now, he pulled one from who knew where in that costume, along with a book of matches.

When she'd lit up, he tucked the matches back into some hidden pocket of brocade and lace and said, "I need you to run an errand for me."

She looked up from her seat on the prop table, flicking ash from the tip of her cigarette. "Yeah? The usual kind?" She'd been moving up, running better stuff for him, and doing courier jobs between his people. Sometimes she even got paid in cash now, outside the tar.

She liked to think he'd keep her on, even if Cyril dropped her. Or, if she decided she'd had enough of Cyril.

"No." His eyes were aimed out toward the stage, watching the scantily clad gimmick pianists play a raunchy, four-armed duet. "No, it's rather different. Do you know Zelda Peronides?"

"Heard of her. She's a fence, right? You want me to run some hooky?" That'd be a step up. And a pinch riskier, for sure. With tar, you could buy off most beat cops if they caught you in possession, but hot stuff was harder to blind a hound to.

"Nothing like that, don't worry." The pianists were finishing up their act. Aristide checked his makeup in the mirror tacked by the curtain rope. "I just need you to take her a t-t-*tiny* message. Her shop ought to be on your way."

"You know my trolley stops?" She ground her cigarette butt into the scarred wood of the table.

"Are you t-t-terribly surprised?"

"If I take it there tonight, after the show, is she gonna be awake?"

"Of course." His eyes moved, fleetingly, toward the audience visible beyond the curtain. "You don't have anything p-p-planned for the evening?"

"What, you mean with Cyril?" She shrugged. "Haven't heard from him the last couple days. Probably busy with his work." She hadn't told Ari what she knew about Cyril and the Ospies. It was always good to keep back things like that; you never knew when they'd come in handy. "Why? You heard something?"

Aristide shook his head. "No. But you're probably right. Mr. DePaul is a very busy man." The pianists bowed. Their instrument slid across the boards as if by magic, but from where she stood, Cordelia could see the crew behind the stage left curtain hauling on the ropes.

"Come by my dressing room after curtain call," said Aristide as the lights began to lower. Twin spots wheeled across the stage and backdrop. The orchestra vamped, waiting on his entrance. Liesl was probably swearing, wondering what was taking him so long. But Ari was a master of stagecraft—he knew the audience liked the anticipation as much as the reveal.

Ari's dressing room door was closed when she showed up. Behind it, she could hear the murmur of conversation. Her knock put a damper on that. When Ari opened the door, he didn't open it wide.

"Would you give us just a moment?" he asked. He had a pair of steel-rimmed spectacles perched on his nose.

From behind him, a low voice—could have been a woman, or a man—asked a question.

"Just another associate." Then, to Cordelia, "Half a breath, really," and shut the door in her face. She wrinkled her nose and leaned into the frame.

Ari wrapped up his meeting within thirty seconds, ushering out a short, broad-shouldered woman in a wide-brimmed hat. She had it pulled low at the front to hide her face. At the back, a few inches of freshly shingled salt-and-pepper hair curled over her neck. She didn't acknowledge Cordelia when she passed.

"Imp-p-*possibly* sorry, darling." Ari drew Cordelia across the threshold and sat her down on his battered velvet settee. He swept up a folder full of papers and paged through it. "I didn't realize she'd be here tonight."

"Who was it?"

His glare came at an angle, over the tops of his spectacles. "Nobody important." The snap of the folder closed the conversation. "This, however"—he pulled an envelope from inside his dressing gown—"rather is."

Cordelia reached for it, but Aristide pulled it away. "Ah! Instructions first. Zelda's shop will be shuttered. There's a b-b-bell rope in the alley. Pull it. One of her runners will let you in by the fire escape. Give this letter to Zelda, and *only* Zelda. Understood?"

"I got ears, Ari."

"Only. Zelda." He sliced the air with the edge of the envelope to emphasize.

"And don't forget to lock the door when you get in." Cordelia rolled her eyes and snatched the envelope away. "Don't worry, Ma. I clock you."

"I'm sure you do." He peeled one of his false eyelashes away, fastidious as a grooming cat. "But it never hurts to take care."

Zelda fronted as an art dealer, and kept a little store in the heart of the southwest quarter, just up Elver Street from Station Way. Cordelia got off the trolley and hiked the few blocks north through the crowds of night revelers until she saw the sign for Peronides Fine Arts and Antiquities. It hung from a wrought-iron hook at a dark second-story window. Instead of ringing the bell at the front, she went down the alley, like Ari had told her, and pulled at a length of tattered rope looped casually from the fire escape.

Nothing happened. She pulled a second time. And a third.

Just as she was turning away, thinking Ari had been wrong and Zelda must be asleep, or out, a thick-armed man in black jersey slipped from an open window and lowered the fire escape. Despite its weight, it moved quietly on well-oiled tracks. She climbed up, taking his helping hand when she could reach it. He fairly hoisted her onto the platform, and slid the ladder up after her.

"I got a letter for Zelda," she said. He said nothing in return, just waved her through an open window. She parted curtains onto a dark room filled with shrouded sculptures and furniture. Muffled voices came through the walls. He came in after her, and pulled the curtains to. Blindly, she followed his grip on her arm. When he opened a door onto bright chaos, she blinked and threw up a hand against the light.

"Marto, what's—oh, stones, just set her in a corner."

Cordelia was duly pushed into an ornate chair with threadbare velvet upholstery. She peered through dazzled eyes at the uproar around her. Marto, the barrel of a man who'd brought her in, had gone to a table at the center of the room, where a woman with nubbly knots of dreaded hair was stretched over the green leather desktop, hissing against the strap between her teeth. Her bloody cotton sailor's shirt was in a pile on the floor. Bruises mottled her torso. A sawbones pulled his curved needle through the flesh of her left breast, drawing the edges of a wound together. A blush boy with a black eye sat in the corner, holding a steaming cup in his hands. He stammered excuses to a small, swarthy woman in culottes and a brocade smoking jacket. The woman had plastered careful sympathy overtop of deep annoyance, but the annoyance looked to be breaking out faster and faster as the blush boy talked.

"Came out of nowhere. Thought they were ACPD, but the uniforms was wrong. All black, no blue. And no badges. We took the hooky in through the back door of the place, like you said, and the madam was real happy with it. Had those rubies round her throat faster than you'd credit. She let us stay on for a little fun, and when we came out—"

Here, the woman in the smoking jacket interrupted. "Out where? The front? Did you come out the back or the front?" She looked like she wanted to slap him.

"Front," he said, meek as a mole. "And the blackboots got us good. One had a knife. Then the real hounds came round to break it up and clocked Duriyah for your gal. We had to scramble, but quick."

The woman in the smoking jacket looked at the wounded runner on the table. "Duriyah's been with me a long time," she said. "And you've only just started."

The blush boy flinched, like he was waiting for bad news. But all the woman said was, "She should have known better than to go out the front. And you both should've known not to come back here!" Cordelia thought the woman really would slap him now. Her hand was stiff, drawn back slightly from her hip. But an intercom crackled from the desk, beside Duriyah's foot, and she whirled to listen instead.

"Hounds coming down the street," said a high, fuzzy voice. Sounded like a kid.

"Everybody shut up," said the woman in the smoking jacket. "Keep quiet. And Marto? The lights."

Marto flipped the switch at the doorway, and the room was plunged into blackness. The only sound was Duriyah's shaky breathing.

Cordelia's toes curled. If she ended up in the trap for delivering a letter she hadn't even read, she'd lay every curse she knew on Ari's curly head. Not that it would do her much good.

Thirty tense seconds later, the intercom crackled again. "S'good. They gone past."

Marto brought the lights back up. The blush boy had his eyes tight shut, his hands like claws around his cup. The doctor's face was unreadable, but he was already reaching for his coat. The woman in the smoking jacket, who must be Zelda, finally got an eyeful of Cordelia.

"And who are you?" she snapped.

"I'm here from Aristide," she said. "I got a letter for—"

"Of course you do. Right now, of *all* times, and he *had* to send a new girl." The scorn in it left Cordelia gaping. "Upstairs. Marto, show her."

Cordelia was ready to smack the envelope into Zelda's palm and be done with it, but Marto took her arm and drew her through another door, into a narrow hallway, and pointed her at a set of stairs that kinked ninety degrees halfway up. He jerked his chin at the steps, and then left her standing at the foot of the runner.

The attic was crammed with dusty artifacts and cobwebbed chandeliers lying at odd angles on the floor. A stuffed leopard growled from behind an ironbound sea chest.

At the far end of the room, where a grand brass bed was pushed against the wall, two women sat in deep conversation. One, dark skinned and heavy around the hips, perched on the bed with her legs crossed. The other had tucked herself into the dormer window, a plain white pyjama shirt pulled over her knees. The curtains were drawn, but billowed in the soft night air. Cordelia was willing to wager open windows were against Zelda's rules, but the stuffy attic smelled powerfully of mold.

"Hello?" She stepped onto the first creaking floorboard.

The women both looked up, startled. Their faces were vaguely familiar, and Cordelia wondered if maybe they were punters. Ari's clients came by the Bee sometimes.

"Who are you?" demanded the woman on the bed. Her northern burr was even thicker than Tory's. "One of Zelda's people?"

Cordelia took a step forward, and both women flinched. She held up her hands. "I got a message, from Aristide Makricosta."

They didn't relax. If anything, they wound up tighter.

"What does it say?" The woman in the window stood and came toward her, bare feet silent against the plain wood. "Is it about Taphir?"

"I didn't open it, all right?" She took the envelope from her pocket and handed it to the younger of the two, who tore the paper with shaking hands. Her companion hurried over, crowding her.

Inside the envelope was a postcard of a hunting party, hounds gathered around the heels of horses. As the woman flipped the card over, Cordelia got a glimpse of Ari's decorative scrawl.

"Charming day yesterday," read the woman in the nightshirt. "Though utterly a wash. The hounds gave good chase and cornered him, but he slipped them in the covert."

It didn't sound good, but the women were smiling. The younger covered her mouth with a delicate hand.

"Oh, blessed stones of the cairn and temple. Oh, Mab, he's out." She threw herself into the older woman's arms, sobbing. Cordelia looked away, embarrassed.

But she wasn't going to get out that easy. The crying woman dragged herself up, leaving wet splotches on Mab's shirtfront, and turned to Cordelia. "Thank you. Oh, thank you so much."

"It's all right," said Cordelia. "Really, it ain't no trouble." She took a step back, angling for the stairs, but the woman put a hand on her arm.

"'The bringer of joy must be given joy in return.'"

Queen's sake, the woman was quoting scripture at her.

"Mab," she went on, "Mab, what have we got left, from mummy's jewels?"

"There's the pearls," said Mab. "But Sofie, that's a bit . . . well, they're a mite showy, nay? Even Zelda said she'll have half a time moving them."

Sofie nodded. "But the earrings, the citrines . . ."

Mab took Sofie's arm and bent to speak in her ear—not even quiet enough to save Cordelia an insult. "She's just gwine to pawn them, Fee. Might as well give her a wad of cash."

But Sofie waved Mab off, and the older woman went to rummage in a knapsack by the bed. "They're not worth much, but won't you please accept what little we can offer?"

Mab returned and opened her palm, revealing two pear-shaped

citrines set in yellow gold, topped with tiny . . . diamonds? Not worth much. Where did this girl come from?

"I really . . . I don't think . . ." Cordelia backed away again, but Mab pressed the stones into her hand.

"It's like Sofie says. You brought brightness to us when we saw dark. It's only an even trade if we return the favor."

So Cordelia took the earrings, with intent to wear them. They sounded like hooky. Pawning stolen goods was stupid unless you knew the right shops. Cordelia did, but her pride was stung and she aimed to prove Mab wrong.

CHAPTER
TWENTY

Insistent pounding on the door forced Cyril's head deeper into the cavern of his folded arms. The top of his desk smelled strongly of leather, and his own rancid breath. He'd spent three days scrounging in the ACPD secretarial pool, looking for scraps he could use on any of the four assistant commissioners. He'd won over Harlee, and Karst was wobbling. Tembu and Eronov he hadn't even tried—they were Taormino's through and through.

His nights he'd spent awake, and largely drunk. Inspiration had not come. Müller remained beyond his reach. His midsummer deadline was a scant few weeks away. He didn't want to find out if there was a penalty for missing it.

Who in the Lady's name could be banging on his door at this hour? He groaned and pulled himself upright, dragging his palms across his face. The clock told him the hour was reasonable; the only thing untimely was his own disarray. He'd shaved last night, at least, at his own peril. His hands had been less than steady.

Another volley landed on the door.

"I'm coming, I'm coming. Mother's tits, give it a *rest*." Why hadn't they just telephoned? They'd have his landlord up here any minute, with this racket.

Damnation. Maybe it *was* his landlord. Cyril wondered what could possibly be so urgent. Opening the door, he was ready to face any number of grim eventualities. He was not prepared to find Cordelia, draped in a fringed calico wrap, holding a bottle of cheap plonk and a grease-spotted sack that smelled of cardamom.

"What are you doing here?" he asked, surprise making him blunt.

"Dragging you out for an airing," she said. "And good thing, too. You're clearly in need of one."

"What—"

But she pushed past him into the flat and closed the door behind her. "Go put on something fresh. And eat these." She put the sack in his hand. "Sometimes I marvel any man survives outside his mother's womb. What have you been doing to yourself these past few days?"

He pulled out a puff of deep-fried rice dough, crispy and still hot, dripping with almond syrup. The steam burned his mouth, but the flavors roused his appetite. "Work."

"Don't talk with your mouth full. It's quitting time. Thought we'd take this to the park." She gestured with the bottle. "But you look more in need of a big meal and strong coffee. Where's good eating around here?"

Cyril swallowed another fritter and licked his sticky fingers. "The Stones and Garter isn't bad." And it was dark and cool. Given the hangover clawing its way up his neck, and the scorching sun outside, the park was the last place he wanted to be.

"Perfect. Now go get changed."

In his bedroom, he chucked his rumpled shirt onto the bed, grimacing at the sweat stains he'd left on the fine white cambric. A splash of bitter lime cologne, a new shirt and collar, and a blue seersucker jacket saw him out the door with Cordelia on his arm. They left the champagne behind.

"You were right," he said, throwing his napkin across his empty plate. "I needed that."

"After one too many all-night-ups, you're not getting anything done worth doing." Cordelia finished her tomato juice and set the glass down. "Feeling up to a little sunshine yet?"

His headache had abated with the food and coffee, and yes, he was. She was right: He'd got nothing done in three days of panicked scheming he couldn't have gotten done in a single, well-planned afternoon.

They walked to the wide lawn above the Loendler Park amphitheatre. A team of bowlers was practicing at the flattest part of the field, white shirts and trousers blinding in the sun. The rhythmic thuds of pins hitting the grass and the laughter of the players came faintly across the green, reassuring background noise. Cordelia spread her wrap in the dappled shade beneath a fragrant linden tree and settled onto her belly, kicking off her shoes. Cyril sat beside her, heedless of his trousers on the freshly cut grass.

If he could just stop time, right here, before everything went pitchforked . . . He closed his eyes and tilted his head back, letting the shivering light play on his eyelids.

Cordelia said his name. He ignored her. She kicked his knee, and said his name again, drawing it out in an exaggerated whine.

"I love the way you say that." He opened his eyes, looking up into the branches of the linden. Pinching his nose, he imitated her. "*Cyrilllllll!*"

She sat up. "Don't make fun," she said, but she was laughing. "Queen's sake, it's getting hot. Wish we'd brought that fizz after all." Lifting her hair away from her neck, she twisted it into a knot. When she lowered her arms, a shifting spot of sunlight struck a golden flash from the jewel at her ear.

"What's that?" asked Cyril, reaching for it.

"Hm?" Cordelia tilted her chin, so he could get a better look at the heavy citrine hanging from its gold-and-diamond setting. "Oh, just some new sparkle. Do you like 'em?"

He cupped a hand behind the stone. Honey-colored light pooled in his palm. "Where did you get these?"

"Why?" she asked. "Jealous?"

"Just curious." He kept his voice calm, but blood roared in his ears. He knew these stones. He'd last seen them casting golden halos against the aged throat of Nuesklend's richest matron.

"Present from a friend," she said. "You ain't the only one I got."

"What kind of friend?" If Ari was paying her in stolen goods now, Cyril would kill him.

She laughed, uneasy, and pulled away from him. "Cyril, what's the matter?"

"Did you know they were stolen?" he asked. He'd kill *her*, if she was brash enough to wear hot jewels around the city. "Those are Minna Keeler's earrings."

The color drained from behind her freckles. Shock or guilt, he didn't know.

"Queen and cairn and temple bells." She put a hand to her mouth. "I knew she looked familiar."

"She?" Cyril caught his voice before it rose. The bowlers were far enough away they wouldn't overhear a conversation, but shouting might draw their attention.

Cordelia realized she'd given him too much. Her bright lips drew to a thin, hard line. She opened the watch hung around her neck to check the time. Her movements were quick and sharp. She stood and gathered her wrap from the ground. "Better go or I'll be late."

But Cyril stood too, and stopped her from leaving with a hand on her wrist. Not hard, not closed, but enough to keep her from stepping away. "Cordelia."

She shook her head. "I can't."

"I don't want to know anything." He relished her surprise, her relief. It was nice to let someone's secrets lie; under Ospie supervision, it wasn't always as easy as this. "I really don't. But—"

Her eyes narrowed, and she tried to step back. Now, he did close his hand. The bones of her wrist pressed against his fingers.

"But what?" she snapped, drawing her wrap close.

"I'm going to need those earrings."

"You're gonna need a new pair of oysters if you don't let me go."

"Cordelia," he said again, lifting her wrist and holding it in front of his face, beseeching. "I need those earrings or I'm scratched."

She paused, searching his face. Her eyes were only slightly darker than the citrines, but much deeper, crackling with intricate flaws.

"Does it got anything to do with me?" she asked.

He shook his head.

"Anybody gonna end up in trouble?"

"No one you know."

That satisfied her. She pulled free from Cyril's loosened grip and unclasped the earrings, one and then the other. Cyril held his palm up to receive them. The gold was still warm from her skin.

———

On his way home, Cyril stopped into the telegraph office to send a message to Müller. A call would have given the deputy commissioner a chance to ask questions. A telegram gave him only two options: come, or stay away. And Cyril left the message deliberately cryptic, with an enticing tone of urgency.

In his flat, he ran a bath, sank into the tub, and propped his feet up on the taps. Despite the ramifications of his actions—chief among which was smoothing the Ospies' path to dominance in Amberlough—he felt a cruel frisson of success at the noose he had prepared for Müller. It was tight, and clean, and excellent work. He'd saved himself. And what's more, he'd done it elegantly.

Would do it. *Don't get ahead of yourself, DePaul.*

It felt good to know he still had it—that sharp, fast thinking, unrestrained by scruples or emotion. The hard flint Central searched for in its agents. Tatié hadn't broken him, and neither had the unionists. He was still good at what he did, even if he wasn't doing it for the right people.

No, he reminded himself. He was doing it for the only people who mattered now. For himself, and for Aristide.

Then, there was the matter of Cordelia turning up with Minna Keeler's stolen earrings. She had probably told the truth, about receiving the earrings as a gift. She couldn't afford them, even secondhand. But from whom? *I knew she looked familiar.* He turned that over, examining it. Sofie's picture had been all over the papers. She must have given Cordelia the jewels; he was sure of it. As payment? For what? Whatever the bargain, someone had introduced them. And Cyril knew exactly who. Ari had been moving refugees for months.

Sinking below the surface of the water, Cyril held his breath until his heart slowed. He'd deal with Aristide later. For now, he wasn't going to let anything dampen his victory over Müller.

Freshly scrubbed and buttoned into well-brushed evening wear,

Cyril hopped a streetcar and held the rail for a few blocks. The tails of his evening coat whipped behind him. At Orchard Street he let go and dropped easily back to the pavement, quickstepping until he shook the momentum of the trolley.

Müller was waiting for him in the Kelly Club, tucked into a corner booth with his back to the wall. "What do you want?" His face was sour, the glass of port in front of him untouched.

"Cold veal and pickle," said Cyril decisively. "You? It's order from the bar here, right?"

"Don't get cheeky, DePaul. This day's been a beast and I'm in no mood."

Cyril put his fingertips to his chin. "Really? Ragtaggers giving you more trouble than you care for? Or is it something closer to home?"

Müller sighed, his nostrils flaring. "Taphir Emerson was released yesterday afternoon, by some damn constable who wouldn't know from. 'A mix-up with the paperwork,' they tell me. And now he's disappeared like an elver into jelly."

Cyril scented Aristide's perfumed hand in this. However angry he might be about Ari facilitating Cordelia's latest foray into lawlessness, Cyril still thanked Ari for sticking this sharp pin in Müller's ass—the last of many. The one that, along with some elegant blackmail, might change his mind about the Ospies.

"Too bad," said Cyril. "And you have no idea where to look?"

"Oh, I have ideas," said Müller. "But getting the force to follow them is like dragging a ram at the end of a rope. It's not going to happen. And don't say you can offer me a better position. I told you, I won't—what are those?"

Cyril had taken the earrings from his pocket and was dangling them over the candle at the center of the table. Their facets winked and flared in the wavering light.

"Pendeloque-cut citrines, set in yellow gold with diamonds—that's the description in the insurance claim made by Minna Keeler, following a recent robbery. A robbery accomplished during the kidnapping of her eldest daughter."

"Mother's tits," hissed Müller, reaching for the jewels. "Where did you get them?"

Cyril drew the citrines away from Müller's outstretched hand. "That hardly matters."

"It matters a great deal, to a police officer."

"What ought to matter more," said Cyril, settling back into the cracked leather cushion of the booth, "is where they're headed next."

"What do you mean?"

"I hear Taormino's latest lover is a bit of a dandy." In the low light, the gemstones shivered like falling drops of honey. "And she's got the means to decorate him. How do you think it would come out if he was found in possession of Keeler heirlooms?"

Müller's eyes narrowed, the crow's-feet at his temples deepening. "Not well for Taormino. The case is too high-profile. There'd be an inquiry; she might be forced to resign."

"Handy for you."

Müller sucked his teeth, but said nothing.

"Less handy," said Cyril, "if the person caught in possession was your wife."

Müller froze. "You wouldn't. You need me."

"Not if I have Harlee and Karst." Half a lie. If he got Müller arrested, the situation would still be precarious. Two out of four assistant commissioners might not get him what he needed. But precarious was better than nothing at all.

Müller's fists clenched. "And what about Taormino?"

"What about her? With you in the trap, and two of the assistant commissioners . . . Most of the department chiefs are already mine. How long do you think Taormino will last, even with Eronov and Tembu backing her?"

Spreading a wide, blunt hand across his face, Müller slumped and said, "You can promise me a clean force?"

"I can't personally vouch for the morals of every officer," said Cyril, "but the Ospies won't take kindly to misconduct. Their system is straight and the change of power should purge most of your troublemakers." It might be true.

"Doesn't sound pleasant."

"You didn't get into police work for pleasantries."

Müller's laugh was a single, dry exhalation. "No," he said. "No, I did not."

CHAPTER

TWENTY-ONE

At the breakfast table, Aristide didn't even get his coffee to his lips. He caught sight of the *Clarion*'s headline and froze with his cup hovering just above its saucer.

Police commissioner pockets stolen goods. Investigation reveals collusion with impeached primary.

Putting his coffee down with a snap of china, he flicked the paper open. The headlining article ran the length of the front page. He was so intent on his thoughts that when Finn dropped a cool, damp kiss on the back of his bent neck, he started violently.

"Sorry." Finn laughed and ran a hand through Aristide's curls. Aristide tipped his head back and let Finn kiss him properly. Water spiked the younger man's freshly barbered hair. He had a towel wrapped around his hips, and that was all.

Utterly delicious, and Aristide had no patience for him. He turned back to the paper while Finn settled into the seat across from him.

Hebrides was scratched. Amberlough had always been very polite about looking the other way, but no one could ignore embezzlement and graft so blatant, not when hard evidence was presented in the trial of the decade. Because there *would* be a trial. And that was leaving out possession of controlled substances and soliciting unlicensed prostitutes. The hounds had been thorough; someone must have been egging them on, coaching them, encouraging them. Someone with a stake in Hebrides's downfall. The Ospies, of course, but who among them could manipulate the ACPD so deftly? This was someone who understood the intricate web of mutually assured destruction between lawmakers, lawbreakers, and Amberlough's police.

"Wind blows cold, your face'll freeze that way." Finn applied butter to a scone with brisk strokes of his knife. "No good for a man who trades on his looks. What's in the paper that's got you so pestered?"

"The same thing that'll be p-p-pestering you at office today, I imagine." Aristide folded the paper back on itself and handed it across the table. He watched Finn's bright eyes flick back and forth across the words.

"Holy stones of the Lady's cairn." He set down his buttered scone and dusted his fingers clean on the edge of the tablecloth.

Aristide pushed back his chair. "Ilse's brushed your suit," he said. "Can you show yourself out?" When Finn looked up, trying to hide his wounded expression and failing, Aristide added, "No rush."

It didn't take the hurt out of Finn's face. Exasperated, Aristide bent over the table and pressed his lips to Finn's forehead. "*Terribly* sorry, but we're both going to be b-b-busy for a while. And anyway, if I spend all my time with you, I'll wear off your shine. So scurry along, my dove, and g-g-get to work."

When Ilse came in to take the breakfast tray and told him, "There's a young woman calling, sir," her expression communicated quizzical disgust.

Aristide wondered who on earth it could be. "Show her in."

Within minutes, a dirty-cheeked girl of maybe twelve was sitting on Aristide's brocade chaise. She held one of the leftover breakfast scones and was gnawing it to bits. Crumbs showered down into the canvas sack of newspapers at her feet.

In his own cupped palm, Aristide held a matchbook from a grisly dive just north of Eel Town. He flipped it open and saw one match missing, and one torn in half. At the corner of the cardboard flap was the message *TIED UP till then*, written in smudged pencil and block letters to disguise the hand.

He took a coin from his pocket and tossed it to Cyril's messenger. "Thank you. Go see Ilse in the kitchen."

There was lots to do before half one: people to see and plans to make, all over the city. The weather was fine enough for springtime plaid—a heather ground crosshatched with pale green and blue. As a final flourish, on his way out the door, Aristide stuck a cheap gold rosette in his hatband. It had come last week in one of the endless bouquets punters sent backstage, and he'd been trying to figure out what to do with it since. He wasn't worried about looking too gaudy in the rough neighborhoods where he was headed—in Amberlough, people knew who he was. And if that failed . . . the cut of his suit might telegraph money, but the tailor who'd constructed it had done so with respect for hidden holsters.

Reflected sunlight bounced off the Heyn. When Aristide

ducked into the Little Camphor Bar, he had to blink spangles from his eyes.

Cross was in the private dining room upstairs. She nodded Aristide into the seat opposite hers and started talking, without preamble.

"I'm not staying in the Foxhole," she said. "Not now. Things are going sour like milk."

"I didn't imagine you would," he said.

"Question is, do you have a full-time spot for me? I can probably get myself back to Liso, if you need somebody there. But to be honest . . ."

"You've been there two years and you'd like to stay at home a while longer, yes. Even with things as they are?"

"Amberlough is where I hang my hat," she said. "I'd like to stick by her while she wades through this mess."

"Then this may be a tricky sell." He'd been turning it over for a while, this idea. Even before Cyril scratched the regionalists. The Ospie threat had been looming for some time, and Aristide always liked to be prepared.

"You want me abroad?" Tired lines pinched the corners of her mouth. "I thought you would."

"Actually," he said, and saw the furrows melt from her face. She'd have them back, and worse, in a moment. "I need someone here. Someone to keep an eye on the Ospies. Preferably from within."

To his surprise, she laughed. "A double agent," she said. "Aren't you lucky you know one already?" She paused, sucked at her teeth. "I'd have to play like I was turning. I mean, I'd really have to turn. And they'd want to use me to spy on the Foxhole. That's three handlers to please at once, Mack."

"I understand if that's somewhat . . . intimidating."

"Nah." She grinned. "Sounds like a thrill to me."

"So you'll do it?"

"I been waitin' for this one my whole life."

Cross's confidence was reassuring, even if she did sound mad. "I'm going to back off from you for a while," he said. "Just so you don't look suspicious. Will you let me know when you're in place?"

She reached across the table and plucked the gaudy rosette from his hatband. "You just bet I will."

His errands took him slowly but steadily south. If he had a tail, he hoped they would admire his efficiency instead of suspecting his final destination. He'd bought most of the foxes on his case and wasn't worried what they thought, but until Cross wormed her way into the Ospie ranks, Acherby's people were an unknown quantity.

He stopped in at I Fa's flat during her morning receiving hours, less for pleasure than for business. She was heavily invested in a few of his ventures, and things wouldn't go well for her if her finances came under scrutiny by Ospie agents. Then he headed down the wharves, rendezvousing with some of his ground-floor operators. Last, before answering Cyril's summons, he went up Elver Street into the heart of the southwest quarter. In the attic of Peronides Fine Arts and Antiques, Aristide sat across from his three frightened clients and told them they could no longer stay in Amberlough.

"But Taphir's safe," protested Sofie, gripping her husband's knee.

"Depends what you mean by 'safe,'" said the boy, putting his hand over hers. "I will need to keep my head down for a bit."

"But that's not hard in this city." Sofie looked at Aristide with huge, beseeching eyes. "Am I right, Mr. Makricosta?"

"A year ago," he said, "you could have remained here, and done very well indeed. But not now. If you wish to stay together, and stay safe, you must get out of Gedda entirely."

"But—" Sofie looked around the room, as if she might find something to counter Aristide's pronouncement.

"Surely you've seen today's papers," said Aristide.

"Papers?" Mab spoke, finally, and her tone was acid. "We've been cooped up in this aerie for nigh on a week now. How are we supposed to get any news?"

He realized they truly didn't know, and he didn't relish telling them. Especially as he knew on whose golden head the blame could be squarely placed.

"Evidence has emerged that is more than enough to remove Josiah Hebrides from office. You can expect a swift decline of regionalist influence in Amberlough. I advise emigrating before doing so becomes impossible."

Exhaustion replaced Sofie's outrage. Her knuckles went white between Taphir's. "Where are we supposed to go?"

"Do you have any friends or relatives abroad?"

"No one I would trust," said Sofie. Mab shook her head. All eyes turned to Taphir's pinched face.

"I have an aunt," he said, "back in Porachis. We haven't spoken in a few years, but she might be worth a try."

Mab rubbed thumb and forefinger along her eyebrows. "'Worth a try' en't exactly confidence-inspiring."

"Have you got a better idea?" he snapped. "I spent the last two days in a lockbox and I don't like the idea of going back. At least we'll be out of Gedda."

A strangled sob escaped Sofie, who put her fist to her teeth.

Aristide smoothed his lapels. "I can arrange for passage to the Port of Berer, and move your money. Mr. Emerson, it might be better to leave any correspondence with your aunt until you make landfall in Porachis."

Taphir nodded, his dark eyes wide and somber.

"I'll be in touch," said Aristide. Brushing attic dust from his trousers, he left Sofie crying between her two silent spouses.

When he gave his last cabbie directions, the woman looked him up and down and asked, "You sure?"

"As a keystone," said Aristide, and climbed into the back of the hack. In reality, he was puzzled, and not a little apprehensive. What could Cyril possibly want? And why now, for queen's sake, when half the rotten Foxhole was probably looking for him with their teeth bared and their blood up? He'd be arrested, if they could find him. Or maybe just shot.

The streets got dirtier, the buildings more ramshackle, as he traveled toward Eel Town.

"Here is fine," said Aristide, when the cabbie crossed the intersection of Solemnity and Cane. She stopped at the curb. He paid twice the fare and thanked her. As she pulled away, he saw her eyes in the mirror, giving him one last doubting look.

The Stevedore was tucked down the back of an alley off of narrow, twisting Rifle Row. Broken glass choked the wet gutters. A steep set of stairs led down from the footpath to a basement door, marked with a tin sign painted in chipped lead white. The air inside reeked of spilled beer and stale smoke.

A few red-eyed patrons cased him when he walked through the door, but evidently found him less interesting than their pints. He checked his watch: one thirty-five. Cyril might be running late. Or he might be dead.

A low doorway at the back of the room led to a corridor that ended in a service stair to the left. At the right, it doglegged. Aristide made the turn and found himself in a second room, smaller and darker than the first, cluttered with tables. The chairs were up at most of them, crooked legs sticking into the air like the feet of dead animals. But in the rear corner, at a table lit by a chimneyed taper, Cyril sat with his back to one wall. A second chair stood empty against the other.

Weaving between the disused tables, Aristide took Cyril's measure. He'd dressed down for the locale—a tweed flat cap and a collarless shirt, an oily rag around his neck. He had the details right even down to his ragged, hand-rolled cigarette. Despite his attire, he was clean-shaven. The circles Aristide remembered beneath his eyes were gone.

"You look well." Aristide lowered himself into the empty chair.

Cyril snorted. Smoke barreled from his nostrils and twisted through the candlelight. "Thanks."

"Will you *please* tell me why we're meeting in this wretched place? You could've come by the theatre. Cordelia's anxious about you. You g-g-gave her a bit of a scare, apparently."

Stubbing out his cigarette, Cyril sat back in his chair and removed his cap. A lock of pomaded hair fell out of place and curved across his forehead. With an impatient gesture, he flicked his head to the side. The movement was ineffectual, but Cyril didn't try again. Aristide had to check his hand from rising to smooth the stray bit of hair. The jerk of the chin, the fleeting irritation—familiarity cut keenly. How many times had he seen that same blond crescent fall against Cyril's brow?

"I hope," said Aristide, looking away, "you weren't planning on an assignation."

"Ari, please. If it was sex I wanted, we wouldn't be in the basement of the Stevedore. No matter who was on my tail."

"Is there anyone?"

"Of course. You don't think the Ospies would give me my

parole. I'm doing good work for my handler, but he doesn't trust me. He's afraid I'm going to embarrass him."

"So it was you. Who scratched Taormino, I mean. And Hebrides, too?"

A self-deprecating smile hooked the corner of Cyril's mouth. "You noticed?"

"I could hardly fail to. Which means Culpepper will notice too. Has she sent anyone after you?"

"Not yet, but she will. I can handle it, don't worry."

"I wasn't."

"That's sweet of you. I'm flattered."

"Cyril, why are we here? Tell me I didn't come all the way across t-t-town to flirt in a dirty basement."

With a sigh, Cyril pushed the stray curve of his hair back. Speaking more to the candle wick than to Aristide, he said, "Cordelia's running for you."

"Yes." He'd been hoping to keep that from Cyril, but there wasn't much one could.

"Our history—yours and mine—isn't exactly secret. Think of how that would look, if it came out Cordelia was in on your schemes."

"It won't," said Aristide, with practiced confidence.

"What could possibly have possessed you?" Cyril's fist curled tight around his tweed cap, bunching it into a tube. "Ari, the whole point was to keep me looking like a respectable Ospie. And you start sending her on errands?"

"She wouldn't take my money," said Aristide. "And I needed her help. What was I supposed to offer?"

"You needed her help? I thought she was—"

"Yes I needed her rotten help!" Aristide cut him off, suddenly overcome. He put his face in his hands and pushed his fingers past his hairline, tugging on his curls until his scalp stung. His burr leapt out like a rat from a sack. "Plague and pesteration, Cyril. I needed her help to keep you safe."

"But you're still using her." Cyril's soft voice didn't take the sting out of the accusation.

Aristide took a deep breath and made sure the next sentence came out smooth. "You're using her too."

There was a tight pause. Aristide could feel Cyril's anger building. When his outburst came, it snatched Aristide's breath with its force and revelation. "Not to move stolen goods for wanted refugees."

"What?"

"Oh don't play innocent; you're no ingénue. Cordelia was wearing Minna Keeler's stolen citrines yesterday. Do you have any idea the kind of trouble that could land me in?"

Blood drained from Aristide's limbs. His hands went suddenly cold and heavy, as if they were cast in lead. "Citrines?"

"Set with diamonds. They're not exactly inconspicuous."

He knew the jewels. He'd told Sofie to hold onto them; they were less valuable than some of the other pieces, and more recognizable. "Cyril, believe me. I never asked Cordelia to move them. I have no idea how she—no. That's a lie. I know how she got them. But if she'd had any sense she wouldn't have accepted."

"Don't," said Cyril.

"What? Call her a fool? You're not falling for her, are you? I thought your tastes were more refined."

Cyril made an ugly, scornful face. "Don't flatter yourself. You're putting me in danger, and you're putting her in danger. She's not going to run anything for you anymore."

"I think that's something she can decide for herself."

"You can't have it both ways, Aristide. Either she's a vacuous tart or she's clever and keen." He shut his mouth and Aristide saw a muscle in his jaw flex. When he spoke again, his voice was quieter and more controlled. "I know which one I'd pick."

"You think she's smart," said Aristide. "You're right. But you can't have it both ways either. Don't come to me and tell me what Cordelia can and cannot do. It's not your place to decide. If you feel endangered by her association with me, then you can end your own with her."

The set of Cyril's shoulders collapsed. "No," he said. "She'll need somewhere to go, when the Ospies take over."

"I can see her safely out of Amberlough."

"Be realistic. Your influence is shrinking with every Ospie gain. You'll be lucky if you can get *yourself* out." He paused, dug his nails into the rotted tabletop.

"Yes?" prompted Aristide.

"I—I didn't want to tell you, but . . ." Cyril ducked his chin to one side, his expression rueful. The same recalcitrant piece of hair fell across his forehead.

This time, Aristide didn't stop himself: He reached out and combed it into place with his fingers. "Didn't want to tell me what?"

Cyril put his hand on Aristide's forearm. His mouth moved, but he didn't speak.

"Didn't want to tell me what, Cyril?" Aristide asked again, almost whispering. He traced the strong, straight line of Cyril's cheekbone and jaw, ending with his fingertips arrayed just beneath the edge of Cyril's chin. He felt an indrawn breath, the movement of Cyril's larynx just before he spoke.

"They're out for smugglers' blood," he said, his tone flat and defeated. "When Acherby's position is firm, they'll be coming after you like a pack after cubs."

There was something false about the sentiment, though the statement was credible. Aristide sighed, tired of Cyril's games, and moved to stand. Cyril's grip tightened and drew him closer, across the table. Aristide felt the warmth of the candle on his shoulder, swiftly eclipsed by the smoke-limned heat of Cyril's mouth on his.

"Mother and sons," said Cyril. Aristide could taste the words, and feel the movement of his lips. "I've missed—"

Aristide didn't let him finish. He put his hands around the back of Cyril's head, digging his fingers into the carefully waxed waves of hair. He pressed their faces close, jaw aching with the force of the kiss. Cyril didn't fight; he reached for Aristide's lapels, pulled him nearer, gasped into his open mouth.

A clatter of dropping crates, and accompanying stream of curses, alerted them to a presence in the corridor. Like children caught at naughtiness, they pulled apart. Cyril's pulse hammered so hard Aristide could see it: The flushed skin of his throat fluttered against the oily calico kerchief.

"I need to go," said Aristide.

Cyril nodded, and looked away. Candlelight picked out his eyelashes like gold filament.

"We can't do this again," said Aristide.

Another nod.

As he walked away, Aristide curled his fists so tight his long nails bit into his palms. The small pain was like a pinch to distract from the agony of a broken bone.

CHAPTER

TWENTY-TWO

Cordelia had barely got into her dressing room before Tory came skidding down the hall and caught himself in her doorway.

"You've heard?" he asked, breathless.

"You think there's anybody in the city who hasn't?" She threw her purse into the corner of the room and fell into her makeup chair. "Afternoon edition of the *Telegraph* had a headline about five inches tall. But they always do lean dramatic."

"I've had to do up a whole new routine. People are sticking close behind Hebrides. I can't feature any jabs at him flying high with tonight's crowd."

"You think we'll have much of one?" She belied her reservations, starting to undo the buttons on her blouse.

"Course we rotten will." Malcolm appeared behind Tory in

the doorway and gave them both an appraising glance. "It'll be a madhouse." He looked down at Tory. "You. Go run your new material with Liesl. She wants to get the beats right for tonight's jokes."

Tory met Malcolm's uncompromising glare. "Malcolm," he said, and then paused like he was struggling. After a brief nod of the head, he was gone.

Malcolm watched Tory go, and while he was distracted, Cordelia cased his profile. He needed a shave. His nails were dirty and wanted paring. The heat backstage had him down to his undershirt, and even that was soaked with sweat. She thought about pecking him for shabbiness, but he sighed and slumped against the door frame, and she couldn't.

"Three bits for whatever's on your brain," she said, hanging her blouse up on a coat hook.

"Just worries," he said. "Same as always."

"I'd wager that ain't true. This is a little heavier than taxes and protection." She let her skirt fall to the floor and didn't bother with a dressing gown. It was stuffy backstage, and it wasn't like what she had was a secret—especially not to Malcolm. "What are you gonna do?"

He shook his head. "I'm waitin' on divine inspiration," he said. "Something might come down out of the mountains and save me."

"Well, for all our sakes I hope it does. A lot of people depend on this place, Mal."

"Thanks so much for reminding me." He crossed his arms across his broad chest. "'Specially since you ain't one of 'em."

She stopped, her lipstick halfway up. "Say that again."

"You got your game with Makricosta—don't think I ain't clocked it. And your swell, even if you ain't knocking him. You're getting too grand for us stagefolk."

"Oh shut your face, you big ape." She painted two perfect arches on her upper lip, and a longer, fuller smear on the lower, then capped the tube. Twirling the chair to face Malcolm, she put one finger in her mouth and drew it out, to clear the insides of her lips and keep her teeth white. It came out with a satisfying pop. Even the added brown of Malcolm's late spring tan couldn't cover the flush that crept up his neck.

"If I was getting too grand," she said, "I'd already be gone."

When she came back after the final curtain she found Cyril sitting at her makeup table, holding a bunch of roses. "I know they're black on the poster," he said. "But do you know what the duties are on Porachin Sables? Besides, they aren't in season."

She took the flowers in her arms. "These are lovely. What's the occasion?"

"The end of the world?" He stood, in one smooth motion, and turned her chair for her. She sat, and let him spin her toward the mirror.

"Cheery." She buried her face in the flowers. The corner of an envelope poked her in the eye. When she pulled it out, Cyril plucked it from her hands. In the mirror, she saw him wave it, then drop it into her purse.

"Read it later," he suggested.

She opened her cold cream and started cleaning away her paint. "How soon will things start sinking, do you reckon?"

"Soon," he said, "and fast."

"Soon and fast enough I should start worrying now? Or can it wait a week or two?"

"Don't worry yet," said Cyril. "But start thinking about what you can do once you can't do this anymore." He tapped one finger on the corner of her makeup table. "Or when you can't run tar. I imagine the Ospie vice squad won't be as easily bought as the ACPD is at present."

"Mother's tits," she said, laughing. "I ain't exactly qualified to do much else."

"I've been thinking about that," said Cyril. He leaned against the wall, beside her mirror, and lit a cigarette. "You've got more than a few of the talents Central looks for in its recruits."

"And a lot of good they'll do me when Culpepper is belly-up under the Ospies' boots."

"Acherby needs agents too," he said. "Ones who know this territory. After all, they'll have to purge the current stable."

Cordelia stopped with half her face smeared in cold cream and turned to look at him. "Sorry, are you trying to turn me Ospie?"

"It's move with the herd or be trampled. And you're a survivor, Cordelia."

"What, like you?"

He smiled ruefully around his straight. "Oh no. I'm just a coward."

She wiped her face clean and threw the cloth to the back of her makeup table. "I'll have to think about it." She didn't like the idea, but she wasn't sure what else she could do. Leave town, maybe, and look for theatrical work somewhere farther south. Hyrosia, maybe. But she was an Amberlinian, born and raised, and Amberlough was what she knew. Still. "Working for the Ospies ain't exactly a sunny proposition."

"Understandable." He blew smoke toward the ceiling.

Someone knocked on her dressing room door. Cyril's head snapped around. When Cordelia got up to answer, he put his hand out. She waited. He moved to the wall beside the hinges and, to her horror, drew a snub-nosed revolver from the inside of his jacket.

"What do you think you're doing?" she hissed. He shook his

head and tipped the short barrel of the gun toward the door. She pulled it open, hiding Cyril from whoever had knocked.

"Do you have a moment?" Ari lounged in the doorway, draped in silk. Transparent with sweat, it stuck in places to his skin. "I've got something you might be interested in."

"Doesn't everybody?" She didn't give ground. "Can it wait a minute? I got company."

He arched one finely sculpted eyebrow. "But I just passed Tory in the hall. And Malcolm's t-t-tied up with punters."

"I'm a busy girl."

"I'm sure you—" He froze, staring over her shoulder. She turned, and saw a sliver of Cyril's reflection in her makeup mirror. Just the edge of his shoulder, the back of his head. In Ari's place, she probably wouldn't have noticed it.

He shoved her aside and came in, shutting the door and leaning against it in lieu of a lock.

"Plague and pesteration," he said, and Cordelia wondered where he'd picked up the northern curse. "What do you think you're doing here?"

"No one saw me."

"If you're so sure, why are you waving *that* around?" Aristide cast a look at the gun like it was a dead and stinking wharf rat.

"No one who?" asked Cordelia. "What's going on?"

"Just a precaution," said Cyril, holstering the revolver. Then, "I'll leave you two. Cordelia, think about what I said?"

Ari looked sharply between them. Cordelia gave him nothing. "I told you I would. But why the snubby? Who's after you?"

Cyril shook his head. "This isn't one of those things you need to know."

"Holy stones," said Aristide. "I think you might tell her enough to keep her out of trouble. Since you're *so* worried about her safety."

"Am I gonna end up scratched?" Cordelia asked, hands on her hips.

Cyril squirmed under her scrutiny, and turned pleadingly toward Ari. "They wouldn't use her—"

"I'm right rotten here," she snapped. "Cyril, am I in some kind of danger?"

"It's possible Culpepper has some foxes out for my blood. I don't think they'd use you to get to me, but just look over your shoulder every now and then. And if you go out alone, let someone know where you're headed."

"Mother's tits," she said. "I knew something like this would happen."

"You'll be fine," he insisted, arrowing a sharp glance in Ari's direction. "Cordelia, the people who are looking for me . . . they know what my sticking points are. And—no offense—you aren't one of them."

"Oh, thanks," she said, ready to ask who was. But midway through an outsized eye roll, she caught Ari sneering. The expression didn't quite cover the faint, dusky blush on his high cheekbones.

"Cyril," he said, "get out. And do try not to get yourself k-k-killed."

Cyril took his hat from Cordelia's makeup table, tipped it to Ari, and pulled it low over his eyebrows. He was gone without another word.

After a weighty moment of quiet, Cordelia turned to Ari. "You wanted to talk to me about something?"

His lips drew into a thin, frustrated line. "Let's leave it for later, shall we? Get dressed and get your things together. I'll take you home."

"Ari, I grew up in the Mew. I can watch my own ass."

"I know," he said. "But please, give me the satisfaction of seeing someone safely to their door."

The next afternoon, when she showed up at the Bee, the whole place was roaring like a kicked hive—funny, that comparison. She collared Garlande, who was still dressed, and asked what the trouble was.

"You mean you don't know?" She put her hand over her mouth. "Mother and sons, I don't think you oughta hear it from me."

"Come on, Landy." Her stomach had gone sour with fear. "What's got everybody in such a fret?"

But Garlande just shook her head. "Ask Malcolm, if you're still talking to him. Or Ari if you can stand it." She turned her back and ran off before Cordelia could shake out an explanation.

Suddenly apprehensive, she kept on down the corridor until she came to Malcolm's office. The door was clogged with a crowd, all shouting and hissing and waving their hands.

"What are we supposed to do instead?" demanded the new tit singer—Mal'd brought on a contentious contralto after he sacked Thea. "What kind of act are you gonna slip in? We haven't got anything."

"Do you run this show?" Malcolm thundered, from the depths of his burrow. "No! So I'll thank you to swallow your tongue. Choke on it if you like. Liesl!"

The conductor, at the edge of the mob, started and dove in. Whatever Malcolm had to say to her got lost in the hubbub.

One of the chorus dancers spotted Cordelia and went white. He elbowed his friend, who gaped, then turned to whisper into the ear of the mime. Within seconds, the whole lot of her cast mates had gone quiet and blanched as a bunch of boiled potatoes.

"What's got all of you so pinched?" she asked, holding her purse to her chest. Something was dead wrong here. Bad wrong.

"Delia?" Malcolm's voice sounded rough in the sudden silence, and there was a stuffy, nasal undertone that made her wonder if he'd been crying. "Get in here. The rest of you, clear off. If you don't hear from me in half an hour . . . well, you'll hear from me in half an hour. For now, keep on like we're doing the show."

"Aren't we?" she asked, pushing through the rest of the cast as they left.

"Come in," said Malcolm. "Shut the door."

Ari was in Malcolm's office, and Liesl, taking up the love seat and the extra chair, respectively. Cordelia reached for the stool under the coat hooks, the one Tory usually used. Malcolm looked pained. Ari coughed and made a little gesture with his hand, outside of Malcolm's view. Cordelia left the stool and stood awkwardly in front of Malcolm's desk. She felt like she was about to have her knuckles slapped by a school teacher.

"What's wrong?" she snapped. "You all look like somebody died."

Aristide closed his eyes and mouthed something that looked like a short prayer. Liesl ran her teeth over her lower lip. Malcolm's face was indescribable.

Cordelia clutched her purse straps. "Who is it?" Then, remembering the reaction when she reached for Tory's stool, she took a sharp breath and choked on it. "Mother and sons. He's not—" She staggered and reached out. Liesl was beside her, suddenly, with a hand under her outflung arm. The conductor guided her to the love seat and settled her next to Ari.

"No," said Liesl, "no, he's not. Damnation, your hands are cold. Malcolm, you might have told her to sit down first."

But Malcolm had the heels of his palms against his eyes, and didn't apologize.

"He's not dead," said Aristide, staring at Malcolm. "But he's very badly injured, and he hasn't woken up. They aren't sure that he will."

"Where is he? What happened?"

"His performance last night was positively stinging," said Ari. "You missed it—costume change, I think—but he'd never done better."

"What happened to him?"

"Well he rubbed a couple cats the wrong way, didn't he?" Malcolm let his fists fall to the top of his desk, rattling pens and empty glasses. "And they scratched."

"What do you mean? What did he say?"

"He destroyed Acherby." Malcolm laid a square of rolling paper out and added a pinch of tobacco. He tried, twice, to twist it up, then slashed it away with the flat of his hand. "Took him apart and dangled his bits up like a carnival sideshow. It was genius. Only, some of the punters got pinned about it and sang to the blackboots. Near as I can put together, he got about halfway home before they caught up with him. The ACPD picked him up around four a.m. and got him to Seagate Hospital, but by then he'd been lying in the gutter a couple hours."

"Holy stones," said Cordelia, reaching blindly with a shaking hand. "Has anybody got a straight?"

Aristide produced his case and offered it around. Malcolm accepted, gratefully. Liesl waved him away. When Cordelia put one of his cigarettes between her lips, Ari handed her a smudged book of matches with a few sticks missing. She lit up with shaking hands and took a deep, smoky breath. Exhaling, she asked, "So. Are you canceling?"

"That's what we're trying to decide." Liesl's expressive hands fidgeted on her knees. "The whole cast is having fits."

"We've had fits before," said Cordelia. "Mal, I know you ain't gonna take that for an excuse."

"I wouldn't," he said. "But it ain't just that. Without Tory . . ." He paused for a steadying drag on Ari's gold-stamped straight. "Without Tory, there's some gaps in the show that need filling. About fifteen minutes, all told. Three acts."

"Drag out some old material," said Aristide. "Two seasons old. No one will remember it."

"Damnation, Makricosta, I know. You've said it twice. But—"

"But *nothing*," said Ari, biting the "t" so sharply Cordelia could hear his teeth click. "Your friend's in hospital. You're shattered, I understand. But plague it all, Malcolm Sailer—" Malcolm winced, and Cordelia wondered whether it was because the northern curse called Tory to mind, or because Ari had used his full name. "—that stage will *not* stay empty tonight. If it does, they've won."

"I didn't realize you cared so much about politics," said Malcolm, tapping a column of ash right onto the floor.

"Malcolm, this is your *livelihood*. At least *pretend* you understand the consequences of your actions." Ari leaned forward, elbows on his knees. "If you cancel tonight's show, you have given them *everything*. If you put on any act the Ospies don't like, they'll know they can attack your stagefolk on the street and close you down."

"Well I can't exactly run a show with my cast in hospital, can I?" Malcolm's nicotine-stained snarl put Cordelia in mind of the yellow fangs of a cornered street dog. "Can't imagine you'd be too thrilled to end up at the wrong end of a cosh, yourself."

"No," said Aristide. "But I'd like it far less if I knew it worked. Put on the show, Malcolm."

Liesl nodded. "He's right, Mr. Sailer. You've got to."

Malcolm didn't look at either of them. He stared straight at Cordelia. She stared back, into the familiar darkness rimmed with red. The skin under his eyes was soft and purple with exhaustion.

She'd kissed him there, in the hollows above his cheekbones. She remembered the faint brush of his eyelashes against her nose.

Looking in his face now was like catching her reflection in a dark shop window. For a moment, she saw a stranger. Then, she saw her own aching need to be alone, to grieve. But when she spoke, despite his desperate eyes, all she said was, "Do it."

CHAPTER

TWENTY-THREE

There were riots, in the week after Taormino's arrest. Not big ones, but enough to get the ACPD hopping in the fourth precinct. Students and theatricals—volatile types—and farther south, in Eel Town, all the Amberlinians who'd operated in the ample shadows of the old administration.

Cyril was insulated from most of it, mewed in an Ospie safe house in a northern suburb of the city, on Van der Joost's orders. He couldn't tell if they honestly wanted him out of harm's way, or if they were just suspicious and keeping a close eye on him. He hoped it was the former. That meant he was valuable, and his work had done them good. And good work meant new IDs and permits and a ticket out, for him and for Ari: the point of the whole endeavor.

The flat's small windows overlooked a narrow alley. Summer weather made it stuffy, so Cyril went around mostly in a cotton undershirt with his braces dangling, smoking perpetual cigarettes. Nita, the girl who brought his papers and correspondence, had also grudgingly delivered a carton of cheap straights. Officially, the Ospies disapproved of Gedda's booming tobacco trade because the majority of the leaves were imported. But some, mostly new temple Hearther types like Nita, objected on moral grounds—that it was a foreign, decadent habit.

Cyril put Nita at twenty or twenty-one years old, newly down from university. He hated her, but hid it with professional skill. During today's visit, she had dropped off a pile of dispatches from his nascent network of traitorous police. It felt good to have informants, especially trapped here until the foxes trailing him could be dealt with. He was just finishing up his reading when the intercom from the front door buzzed. He tapped the button, dropping a fine spray of cigarette ash across the grille. "Yes?"

"A woman here to see you, sir." The doorman was one of Van der Joost's people. "Mr. Satzen brought her by."

Cordelia. It had to be. And something must be wrong. The note in the bouquet of roses had said "for emergencies." Inside was the exchange for Rudolf Satzen, an Ospie courier. He hadn't meant for Rudy to bring her here, just to act as a messenger. But Cordelia probably always got what she wanted, in the end. "Send her up."

He heard the lift mechanism wheeze behind the walls, and within a minute, footsteps in the corridor. He waited for her to knock, but instead, the door handle rattled. It was locked, but she kept at it. Then she knocked, like she was trying to hammer through. He ground his cigarette butt into the ashtray, stretched his braces back over his shoulders, and went to let her in.

Through the peephole, he caught her in profile, her hand to her mouth. When he turned the lock, her head snapped around and she nailed him with a glare straight through the glass. Suddenly, he worried he would need the help of the heavy across the hall, the bruiser set to guard him from anyone who made it this far with murder on their mind.

When he opened the door, she pushed past him wordlessly, but stopped just a few steps past the threshold.

"Have a seat," he said. "Can I get you a drink? No gin, but there's rye, and I think a bottle of sherry."

"No." She didn't turn to face him.

"What's wrong? Do you need help?"

"Not from you." The line of her shoulders was tight and shaking. "That's what I came to say."

Damnation. "What can I do to change your mind?"

She whirled on him, and he realized she'd been crying. "I don't know," she said. Her eyes were sunken and crazed with red veins. She looked like she hadn't slept in three days. "Can you raise the dead?"

A jolt of fear lanced through him. "Who?"

"Nobody you know." Disgust twisted her mouth. "You thought it was Ari, didn't you?"

He sat at his desk, heavily, unwilling to admit his relief.

"Stones, Cyril," she said. "How do you keep this up?"

"How? I would think you of all people would understand. I keep it up because I do what's necessary."

"You're nothing like me."

"Whoring? Selling tar? You've done ugly things to survive."

Her snort was eloquently derisive. "You ain't surviving. Your heart's beating, sure, but there's nothing left inside it. Least I been honest about my ugliness. All these lies, they're hollowing you out."

"What lies?" He flung his hands up. "You know exactly who I am, what I'm doing."

"I didn't say you lied to *me*." A curious softness came into her eyes, unbearably like pity. "Whatever they said to you, whatever they told you they'd do . . . There were other ways, Cyril."

"Like what? Central couldn't keep me safe in Tatié. You think they could keep me safe in a coup?"

"Ari would have hidden you in a second, sent you out of the country. He still would, if you asked him."

"I don't think so." Anyway, he wouldn't have to.

"Why not? Mother's tits, Cyril, he loves you like pigs in slop."

"Because he's not an idiot. And because I'd never ask him to."

"What, you're too proud?" The pity in her eyes dissolved. "You've always gotta be the one pulling other people off the tracks, is that it? Well, Cyril DePaul, I can get my own ass out from under the train. So go help somebody who really needs you."

She slammed the door so hard, his stack of dispatches jumped and began to slide off the desk. The papers went one at a time at first, then built to a cascade. He let them fall and spread in a white fan across the floor.

He was still reeling from Cordelia's refusal when he got the call.

"Hebrides is dead," said Van der Joost. No preamble.

Cyril pressed the receiver to his cheek. "What? How?"

"Heart attack."

He'd envisioned assassination. Suicide. The truth caught him off guard. "Really?" But of course. Hebrides's heart had always been tricky. Rich living in the last decade had made it worse, and impeachment wouldn't have done him any favors. "What now?"

"Some arrests. The chain of succession, the first three links: Almstedt, Scott, Demotchka. Leave Koryon—he's one of ours. And bring in Culpepper so we can get those agents off your scent."

He said it casually, but Cyril was under no illusions. This was a test he couldn't afford to fail. But he had to ask: "On what charge?"

Van der Joost's pause was nearly imperceptible, but it spoke volumes of mistrust. "You have Müller in your hand. Do you need one?" He ended the call without waiting for an answer.

For a long while after, Cyril brooded over the last of a cheap bottle of rye, thinking about what Cordelia had said.

Aristide was smart and capable and sometimes—often—ruthless. Left to his own devices, could he have gotten himself out of this mess? Or would he have been overconfident, and left it too late? Was Cyril really doing good, or just showing off?

Maybe he should have said something to Aristide after all, about his bargain with Van der Joost. He almost had, in the Stevedore. But it wasn't a surety, and Aristide would have torn him up and down for agreeing to the terms. But what terms would Aristide settle for? Only his own. And those might not get him out of Gedda safely.

Unless Cyril could convince him. Or bribe him. Or maybe, like Cordelia said, even just *ask*.

He picked up the telephone receiver. Pinching it between his shoulder and cheek, he used his free hand to turn the dial. He held his whiskey in the other, ready to douse any second thoughts.

"Sola's Oyster Bar." The woman on the other end of the line had a smoky, inviting voice. "What can I do for you tonight?"

"Reservation for two. Say, one o'clock? Have you got a private dining room open then?" They would let him out of the building, if he said it was for work. Maybe they'd send Rudy with him. That wouldn't be a problem.

There was a quick pause as the maitre d' checked her list. "I do. Whose name shall I put down?"

He gave her one. Not his own, obviously. "And if you don't

mind, will you ring my assistant with a reminder an hour or so before?"

"Absolutely. What exchange shall I use?"

He gave her the line for Culpepper's office, and hung up.

When Memmediv entered the room, the strains of a crooner and big band came with him from the public bar. He paused for a beat on the threshold, eyeing Cyril warily.

"Close the door, please," Cyril said.

Memmediv did, with careful movements. "You are not Karl Haven."

"No one is, not even Van der Joost. He's a fiction. And he was useful: Here you are."

"Well played, Mr. DePaul." Memmediv inclined his head. "Very well played."

It was that dark, luscious dialect that should have set Cyril's hackles up from the beginning. Memmediv wasn't a disillusioned Tatien expatriate; he was furious. A state-loyal fanatic who'd kept his hatred of Amberlough so well hidden Culpepper had brought him right into the warmest part of the Foxhole.

Years in the profession had given Cyril a keen sense of irony—espionage could be as good as tragic dramas. He hadn't acted on facts, setting up this meeting, but on the sense that Memmediv as the Ospies' mole was so bitterly perfect it had to be true. And he'd come running at the sound of Van der Joost's work name. So that proved something.

"Have a seat," said Cyril, gesturing to the empty chair across from him. There was no food on the table, but he'd ordered a bottle of dry white wine. Two glasses waited, empty. Cyril lifted the bottle.

Memmediv let him pour, but didn't pick up the glass when it was full.

They stared at each other. Cyril was keenly aware of the balance of power. Scant months ago, he'd outranked Memmediv by several leagues. After all, Cyril was—or had been—one of Culpepper's best agents, and a division head, while Memmediv was just her secretary. But Memmediv had been spying for the unionists since . . . well, Cyril didn't really know. And he'd blown Cyril's cover as coolly as Cyril would have broken his. It was Memmediv's fault Cyril was here, now, and needed a favor.

Turning his wineglass, Cyril breathed in the green, mineral nose, and sipped. Only then did he say to Memmediv, "How long?"

The other man blinked slowly, shuttering a cold, blank gaze.

"The Ospies, Vasily. How long?"

Memmediv's lips pulled tight across his teeth. "Two years, give or take some weeks."

Cyril had been in Tatié, when Memmediv turned. Not that he would've known, to stop it. "And Ada still doesn't suspect anything?"

"Of me?" Memmediv's crooked eyebrow telegraphed insult. "Of course not. You . . . have not been so careful, Cyrilak. The whole city knows whose side you're on. You used to be better than this."

Cyril bristled at the Tatien diminutive, and more, at the truth of Memmediv's insult. But he tamped down his irritation and continued. "You still have access to her papers?"

"Not *all*," he said, drawing his fingers in tantalizing arcs around the base of his wineglass. "Not *officially*."

"Semantics," said Cyril, dismissive.

The corner of Memmediv's mouth curled up slowly, like burning paper. He lifted his wine and drank without comment.

"Look." Cyril hunkered forward on the table. "With Hebrides dead, Van der Joost wants me to bring in Ada."

"And why, then, do you need me? You're the man with the paddle." Hovering one lean hand above the table, he twisted his wrist as if manipulating a marionette. "I hear Konrad is very pleased with your work so far."

"He may be pleased," said Cyril, "but he doesn't know Müller. The man won't hold Ada without charges. He's an honest cop, mother love him. And I played on it to bring him over."

Memmediv sneered. "You blackmailed him, DePaul. Don't try to elevate it."

"The blackmail was a clincher," said Cyril. "But I promised him an aboveboard police force. If I can't give him that, he's gone." He could feel an angry flush rising up his neck. Memmediv saw it, and graced him with an infuriating, thin-lipped smile.

"We have him." The "h" was guttural. "He is commissioner by the grace of the One State Party. His wife is involved with an undesirable alien, a known associate of smugglers and deviants. He cannot afford a false step."

"He can't," agreed Cyril. "But people don't care about consequences when they've been pushed and pushed and pushed. I'm trying to reel him back, Vasily, not shove him off the cliff. Keep testing him and eventually he'll jump on his own."

"Like you did?"

Cyril set his wineglass down with deliberate care. "Excuse me?"

"Culpepper did not mean to push you."

"We're not here to talk about me."

Memmediv didn't acknowledge him. "She should have known. Bowing and scraping to Tatié, to the very people who nearly killed you? Then the desk work: humiliating. And just as you resigned yourself and started to get comfortable, she dragged you back into the field. You were like a child who fears the water, after nearly drowning. And she just threw you in." He flicked his fingers over his wineglass. Softly, so that Cyril almost missed it, he added, "Splash."

Cyril sat back and crossed his arms. "She's good at her job."

Memmediv's laughter was quiet, rich as velvet. "She's a fool. *I* suggested you, for the Landseer action."

It came to Cyril then, like an anagram resolving. Memmediv had *groomed* him. His anger was swift, scorching, and bitterly impotent. "She *listened* to you?" he hissed. "*Why,* for queen's sake? You're a secretary. What do you know about espionage?"

"As it happens, more than anyone thought. She listened to me, DePaul, because she loves me."

The echo of Cordelia's accusation raised gooseflesh on Cyril's arms.

"What did she say?" Memmediv went on. "Oh, yes, 'Good idea, Vaz. Let's get him back out there. I'm sick of wiping his drool off of you.'" He blinked again, slow and flirtatious. His long, dark lashes cast momentary shadows over his cheekbones. "She has a jealous streak, our Ada."

Cyril said nothing.

Crow's-feet deepened at Memmediv's temples as his smile spread. "Now," he went on, "you need something from me. If you ask very, very nicely, perhaps I can be persuaded to help you."

"If you help me, you help the unionists. Isn't that what you're after?"

"Whatever it is you're doing," said Memmediv, "you'll find a way; Konrad has you by the jewels." He cupped one hand evocatively. "But other ways may be harder than this, less elegant. And you would look so sweet, begging on your knees."

PART

3

CHAPTER

TWENTY-FOUR

On the first truly sultry evening of the year, Aristide sat under the candy-striped awning of the Crane Gallery on Talbert Row, buttoned into a linen suit of summery white. Waiting for Finn's trolley, which was late, he was moments from slipping away to make a few telephone calls and disappearing into the night.

The affair had been pleasant enough. But these days being what they were, there were more important people Aristide could be spending time with. Dalliances were for peacetime, and with the Ospies ascendant, this was no such thing.

His runners were reporting sharp drops in business due to unionist intimidation. After Tory MacIntyre's run-in with the blackboots, Aristide could see why. Cordelia had thrown Cyril over entirely after the incident, and had nothing good to say about him since. It was ridiculous, but without her little asides about Cyril slipping into conversation, Aristide felt shut off from something he hadn't even known he wanted. On top of it all, Cross was still incommunicado. He was beginning to worry something had gone wrong with her transfer of loyalties.

Before he could descend into further nervous calculation, the 8:15 trolley slid into view down tree-lined Talbert Row. Its bell clanged brightly, scattering automobiles. Aristide ground his straight into the ashtray, adjusted the amethyst studs at his cuffs and ears, and took a moment to preen in the window. As he straightened his tie bar, the trolley slid up to the curb and deposited a tipsy redhead on the corner. Finn's shoulders were dusted with glitter, and there was a garish rosette pinned to his lapel.

"Mr. Lourdes." Aristide pulled out a chair for his companion. "You're late. And there's confetti in your hair."

"I was out with a few of the folk from the office." Finn rubbed sheepishly at his coif, leaving it in disarray. His efforts did nothing to dislodge the rainbow spangles. As Aristide settled into his own seat, he got a better look at the gaudy loops of gold ribbon and tinsel erupting from Finn's buttonhole.

"And what's this?" he asked, reaching for it across the table. He kept the question from coming out sharp, just barely. That rosette was familiar.

Finn tugged it free and handed it over. "I was just . . . it's my birthday. A few of the folk in the office took me out for drinks."

"A p-p-*party*," purred Aristide. "How *nice*. Who was there?"

"Oh, I don't think you'd know any of them."

"I think you'd be surprised. Names, Finn." He knew he sounded curt, but things had just taken a very interesting turn.

"Well, Amelia was there, and Dugan—both from the bursar. Merrilee came for a bit—"

"Merrilee Cross? You know her?"

"I wouldn't call us friends," said Finn. "I only just met her a few weeks ago—she's been away on business. But she's nice enough. She came by as we were leaving. It seemed rude not to invite her along."

"I'm sure it d-d-did."

"Ari, is something the matter? Have I done something wrong?"

"What? Oh, no, darling. In fact you've been quite terribly clever." He pinned the rosette back in place and leaned the extra inches across the table to kiss Finn on the tip of his freckled nose. "I d-d-don't know what I'd do without you."

"That's quite nice," said Finn. "You know, I was getting a feeling you might drop me soon."

"D-D-Drop you?" Aristide put a dramatic hand to his heart. "I'm *wounded*, Finn. P-P-Positively shot through the heart."

"*You're* wounded? Think how stung I felt."

Aristide took Finn's hand in his and squeezed it. "Would you be *awfully* p-p-put out if we skipped dinner altogether? I suddenly feel a great need to do imp-p-possibly wretched things to you."

"They fed me a bit," said Finn, "at the party." He blushed, but his smile was wicked. "I could wait on dinner. Maybe even until morning."

"Excellent." Aristide pulled him to his feet. "I hope you like shirred eggs. Ilse's are d-d-delicious."

Finn laughed and flirted like a Princes Road harlot the whole ride back to Aristide's flat. Wine or birthday gaiety made him vivacious. But as soon as Aristide closed the door behind them and slid the bolt, Finn's smile dropped away.

"I'm not an idiot, Ari," he said.

Aristide paused, his hand still lingering on the lock. "Nobody said you were."

Folding his arms, Finn nailed Aristide with a stern look. "What's your connection to Cross?"

"Nothing you need to know about. Care for a d-d-drink?" He didn't wait for an answer. Finn tailed him into the parlor and, while he poured single malt into two tumblers, continued to harangue him.

"You're using me to send messages," he said, tearing the rosette from his buttonhole and holding it high. "Do you realize the kind of trouble I could land in? It's not like it was; I can't afford to be caught out aiding smugglers. And she is a smuggler, isn't she?"

"*I* am a smuggler," said Aristide. "*She* is my associate." He capped the decanter and set it at the back of the bar. The crystal snapped against the mirrored shelf, harder than he'd meant it to. He turned to Finn, a glass in each hand. "Drink. Relax."

"I won't rotten relax," said Finn, "until you tell me you won't do that again."

Aristide rather doubted Cross meant to send any more messages in such a flashy, obtuse manner. She was just marking Finn as a channel; it was up to Aristide to figure out the manner in which he might be used. But that wasn't what Finn wanted to hear. Instead, Aristide asked, "Are you frightened?"

"Yes, Ari. Of course I'm frightened. The country's falling apart and you're using me to run who knows what right under the Ospies' noses. You're being reckless, and I want no part of it."

"Don't you?" He set the glasses aside and stepped closer.

Finn's eyes flickered, but he held his ground. "No."

"Are you sure?" Aristide closed, and took the rosette from Finn's suddenly pliable fingers. He used the gilded frippery to trace a line up the front of Finn's waistcoat, to follow the curve of his throat and tip his head back. "Don't you think you'd like it? Helping me do d-d-*dangerous* things?"

"You should have told me," said Finn. He was breathless.

"Why?" Aristide leaned forward, put his mouth against Finn's ear. "Would it have made a difference?"

"I know that office, Ari. There are better ways to send a message than this." He dashed the rosette from Aristide's grip.

Aristide grabbed his wrist instead, pulling Finn into his body and curling over him, speaking into his neck. Finn's pulse beat against his lips. "Like what?" He let his tongue curl elaborately over the "L," striping the warm hollow of Finn's throat. "Why don't you tell me?"

"There's—there's a procedure . . ."

"Yes?"

"For agents like Cross . . . she—ah!"

Aristide's grip on Finn's wrist had gone very tight. He let go and pushed Finn back until his knees buckled against the sofa. "Go on," he said, settling on the floor between Finn's thighs. His fingers knew their own way around buttons and zippers, so he could stare Finn straight in the face. Desire made the boy's pupils into inkpots, swallowing the gray center and leaving only a halo of gentian around the black. "Go on; I'm waiting."

"Um. Cross is . . . she's inactive, but she's . . . on retainer. They call it . . . oh, perdition. They call it 'hobbled.' Like a horse." He swallowed, larynx bobbing beneath whey-pale skin.

"That means nothing to me." Aristide made small, slick circles with his thumb. Finn cursed. "Explain."

"She's not on an action." He spoke carefully, with long pauses in between his words. When he finished the sentence, he took a shuddering breath. "But they want to keep her close, in case they need her."

Aristide dipped his head, letting his breath out. His mouth was so close to Finn's prick he could feel the heat of it. "And?"

"They pay her expenses—" He choked. "She's got . . . she's got to turn them in at the beginning of the week. Every week. Please will you just—!"

"I still don't understand," said Aristide, pausing to put the tip of his tongue out, to taste Finn for just a moment, "what exactly this has to do with me."

Finn's hands jumped, fluttering close to Aristide's face, then curled into fists on his own knees. His words came out strung together, in a gasping rush. "Hobbled agents put in their reports at the beginning of the week. At the end we put out a memo about departmental expenses. *Somebody's* got to collate those reports and write up the memo. Plague take it, do you understand *now*?"

Inhaling, long and slow, Aristide could feel the air move across his palate. He knew Finn could feel it too, in more sensitive places. "Clever boy. So d-d-*devious*."

Finn made a strangled sound and clenched his fist in Aristide's hair, pushing desperately. But Aristide held his neck stiff, unwilling to be directed. He wasn't finished yet.

"Tell me . . ." he said, tipping his chin so his curls fell around his face, tumbling over Finn's spread thighs.

"Tell you what?" Finn's spastic grip stung Aristide's scalp.

"In between reports. How do we talk if something urgent comes up?"

"If it's on her end, she can—she—"

Aristide's hands, resting on the top of Finn's thighs, slid inward and up. "What can she do?"

"Ask for emergency funds." He shifted into the pressure of Aristide's hands, caught his breath. "She can put the message into the request form."

"And if I need to talk to her?"

There was a scrambling pause before Finn attempted to answer. "I—I—ah! I can—"

"You can what, Finn?" He let it come out sharp, and pulled his hands back. Finn slipped down on the sofa, chasing his touch.

"An audit," he said, desperately. "I can audit her expenses."

"Hmmm." Aristide kept his lips closed but soft, ready to give in. "Plague take it, what now?"

"Nothing," said Aristide, casting a treacle-slow glance upwards to meet Finn's pleading eyes. "Only I never knew accountancy could be so thrilling."

Finn's snarl was like a wounded animal's. "Oh, shut up!"

And though Aristide usually gave the orders in his own boudoir, this one he obeyed.

In the morning, Aristide rang for his breakfast from bed. Finn didn't wake, even when Ilse budged the door open with her hip and settled the tray over the folds of the duvet. The *Morning Telegraph* and the *Clarion* were folded into neat bundles next to a dish of shirred eggs and a pot of steaming coffee. Aristide poured himself a cup while Ilse folded Finn's abandoned trousers briskly over her arms. "I'll get these brushed and pressed," she said. "Looks like last night took it out of him. You ought to be a little gentler, Mr. Makricosta."

"Hmm?" Aristide looked up from stirring sugar into his coffee. "Oh, he'll be fine after he's had a bite to eat. Perhaps a few layers of powder before he goes out." Bruises spattered Finn's neck like crushed berries. Aristide swept his thumb across the red-and-purple skin.

Ilse cleared her throat. "Will that be all, sir?"

He nodded absently and picked up the *Telegraph*. Flipping it open, he scanned the headlines. Peace negotiations in Tatié—no doubt the Ospies were turning their attention to Amberlough, and Moritz had got the order to redirect resources from the border dispute. Aristide didn't bother with the article below the bold type—his spectacles were in the parlor. He set the *Telegraph* aside and picked up the *Clarion*. Though he kept his face from showing his surprise, the breakfast tray jumped across his knees.

"Sir?" Ilse lingered in the doorway, watching him.

"My spectacles," he said, deadly calm.

"Where did you leave them?"

"Parlor. By the wingback chair. Now, if you please." Even without corrective lenses, he could read the two-inch headline perfectly. *Culpepper in custody*. Plague it all, this was why he needed Cross in the Ospies. So he would know when things like this were happening. Squinting, he read painfully through the first paragraph, then cursed and threw the paper aside. If the *Telegraph* hadn't put this story on the front page, it meant they were in the Ospies' pocket. The editor had always leaned radical; with Hebrides dead and Acherby on the rise, he must be happy as a maggot in a midden heap.

Finn stirred, blinking sleepily from the depths of his pillow. "G'morning."

"I think you'll find it isn't." Before Finn could ask what he meant, Ilse returned. Finn blushed and buried his face in the linens. Ilse smiled at Aristide and rolled her eyes. He took his spectacles without returning her bemused expression. "Thank you. That will be all."

She slipped away. Aristide set the breakfast tray on the bedside table and turned to Finn.

"Your offer," he said. "It still stands?"

"Hm?"

Well, he hadn't even remembered his name, toward the end of the night. Of course he needed a little reminding. "You'll act as go-between in my communications with Merrilee?"

That erased the saintly peace sleep had leant to Finn's expression. He looked pained. "Ari, I—"

Snatching the *Clarion* from where he had thrown it, Aristide shoved it under Finn's nose. "I can't afford to be surprised like this again. There are things at stake I'd rather not risk."

Finn's eyes moved as he read. His mouth fell open. "Plague and pesteration . . ." Then, scrabbling into a modicum of comprehension: "But Cross can't possibly help you now. The Ospies will take the Foxhole. They're the ones who've had her arrested, I'd wager a year's pay."

"Of course they will. But Cross is one of them." A small secret to part with, and not dangerous to Cross, not now.

"*What?*"

A thought struck Aristide then. "Will they keep you?"

"Cross, an Ospie?"

"Finn, will they *keep you*? In the bursar, will they?"

"Um." Finn shook his head, like a horse scaring off flies. "Maybe not forever? But they can't exactly sweep the whole place clean and go without. I imagine it'll take a few weeks to even get down to us accountants."

"A few weeks is plenty of time. Finn, *please*."

There was a pause Aristide could have measured with a yard-stick. "I don't want to know what they say."

Aristide let out the breath he'd been holding. "I won't tell you. And all the messages will be in code." Gathering Finn into his arms, he petted a stray piece of orange hair back into place. "Perfect, b-b-brilliant boy," he said, kissing Finn's forehead. "What would I do without you?"

CHAPTER
TWENTY-FIVE

Cordelia went with Malcolm to pick up the ashes from a cremato-rium in the northeast quarter. The box was small, but no smaller than any of the others lined up behind the counter. Malcolm wouldn't carry it, so she tucked it under her arm.

"Glad we don't have to see his face again," said Cordelia, as they waited for the trolley. "The way they marked him up . . . I could hardly stand going to visit him in hospital. Those bruises . . ."

Malcolm made a small sound. She changed topics.

"We gonna do a funeral or something?" she asked. "For the rest of the folk at the Bee? He didn't have no family in Amberlough, that I knew." He shrugged, his shoulders stiff. "Queen's sake, Mal. Say something."

"What do you want me to say?"

"'Sorry' would be a good start."

"Sorry? What for?"

"Being an ass? There's more important things going on right now than you scowling over my knocking Tory. Jealousy ain't flattering, especially not now."

"You think that's why I'm bruised? Get your head out of your rear, Delia."

"It's just I can't help thinking we'd be a little kinder to each other if you weren't still so pinned about it."

"We really gonna talk about this right now?"

"When else? He was our friend—*our* friend, Mal—and now he's dead, and I ain't gonna scrap with you over him anymore, y'understand?"

He opened his mouth, but the trolley bell cut off whatever he'd been about to say, and he didn't try again.

They got on board and struggled to the back. Even with all the windows cranked wide, it was close and stinking and far too loud to talk. Instead, Cordelia let her hand drift toward Malcolm's. He curled his fingers into a fist, but she was patient. Eventually, he relaxed, and covered her knuckles with his palm.

"Where are we headed?" he asked.

"Let's go to mine," she said. "I got a bottle of gin—if you promise not to throw it across the room. We can light a couple of candles and set out an extra glass." She put her free hand on the little brown box, where it sat on her lap.

When Malcolm didn't say anything, she looked over to see if he was angry. But she caught him swallowing, hard, his eyes aimed up like he was wearing mascara and trying not to let it run.

Cordelia climbed out of sleep to the sound of frantic hammering on the door of her flat. She'd gotten a new lock, with a chain; it rattled on the freshly painted drywall. Cordelia hoped it wouldn't scratch. She'd fixed the place up nice with the cash coming in from Ari's tar.

Her mouth was dry, her eyes gritty. She hurt all over, with grief and sore muscles. Malcolm took up most of the small bed, forcing her to sleep cramped up. There was a reason they'd always stayed at his.

"I'm coming," she said. Her voice came out a rasp. The racket didn't stop. "Hang it," she shouted, "I'm coming! Don't break down the door."

Malcolm rolled over and rubbed a hand across his face. "Mother's tits. What time is it?"

Cordelia looked out the window and got a smarting eyeful of sunrise colors. "Too early." The banging on the door doubled. "I swear, I'll ram their own fist up their ass."

She grabbed the discarded sheet from the floor—the night had been hot, and Malcolm was better than a radiator. Wrapped in threadbare cotton folds, she shuffled to the door and undid the locks. Opening it a crack, she saw Tito in the corridor. His thin, brown face was pallid. A streak of soot marked one cheek.

"Tee," she said, through a yawn. "What're you doing here?"

"Mr. Sailer in?" he asked. "He weren't at his flat, and I didn't know where else to try him."

Springs creaked behind her. Malcolm called out, "Dell, who is it?"

"Mr. Sailer?" Tito bobbed like a buoy, trying to get past Cordelia. She stepped back and let him in.

"Tito?" Malcolm pulled a pillow over his tackle and sat up. "D'you know what time it is?"

"Sorry, sir, but you've gotta get down to the Bee. Now."

That was all he needed to say. Malcolm snatched his trousers from the foot of the bed and stepped into them, flinging modesty aside with Cordelia's pillow.

Cordelia took a little more convincing. She grabbed Tito's sleeve and pulled him to the dormer window. "Sit," she said. "I'll make some coffee." She had a gas ring now—a good one.

"Ain't time for that, Miss Lehane." He shook free. "Get your clothes on if you're coming."

"Will you at least say what happened?"

The card boy cast a nervous look over his shoulder, where Malcolm was tugging his undershirt over his head. "Blackboots," he said. "They busted the place up. Tried to set a fire."

Malcolm's head popped out of his collar. "What?"

"Didn't spread, sir." Tito held his hands up like he was apologizing. "Just . . . the marquee's a little scorched, and the lobby—"

Malcolm didn't wait to hear more. He snatched his watch and wallet from the bedside table and was gone. Tito scrambled after him.

"Queen's cunt." Cordelia threw her sheet aside and dressed in a hurry. On her way out the door, she took the small brown box of Tory's ashes and put it in her purse. He'd want to be there, if the Ospies hadn't got him burnt up first.

They took a cab. Malcolm never took cabs. This early, traffic was light and they reached the Bee just as the sun was coming up in earnest.

"Mother and sons," said Malcolm, letting the oath out like a breath he'd held too long.

Soot and smoke streaked the front of the building. The gilding had peeled from the double doors, showing wood burnt black. White paint splashed the wreckage with an Ospie quartered circle in a circle.

The fire had started in the ticket booth, where the glass was broken in the front. "Figure they threw it in that way," said Tito. "Lucia got here early to tidy up, and called the hounds. They sniffed around but weren't much help. Blackboots own 'em now. She rang up Ytzak after they'd gone. He says he thinks it were some stupid kids with a handle of white blinder stuffed with a rag. Anyone cleverer would've used gas or paraffin. He says."

"Does he?" Malcolm stepped across the gutter and crossed the footpath. He ran a thumb along the charred counter of the ticket booth. "Guess we're lucky, then."

"We gonna do the show tonight?" asked Tito.

"Don't be an idiot," said Cordelia. "Of course we are."

Malcolm didn't say anything.

CHAPTER

TWENTY-SIX

"Thanks for coming," said Cyril, after the waiter had left them alone with their drinks.

The dim lights of the Crabtree House slid over Cross's silvery hair as she nodded. "It's been a while since I dropped in at the Crab. It's changed a lot."

"You could say the same about most of Gedda."

She shrugged. "The seeds were there. Even before I went off. You know they were. Bless Amberlough, but our state takes first prize at putting the squeeze on. There were times I was glad to be in Liso—at least there everybody who wants you dead will say it to your face. Here it was all—"

"Shake with the right, shoot with the left?"

"You said it."

"Makes emigration sound like a treat, almost."

"Better hurry if you're going." She looked into her whiskey like it would solve her problems. "From what I hear, the Ospies are coming up with a whole set of travel restrictions. And I hear a lot; Veedge has me working Ins and Outs under the new management—you heard Koryon appointed him emergency director?"

"I heard." Cyril wondered how Van der Joost would feel about Cross's nickname. Probably nothing could really get him pinned, now that he had his little puppet in place. Koryon had been fourth in line for Hebrides's position, and only too happy to follow Ospie orders.

"Technically, I'm still hobbled," Cross added. "At least in the official Foxhole books. They said it's for my protection—never know who might be pinned over one of Ada's people switching sides—but I figure they just don't want to pay me regular."

"That's how they're doing mine as well. Expenses, no extra. I have to be on my best behavior; if the Ospies freeze my assets, I'm scratched." There were better reasons, but Cross didn't need to know them.

She made a face. "Bit-pinching fishwives. At any rate, Veedge brought in a bunch of new division heads. I'm under Nikita Krahe, doing customs and immigration. It's a mess for now—old protocol, new orders, lotta spats over nothing. But watch out when they get it ironed flat. Things'll change fast."

"How'd you end up with the beat?" Cyril asked. "Ins and Outs, I mean."

"I was doing it in Liso," she said. "Monitoring trade. Since the Spice War, it's been a murderer's game over there, and they've got some interesting folk fighting up through the ranks. Just looking after Amberlough's assets in rough country."

"So, what do you do now? Catch smugglers?" He kept his hands relaxed around his glass, but inside his brogues he curled his toes tight.

"Just assessing the climate. Veedge wants everybody acting nice when the primary reps take a dive and the Ospies level with new regulations. He says I might be up for a promotion if I do good work."

"'Take a dive'?"

"Yeah. Acherby's got a deal with them—they drop out of office and he consolidates power. They get plum positions in his new government."

"What's going to rattle folk? Besides the obvious."

"Cargo limits," she said. "Ospies want to keep Gedda's goods in Gedda. Anything going upriver is golden. But you try to take it out of the country, the taxes'll scratch you. Ask me, the salt folk are going to be madder at the riverboat captains than they are at the unionists. There'll be fights at the docks for sure."

"So public opinion isn't a big concern."

"Not on that front," said Cross. "But the rest'll be a tougher sell. It'll be a lot harder to travel abroad. Lot of paperwork, and you'll have to get bureau approval and a permit. Hope you weren't looking to go on holiday."

Cyril put his face in his hands. "Queen's sake."

"It's not her you oughta be praying to." Cross checked her watch—she wore it at the wrist, like a soldier. "'Tits. I gotta get moving."

He waved her off. "Of course. Thanks again. It's good to talk to somebody who clocks me."

"Anytime." She swallowed the last of her whiskey, picked up her briefcase, and slipped her straw cloche into place. "See you around."

On the top floor of a vacant office building in the northeastern quarter of the city, Aristide waited for Cross. He sat with one hip hitched up on a sawhorse, trying not to check his watch. He'd already looked at it twice in the last five minutes.

She was late. Very late. And he was worried. He needed the papers she was bringing, for himself and several clients, and he knew of no other way he could get them.

Just as he reached for his watch again, he heard the stairs squeak. He put his hand on the pistol holstered under his arm. Half a minute later there was a knock on the door—two long scratches, four quick taps. Cross's signal. Rendezvous four. It was her.

Aristide twisted the lock. The open door revealed Cross in a high-collared summer jacket and a cloche pulled low over her forehead. The brim cast concealing shadows across her face. He shut the door behind her and relocked it, then turned to watch her pick her way through construction debris. Though the streetlights would keep anyone from seeing in the single window, she stayed well away from the glass.

"You're late," he said. "What happened?"

"Friend in need," she said. "Cy wanted to jaw a minute. He looks like a steaming pile these days. Couldn't say no."

"My, my," he said, carefully bland. She was baiting him. "I have missed your . . . c-c-colorful language." If Cyril looked bad he was probably drinking too much. And not sleeping.

Cross snorted, like she hadn't noticed his evasion. "Nice to see you too, Mack."

"Mr. Lourdes's reports are very thorough," he said, relenting and kissing her cheek, "b-b-but there's nothing like the genuine article."

"Nice boy. Is all that bumbling and sweetness honest, d'you think, or an act? If he's putting it on, I'm impressed."

"I think Mr. Lourdes is much sharper than he seems, at first blush."

"Blush," said Cross, and laughed—a single, blunt sound. "He does do that. Anyhow, lucky you. Wish Cy'd play matchmaker for me."

"P-P-Please, Merrilee. I make my own matches."

"Speaking of." She pulled a crumpled cigarette from the pocket of her slacks and lit it. The pop of the struck lucifer was loud in the hush of the vacant building. Exhaling a draconian plume, she said, "He's come in rotten handy, Mr. Lourdes."

Aristide relished the irony. Cyril had used Finn so casually as an entrée to the Bee, after his own treachery had curtailed his freedom of movement. Now Aristide was turning the trick around on him. Slight guilt, of course, for making pliable Finn into a tool, but desperate times and all that. "Did you have any trouble getting the papers?"

Cross laid her briefcase across the sawhorse and unlocked the catch, revealing a slim folio and a block of gray putty. She handed the folio to Aristide, who flipped it open and smoothed his hand over the blank travel permits.

"They were a breath to snatch," she said. "There's loads of 'em lying all over the place."

"Gorgeous," he said. "Did you manage to get a good impression of the new seal?"

She pulled the block of putty from her briefcase. "You'll have to find a printer to work up a proper stamp. These don't have Krahe's signature or anything. I did get a sample, though. Do you have somebody with a steady hand?"

Aristide tucked the folio into his jacket. "I know just the person, yes."

———

Zelda Peronides had gone to ground in a warehouse at the worse end of the harbor—not far from Central's dockside facilities, if Cyril was to be believed. Aristide hoped she was keeping a low profile—with Culpepper in the trap, who knew what sort of person was running the Foxhole these days.

He found her in the foreman's office overlooking the echoing cargo hangar. She was living there, and hadn't left for days, probably. Balled-up napkins and grease-stained bags littered her desk. The smell of stale coffee and sleep sweat lingered in the stifling space. Zelda herself, usually so glamorous, had replaced her silk and velvet with a sleeveless jersey dress in brick red. The color would have suited her, if she weren't so wan and haggard.

"Ari, darling." She'd been chain smoking—her voice was dry. "How nice to see you. It's been ages. Not the best time, though."

He kissed both her cheeks. "I need to falsify some documents."

Her frown was delicate. "I'd like to be tactful, darling, but you're wretched at forgery."

"Yes, but your p-p-people are very good."

"Flatterer." She smiled, catlike, and a little of her old pizzazz sparked back into her expression. "They're also very expensive."

"Even for an old friend?"

"Times being what they are," she said, and waved an expressive hand rather than finish the sentence.

He lit a straight, nonchalant. Only when he'd breathed out did he say, "I'll b-b-buy the Keeler pearls from you."

She scoffed. "That's not payment."

"Oh, don't be unreasonable. You can't *move* them, Zelda! Even unstrung they're easy to p-p-pick out from the chaff. That shade of gold isn't exactly inconspicuous, and each one is the size of an eyeball." Only a mild exaggeration. "I'm doing you a favor."

"And what are you planning to do with them?"

"I'll wear them, for queen's sake."

"And get arrested? You saw what happened to Taormino."

"I'll wear them when I'm at home," he said. "Will you sell?"

"All right." She flapped her hand. "All right, yes, I'll sell. Your neck in the noose, not mine."

"My neck in the necklace, too." He stroked his throat, as if the pearls already hung there.

Zelda rolled her eyes, crazed with red veins that gave her expression a mien of lunacy. "What are my little scriveners copying out for you?"

He slapped Cross's folio onto her desk. "I'm not a fool. I know you'll keep a batch for yourself. I don't mind as long as you c-c-cut me in. And as long as you're *exceedingly* careful who you sell them to."

"I'm always exceedingly—"

"Zelda, I'm serious. They were difficult to acquire, and I don't want to risk anything like it again so soon."

She picked up the folio and let it fall open. As she read, her carefully plucked eyebrows—growing a bit ragged around the edges, now—rose by steady degrees. "Aristide Makricosta," she said, articulating each syllable like a scolding nursemaid. "How did you come by these? And what exactly are they?"

"The Ospies are going to introduce exit visas."

"They don't have that authority. The parliament would need to vote on it."

"Don't be thick," he said. "You know where we're headed. We'll be lucky if there's a parliament left by the next session."

"How many do you need?"

"Right now? A dozen or so."

She shuffled the pages of the travel permit back in order and slipped the folio into a drawer of her desk. "Anything else, while you're here?"

"Yes, as a matter of fact. Can you draw up some false identification for me?"

"You have about seven aliases already," she said. "What could you possibly need an eighth for?"

In fact, he had twelve, but what Zelda didn't know, she couldn't divulge. "It's not actually for me."

"Oh?"

He pursed his lips. "Zelly. Don't be nosy. It's so very c-c-common."

The look she gave him would've stripped paint off a ship's hull. "Who am I filling it out for?"

"The name doesn't matter," he said. "Just call him . . . oh, Darling. Paul Darling." He wanted to correct himself; that was a ridiculous pseudonym, and a whisker too close to the name he wanted to elide.

She slotted the paper into her typewriter and typed it out. Then, "Height?"

"Five feet, seven inches."

"Weight?"

Warm, fidgeting. Corded muscles softening with desk work. Zelda's gaze flicked up at his pause. "Eleven stone."

"Hair?"

"Blond."

She stopped writing, and stared at him. "Eyes?"

She'd figured it out. Of course she had. "Blue."

She bit her lip. It was already raw with anxious abuse, and split beneath her teeth. Then, incongruously, she giggled. "A roto print of Solomon Flyte. Oh, Ari. It's good to know you're a fool in love, just like the rest of us."

"Laugh again," he said, leaning close, "and I will p-p-positively *kill* you."

Her cruel smile faltered, and he thought she might believe him. Excellent; she should.

CHAPTER

TWENTY-SEVEN

By the time Ari found her in her dressing room, Cordelia was holding herself together with a twist of thread and a prayer. Builders had got the fire damage fixed in a few days, but there'd been more vandalism in the last week, and the cast was getting hassled every night on the street. No one wanted to leave the theatre at the end of the evening, and some of them were solving the problem by not coming in at all. The show was down to bare bones, with a dwindling chorus line and one too many repeats and old numbers.

Malcolm spent most of his time locked in his office, drinking the bar's ballast and going over his unhappy accounts. She'd just left him, half-drunk and all raging, to glue on her pasties and get ready for another grueling night. Ari didn't knock, and caught her topless with a bottle of gum in her hand.

"Need something?" she asked.

"You're crooked on the left," he said, tipping his chin.

She swore and peeled the swatch of glitter from her breast. "Ari, I ain't got time for your sass. Curtain's up in fifteen minutes."

"And you're not on for thirty. I'm the one who should be worried, and do I look it?"

"This is what I mean." She replaced the pastie, straight this time. "What's going on?"

"Will you pick something up for me?"

"Where?"

"P-P-Pyck Street. Do you know the Quayside Fish House?"

"Rough," she said.

"You're not afraid."

"No," she said. "I ain't." She hadn't been afraid of anything he offered her, not since Tory died. She was mad at the Ospies, at the blackboots who'd beat him, and even at Cyril, who'd only offered her a way in to keep her safe. So mad, she'd come to Ari and offered to go him one better than running tar. The letter to the women in the attic, that had been small change. Now it was coded messages, money, guns with the serial numbers filed away.

"There will be a man waiting for you at the bar. Red skullcap and waxed mustaches. He has your description."

"Got a little ahead of yourself. What if I'd said no?"

He cocked an eyebrow, exaggerated with dark paint.

"All right," she said. "You're right. But what, you busy with something else tonight? Please say it's more important than shuckin' your oysters with some soft-bellied blush boy. You still seein' copper top?"

"Off and on," said Aristide. "But no. I have an appointment with a client. Only time we were both free. Unfortunately, also the only time Zelda's man could make a drop."

"Peronides? So it's hooky I'm moving."

He paused to consider the question. With his garish makeup, and a stocking cap over his pin curls, he looked like a mannequin wearing a carnival mask. "I suppose it's stolen, yes."

"Leave it with Narita? The usual spot?"

"If you please. And ask her to wait with it. I'll be by, late, to pick it up." He turned to go, then stopped at the doorway and looked back. "Cordelia . . ."

"Yeah? What?"

"Thank you."

She shrugged one shoulder. "If you want."

He half-smiled and left her alone. As he walked down the hall, she heard him start to sing a scale: up eight, down eight, and then one-three-five-eight-five-three-one. His smoky baritone echoed through the thin backstage walls. Usually, he'd have had two or three other singers jumping in to sing harmony for warm ups. But he didn't rouse even one.

Cordelia faced the mirror and started in with her lipstick. Cyril was right: She'd have made a clever fox if she'd gone over. But she wasn't going to. Tory was dead, Malcolm was falling apart, and the blackboots had chucked a bomb into her theatre. Amberlough wasn't safe for stagefolk at night. The Ospies were picking apart everything she loved and knew and lived for, and she aimed to pick back.

The man with the waxed mustache bought her a glass of dark beer. They put on a good show of flirting. Leaning close, he put his arm around her shoulder and spoke into her ear.

"Hang your purse up."

She giggled and pushed him away. There were thief-proofed clips on the underside of the bar. Snagging the strap of her handbag in the clip nearest his knees, she let it swing over to him. When the bartender had his back turned, and the crowd was mostly facing away, he pulled a package from inside his jacket. He moved so smooth, so fast, she missed the moment it went into her purse.

He bought her another drink. They lingered. Then, he checked his watch and swore. "Wife's gonna hide me."

Cordelia pretended offense, and wouldn't speak to him as he left. She scowled over the last of her beer. The bartender gave her a sympathetic look. She left. The whole play took half an hour, at most, and then Cordelia was out the door with her handbag a damn sight heavier than it had been.

She didn't look inside. No point—it was wrapped up, and she didn't want to know what it was, anyhow. Just wanted to get it safe to Narita.

Pyck Street ran north to join up with South Seagate at the end of the trolley line. Cordelia struck out along the fringes of Eel Town, walking quick past cheap hotels, dodgy kebab joints, and brothels that catered to sailors who couldn't be assed to make the long trip north to the first precinct's regulated red light district. Most of the houses down here weren't licensed, and the ones that were did a lot of off-the-books business: kidnapped kids and foreigners. Crooked pimps had always slipped through Taormino's well-greased fingers.

"Hey you, copper top!" A drunk Niori seaman waved at Cordelia from a piss-stained doorway. "How much?"

She ignored the catcall and pressed on, wishing for a scrounging cabbie stupid enough to brave the dregs of the fourth precinct. Maybe she ought to have taken the shorter route, straight through Eel Town on Cane Street. Seedier, but maybe faster, and she might already be home.

Caught up in worrying, she didn't see the hound until she'd already run into him.

"Watch it, dolly," he said. "All that hurry won't do no good if you fall and break your skull." His truncheon whistled past her head, but long practice kept her from flinching. The hounds liked to snap at kids from the Mew, and kids from the Mew learned quick not to snap back. But they also learned hounds followed the smell of fear. Cordelia didn't give him anything to scent.

"I'll be careful," she told him. "Thanks."

When she moved to walk past, his truncheon struck her hard across the breasts. Hissing through her teeth, she stopped and waited.

"Hold on a minute. Which house are you from?"

"I ain't from a house," she said.

"So you're freelance? Let's see your license."

"I don't hire out," she said. "I'm just passing through on my way home."

"From where? You work one of them big ships on the docks? I doubt it. License." He grabbed at her handbag.

She snatched it back. "I told you, I ain't got one."

"So you're a hack." He said it so calmly, she didn't expect the blow. It slugged like iron straight into her belly. Her knees cracked on the pavement. As she fought to yank some air back into her lungs, the hound scooped up her handbag.

"How much you want?" she asked. No use trying to convince him she wasn't for hire, not now. "I just got off work and I got a stack stuffed in my garter. Take it all." *Just don't open the bag.*

"More'n my oysters is worth, pigeon pie. New commissioner's coming down hard on us that likes a little side dish with our roast."

Hidden by her hair, Cordelia cased the street. There weren't any other hounds she could see, and most of the whores and their hangers-on had scuttled when they clocked this one.

He popped the clasp and opened her purse. "Though maybe I'll have a look in here, just to find out what else's on offer. You was awful grabby about it. Something in here I shouldn't see?"

She launched herself forward, taking him out at the knees. Last time she'd fought she'd been a scrawny kid going after other feather-weights. The resistance she met when she went at the hound surprised her, and she bungled. He tilted to the side and tripped, but he didn't crash down like she'd planned. His truncheon struck the side of her head and things splashed white, bright as a powder flash. She didn't let go. Right at a level with his tackle, she opened wide and bit.

He screamed like a baby and lost his balance, fell backward and dragged her along. She was up, and yanking her handbag from him, but he managed another swing of his truncheon and caught her across the wrist. There was a crunch like gravel under tires. Cordelia lost her grip. While the hound recovered, she lashed out with her other hand and scratched him across the eyes, then scooped the bag up and ran dead into Eel Town, looking for a crooked alleyway to hide in. Behind her, the hound blew his whistle.

She made it half a block before his partner came running, with four blackboots at his heels.

Cyril slept better now, back in his own rooms on Armament. With the windows open he could smell the roses blooming in Loendler Park, and pretend it was just another summer. So he was dead gone when the lights came up, and couldn't claw himself awake before the foxes grabbed him.

He'd hauled a few targets out of bed in his time—he knew the routine. But the experience was different when he was the one blearily thrashing in a tangle of sheets and grabbing hands.

While he was still blinking, somebody snatched him by the hair and pulled him upright. He went limp and let them haul him, then lashed out with a sharp elbow and caught his assailant in the belly. Still blind, he dove for the foot of his bed and rolled free. The frame bruised his ribs.

Before he could stand, a second attacker landed a kick in the center of his body. He curled around the blow and felt his breath rush out.

"We'd prefer if you came quietly."

Cyril tried to stand, but the man who'd kicked him stomped him back down. He heard the crack of his skull on the floor like a distant gunshot.

"The boss just wants to ask some questions," said the first fox. He leaned over Cyril's bed, weight on his hands, head hanging. His words sounded strained with lack of air. When Cyril spoke, he sounded much the same.

"Well he could've asked, couldn't he?" He wanted to sit but stayed where he was, wary of another blow. "I'd really have preferred the telephone."

"Good evening, Mr. DePaul." Van der Joost had made himself comfortable in Culpepper's office. The desk was organized in a careful grid, and he'd replaced Culpepper's seat with a low-backed chair that displayed his ramrod posture to best advantage. Memmediv stood just behind him, looking unfairly poised for whatever ugly hour it was.

"Skip the pleasantries, Veedge." Cyril had the satisfaction of catching Van der Joost in a double-take, pale eyes flashing under paler brows. "Why am I here? What time is it, anyway?"

"Quarter past three." Not that anyone would have known from

Van der Joost's appearance—his suit was freshly pressed, his thinning hair combed neatly to one side. Cyril, on the other hand, felt rumpled and sandy-eyed. The foxes hadn't even let him dress—he had a lightweight mackintosh over his pyjamas, and that was it. His stomach still hurt, too.

Van der Joost held up a hand. "Mr. Memmediv, the packet, if you please."

Memmediv handed over a bundle wrapped in brown paper, tied with twine. The front was torn open beneath the binding, showing a slash of red.

"Recognize these?" Van der Joost set them on the desk, in front of Cyril.

The knot was tight, and Cyril struggled with it. Van der Joost slid a steel letter opener from his stationery box and sliced the string. Cyril thought he'd hidden his flinch, but Van der Joost's smile told him he hadn't managed it well enough.

Unfolding the paper, where it wasn't shredded, Cyril revealed a stack of documents. He leafed through them, reading names—none he recognized, but that didn't mean anything. These were false papers, versions of the travel permits Cross had mentioned. Each was marked "approved," in scarlet ink, with the newly modified national seal below. They must have gotten an impression of the stamp. Cyril might not have known the papers were forged if they hadn't been sitting between him and Van der Joost at quarter past three in the morning.

"Never seen them before," he said, pushing the pile away.

"So you weren't involved in leaking them to the black market?"

"You know me," said Cyril, forcing himself to lean back in his chair, relaxed. "You know why I'm here. Why would I jeopardize that?"

"Perhaps I don't know you as well as I thought. Reading a man's file does give one certain insights, but it sometimes fails to communicate the nuances of his character."

"You told me to toe the line; I toed it. I have done nothing but what you asked." He crossed his arms, drawing his mackintosh tight around his chest. Pinning Van der Joost with a bleary, small-hours glare, he added, "Frankly, I'm insulted by your suspicion."

Van der Joost gathered the papers up and tapped them against his desktop, straightening the edges. "But you understand it."

"No," said Cyril. "I don't. What does this have to do with me?"

"Shall I tell you who the police caught carrying these papers tonight?"

Cyril shook his head, bewildered. "A runner? I don't know."

"One Cordelia Lehane, with whom I believe you are associated in some capacity. Your . . . *mistress*?" Condescension coated the word like slime.

Damnation. It was satisfying, in a small way, to know Aristide had his own plans. But Cyril couldn't appreciate the irony of their mutual destruction; he was too busy scheming frantically, recalibrating his own strategy.

Cross worked Ins and Outs. Cyril would wager anything she'd ferried the original documents to Aristide. And he'd wager anything twice the foxes had hauled her out of bed tonight, too. If she'd been there in the first place.

Aristide and Cross were partners. And Cordelia was probably giving up everything she knew under torture. Pressure built behind Cyril's eyes. He ground his teeth against it, unwilling to give Van der Joost the satisfaction of seeing him weep, even in frustration. "I didn't know."

Van der Joost sighed, suddenly, and looked at Cyril with concern. "DePaul, I hope you're telling the truth. We had a very tidy bargain. I'd like to think you weren't fool enough to break it."

"I *am* telling the truth." Cyril leaned across the desk and looked Van der Joost full in the face. "I swear I am. If I can prove it, does our agreement stand?" If he could prove Cross's involvement without linking her to Aristide. If Cordelia didn't give away everything when they started sliding pins beneath her nails.

"If you can prove it, perhaps. But it will be tricky. And forget about the same thing for your *friend*." Van der Joost's tone lent the word a vulgar connotation.

Well. If Cyril could get out of Gedda, that was enough. Aristide obviously hadn't been banking on his help, and would have some sort of secondary plot in motion now that his first had come undone. He would get out safely. Cyril just had to save his own skin now.

"Memmediv." Van der Joost handed the pile of papers back. "Burn these. And tell Customs and Immigration to start drafting a new set of permits."

Memmediv glanced pointedly at the clock. "Now, sir?"

"Soon begun is sooner done."

"Yes, sir." He disappeared through the double doors.

"Are you going to hold me?" asked Cyril. "Because I'd really prefer my bed to a cell."

"You're free to return home," said Van der Joost. "But not, I'm afraid, completely at liberty."

"House arrest? How am I supposed to—?"

"You will be allowed to move about the city, with an escort. But I wouldn't try anything *adventurous*, if I were you. We will ask you back for further questioning, at which point you may present any evidence in your favor, as regards your involvement in this leak."

Cyril's grin felt tight. "I can't wait."

CHAPTER

TWENTY-EIGHT

Aristide's plans changed rapidly after the leaked papers were discovered. Who knew how long Cordelia would hold up under Ospie interrogation? He needed an out that didn't require international travel. The scheme was already laid for his exit from Amberlough, but he lacked a destination.

He had been scouting places where his money would be worth triple and out of reach of anyone who might like to freeze his assets. Places no one asked expatriates many questions. Now he was hemmed in. In such a bustling international port, the Ospies would be on watch for fugitives. The northern border, though . . . Now there was an opportunity.

So he visited a lawyer in the southwest quarter, a discreet, squirrel-faced woman who specialized in inheritance law. Aristide had never sent so much as a postcard home after leaving Currin. But he'd been an only child—there was no one else to take the farm after his father died. Which he had done, according to the records, almost five years ago. The waiting period was nearly run out, but not quite; the state of Farbourgh hadn't claimed the farm as abandoned property. It still belonged to Aristide. Or, more accurately, to Erikh Prosser.

Along with the deed, the lawyer procured a copy of Aristide's birth certificate. After all, he couldn't identify himself as the beneficiary of his father's will under his stage name. The lawyer labored under the misapprehension that Aristide was acting as a factotum for an ill and absent friend. He did not disabuse her.

At home, he buried the papers under a pile of books on his bedside table and traded his town clothes for a jersey robe and slippers. Shoulders hunched around his ears, he went to pour himself a very stiff drink indeed. Though he was not in a habit of drunkenness, this was a special occasion.

He was happily on his way to forgetting who he really was when Ilse knocked on the parlor door and announced Finn had arrived. "Show him in," said Aristide, rising unsteadily to pour another glass of brandy. His limbs moved half a beat more slowly than his brain. Liquor splashed across the bar.

"Ari?"

"Finn, darling. *Do* come in." The brightness of his own voice pained him.

"I've got a message from Cross." Even Finn's frown managed to be endearing. He was like some kind of spaniel puppy, all liquid eyes and sweetness.

"I'm sure it's nothing good." Probably it would be the last. She wouldn't stick around the Foxhole after this. "B-B-Brandy?"

"Ari, are you drunk?"

He tried to stopper the decanter and missed by half an inch. Cork squeaked against crystal. "Whatever gave you that idea?"

"You're slurring a bit." Finn took one of the glasses from the bar and sipped. "This is too good to waste on you in your state. Come on. Let's get you to bed."

"Oh, please," said Aristide, desperate for distraction. "Let's."

Finn was briskly nursemaidish, despite Aristide's amorous attentions. As the consequences of several large brandies in quick succession made themselves apparent, those attentions lapsed into idle fingers and occasional kisses. Aristide's eyelids felt heavy. The room was very warm.

"Would you like to see Cross's dispatch?" asked Finn.

"Lady's sake, no." Aristide put his hand across his eyes. "Not until I'm sober. I look abysmal when I weep."

"I can go, if you want to sleep it off."

He curled his fist around the hem of Finn's waistcoat. "No. Stay. I want you to stay."

Finn sighed. "Well, would you like me to read to you?" He shifted, reaching for the pile of books on the bedside table.

"Oh," said Aristide, remembering what was beneath them. "No, no please—"

But it was too late. "Who's Erikh Prosser?" Finn's pronunciation of the tricky given name was flawless: the high "i" at the front of the mouth, with the pharyngeal consonant at the finish. Most people, even northerners, would have gone for plain "Eric."

"Client of mine," Aristide extemporized. "Owns some land up north where I have . . . interests."

"Good luck to him, hanging on to it."

"What do you mean?" Aristide peeled his eyes open and looked up at Finn, who was scanning the deed to a rocky scrap of meadow in the Currin Pass.

"Erikh's a Chuli name. You think the Ospies are going to let the Chuli hold onto any of their assets? Won't even let them stay in Gedda, most like. Push them across the border to Enselem, who don't want them either."

"Well, nobody's exactly t-t . . . treated them with kindness," said Aristide. Weighted with brandy, his tongue bungled the false stutter. "The Chuli. Don't see why they ought to expect any different now."

"I suppose you would know, wouldn't you?"

"Pardon?" He rolled heavily onto his back. Finn had set aside the paperwork and was watching him.

"I clocked you long ago." Finn drew his fingers through Aristide's loose curls. "You're an half-caste, aren't you?"

"Mmm." It wasn't meant as an answer—he didn't want to talk about it. But Finn went on.

"You can pass for Hyrosian, under your stage name. But your skin's a little too tawny, and you've got a Chuli nose." He traced the feature of interest with a fingertip. "And sometimes those northern curses slip out. When you're upset. Or . . ." He turned pink. "Other times."

Aristide gritted his teeth, furious to have years of reinvention stripped away. Suddenly, his verbal affectations—the conscious stutter and retroflex consonants, the aspirated glides—seemed glaring: clear markers of the work he'd put into eliding his native burr.

When he put on his performer's smile, it felt like baring his teeth. "Darling." He reached up and patted Finn's cheek. "You are absolutely *wasted* in the bursar."

Finn turned his head and kissed Aristide's knuckles. "I always did toy with the idea of applying for a transfer. Can I use you for a reference?"

"Feel free," said Aristide, sourly. "Though I doubt it'll do you any good."

"Oh, that's all right." Finn wrapped his arms around Aristide's shoulders and didn't seem to notice how stiff they'd gone. "When they sack me, I'll come work for you."

Finn left a manila envelope on the bedside table, overtop the property deeds. When his head stopped spinning, Aristide slit the seal and pulled out a copy of Cross's latest expense report. Applying the key got him three terse lines.

reps gone tmrw. blown but im out. dont ask favors.

He crumpled the paper and climbed out of bed holding it in his fist. The grate in the bedroom was cold, and in the parlor. He stalked to the kitchen, where Ilse was putting together a plate of smoked salmon and sliced pears—a late lunch before Aristide went down to the Bee.

"Peckish?" she asked, winking.

"Peevish," he corrected. "I need to use the range."

She stepped aside. He turned on the gas and let it hiss for a moment, then lit the burner. Cross's code withered into flame-edged, blackened curls. Aristide let the scraps fall onto the stovetop.

"Oh, that's all right." Ilse side-eyed him over her cutting board. "I need to clean it anyway."

"Sorry." Cowed, he swept the ashes into his cupped palm and dropped them in the wastebasket.

She handed him his plate. "Go on. Get out before you muck the whole place up."

As he ate, he turned Cross's message over in his mind. This piece of news—*reps gone tmrw*—meant it was time for him to leave as well. Tonight would be his last night at the Bee. It was, perhaps, foolish to take to the boards with so much at stake. But if he was going to say goodbye to Amberlough, he was going to do it right.

He made a vital telephone call, to one of the *Clarion*'s distributors, and passed on a code word. Then, with lunch dispatched, he dressed and went to catch the Temple line. He wasn't wild about the prospect of his commute. Over the last month, he'd been squeezed between blackboots on the trolleys one too many times, suffering snide comments and derision and, on one memorable occasion, an Ospie pissing on his shoe.

Temple Street was pasted from Baldwin to the bay with ugly propaganda posters. A few of the storefronts had gray-and-white bunting over the doors, or the quartered circle within a circle, white on a field of slate. Several of these had suffered vandalism. One was burnt black, the windows burst into sparkling shards across the footpath.

Repairs on the Bumble Bee had the marquee looking even sharper than before. Aristide didn't know what Malcolm had paid, or if he could afford it, but suspected that the answers were "too much," and "no."

He went through the front of the house. Malcolm didn't like them to, but Aristide had never cared. When the black-and-gold weight of the doors swung shut behind him, he stood for a moment in the dark foyer, breathing stale smoke and the scent of mingled perfumes—the smell of the audience. His audience.

In the theatre proper, he tipped his boater to Ytzak behind the bar. Then he retreated to his dressing room to prep and warm up.

Sitting at the mirror, haloed by a half-circle of brilliant lights, Aristide stared at his reflection. His mother's Chuli nose. His father's jaw. He looked harder, putting his face closer to the glass. A loose curl, falling past his chin. Plum lipstick over a practiced, gap-toothed smile. Faint laugh lines at the corners of his eyes, earned rather than inherited.

Finn had stripped away every artifice of Aristide's constructed self, tearing through the ribbon and tissue like a child opening his Solstice presents. It left Aristide raw and furious. Cyril had always treated the package with more deference—never even shaken it. Perhaps because he already knew what lay inside, didn't care, and respected—preferred?—the character Aristide chose to present.

This man in the mirror was the man Aristide wanted to be. A man he'd made. A man who would be gone tomorrow, and not to some breezy foreign clime with red sand beaches.

He lifted an ivory comb from the cluttered makeup table and swept his hair down over one shoulder. Glossy curls twined between the teeth, dark as chestnut cases. Avocado oil every night, the careful teasing out of knots . . . He worked hard to keep it soft. And still, no gray. As he wound each pin curl and fixed it into place, he drew the coils through his fingers and tried to fix the sensation in his memory. It had taken years to grow it out. If it got this long again, he doubted it would be as thick and dark and free of silver.

Once his stocking cap was fixed in place, he opened a tube of white grease paint and slicked it over the contours of his face. Then powder, to set it. Talcum rose in ghostly tendrils from the pouf. Thin, black eyebrows drawn over the angles of his own. Rouge, high on his cheekbones. Red paint in a perfect bow to accentuate thin lips—long practice let him shape his moue with little effort.

As he pressed the corner of his second set of feathered lashes into place, he heard a distant shout. A crash. The thin walls of his dressing room bucked and shuddered. Wiping tacky fingers on a tissue, he stood and took a step toward the door. It flew open just before he touched it, and he staggered back.

"Raid!" Liesl's knuckles were white on the door frame. "They're looking for ballast, but they'll take anyone they want. Go, now."

He didn't need to be told twice. Liesl peeled away and ran down the corridor, hammering on doors and flinging the chorus from their communal makeup table. As the chaos swelled, Aristide shucked his dressing gown in favor of the sweaty black jersey he wore for dance rehearsals. The straw boater covered his stocking cap and shadowed his painted face. He jabbed a pin through the hat to hold it in place, and to use as a weapon in a pinch.

Cast and crew buffeted him from one side of the corridor to the other until he started throwing elbows. They didn't have nearly what he did to lose. There'd be hounds at the stage door and the front of the house. That left one option. He took the stairs to the costume loft three at a time, hauling himself up by the bannister. It was dark up here, and stuffy. The ceiling sloped to a row of long, grimy windows below the eaves. They were open onto the alley to catch the sea breeze.

Aristide had cased the Bee long ago for good escape routes—his sideline had never been a safe one, even at the best of times—and these windows were his insurance against capture.

He was halfway out and hanging onto the gutter when the hounds burst into the backstage corridor. He couldn't see it, but he heard it. As the whistles shrieked and the stagefolk screamed, Aristide bellied onto the scorching tiles of the roof.

He came down to the street near the Heyn, jumping the last few yards from the bottom of a fire escape off Waxworks Road. Across the river, he stopped in a rickety teahouse to wash his face and make a few telephone calls.

The proprietress, an Asunan woman with a seamy face, knew Aristide by sight, but it was her nephew with whom he'd made his arrangements. Said nephew was absent, and it took several minutes of frustrated mime to make her understand that he needed the telephone.

After he hung up on his final factotum, he found a steaming cup of honeyed white tea at his elbow. Redolent with ginger, it cleared his head and sinuses.

When the telephone rang with a return call, he snatched it with the speed of a striking viper. "Yes?"

"They're on the up-and-up," said the man on the other end. He was a mid-level bureaucrat with connections to the ACPD. "Really looking for ballast; word is the Ospies tried to buy Sailer out but he wouldn't take the money. So they got him another way."

"Damnation."

"They're not onto you yet," his contact continued. "Not as far as I know."

Relief poured down his neck and back, uncoiling knotted muscles. Cordelia was still holding out. "Thank you. Excellent. Good work."

"Don't mention it. But listen, if the blackboots have Lehane and she breaks, they might act without me hearing."

"I understand." But it wasn't enough to tense him up, not yet.

Waiting for his second call, Aristide had a leisurely game of mahjong with the old auntie. They used his bobby pins as betting sticks. She trounced him, and he ended the game with his hair springing wildly around his head. They split a second pot of tea. The telephone rang. This time, Aristide's pace was less frenetic. He levered himself up from the brass-topped table and went behind the beaded kitchen curtain to answer. "Did you get him?"

"Sure did." The woman sounded pleased with herself. "But his bail was pretty dear."

"You'll be reimbursed. Did you take him to mine?"

"Yeah. The maid didn't seem too pleased."

"I'm sure she isn't. Thank you, darling. You've been a treasure." This time, he hung up first. Before he left, his hostess served him jellied plums. He thanked her—it was the only Asunan he knew, outside "hello," "goodbye," and a few choice curses. They bowed to each other in the doorway and he left her as the moon rose above the Heyn, turning its currents to chrome.

Hunched in Aristide's wingback chair, Malcolm Sailer clashed with the decor. He had a split lip and a bruise blooming high on one cheek. A tuft of black thread showed where one of his buttons had been torn away.

"So these *are* your digs," he said. "I was startin' to wonder who'd bailed me out."

Aristide swept across the parlor to the bar. "B-B-Brandy?"

"Yeah." Malcolm held out his hand for the snifter.

Aristide obliged him. "Drink that down. I'm just going to go and ch-ch-change." He ditched the jersey in his bedroom. It was grimy from his cross-town adventures, and would need a wash. Or would have, if he ever planned to wear it again. When he returned to the parlor, it was in belled silk culottes and a smoking jacket.

"Fancy." Malcolm's efforts had lowered the level of his drink considerably. "Fit right in with your surroundings now. Like one of them bugs that look like sticks."

"I think I'll choose to interpret that as a c-c-compliment."

Malcolm set his brandy on the coffee table and put his head in his hands. "I'm scratched, Ari."

"So they found the ballast?"

"You don't even know the worst of it yet."

"They tried to b-b-buy you out," said Aristide. "I heard." He sat on the sofa and tucked his feet up. "You should have taken the money. Shall I ring for some supper? To be honest, I'm absolutely famished."

Malcolm's face went pale, but he swallowed his shock. "I don't remember the last time I ate." He picked his brandy up again— considered it. "Not a real meal, anyhow. I think Delia put a couple eggs in me . . . yesterday? Say, you ain't seen her, have you? She was running late to the show tonight, and then the raid . . . You don't think she got drug in, do you?"

Aristide fanned his nails across the upholstery and examined his manicure. "Malcolm . . ."

"Only, I know she was doing errands for you here and there, and if they caught her with anything I don't wanna think about what might have happened."

Aristide took a deep breath through his nose. "Malcolm, Cordelia . . . well, she was moving more than tar, this last week or two."

Malcolm looked up from his knees. "What do you mean?"

"She'd started carrying messages, and a few other things. Since T-T-Tory died."

"And?"

"She was caught ferrying sensitive documents between two of my contacts. She's been in custody since late last night."

The stillness that crept across Malcolm's brawny shoulders was a warning. Seconds later, the snifter popped between his hands and he started bleeding on the carpet. Aristide shook out the hand- kerchief from the pocket of his smoking jacket and handed it over.

"Where is she?" His fists clenched around the cloth and turned it red. "Get her out."

"I can't," said Aristide. "I don't know the right people anymore, Malcolm."

"You got me out."

"That's d-d-different and you know it. That was money. This is statecraft."

Malcolm let his head fall back. His dark hair left an oil stain on the upholstery. "Mother's tits. Everything. They're taking every-thing."

"Like I said: You should have j-j-jumped on the buyout when they offered it."

"You think I haven't figured that out by now?" Blood seeped between Malcolm's fingers and dripped onto his trousers, disap-pearing into the weave of the dark wool. "But Ari, that's my life's work. Don't you understand?"

"Believe me," said Aristide, suddenly immensely tired. "I do."

"I can't afford the fines for stocking ballast," said Malcolm. "They know I can't. I wouldn't sell out, so they're gonna ruin me."

"What do they want the Bee for?"

"Picture house. Showing jingo flicks."

Aristide waved an indifferent hand "No one will come."

"That's not the point. They just want us shut down. Doesn't matter if they bring in punters. They don't need 'em." He uncurled one hand and hissed as sticky wounds reopened. "Poor Dell. Queen's sake, Ari, ain't there nothing you can do?"

Aristide shook his head. "Again, I'm sorry." It was true. He'd come to rather like Cordelia. To trust her. And here she was ar-rested on his account, probably holding out like a skint blush boy to keep him safe from the Ospies. Must be, or he'd be behind bars by now as well. He didn't like to think what they'd have to do to make her talk. "You have no idea how much."

"Don't I?" Malcolm stood and balled Aristide's handkerchief between his bloody fists. "She was my girl." He tossed the red-splotched rag onto the coffee table and stalked out.

Aristide stared at it, bereft of words. Finally, his growling stom-ach spoke for him. He lifted the little glass bell from its bracket and rang for supper.

CHAPTER
TWENTY-NINE

Cordelia's wrist was swollen up, purple and black, and she could feel the edges of crushed bones grinding just beneath the skin. Nobody had offered to splint it. Nobody had offered her water, though her voice had given out with answering the same questions, over and over. Nobody would even tell her what time it was. There weren't windows, wherever they'd brought her, but from the sticky dryness of her eyes and the exhaustion making her head pound, she guessed it had to be well into the next day. Maybe evening time. She hadn't gotten more than half an hour's sleep together, and usually less.

But she hadn't told them anything, because she wasn't a bird. One sleepless night wouldn't get her singing.

They hadn't put her in a cell, at least. Just a room with four bare walls, a chair, a table. Men came in, asked questions, left. The light stayed on. Sometimes she heard footsteps in the corridor, sometimes muted voices.

She was just starting to nod off again when the door opened and a new sculler came in. Not one of the stout, clerk-faced types that had visited her so far. He was tall and on the thin side, hair clipped close. A badly set break had put his nose crooked. He wore a plain, dark suit, jacket unbuttoned over a rumpled white shirt. No waistcoat. When he pulled the jacket off, his sleeves were already rolled up past the elbow.

He stood across from her, leaning in. Didn't say anything. She could see the sinews of his forearms ridged beneath the skin. And she saw them tense, seconds before he turned his hands and hooked his fingers underneath the table's edge. Cordelia scrambled from her chair, but not fast enough. The falling table struck her knee. She reached out to catch herself, forgetting her broken wrist. When she came down, her vision went white. Pain sent electric sizzles through her body.

Opening her eyes, she realized she was lying on the floor, curled up like a baby around her throbbing arm. The thin man stood over her. Down here, she could see the scuffed toes of his boots, and guessed there was steel behind the leather. She thought of her sister, whose man had got her in the belly with boots like these, and the long three days it had taken her to die.

"You gonna ask me any questions?" She squeezed her eyes shut. It was easier to sass him if she couldn't see. "Or you just gonna start kicking?"

She heard hobnails scrape on wood. Gritting her teeth, she pulled into a tighter ball. The blow was a long time coming, but the thin man would've been good on stage: He knew the value of anticipation.

She held out until the knife. It was a good run, she thought. Might have given Ari time to get out of the city, even.

Sometime after the thin man broke her nose, but before her left eye had swollen shut, a dumpy sculler in a gray suit came and sat across from her, his hands folded primly in his lap. He looked like a pudding, pale and soft, his thinning hair combed neatly over his scalp.

"Hello Miss Lehane," he said. "I'm Konrad Van der Joost. My colleagues tell me you've been somewhat reticent during your questioning."

She didn't have the energy to talk smart, so she didn't say anything.

"Your silence is unfortunate, for us and for you. We are attempting to bring a criminal to justice, and I'm sure you are more than ready to go home."

Home. She didn't rotten have one anymore. Not in this city. Not with people like this in charge of things.

"Why don't you tell me who gave you those papers," he went on, "and we can all get exactly what we want out of this."

"Why don't you stroll off," she said, summoning the last of her attitude, "and leave me with my friend here." She jerked her chin at the thin man, who stood at Van der Joost's shoulder. "We was getting along just fine."

"Regrettably, Miss Lehane, I will not be strolling anywhere. But please don't let my presence interrupt your rapport with Rehimov." He waved the thin man forward with two fingers. Cordelia braced herself, sinking down into the solid foundation of her chair. She latched her good hand under the seat, holding on, but Rehimov grabbed her wrist and yanked her fingers free. One of her nails splintered and she yelped. Van der Joost pursed his lips.

"Now," he said, as Rehimov pinned Cordelia's hand to the table. "You have ten fingers, and each finger has three joints. That's . . . well, it's thirty, technically, but the last joint of the thumb is always difficult, or so Rehimov tells me. So let's say twenty-eight. I thought we'd start with your good hand, and only move on to the broken one if we have to."

Cordelia realized what he was getting at, and tried to stand. Rehimov sat in her lap, pinning her to the chair, her arm lodged against his ribs. She could feel the grain of the wooden tabletop under her palm, and scrabbled at it, breaking more nails. Rehimov put his own hand over hers, stretching her pinky finger flat. A cold, thin weight came down on her first knuckle.

"Twenty-eight joints," Van der Joost repeated. "That's twenty-eight chances to answer one simple question. Who gave you those papers?"

She reeled back, gathering momentum, and slammed her head into Rehimov's spine. He grunted and gave, but not enough. She was trapped.

"Miss Lehane," said Van der Joost, irritation creeping into his voice at last. "Patience is not one of my strongest suits. If you think I am toying with you, I suggest you revisit that assumption."

She couldn't see Van der Joost nod, or give his silent order, but she felt Rehimov tense, saw his shoulders move. The tip of his knife slid into her knuckle, separating the bones and cutting neatly through the tendons. He did it so quickly, the first of her twenty-eight chances was gone before she even started screaming.

When she subsided into sobs, her cheek resting between Rehimov's shoulder blades, her tears soaking through his shirt, Van der Joost cleared his throat. He had mastered his irritation, and spoke as calmly as he had before. "So, Miss Lehane," he said. "Tell me: Who gave you those papers?"

CHAPTER

THIRTY

As he prepared to leave, Aristide opened his tall glass parlor doors onto the balcony so he could listen to the city's anger. He had friends down there. Lovers. Associates. As he made his final circuit of the flat, he stopped and stared at Baldwin Street.

The crowd had not begun as a riot; it had started with puppets, costumes, songs. Students and artists and actors, the denizens of Baldwin Street and the theatre district, giddy and frightened, acting out. But the comical effigies they had burned earlier were at the bottom of heaped bonfires now, beneath smoldering mattresses and motorcars. Aristide stood at the back of the balcony, listening to the chanting and catcalls. Across the street, a woman in lace knickers and a defaced Ospie jacket—how had she gotten ahold of that?—hefted a gray-and-white banner and hurled it across a pile of burning detritus. A rock careened out of the crowd and smashed the windows of the dress shop behind the conflagration.

Aristide was on the second story, near enough that the protestors could throw things if they wanted: a fact he was counting on.

"Mr. Makricosta?" He turned and saw Ilse lingering at the parlor door. Her face had a sick green tinge around the lips. "Sir, there's some folk come to the service entrance with a . . . well . . . they asked for you."

"Ah. Yes. Go to the kitchen, Ilse, and stay there. I'll take care of it."

She nodded and fled.

Two men with shipyard muscles waited at the bottom of the service stair. Between them, they carried a laundry basket. From the way their arms were straining, it weighed nearly as much as either of them.

"Come in," said Aristide. "Can I help you carry?"

The three of them got their burden up the stairs and into Aristide's flat with no small amount of cursing. He directed them with jerks of his chin to the parlor, where they set the basket down.

"Did you have any trouble," panted Aristide, "getting here from Pellu's?"

"Did we?" One of the men wiped his forehead with a striped kerchief. He had a cut over his eye. "Had to fight our way through like it were a war."

"Thank you," said Aristide. "Wait here for just a moment." He went to his office and came back with two fat envelopes. "You were never here, understand?"

"We know the routine." The second workman tucked his payment into his canvas jacket. "In, out, and nobody the wiser. Good luck with 'im, whatever you're planning."

Together, they wrestled the linen-wrapped contents of the laundry basket onto the sofa. Then, the two men left and Aristide was alone with . . . well. He pulled back the sheet and stared into a face almost like his own, slack with death.

About a week ago, a friend in the Royal Arms Paupers' Hospital had tipped him off to an anonymous Chuli corpse, which he'd claimed and passed on to a colluding undertaker, one Mr. Pellu. The dead man matched Aristide's height and weight, roughly, and his bone structure was similar. Charred beyond recognition, that was all they'd need. He didn't have the same charming gap in his teeth, but Aristide's dental records were not on file anywhere the Ospies would find them, and neither Amberlough's coroner nor her assistants had intimate experience with his smile.

Though Pellu had kept the corpse on ice, a week of death had done its work. The flesh around the man's eyes had sunk into his sockets, and a faint smell of corruption clung to him like rank cologne. But the fire would take care of that, and burn away the gaping knife wound in his gut.

He arranged the dead man on the sofa and, when his body was propped upright, paused to touch his cheek.

"Thank you," he said, feeling only moderately foolish. The poor creature had probably been stabbed anonymously in an alley and dumped for the night nurses to find. A senseless death, but at least now it wasn't entirely without purpose.

Aristide slipped out of his dressing gown—Niori silk embroidered with explosive peonies—and wrapped it around the dead man's shoulders. His slumped body was otherwise naked, stripped of any identifying clothes or effects. If anything remained after the fire, it would be scraps of Aristide's robe.

In the kitchen, Ilse was washing the breakfast dishes. Aristide almost laughed. He started opening drawers, shuffling through foreign implements. Finally, she put down her rag and rounded on him.

"You're making a mess," she said. "What are you looking for?"

He bit the inside of his cheek. "Shears."

"Why?" She wiped her hands on her apron, leaving wet splotches.

His hand moved, unconsciously, to the braid hanging over his shoulder. He forced it back to his side, but she'd seen him.

"Ah. I'll get my sewing kit."

She passed him on her way out, and he caught her arm. "Thank you. And . . . I'd avoid the parlor."

In less than a minute, she was back with a comb, a pair of bright silver shears, and a smaller set of thread snips.

"You should've asked," she said. "If you try to do it yourself, it always comes out crooked."

"I don't need anything fancy," he said. "Just . . . take it all off."

She lifted the braid and he shut his eyes, as if that would stop him feeling the bite of the scissors. But it didn't come.

"You're sure?" she asked. His scalp prickled as she hefted the weight of his hair.

"Just do it, Ilse. I haven't got much time."

She *tch*ed. "No need to be so snappish." Then, without ceremony, she sliced clean through his plait.

He sent her home after that, with another one of the dwindling stack of fat white envelopes from his safe.

"It might be for the best if you got out of the city for a while," he told her. "You have an aunt who lives in the weald, don't you?"

She nodded, and pocketed the cash.

"Go to her. Don't come back if you don't have to, not for a month at least. Are all your things out of the flat?"

Lifting a voluminous handbag, she said, "This is the last of it. Most I took home on my night off."

"Good girl." He looked around the office once more and squeezed her shoulder. "Now, stroll off. Do you have a gun?"

She shook her head.

"Do you want one?"

She shook her head again, more violently.

"Well, be careful. Take a hack if you can find one. There's more than plenty in there for the fare. Now, go."

And she did.

Left alone under the high ceilings of his flat, Aristide changed into a cheap suit of itchy brown wool—the kind of thing a farmer might wear, on his one big trip to the city—and secreted a snub-nosed revolver in his pocket.

In his scuffed white canvas duffle, there was a heavy overcoat, because the nights in Currin would already be cold, and getting colder. An oilskin, for the relentless rain and mist. Other clothes and sundries. And at the very bottom, sewn into the lining, a rope of golden pearls he couldn't sell but couldn't bear to burn. The rest of his jewels had been converted to more liquid currency.

He emptied his safe into the sack as well—a few more envelopes of cash to use as needed. An emergency roll of large bills wrapped inside a few disguising smaller denominations. And a thin packet he slipped carefully against the side of the duffle, curving it with the canvas so it wouldn't wrinkle.

He set the bag by the service stair and went into the kitchen. Ilse had ordered a drum of paraffin, at his request, last week. Aristide dragged it out into the parlor, where his doppelgänger rested on the sofa. With a heave, he toppled it over at the dead man's feet. Oil soaked the carpet, wicking through the thick white pile.

Aristide dragged the barrel across the room, letting the last of the stuff drain out. Outside, glass broke. He could hear the crash over the noise of the crowd. Then, the high keening of an ACPD whistle. He had to hurry, before the hounds and the mob really got into it.

He left the barrel by the sofa and went to the bar. Set behind the brandy and port, there was a bottle of white blinder—grain alcohol. He tucked it under his arm, settled into his secondhand boots, and stopped to look around one last time.

The corpse in his flowery dressing gown reclined against the arm of the sofa as if asleep. Above him, crystals on the chandelier swayed in a breeze off the street. A bouquet on the coffee table dropped a petal. When Aristide breathed deep, hoping to catch the last, lingering scent of flowers, of cigarette smoke and perfume, all he smelled was kerosene.

A gunshot in the street shook him out of his reverie. He went down the service stair, shouldering his rucksack, and paused in the alcove to light a cigarette and open the bottle of liquor. Wrinkling his nose at the fumes, he took a scrap of calico from his breast pocket and stuffed it into the open neck of the bottle. Then, pulling a broad-brimmed felt hat low over his eyes, he went out into the alley, and from there, to the street.

He held a hand to his face to keep his cigarette safe from careless elbows. It didn't stop the crowd from stepping on his feet or shouting in his face. At the south end of the block, a cordon of ACPD officers fought their way forward with truncheons and heavy coshes. Aristide headed for the center of the street. There was a makeshift podium built from a chair set on stacked shipping pallets, where students had been making wild orations earlier in the day. Aristide looked around swiftly and levered himself up. Exposed for an uncomfortable moment to the gazes of the rioters and the police, he lit the rag of his makeshift bomb with his cigarette, took aim, and hurled it over his own balcony.

Blue-and-orange flames exploded between the decorative wrought iron. One of the hounds blew a whistle, but Aristide was already down off the podium and pushing his way through the crowd. He didn't stop until he hit the end of the block and could duck around the corner. Pressed against the sun-warm brick of a kebab shop, he looked back the way he had come. Fire filled the windows of his flat and licked out the open doors, reaching for the third story. Pity he couldn't have warned his neighbors. But un-canny foresight might have made his subsequent tragic death sus-picious.

The mob thinned out off of Baldwin Street proper. Looters were at work already, shattering shop windows and hauling off their spoils. Aristide kept one hand hooked in his jacket pocket, ready to reach for his pistol if anyone looked at him wrong. No one did; they were all preoccupied with their politics and thievery.

Loendler Park was worse than he'd hoped. He should have known. Radicals of all persuasions loved to use the bandstand for their speechifying.

Still, he found the girl he was looking for. They'd agreed to meet here, pending Aristide's signal: the call he'd made yesterday afternoon to his contact in the office of the *Clarion*.

She was pressed against a crooked tree in the center of the ramble, her bony back flush with the bark. She kept her shoulders crunched up near her ears, as though she wanted to sink into her own body like a tortoise and hide. The noise outside the tangled branches was incredible.

He slipped in beside her and nudged her with his foot. "Two parts rotten day, ain't it? Shame to waste weather so fine."

She jumped, her face slack with panic. She didn't recognize him; good. Before she could run off, he grabbed her wrist and crouched down so they were face-to-face. "Darling," he said, letting the curling rhythm of the central city come out once more. "It's me. The gentleman from Baldwin Street. Remember? You brought me a matchbook. We made a deal."

"I'd come meet you if Miz Kay told me, and only if she used the password." She swallowed and looked around them at the crowd. "Damnation though mister, why today?"

"Because no one will see me hand you this." He put his rucksack between his knees and pulled out the thin packet, sealed tight and tied with string. The paper seller reached for it.

"Ah-ah." Aristide tugged it away. "Instructions first. The gentleman who gave you the matchbook. He buys his papers from you, yes?"

She nodded.

"Put this packet in tomorrow's paper. Not when he buys it, understand. You *must* plan ahead. He's being watched. Don't be ostentatious."

"What?"

"Don't make a show out of it."

"All right, but what if he don't buy tomorrow's paper?"

"Put it in the next day's paper. And the next. And so on, until you've passed it to him."

She crossed her arms. "What's in it for me?"

He took out one of his white envelopes and stacked it on top of the packet. "There's more in here than you'll see the rest of your career, if you stick to selling papers."

She reached out again, with a filthy hand. He jerked back. "What a wretched habit," he said. "Why don't you wait to be handed things?"

"Aren't you in a hurry?" she snarled. "What else do you want?"

"Hit me."

"What?"

"Hit me. Here." He pointed to his right eye. "Careful, though. Don't hurt yourself." When he showed up at the train station to book his passage north, he wanted to present a bewildered bumpkin fed up with manic city life. *This is really the last straw, sir, I tell ya.* Besides, a black eye would further obscure his identity.

But the paper seller didn't ask for reasons. Before he had a chance to brace for it, her bony knuckles landed an expert blow between his cheekbone and his eyebrow. He fell to his rear on the pavement.

"Very good," he said, when he'd recovered the power of speech. It had been a long time since anyone struck him.

"Thumb on the outside," she said, "and punch from the shoulder. I ain't some kind of powder puff."

"No one said you were." He stood, clearing his weeping eye, and handed her the packet and the envelope of cash. "Go back home, or wherever it is you live. Get off the street until things clear up."

She nodded, and was gone. He didn't worry about whether she would follow orders. She was ambitious, and stupidly brave. The streets of Amberlough were peppered with children like her. He'd been one, once—a little older than the paper seller, but that just proved her precocity. Cyril would get his message.

CHAPTER

THIRTY-ONE

After Cordelia told them everything she knew, a doctor-type came to bandage her bleeding stumps—she'd lost two fingertips before she folded.

When the sawbones was done, he gave her a shot of something that knocked her out for a few hours. She was struggling to sit up, cursing at broken ribs and bruises, when the hinges of her door squealed. Flinching, she hissed at the pain.

"We're transferring you." It was a man she hadn't seen before, and probably wouldn't see again, the way things were going lately. A new face every time they sent for her, and none of them kind.

"Come on." He waved her out the door. "I got more coming in every minute for questioning, with the mess outside. We need all the room we got."

Blackboots thronged the corridors, jostling her until she went dizzy. From behind the placketed iron doors she could hear muffled shouts and pleading. She hobbled along like an old lady and hoped there was a lift. She couldn't have managed stairs.

They put a hood over her face before they took her outside. Through the burlap, she got a good gulp of sea breeze, flavored with rancid garbage and . . . smoke.

"What's burning?" she asked, but didn't get an answer.

The bumpy ride in the back of the van took an age. Each time the tires struck a pothole, waves of nausea broke over her, from the drugs and the pain. The driver's maneuvering slacked off the longer the ride went on. Shackled in the back of the transport van, she could hear raised voices from the driver's compartment, but couldn't make out what they were saying.

Something struck the side of the van, once. She startled away just as they took a sharp turn, and sprawled across the floor. Her broken ribs burned, but the lingering remnants of morphine kept her from caring much. The purple lump of her shattered wrist was beyond regular hurting by now. Everything from her shoulder down felt like she had molten metal on her bones. All she wanted was sleep. The smell of smoke followed them as they drove, growing stronger, then fading, but never leaving the air entirely.

It took so long to get where they were going, she was surprised when her minders opened the rear doors and she found they were still within the city limits. Outside the Department of Corrections, in fact. Then again, maybe the place they'd brought her from was somewhere out in the weald, or on the sea cliffs. They could have been keeping her anywhere.

"City's gone crazy," said one of her minders, talking over her head to his partner. "Brains leaking outta their ears, you'd think."

Cordelia remembered the blow to the side of the van, the smell of smoke. She risked a look over her shoulder, back toward the central city, and saw the orange glow of fire against the night sky.

"Eyes front, copper top." One of her minders shoved her forward.

Whatever was going on in Amberlough, she got a tiny glimpse of it inside the DOC. Uniformed officers scrambled around the corridors, screeching orders at one another. Telephones rang at desks and behind doors. She wanted to cover her ears and lie down, but her two guards moved her along, winding through crowded, noisy hallways until they found the proper office.

She didn't have a good sense of what happened next, but it seemed whoever they needed was out, or busy. Time skipped oddly as exhaustion and agony overtook the drugs she'd been given earlier. Whenever she blinked she felt as if she'd missed whole minutes. Eventually, after a flutter of her eyelashes, she found herself sat in an uncomfortable wooden chair in a noisy corridor, cuffed to a cold radiator by her good wrist. Her severed fingertips throbbed with her heartbeat. Both her minders were gone.

A noisy group of officers came shoving down the center of the hall, scrabbling around one man like a litter of hungry pups. He held his shoulders as if he was sick of their assault, his hands up high to ward them off. Light from the overhead sconces flashed off his spectacles. She recognized that face, lean and hawklike, ashy with fatigue.

He'd already passed her, and was still walking. She had to grab the chance. "Commissioner!"

He stopped. She couldn't see if he turned—he was hemmed in by flunkies. They started to move on again, and she shouted his name, more desperately this time, with less formality. "Alex!" Her voice broke on it. He'd never recognize her. Not after one night of drinks and flirting. Especially not with her face rammed in like this.

Dry, cool fingertips touched her jaw and she jerked back, not realizing she'd closed her eyes.

"Ma'am? Ma'am, are you all right?"

One of the hounds was tipping her face up to catch the light. She squinted, and saw the shine of Müller's spectacles over his shoulder.

"Alex," she said again. Müller tipped his head, staring at her with a wrinkle between his eyes. He didn't remember. His flunkies started ushering him away. Cordelia stuck out her foot and tripped him. One of the officers kicked at her ankle and she cried out.

"You." Müller's voice was cold. "Don't you dare. Officers in this force do not strike prisoners. Not on my watch."

Cordelia bit back a sob of gratitude.

Müller crouched at her feet. He took off his spectacles and looked at her, so close she could smell the bitter remnants of his aftershave.

"Ah," he said. She looked into his eyes. "The Kelly Club. You drank a dry white, didn't you?"

Cordelia, who couldn't remember what she'd poured down her chute, nodded. "Yeah. You tried to slip your hand up my skirt under the table."

A flush crept past his collar, and he glanced at his hangers-on like he was daring them to say something. None did. "Cordelia, right? What happened?"

"Whole mess of things."

He ground his teeth, looked around at the people scuttling down the corridor, at the officers waiting for him to stand up, and said, "Let's go someplace quiet, and we'll get you sorted out."

It sounded like a pickup, but she was miles beyond caring.

———

"I really can't spare the time," he said, shutting the door behind him as they ducked into a borrowed office. "Those daggers they were looking at me . . . all deserved."

"What's going on?" she asked, sinking gratefully into the leather chair behind some police captain's desk. "Why all the ruckus?"

"You mean you don't know? I'd have thought you'd been out in the worst of it, looking like you do."

"I ain't been out since . . . late last night?" she guessed. "Or maybe the night before? What day is it?"

He didn't answer. "What'd they cart you in for, then, if you weren't brawling?"

Rubbing her good wrist against her dress, trying to erase the memory of the steel cuff Müller's deputy had cut away—and more, the thin, cold edge of Rehimov's knife—she spoke to her knees instead of to him. "Some big stuff. I been—I don't know where. The Ospies wanted to find out what I knew."

A muscle in his jaw tensed, but he didn't press her further.

"What are you doing at the DOC?" Her question sounded odd in the silence. "I thought this was just for stamping and stocking the criminal set. Getting 'em ready for the trap."

"Headquarters was . . . compromised." He put his hands in his pockets. "I told you. There's rioting everywhere. Three of the primary representatives stepped down. Acherby's assuming control of the whole country."

"Mother and sons." She let her head fall against the back of the chair. "He can't."

"He did. Nothing we can do about it."

"Swineshit." She sat straight again, breathless with the effort but filled with anger. Müller just looked at her with badly shuttered pity and she fell back, winded. "I don't wanna believe that. Bet you don't either."

"You know what I want?" He sat on the corner of the desk and stared across the room, talking to a cork board pinned with notes and scraps of colored paper. "I want a force that isn't sour through with crooked hounds. I want a state that works the way the law says it should."

"And you think you're gonna get it? Is this it?" She lifted her good hand—what a joke, good hand, when she was missing pieces off it—to indicate the chaos of the riots, then spread it wide to show her chopped-up fingers. Ragged spots of red showed through the cotton bandage. "Is this?"

Müller went green, finally figuring out her arrest hadn't exactly been by the book. "Of course not. DePaul promised—"

"Oh I'm sure he did." She spat. Strings of pink saliva slashed across the green leather desktop. Müller, to his credit, didn't flinch. "If you believed all that, you're gonna get what's coming to you."

He stared at her, fierce and unblinking. When she didn't shrink, his face turned tired and he stood.

"Come on," he said.

"Where?"

"I can put you in a cell overnight—"

"You rotten think you will."

"You didn't let me finish," he said. "They're going to transfer you, all right? Into the city system. I can get you out on parole tomorrow. But you don't want to get mixed up with the scullers coming in off the streets tonight. I'll put you on your own, safe, and in the morning I'll handle everything."

She lowered her chin, chastened. "Thanks."

He took her out into the hall and flagged down a junior officer. "Put her in one of the small cells. Alone. Have somebody splint that wrist, and get her a clean smock, too."

The hound nodded and took Cordelia's good arm. Before he could haul her off, she grabbed Müller's sleeve.

"How come you're doing this for me?" she asked.

"What, it's not enough?" The line of his shoulders went taut. "You gotta ask questions?"

She shrugged her least-painful shoulder. "Just . . . you gave me that line about crooked hounds. And now this."

"It's like you said." He took off his spectacles and wiped them clean with his handkerchief. "I'm not going to get what I want, so . . . I better do what I can."

True to Müller's word, Cordelia was out of the trap by morning, let free on parole she had no plans to obey.

The Station line took her straight from the DOC to Mosley Row, by way of the capitol. Crumbling gashes of bare earth marked the sloping green lawn. A unionist banner hung from the front of the building, but someone had set fire to a corner, and fingers of soot climbed the gray field to streak the quartered circle within a circle at its center.

When the trolley neared the river, she looked up at Bythesea Station. Dawn touched the white marble of the terminus and turned it crimson. As she watched, a pennant unfurled from the top of the station arch, its gray folds colored by the bloody light of sunrise.

The walk up Mosley nearly killed her. She hurt so bad she hardly noticed the sideways looks folk gave her on the footpath. Small wonder they did. When she reached her tenement and saw herself reflected in a ground-floor window, she looked like she'd been rumbled by an angry stevedore in the full swing of a boozy rage.

She realized she didn't have her keys—the Ospies hadn't given back her handbag—and she had to ring the buzzer for the land-lady. The old woman opened the door a bare few inches and peered over the chain lock. When she saw Cordelia, all the blood went out of her face. "Mother and sons."

"Got caught in the riots," Cordelia said, but the old woman was already shaking her head.

"They come two nights ago and tossed your rooms. Girl, I don't know what you been up to, but I can't keep you around."

"Miz Ess . . ." Cordelia held out her hands, cut up and splinted. "You don't understand."

"I don't wanna," she said, eyes going round. "I'm sorry, but I don't want nothing to do with it."

"Can I at least come in and get my stuff?"

The old lady wrinkled her nose in consideration. "Fifteen minutes, all right? Then I don't want to see your head nor tail no more."

"Thank you."

The door shut, and the chain rattled against the lintel. Ms. Ess opened up and stood back to let Cordelia pass.

She hauled herself up the four flights to the attic, pausing at each landing to suck painful breaths into her broken chest, knowing she ought to be lying down. In fact, when she got up to her flat—door broken down, or she wouldn't have been able to get in—the first thing she did was collapse on her bed. Stuffing puffed out of gashes in the mattress. From her horizontal vantage point, she cased the damage.

Her little gas ring was trampled into bits. Her three chipped plates were broken, and her mugs and glasses. Clothes lay muddied and wrinkled across the bare wood floor. But they hadn't found anything, because there was nothing in her flat to find.

She wondered what her dressing room at the Bee looked like. Probably about the same. Maybe worse. But there was nothing there either. She didn't keep the hooky around long enough to store it, or the tar.

It wasn't until Ms. Ess came clumping up the stairs and hammered on the remains of the door that Cordelia realized she'd dropped off. Her mouth tasted like she'd eaten something foul scraped out of an Eel Town gutter.

"I said fifteen minutes." Ms. Ess came into the flat and moved to roust her out of bed. Cordelia jerked away from her touch, but the landlady was more careful than Cordelia would have given her credit for.

"It ain't about you, hon." The older woman picked through the mess on the floor until she came up with a crocheted grocery sack, and started cramming clothes into it. "You've always been an all-right tenant. But the last thing I need's blackboots tearing up my building. You understand, don't you?" She tucked a final pair of stockings into the string bag and handed it to Cordelia. "There. I'll try and tidy it up once you're gone. If you find you're missing anything important you can always send a wire."

Cordelia's head sank to her chest. A wire. Stupid sow. She might as well invite Cordelia back into her house. But all she said was, "Thanks, Miz Ess." Holding her string bag hooked over her elbow, she went down the stairs as slow and wincing as if she were an old lady herself.

CHAPTER

THIRTY-TWO

Van der Joost had the shades drawn in his office against the morning sunlight on the harbor. Despite the scorching weather, he wore his plain, dark suit like a uniform.

By contrast, Cyril's blue seersucker was stained at the front with oil, dusted with jail dirt, and past the point where wrinkles added to its charm. He'd slept in it, on a hard bench in some suburban lockup, wondering why they hadn't dragged him straight to the Warehouse. The ride down to the Foxhole through burnt and bloodied streets had given him some idea. He was almost glad they'd arrested him before the riots really got under way.

His minders hauled him in front of Van der Joost's desk. He'd had the same two goons on his case since yesterday morning—Moore and Massey were the names he'd wheedled out of them, though the comedic alliteration made him suspect pseudonyms. They were all right—he'd played a few hands of cards with them in his cell.

"Rough night?" he asked, casing Van der Joost's dark circles and sagging face.

"Ah, Mr. DePaul." Van der Joost closed the report he had been reading and set it aside. "Have a seat. Coffee?"

He was dying for some, but he shook his head. "I'm sure the stuff around here's gone down in quality since your people took over. Let's just talk, and then I'll get out of your hair."

"Very well." He selected a stack of papers from his inbound mailbox. "Our staff at the interrogation facility extracted some intriguing information from Miss Lehane."

"Did they?" Under the table, Cyril balled his fists.

"She implied that at one time you were . . . *intimate* with her employer, and seemed to think this intimacy may have continued until recently." He said the word like he was picking it up with tweezers.

Cyril wanted to reply with something facetious, but his mouth had gone dry. "She was mistaken."

"We can discuss that later. For the purposes of this investigation, your precise activities with Mr. Makricosta are irrelevant. We're more concerned about his access to sensitive government materials."

"I don't—"

Van der Joost rode over him. "Naturally, we would prefer to question Mr. Makricosta himself about his acquisition of the travel permits."

"Naturally."

"Unfortunately, he was killed in yesterday's . . . disturbance."

"Oh." He should have drawn a breath, but forgot. His next words came out a little too forced, airless. "What a shame."

"But we must press on with the investigation," said Van der Joost. "Don't you agree?"

"Of course."

"Let's begin with the obvious. Did you pass the papers to him?"

"No. It had to be Cross."

"Preliminary investigations suggest they used a middle man."

"Konrad, please. I didn't even know this was going on. I haven't—hadn't seen him in weeks."

"But you *were* assisting each other. Lehane says he put the two of you in contact; that he paid her to act as your companion. Surely you felt an obligation to reciprocate."

"I'm a very self-interested man."

"Are you? Lehane says you tried to turn her, to keep her safe. And what about that second set of papers, for your . . . friend?" He knew, and Cyril was undone. Van der Joost kept asking questions, but really, it was already over. Some of the questions, Cyril would have preferred not to answer, but he did. Aristide was dead. What harm could these indiscretions do him?

Under all of it, Cyril wondered if Aristide's death wasn't really an assassination. The riots would have been an excellent cover. And despite what Van der Joost had said about preferring to interrogate Aristide himself, maybe the Ospies had decided he was more trouble to them alive than dead. That they could get their information elsewhere. From Cyril, for instance.

When the questions were done—two hours later, nearly, and he was starving and thirsty and wished he'd said yes to the damn coffee—he walked stiff-backed out of Van der Joost's office and went straight to the washroom, so fast Moore and Massey had to jog after him. Locking the door in their faces, he collapsed onto the toilet seat and folded over his knees, weeping noiselessly, drawing jagged breaths through his mouth.

For two minutes, he let himself go on in a silent, mourning

howl. Then—though he could have stayed all afternoon with his cheek resting on the cool tile—he washed his face at the tap and combed his hair back into place. His eyes were rimmed with red, but they'd been like that for weeks. He couldn't remember the last time he'd slept through the night.

No, that was a lie. It had been months ago, in early spring, wrapped in moiré silk while a rainstorm peppered the windows of Ari's flat.

He clenched his jaw to keep grief at bay.

His minders stuck him in a locked, empty office while Van der Joost figured out what to do with him. Cyril didn't hold out much hope—he'd probably end up in the Warehouse, with his knees broken, telling them the same thing he'd just told Veedge. Eventually, they'd kill him and dump him into the harbor.

The lock rattled and Cyril looked up wearily, already gathering himself for his inevitable, ignominious demise.

"Good morning, Mr. DePaul," said Finn. "Do you have a few minutes?"

Cyril blinked, sure he was hallucinating. Lack of sleep combined with terror had caused stranger things than the magical appearance of an accountant, bearing coffee and buns. "Um. I suppose."

"Good." Finn looked back over his shoulder and said, to Moore and Massey outside the door, "I'll just be a moment. You can go ahead and lock the door."

He set the tray down on the bare desktop in front of Cyril, who threw away pride and tucked in. The coffee was bad, but the buns were filled with raspberry jam.

"How did you get in?" Cyril asked, when he was done eating. He cupped the mug in his hands, letting steam warm his face.

"Cross was passing most of her communiques through financial correspondence. I told them the Office of the Bursar wanted to ask you a few questions."

"You're sharp," said Cyril. "Why are you really here?"

"You've heard about Ari, haven't you?"

Cyril nodded, stiff-necked.

"I saw a picture of it this morning," Finn went on, "in the *Clarion*. There's a whole spread in the center roto—photographs of the riots. His building, burning up like a Midwinter bonfire. I called around—coroner said they'd identified his body."

Looking across the oily black surface of his coffee, Cyril felt equally burnt and bitter. "So?"

"Well I went down there, didn't I? Wouldn't you?"

"Of course I wouldn't!" He pushed the breakfast tray away, suddenly nauseous. "He's dead, Finn. What did you think you could do?"

"Look, who told you he'd died?" Finn leaned across the table. "Was it someone who knew him?"

"No." In spite of himself, Cyril heard an edge of curiosity creep into his voice. "No, it wasn't. Why?"

"You don't honestly think he'd die in such a spectacularly stupid way, do you? Burnt to death in a riot, sleeping on his own sofa? No. He had to get out of Amberlough. And now, no one's going to look for him."

Halfway through Finn's theory, a tinny whine started up in Cyril's ears. It grew until he could hardly hear what Finn was saying. "Stop," he said, part to the noise, and part to Finn. "Stop it right now."

"He's alive, Cyril. The body . . . there's no gap in the teeth."

Cyril took shallow breaths, trying not to imagine the blistered lips, pulled back from a white grimace. "One." He held up a finger. "You're insane. Two, if this is true—which it probably isn't, see number one—you shouldn't be telling anybody. Least of all me. Why *are* you telling me?"

"I thought . . . I thought you'd want to know. I'd kenned you two were sparking, or used to. It seemed the decent thing to do."

"That's not all. Nobody in this city does things just because they're decent."

"What an awful thing to say."

"It's true. So tell me why you're really here."

A flush crept past Finn's collar, climbing to his face. "I—I need your help. To get away from Amberlough."

Cyril put his elbows on the table and his face in his hands. "I can't believe we're talking about this. You do realize I was just arrested, and will probably end up executed for treason? How can I possibly help you?"

"Ari said you might be able to, if I ever needed it." He lowered his voice and leaned across the table. "I need to get out of the city. But I need false papers."

"And how am I supposed to get you those?"

"You know people! Tell me who to talk to." Finn's eyes were wet and angry. "I don't know why he didn't tell me. About the fire."

"People who fake their own death usually don't tell anyone," said Cyril. "It defeats the purpose of the exercise."

"It's just . . . I know he can't have left me here. Not after—"

"After what?" Cyril knew his sneer was ugly; he could feel it pulling at the muscles of his face. Did Finn really think Aristide loved him enough to spirit him away from Amberlough?

But Finn shook his head. "Listen, I'm not trying to travel abroad or anything. Just up north. I think he's in—"

"Mother and sons, don't tell me!" Fear twisted Cyril's guts into a knot. "Finn, if he's really alive, the last thing I want to know is where he's hiding."

The accountant cringed, turning redder. "Sorry! I'm sorry."

"No. *I'm* sorry. I can't help you. Goodbye."

Finn pushed back from the chair and knocked on the locked door. It swung open, but before he could leave, Moore sent him back in for the ceramic mug and plate.

"Don't want him getting crafty on us," said the goon, and laughed.

"We're taking you home," said Moore, when they finally came to fetch him. "Don't think I like it, but with the scullers they brought in yesterday, there's nowhere to put you. And they don't want you dead yet."

"Well, that's a relief." Cyril stood and tugged his jacket straight. "Shall we?"

On the drive they passed street cleaners hosing stains and litter from the pavement. The gutters ran with charred garbage and who knew what else. Ground-floor windows gaped glassless onto the street, and divots marred the trampled lawn of the capitol. When they pulled up out front of his building, he looked across the street at Loendler Park. Ugly graffiti marked the Sergia Vailescu Arch, and footprints flattened the flowerbeds around it.

The paper seller leaned against the granite, her back to the slogans. She had a sack of copies of the *Clarion* hanging at her hip and more stacked by her feet. She squalled out the headlines— *Riots sweep city, hundreds in jail,* as if anyone needed to be told.

"Let me get a paper before we go up," said Cyril.

Massey looked at Moore, and Moore looked at Massey. A shrug passed between them. They followed him across the street, breathing heavily on the back of his neck. The paper seller looked about ready to bolt, but Cyril put on his brightest smile and knelt next to her.

"I've got correct change this morning," he said. When he reached for his pocket, he saw Moore and Massey do the same.

"Why don't you pay for my paper," he told them, over his shoulder. "If you're that nervous."

Massey narrowed his eyes, but Moore put a hand on his shoulder. "He's right."

Good to see all those late-night card games had worked their magic. At least they trusted him this far. He handed the girl his money and she reached for the bag of newspapers under her arm. Shuffling quickly through them, she selected one seemingly at random from the center. But the way her hand had lingered, the stroke of her fingers along the folded newsprint . . . She'd been *counting*.

The weight of the paper still surprised him. There was something hidden in it, stiffer than the cheap gray pulp. When he glanced up, the girl's face was a closed door, unrelenting in its indifference.

"Stroll off," she told him. "I got sheets to sell."

Cyril had to wait at the threshold with Massey while Moore swept his flat for guns, knives, and other sundries, but eventually they let him in.

"At last," he said. "I'm dying for the toilet. Excuse me?"

Massey followed him but thankfully stationed himself outside the door. Cyril took his newspaper in, giving his guard a sheepish shrug.

"Leave the door unlocked," said Massey. Cyril rolled his eyes but followed orders. He flipped the lid of the toilet back for an authentic clack of porcelain, then lowered it more quietly and sat with the paper on his knees.

There was indeed an impressive center spread of riot photos. Bleeding faces, broken windows and there, in the upper left corner, a shot of Aristide's block of flats ablaze.

Set against the glossy black and white of the rotogravure was a thin packet, tied with string. He untied and unfolded it, hoping the crackle of paper sounded like turning pages.

Inside was a manila folder, and in the folder were several documents. The first was a handwritten letter. He read it through but left it sitting where it was, as if touching it would be some kind of contract. He scanned past the final lines and dropped to the complimentary close—more than complimentary. It was the hardest part of the letter to read. And Cyril wished, with a fervor that surprised him, Aristide had ever said the words out loud.

Only when he had read the letter a second time did he pick it up, skimming his fingertips along the edges of the paper. Behind it was the document Finn coveted so keenly: ID papers, and an exit visa under a false name—a name that wouldn't send up flares at the train station. *Paul Darling.*

He wondered if he'd need to sign anything, if he should start practicing.

Without any conscious decision, he had started planning his escape. He made himself stop, put down the papers—*Five feet seven inches, ten stone, blond hair, blue eyes*, that was *him*—and think.

Something about it bothered him. Not about the packet from Aristide—the papers were perfect in every detail, and the letter, well. . . . But something Finn had said scratched at the back of his brain like a tabby cat, trying to get in.

I don't know why he didn't tell me. I know he can't have left me here, not after—

Not after what? Their affair? He'd assumed that was what Finn meant. Assuming was bad technique. Still, even Culpepper would have conceded that Cyril had had a harrowing few days; he wasn't in peak condition. Only now, with a modicum of hope restored to him, feeling halfway human again, did he realize his error.

Finn wasn't talking about the affair. He was talking about something significantly more important. Something he'd done for Aristide, that ought to have earned him a place in Aristide's escape plan.

Cross was passing most of her communiques through financial correspondence.

Preliminary investigations suggest they used a middle man.

It was elegant work, and it must have been Finn's idea. Aristide wouldn't have known the intricacies of the bursar well enough.

The secondary implications of this revelation seeped into Cyril's clean astonishment like oil from a ruptured tanker.

Finn was a loose cannon. If he'd buttonholed Cyril at Central to reveal Aristide's faked death and plead for false papers, he was blind and stupid with fear and infatuation. Clever codes and tradecraft didn't mean he wouldn't hang himself scrambling to get out of the city. He was already under surveillance; the Ospies would figure out something was askance. Queen's sake, as soon as crosstalk started up between the departments, and it came out Finn had been jawing with Cyril, the foxes would scent blood.

There was another piece of paper beneath the ID papers. Cyril slid the stack of documents aside and picked it up. He read the first line and panicked, unsure where to put his eyes. He clenched his fists and balled the note up. Edges of the crumpled paper bit into his palms.

All he'd seen was *5 a.m. northbound from Bythesea*, and then fragments, farther down: *friend will meet you*, and *by car from there*.

Instructions. Not a location, but enough to put Aristide in serious danger if Cyril read them and talked. So he didn't read them.

Finn knew where Aristide was. Knew exactly. Under torture he would give it up, and they *would* torture him. Cyril, on the other hand, knew nothing except what Finn had told him: north. And that wasn't enough, or shouldn't be.

He flushed the instructions, folded up the paper around the false ID, and washed his hands. Out in the hall, he yawned, hugely—not even faking it.

"Do you mind if I turn in?" he asked. "I don't think I've slept in three whole days."

"Makes my job easier," said Massey. "Go ahead."

CHAPTER

THIRTY-THREE

Cordelia went to Malcolm's place. There was nowhere else for her to go, not really.

He lived between the train yards and the wharves, not too far from the end of the Seagate line. By the time she got there, the promise of the red sunrise had played out. A front piled up over the harbor, lashing the Spits with whitecaps and lightning.

She let herself in and sat at the bottom of the staircase to catch her breath. It took her a good long while to make it up the two flights—longer than it had taken for her to do twice the distance back home. When she knocked on his door, she was seeing spots and shivering. He didn't answer. She banged again, and called out his name.

There was a drawn-out silence. She slid to the floor, crumpled against the door frame. "Malcolm Sailer," she said, her voice squeaking in her worn-out throat. "Open this rotten door or I'll know why."

Nothing.

Cold, slippery fear slid through her exhaustion, masking her pain. She reached up with her shaking, bandaged hand and tried the knob. It twisted easily, and the door swung open.

Nobody in this part of town left their door unlocked.

Clawing her way upright, Cordelia staggered into Malcolm's flat. It wasn't a big place—three rooms, and two of those barely more than closets—so the smell hit her fast. Butcher-shop stink: iron, copper, salt. A sour trace of shit.

The door to the bedroom was closed. She took a step toward it, but caught a sight out of the corner of her eye and turned.

In the kitchenette, Malcolm leaned back in his chair like he'd passed out. His mouth hung open, and there was an empty bottle on the table. A shred of her felt relief—he'd just been drinking, probably lost hold on his bowels . . . But she wasn't that stupid.

Closer up, she saw the cabinets behind him were spattered red. His right hand hung limp where the revolver had dragged it down. The gun lay half-in, half-out of a puddle of congealing blood.

Cordelia sat down, hard, in the chair opposite Malcolm's corpse.

A copy of the *Clarion* sat beside the empty bottle, doubled over and creased flat to show a chunk of midlist news. The article was headlined *Bumble Bee busted for ballast*. Malcolm's haunted mug shot stared out from between columns.

She could see him, almost, rubbing his thumb over the print, drinking himself down to the bottom of a handle of who knew what. Had he wondered where she was? Had he known? Ari might have told him, if he'd asked. What had finally put the revolver in his hand?

Her breath hitched, and the pain made her see stars. She

couldn't cry. It hurt too much, and it wouldn't get her even with the Ospies.

She tried to think what would. And somewhere in between explosives and assassinations, she drifted off into a red haze of sleep.

When she woke up it was dark and the storm was going full-tilt outside the kitchen window, pelting the glass with wind-driven rain. Lightning seared the room flashbulb-white, making the whole gory scene like something out of a moving picture.

Cordelia straightened, stiffly, and cased herself. Her body hurt worse than ever, but sleep had done her head and heart some good.

While she'd dozed and dreamed about revenge, something in her broken chest had changed. Not her ribs, not a muscle or an organ, but something deeper and more vital. It had turned hard and crooked, like a fracture healed up wrong.

The Ospies had killed Tory. The Ospies had taken the Bee. The Ospies had driven Malcolm Sailer to swallow a bullet. Cordelia wished he'd saved the lead; she would've liked to put it square between Caleb Acherby's eyes.

And who said she couldn't? Maybe not right away, and maybe not on her own. But she had time, and she knew people. Running for Ari had put her in touch with all sorts—money launderers and gunrunners and folk in every seedy trade imaginable. Not just small-timers, either.

They'd be nervous, sure, and rightly so. Her own smashed face was reason enough. But they had no love for the Ospies, and Cordelia had talked punters around to some wild schemes. Maybe not so wild as this, but what did she have to lose?

Her life. But she'd given that up for gone sometime yesterday, under the thin man's steel-toed boots.

CHAPTER

THIRTY-FOUR

Cyril didn't have a lot of time to plan, and the options available were limited. What he did come up with was half plot, half prayer—inelegant and brutal.

Night came more quickly than it would have a month ago. Summer was waning. Outside the window, the sun sank behind the iron fences of Loendler Park, and the cherry trees on Talbert and Blossom. The flowers were long gone, and the leaves had lost their springtime vibrance. The season felt tired. Cyril felt tired. He was relieved, in a way, to be bringing the whole mess to a close.

Even after sunset, he waited. Best to let his watchers grow weary, lose their edge. Besides, if a call came through and no one was there to answer it, he'd have the hunt after him sooner than he wanted. They played another hand of cards. He was getting sick of cutthroat.

Around half past two, someone rang and said they were ready for Cyril at the Warehouse.

"Let's have a toast," suggested Cyril, as Moore and Massey got ready to go. Both of them wore heavy nine millimeters in shoulder holsters. The guns shifted against their chests as they thrust their arms into the sleeves of their coats. "To my last night of freedom. Possibly, of life."

"A toast?" Moore laughed. "Why can't they all be like you?"

"We're on the job," said Massey, nervous.

"Shut up, Mass. One shot won't kill you."

"Bend your knees a minute," said Cyril, nodding to the sofa. "I'll be right back."

In his office, he poured three glasses of whiskey. Two of them got a spoonful of potassium cyanide, which Moore hadn't found in the liquor cabinet because Cyril disguised it in a sugar bowl. He always drank his liquor neat.

Back in the parlor, he offered the glasses around. Cyril said something inane about dying cleanly, and then they drank.

When Moore and Massey lay on the carpet, white vomit leaking from their mouths, Cyril went about his business. He changed into one of his winter suits—the charcoal gray would blend better with the shadows. It was too warm, but it wasn't permanent. His old service pistol and matching suppressor were in the spare bedroom with the rest of the weapons Moore had gathered in his security sweep. Cyril took Moore's shoulder holster and fit his own gun into it, then pocketed the suppressor. The false ID papers he put inside his waistcoat, pressed against his ribs. The letter he folded crisply into a small square and tucked into his ticket pocket. From beneath the washroom sink, he snatched a bottle of peroxide, and stuck it in a paper sack.

The city was quiet as an abandoned film set—curfew, he realized. There would be a curfew, after yesterday's riots. Well, good: no one to see him in the streets.

Finn lived in a row house off of Clifftown Road, north of the boring end of Princes Street—near the terminus of the Ionidous line. He'd looked it up earlier in the telephone directory. The neighborhood was shabby but clean, and mostly free of riot damage. Nothing up here to loot or deface. But lots of windows, and no black cars. Finn's tail would be indoors somewhere, with a good view of the street. Fine. Let them see Cyril walk in. They wouldn't get a good look at his face, even with binoculars. Not at this time of night, with his hat pulled low. He was just some sculler coming home late.

With the sack of bleach under one arm, he walked up to the door and reached for fictitious keys. Feigned surprise. Patted his lapels, as if looking in the pockets of his waistcoat. Finally, he pressed the buzzer for Finn's flat. Pressed it again. On the third, extra-long buzz, he got a sleepy answer.

"Sorry about this," said Cyril. "I, uh . . . I seem to have forgotten my keys."

The lock on the door clicked open, and Cyril let himself in and up the twisting staircase. The list of names on the buzzer panel had given Finn as the third floor. On the tiny landing, Cyril dodged a bicycle and an empty coal scuttle to knock softly on the door.

After a second, slightly louder knock, the door cracked and Finn blinked out from behind the chain lock. "Cyril?"

"Shh. Let me in."

The door closed, then reopened to admit him. Finn's dressing gown was hastily tied over rumpled pyjamas. "What are you—wait a minute. That was you, wasn't it? Who rang the bell?"

"Of course it was." He made sure of the lock, then ushered Finn into the kitchen and turned on the light. There were linen creases in the accountant's cheeks. "Listen, there's not a lot of time to get everything straight."

"What? Wait, how did you get here?" The sleepy squint dropped from Finn's face. "Pesteration, you weren't followed, were you? Did anyone see you come in?"

"Oh, *now* you care who sees us?" Cyril rolled his eyes. "No, I wasn't followed. Give me a little credit."

"Why are you here?"

Cyril flipped his jacket open and started unbuttoning his waistcoat. Finn looked doubtful, until Cyril produced the folder full of papers.

"For you," he said, slapping them onto the counter. "Cross passed them on. From an anonymous benefactor. I think we both know who."

"When was this?"

"After our . . . meeting the other day. You were right. I was wrong. Don't let it go to your head." He glanced at the clock on the kitchen wall.

Finn picked up the folder and flipped it open, examining the documents. "Why didn't she just give them to me?"

"For a number of reasons," said Cyril, "none of which we have time to discuss."

Finn's eyes raked him with suspicion, like jagged bits of stone. Cyril made himself give a little shrug. Finn dropped his gaze. When he turned the first page, a wrinkle seamed his forehead. "This . . . um . . ." He tapped the paper with his forefinger. "This doesn't match my description."

"Don't blame me," said Cyril. His fingers itched for a straight, but he hadn't brought any. "This is what Cross gave me. Anyway, you're about the right height, if you don't slouch."

Finn put his shoulders back and lifted his chin. It brought his eyes nearly level with Cyril's, where they lingered for a moment before flicking up and down. He tilted his head and pursed his lips, and Cyril knew he'd been caught out. But before he'd even had a chance to breathe—to apologize, explain—a worse realization struck him.

There was one crucial detail he had missed. One thing that ruined his entire rotten plan.

He had seen the name on those false papers.

He wanted to be sick. Horror and bile crept up the back of his throat, threatening to choke him. He'd been so careful with Aristide's instructions, not to read them, not to let Finn tell him where Aristide had gone. He'd meant to save Finn, and doing so, save Aristide.

But he'd read through those papers—thrilled like some giddy schoolboy to see his own description, to see the silly wordplay work name: Paul Darling. DePaul, darling. He could almost hear Ari purring it out.

He'd been so worried about Finn breaking under torture, so keen to send him out of the city. He'd never thought about the possibility he himself might break—he hadn't thought he had anything to sing about. But if he gave them that name, they could trace every move Finn made on his journey north, and it would be as good as if Cyril had led them to Aristide himself.

Once, he would have been confident he could keep the secret, no matter what they did to him. Before Tatié, when this was all a game. But he no longer held those illusions.

"Cyril?"

He blinked. Finn was staring at him, still holding the damned papers. "What?"

"I said, these were meant for you, weren't they?"

"I'm . . . I'm sorry?" He marshaled his thoughts around a single, unpleasant certainty. He knew how to solve this problem.

"Ari meant these papers for you. So you could come to him. I—I knew you'd been lovers but I never thought . . . Why are you giving them to me?"

"Because you need them," said Cyril, knowing very shortly, Finn would not. "I know about the memos. And someone's going to figure it out, sooner or later. You know where Aristide is, and if they question you, you'll give him up." Finn opened his mouth to protest, but Cyril cut him off. "No, it's true. Whatever novels you've read, or whatever the pictures have you thinking, people don't hold up under torture."

"Not even Central's foxes?"

"Sometimes not even them."

"So you're taking the fall for me?"

Cyril didn't say yes, didn't nod, but Finn seemed to have answered his own question.

"Holy stones, Cyril, I don't . . . I don't know what to say."

"Don't say anything." He set the paper sack on the counter. "Peroxide. It's not perfect, but it'll get you on a train."

"To where?"

"You know where." He handed Finn the bottle of bleach and didn't look him in the eye. "Get started."

He waited until Finn was bent over the bathtub, rinsing the peroxide from his brassy blond hair. There was no need for him to see it coming.

The noise of the shot against the cast iron made Cyril's ears ring. He felt a tug at his jacket, and turned to see the bullet buried in the washroom door. It had ricocheted and cut clean through the outer layer of his clothes, leaving his waistcoat intact. He let out a small breath, like a sigh but not quite, and stepped toward Finn's limp corpse.

Water from the tap made his viscous blood curl like worms. Gray pieces of brain moved with the current, jostling bone fragments and bits of chipped porcelain. Finn's head drooped below the rush of water. Cyril didn't fish him out—his face would be a mess.

He let his hand linger, for just a moment, between Finn's shoulder blades. The accountant had removed his pyjama top to rinse his hair. The skin of his back was still warm. Cyril's fingers covered scattered freckles, tracing them like points on a map. Poor idiot.

No. Not an idiot. Obviously clever, to have come up with the memo scheme, to have run messages for Ari all this time right under the Ospies' noses. So not an idiot. But a tool. A tool, for people he'd trusted and loved.

"Some people just aren't cut out for it," said Cyril, taking his hand away. He wondered who he was talking to. More importantly, who he was talking about.

The thing was, he could leave now. He wanted to kick himself. He'd planned this all wrong, expecting to end up in custody when he should have been expecting to run. What had Cordelia said? *You've always gotta be the one pulling other people off the tracks.* He had always thought of himself as selfish. Maybe he'd had the wrong idea.

Irrelevant now. He could take the papers and go . . . North, someplace. Damnation, he didn't need to find Ari, not right away. He just needed to get out of Amberlough and go to ground.

There was a chance. If he could make it to Bythesea Station

before the Ospies realized Moore and Massey had failed to report . . . He didn't want to let himself hope. It had ended so bitterly the last time, and seemed so heartless now, with Finn hanging dead over the lip of his own bathtub.

And yet.

He stole the bicycle from Finn's landing, careful not to let it rattle against the bannister or the steps as he carried it down. A little scouting revealed there was a back way out of Finn's building.

He took side streets in a roundabout route to the river, which he crossed. There were myriad ways into Bythesea from the south, through the train yards, but if one approached it from the direction of the central city, ingress was limited to the two sister bridges of Seagate and Station Way. If the Ospies were onto him they'd be watching both of those.

If the Ospies were onto him he'd be lucky to get out of the city at all.

He rode up to the high wrought iron gates of the station's western entrance, casing the approach as he went past. No one lingering . . . wait. Black bowler pulled low, smoking a cigarette just outside the revolving doors. The man's eyes were sharp under the brim of his hat. Some sculler taking a smoke break? Or was he waiting for someone of Cyril's description?

Hopping off the bicycle, Cyril deposited it in the rank against the gates, not bothering to lock it—he didn't have the key. He tried not to look at the man in the black bowler as he passed, but he did allow himself a deep, audible breath when those sharp eyes stayed on the street and didn't follow him through the spinning panes of the door.

Approaching the ticket counter, he hooked his thumb into his ticket pocket, where it brushed Ari's letter. He had the folder under one arm, and wished he had his briefcase instead. Traveling without luggage wasn't exactly inconspicuous. Still, it couldn't be helped, and he was already here.

This early, there was no queue at the ticket counter—wouldn't be, not for a few more hours. He approached the glass wearing what he hoped was the weary but charming smile of a man resigned to early travel.

The teller yawned and looked up from a crossword. "Help you, sir?"

Suddenly, he was viscerally glad he'd seen what he had of Aristide's instructions. "The five o'clock, northbound."

"How far?"

He tried to disguise his hesitation, wondering where he was supposed to get off. "Farbourgh City," he said. It was somewhere to start. "Second class." All he had was the money in his wallet, but in this suit he would stick out in a third-class compartment.

She started to make up the ticket, but caught herself halfway through. "Damnation. I forgot. Do you have your papers?"

"Must be hard," he said, handing over the folder, "with all these new regulations."

She started scanning the first page. "Like you wouldn't believe, Mr. Darling." Obviously reading from a cue sheet tacked to the inside of the glass, she asked "What's your reason for traveling to Farbourgh?"

"Business," he said. "I'm invested in a friend's venture and he wants to talk in person."

She nodded, uninterested, and turned the page to the physical description. She read it through, looked him up and down, and passed the papers back. "All looks fine to me. Let me just finish with the ticket and you'll be on your way."

Adrenaline pumped through his veins, making his limbs weak. She slid the ticket under her little window. He reached for it, thrilling. He'd done it. He'd absolutely—

In the reflection of the ticket counter's glass, movement caught his eye. Half turning his head, already knowing what he would see, Cyril looked over his shoulder.

The man in the black bowler came through the revolving doors, flanked by two other men, much bigger. There was a tense moment, stretched thin and sharp as wire across the gold-flecked expanse of marble floor.

Cyril dropped the folder. When he ran, loose papers flapped behind him like startled birds.

Coal smoke burning in his lungs, Cyril took the stairs down to the platform three at a time, leaping the final distance to the tile. Travelers were few and the rails were bare—the five o'clock wasn't due for another fifteen minutes. That left the end of the soaring glass enclosure, open onto the train yards. He jumped from the edge of the platform. A fraction of a second later, a shot rang out, and he heard ceramic shatter. A woman screamed.

He landed badly, slipping on the oil-stained concrete around the rails, but caught himself and leapt into a sprint. He tried to keep under the lip of the platform. Bullets cracked into the ground at his heels. A chip of concrete struck his calf, and he felt a sting and a trickle of hot blood tracking down toward his shoe. They were aiming to stop him, not to kill.

As he ran, he drew his pistol and rammed the slide back. No time for the suppressor now, and no need. There was an obvious answer here. The Ospies had clearly caught him. He'd be dragged back to the Warehouse and questioned. He wouldn't survive it. So why not just . . .

He skidded to a halt, just short of the open end of the platform. A stiff breeze came up off the harbor, whistling through the aperture. He turned and saw his pursuers gaining. He had the gun half lifted—could already taste the steel and oil, faintly laced with his own sweat.

When he hit the ground, his own consciousness surprised him until, dizzily, he realized he had never put the pistol between his teeth. They already had him cuffed by then, the men who had come from behind, from the yards.

He cursed himself for stopping and turning, for not shooting while he ran.

"Swear all you like," said one of his captors. "Won't get you anywhere."

Cyril took him up on it, spitting every foul word he knew until he broke down into helpless sobbing.

CHAPTER

THIRTY-FIVE

Aristide had trouble on the train; his back ached, and the seats were hard. It had been too long since he did something uncomfortable: He had gotten soft. He promised himself five minutes of intense self-pity, then resolved to move on.

Once upon a time, he had been inured to indignity. With the boneless resignation of a dog, he had lain on hardwood floors, blanketless. He had slept his way through the ranks of producers and financiers it took to pay rent and earn a place onstage. He had cut throats and sold bad tar and done whatever it took to get ahead. Because he knew once he reached the top he would never have to do any of it again.

Yet here he was at forty-two or some odd years, crammed in

third-class, headed back to the place he had done every demeaning thing on earth to escape.

He found five minutes of self-pity wouldn't cover it.

When the train pulled into Farbourgh City, he stood and stretched and rubbed his dry eyes. He wanted nothing more than coffee and a newspaper, but he hadn't the time. The local for Currin left in half an hour, and he still had to find his contact and give her instructions.

On the platform he pulled his collar up against the damp wind. The station here had a dark, flat roof that gave him no sense of the weather outside. Still, under the coal smoke he smelled rain. When he reached the doors of the station, it was indeed pissing down. A sea of black umbrellas ebbed and flowed in the open square, sifting around the stalls and carts of the Station Market.

Aristide had only seen this place once before, on his way out of Farbourgh. He remembered being astonished at the number of people, the goods on display. Now, it left him underwhelmed. Shabby merchants selling oily fried food and hard pasties . . . and there, just on the far side of the street from the station gates, a woman hunched underneath the awning of a fruit stall.

He browsed through her selection of pears, apples, and waxy oranges still green around the stems. Lifting a disappointing citrus, he said, "They're fresher in Amberlough City."

She looked up—not too sharply, but he had caught her attention.

"I get them straight off the boat," she said. She had the velvet burr of an urban Farbourgere, colored with something foreign. "When they come up the river."

"I know a man who can get you better," he said.

"I got a man," she said, irritated.

He let himself smile, slightly. "I know. You've got the best."

She cocked her head, pinning him with a suspicious glance. Then, a faint dawn of comprehension. "They told me you'd come."

She had no idea who he was, not really. She thought he was one of his own agents. So much the better. "Did they tell you what to do?"

She pulled a ragged brown envelope from beneath the grapes and handed it over. "Papers, and your ticket."

He put it into his jacket, then handed her a folded bill. "Thank you. And the other thing?"

"The grease-paws at the garage have an auto ready for him."

"He'll be here soon," said Ari. "Maybe tomorrow, maybe not for a week or so. He knows to look for you. He'll make a gibe about the oranges; ask to see his scar." He hadn't prepped Cyril for that. Which meant no one else would be expecting it, if they turned up instead.

She made a face. "That's a bit—"

"It will be right here." Aristide drew a finger down his abdomen. "If he doesn't have one, don't tell him anything."

A sharp whistle sliced the misty air. Aristide reached for his watch and realized he didn't have one. He checked the clock above the station.

"Must run," he told her. "Remember: the oranges, the scar."

She gave him a sharp nod, and turned back to her wares.

The platform at Beckover was exactly as he remembered it, though the boards were newer: just a pallet set up by the tracks to keep travelers' feet out of the mud. He was the only person disembarking. The train sighed steam and pulled away with a groan of steel on steel, leaving Aristide standing alone in the dusk. It came quickly in the Currin Pass, especially at the waning end of summer. As soon as the sun slipped behind the peaks of the Culthams, the temperature dropped and the air turned heavy with dew. Gentian light softened the edges of the crags and made the streams run black and spangled. A distant herd of sheep—pale smears in the gloom—trotted home over the tussocks of tangled grass that grew up the steep hillsides.

Time telescoped; he was a boy again, filled with the urgent despair of the young. He turned back to the tracks, but the train was gone. All that remained to him was the muddy road switchbacking up the mountain. He shouldered his bag and started up the path to his father's house.

It was exactly as small as he remembered it, and even shabbier. The dirty thatch needed changing, and the whole structure sagged in the center like a swaybacked horse. The single step was splattered with bird droppings and lichen. Aristide took it like a gallows march and put his hands to the door, letting his forehead fall against the damp-slimed wood and chipping paint. The hinges squeaked, and he went forward into darkness.

Fumbling, he found an oil lamp on the table and lit it, with a match from the dwindling pack Cyril had sent from the Stevedore. He set the chimney over the wick and the flame leapt up, showing swathes of cobwebs. A bird stirred in the rafters.

The mattress in the corner was old and flat, and when Aristide sat on it, the rope ties of the bed frame creaked. A few drops of rain rustled on the thatch, building into a steady patter.

It was colder inside than out, but he had no peat for the stove. Tomorrow. He would do that tomorrow. The thought filled him with exhaustion. He had not dug peat in almost thirty years; he had promised that he never would again.

He had escaped this house once, and he would do it once more. It would be easier. He was wiser now, and he would not be alone.

Closing his fist on the grubby pack of matches, he curled around his clenched hand and shut his eyes. Fully dressed and freezing cold, he lay awake and waited for morning.

CHAPTER

THIRTY-SIX

Cyril lost track of time; they left him in a windowless white room and didn't turn off the light. A fly had got in somehow, and careened against the bare bulb over and over and over again.

He thought it had been about a day. He was hungry, his throat dry, whole body aching. But when the blackboots came to haul him out, he fought, and they weren't gentle either. By the time they dragged him up the stairs, he could hardly see for the blood pouring into his eyes. Blinking the sting of salt away, he found himself in a chair opposite Van der Joost. In the back corner of the room, a thin man with rolled-up sleeves picked at a loose thread in his shirttail.

"Mr. DePaul," said Van der Joost. "I'm glad you made it to our meeting after all."

"Veedge," said Cyril, and spat blood on the table.

Van der Joost cleared his throat and smoothed a stray wisp of thin hair back into place. "You didn't hide Moore and Massey's bodies very well. In a hurry, were you?"

"You could say that."

"You must have been a very good agent, once."

"You've read my file," said Cyril.

"Indeed."

"And what do you think?"

"I think your poor sister will be awfully upset if you disappear."

A spike of fear, honed with guilt, stabbed him through. He hadn't reached out to her, first because he wanted to get out of this mess himself. She wouldn't have to sneak him dinner this time. Then, when it was too late, he didn't ask because he didn't want to tar her with his own treachery, his own failings. Well, she'd been splashed with that brush anyway, and now it was too late to warn her.

"Better than if I'd been hanged for treason," he said, with sour humor dredged up from somewhere in his cramping gut. "It'd wreck her diplomatic career."

"You should've thought of that before you leaked confidential documents to a black market profiteer."

Cyril snorted. A dizzying trickle of blood made its way from somewhere high in his nose and slipped over his lip, into his mouth. "I haven't even confessed."

"I think we can both agree your attempted flight was confession enough."

"So you're gonna bag me and tag me?" Van der Joost's bland face assumed an expression of distaste at Cyril's purposefully coarse language. "I'm a little disappointed in your—"

The blow to the back of his head wasn't really a surprise. He'd been expecting it since he sat down, with the thin man lurking behind him. Pinpricks of white and purple-black sparked across his field of vision. He forced a smile and felt his swollen lip crack.

"There," he said, tossing a bit of bloody, displaced hair out of his eyes. "That's more like it."

"Some things have come to light," said Van der Joost, "regarding Aristide Makricosta's involvement with a certain employee of the FOCIS. One Finn Lourdes. A friend of yours, I think?"

Cyril turned his face away. The thin man pushed it back.

"I knew him."

"'Knew'?"

Cyril didn't say anything. A slash of movement in the corner of his eye gave him half a second's warning. The fist in his hair hurt, but he managed to angle his chin so he hit the table with the meat of his cheek and not his nose.

"Hmm." Van der Joost watched him as he recovered from the blow. "I was hoping we could make this quick. I have a lunchtime meeting. However . . ." He looked over Cyril's shoulder. "Rehimov, will you see to him? I'll be back in a few hours to check on your progress."

Whatever motion the thin man made, it must have satisfied Van der Joost. He gathered his leather datebook and pen and set his hat on his head. "I'll be seeing you, Mr. DePaul."

"See me? Sure." Grinning hurt his face. The satisfaction was worth the pain. "But you won't hear a thing."

Cordelia stayed in Malcolm's flat overnight. It wasn't like she wanted to, but it was wet out on the street. Besides, if they weren't after her yet, they would be soon. She needed to keep hidden. And more than that, she needed a day or two to lick her wounds.

So she closed the bedroom door and shoved a blanket underneath it, trying to keep out the stink of blood and shit. Raiding Mal's drawers gave her enough white cotton for a bandage. Nauseous to the bottom of her stomach, she used her teeth to unwrap the grimy cloth from her cut-up fingers. Dried blood made the fabric stiff, and flaked off in rusty crumbs as she peeled the layers away. As she got closer to the skin, the blood was fresher, sticky and bitter. She gagged, but kept pulling cloth away.

The wounds were clean, at least, and she meant to keep them that way. She took Malcolm's good belt from its peg on the door and put it between her teeth. In the washroom, she turned the taps to hot and bathed the stubs of her fingers with lye soap. By the time she was done, she'd bitten straight through the leather.

Like a dead woman, she slept flat on her back without a twitch. When she woke, it was light out—the middle of the morning, from Malcolm's clock, but it probably needed winding. She lay in his bed, smelling him: sweat and hair tonic and cheap cologne. If she closed her eyes, it almost seemed like . . .

No. She sat up, gasping at the grinding pain in her chest, and put her feet over the edge of the bed. She wouldn't close her eyes, and she couldn't play pretend.

She'd always kept a compact in Malcolm's bedside drawer, and it was still there (next to a wad of cash she wasn't too proud to snatch). The bed of powder was cracked, but the makeup covered the worst of her bruises. There would be plenty of people walking around the city with rammed-in faces today, anyhow. The fingers were easy, too. She hauled Malcolm's khaki overcoat from its hook; the pockets were deep. Her eye-catching hair she twisted up and covered with Malcolm's brown felt hat. Pulling it low to hide her face, she made for the door.

Though she tried not to look, she couldn't walk out on him like that. Not when she was leaving him for the last time. Swallowing against the smell, she stepped into the kitchenette. The blood on the floor had dried tacky and tarry brown. There were already flies. Though Malcolm had shoved the gun in his mouth and kept his face of a piece, she couldn't pretend he was sleeping, or passed out.

Picking up the paper in front of him, she stared at his picture. He looked so *tired*. When she touched the newsprint, at least his cheek wasn't cold. She didn't want to feel him like that, when he'd always been hot as a radiator to the touch. As she ran her fingers over the photo, something in the column caught her eye.

"A cinema." She shook her head, disbelieving. "An Ospie picture palace. You stone-sucking half-wit." It sounded angrier than she'd meant it to, but she'd realized what she wanted to do, and the rage felt good.

Dropping the paper, she knelt to pry the gun from Malcolm's death-hard grip. As she uncurled each cold finger, she gritted her teeth and told him, "You always gave up on your fights too soon."

The chemist round the corner let her stand behind his rows of pills and powders and use his 'phone to call up Zelda Peronides. No one answered at the shop or the docks, so she tried the emergency exchange Ari had given her and told her never, ever to use. Not even in an emergency, if she could help it. It got her a gruff male voice, two rounds of pass codes, and eventually, the woman herself.

"Who is this again?" Zelda's voice was rough and deep—Cordelia figured she sounded about the same. Too much action, too little sleep.

"Ari's red-haired friend. We only met once or twice. But I got a little project and I need some help."

"Is there money in it?"

"Some."

"Will I laugh or cry when you tell me how much?"

"Depends how much you need it."

With a lot of exhausting double-talk, they set up a meeting that night on the edge of the southwest quarter; not quite in Eel Town, but not quite respectable, either. Cordelia killed time nursing one long pint in a dark booth at the Hare's Tail, alternating with some laudanum she'd pocketed at the chemist.

After the sun went down, she made her way to a nameless dive off Solemnity Street. Zelda sat in the back, dressed in frumpy dark clothes, peering over a glass.

"Ah yes," she said. "I remember you. Ari's runner. The stripper at the Bee."

"I'm flattered." She wasn't.

"What happened to your hands?"

"Busted." Cordelia lifted her broken wrist, swollen where her fingers peeked out from the splint. Then, her other hand. "Cut."

"Hmm." Zelda pursed her lips. "And what exactly do you need?"

"Dynamite."

"Of course you do. How much money have you got?"

Cordelia plunked most of Malcolm's cash down on the table. It wasn't a lot, and she'd skimmed some off the top just in case she needed it later. Zelda thumbed through the stack and made a face.

"This would buy you approximately enough to detonate a birdhouse. And I imagine you're aiming for something a little larger than that."

Cordelia ground her teeth. "All right. How much?"

"For what? The capitol building? Bythesea Station? Whatever it is, you can't afford it."

"Just give me a number. I'll make it work."

Zelda folded her hands and stared across the table, looking at Cordelia like she was a crossword, and there were a couple letters missing from the toughest answer.

"I know I shouldn't ask," she said at last. "And you certainly don't have to say. But does it have to do with that little Ospie face-lift they're proposing for the Bee?"

"Mother's tits." Cordelia sagged. "Did everybody know but me?"

"They *were* keeping it rather quiet, darling." Ice rattled as Zelda tipped her glass. "Though I must say I'm surprised that Ari didn't tell you."

Cordelia was more surprised—and shattered—that Malcolm hadn't said a word. She wondered if he'd known when they were fighting, and held it back to spite her. Or if he'd only found out once they were sparking again, and wouldn't tell her out of fear she'd leave.

"Lady's name, it will be grim." Zelda lit a cigarette, then offered one to Cordelia, who snatched it so fast she had to apologize.

"What will?" she asked, once she'd taken a drag. Breathing deep made her sore chest scream, but the shag sent waves of dizzy relief through the rest of her body.

"The blackboots showing patriotic flickers there. The Bee was the very best of its kind." Zelda sighed smoke. "I wish I could see it all as it was, one more time, before . . ." She spoke the last of her sentence with her mouth around her straight, and broke off to inhale.

Cordelia knew an opening when she saw it. She leaned close enough she could hear the soft *furze* of burning paper. "Well, you can't. And you won't for a while. Maybe forever."

"No. You're right." Zelda stared at the red tip of her cigarette, and the light of it made her dark eyes glisten like oil. "There's a story they tell in Hyrosia, about a queen who built the most beautiful palace in all the world. She filled it with exquisite art and rare animals, and a harem of a thousand perfect catamites. It was paradise on earth. Until a neighboring queen grew jealous and attacked."

Cordelia's focus narrowed. The sudden rush of tobacco, on top of her exhaustion, made her grasp at the threads of Zelda's story to stay in the moment. "What did she do?"

"She burned the palace and everything inside it, herself and her lovers included. When the rival queen arrived, there was nothing but a pile of smoking ash."

"Well," said Cordelia, "I ain't a fan of suicide. But the rest of it sounds all right."

"I can give you a name," said Zelda. "He'll come down on price if you haggle, and if you still can't pay, he might take a marker. He bears no love for the Ospies. Give him a kiss from me."

"Thanks a heap." Cordelia stubbed out the butt of her straight and stood to leave. "I'll give him two."

CHAPTER

THIRTY-SEVEN

Aristide waited a week. He got friendly with Farah Akin, the woman who owned the dry goods store at the mouth of the pass. She gave him a loaf of currant cake, the first time he visited her shop.

"To welcome you, like, Mr. Sangster." That was the name on his new papers. Memories ran long in the mountains. He couldn't afford to keep his old Prosser identity, though he had the identification on hand if anyone got pinned about the property.

The cake was heavy, and too moist. But he ate it, because sweet things seldom turned up in Currin.

The next time he came down to the store, Farah gave him a telegram that had come up from the city. The Akins had the only wireless receiver for miles.

No oranges stop Maybe next week stop

"Do you like them?" Farah leaned across the counter. "Oranges? We rarely get them in. Only around solstice, usually, and even then they're green and tart. The dates, though . . ." She scooped some from a jar behind the counter and poured them onto the counter. "They're my favorite. Can't imagine they'd be any better fresh. Care to try?"

Aristide took one of the sticky fruits and put it into his mouth, so that he did not have to speak. *No oranges.*

"You've gone pale, Mr. Sangster. Not to your taste?"

"No," he said, pulling the pit from between his teeth. "They're delicious. I'll have some to take home. And a few ounces of shag."

"Any more rolling papers?"

"No, thank you. I've still got some from last time."

She clucked and shook her head. "Ought to start smoking a pipe. You're not cityfolk any longer. It'll save you money, too."

Underneath the humdrum of commerce, Aristide's mind jumped from one possibility to the next. Cyril had misunderstood the directions, or made a mistake. Or he had been caught and tortured or—even worse—gone over to the Ospies entirely, in which case staying longer in the Currin Pass put Aristide in more danger every day. Very worst of all, he had read the letter and laughed.

Aristide smiled through the rest of his transaction. He flirted a little. Farah tipped a few extra dates into the paper sack before she folded the top. By the time he walked out, the mask of his face felt stiff. Among the brooks and gorse and muddy stone, he let the façade fall. His own weakness broke his heart, and frightened him.

By the end of his walk home he was desperate for a cigarette. Inside the cottage, the heavy stove had kept most of the banked fire's warmth. The small space was dry and cozy. Aristide scowled at its rustic charm—such a slim reward for cold nights and lean comforts.

Hunched over the table, he tried to roll a twist. He was not good at it. After three bad tries he curled his hands into fists and closed his eyes against stinging pride. He had been good at everything he needed to be, back in Amberlough. He'd had everything. Now, all he wanted was *one rotten cigarette*, and—

His next attempt wrapped up perfectly, and a cold weight settled in his stomach. He hoped he had not made some terrible bargain. There were more important things to hunger for.

Instead of smoking, he fed another brick of peat to the stove and opened the vents, then collapsed onto the squeaky cot in the corner. Lying on his side, he watched flames lick at the edges of the cast iron grate.

The play of light and shadow lulled him half into a dream, more memory than imagination. Rain swept the pavement outside the Bee, turning into steam when it struck. Fog curled around the crowd's ankles. Aristide stood beneath the marquee with his collar turned up, waiting for a hack.

They saw each other at the same time, through the milling crowd. In that look, there was professional assessment, followed by a swift and startling realization, not wholly welcome. Aristide saw his adversary's eyes widen. The man stepped back, not by much, then squared his shoulders and lifted his chin. Aristide wondered what small tells his own body had given.

They'd had a choice, when they met, but neither of them had made it. They were both tightrope walkers, by trade. It had just been another line to tread.

Lucidity stole over Cyril, pulling him from a hallucination he couldn't quite recall on waking. He had been sunk deep in insulating fantasies for days. Hide-and-seek with Lillian at Damesfort.

Lazy, golden hours of skipping class at university. Rain on the windows of the Citadel, the hotel where he had begun his liaison with Ari.

He slid from one to the next before he could remember: His capture made Lillian vulnerable. His indiscretions at university had funneled him into a career that ended here. And he would never see Ari again.

The scent of the docks cut through clots of blood in his aching nose: oil and damp and the meaty tang of brine—sharp enough to wake him from his daze. Sight returned more slowly than his other senses; if he hadn't smelled the ocean, he wouldn't have known they'd moved him. It must be high tide, for two reasons: The water covered the stench of the city's dross, and they had brought him out to kill him.

Bodies were only dumped from the back door when the currents would carry them out and dash them against the Spits, battering them until they fell to pieces. No identifying features, if they ever washed up. They didn't tend to.

There were two blackboots out here with him. He didn't recognize either of them from his interrogations—just drudges, probably. One was screwing a suppressor into the barrel of his gun. The other was talking, and his words gradually worked themselves into sensible order.

"—ought to go through and just see if there's anything worth taking," he said to his partner.

"Don't be stupid." The suppressor spun. "They'd have searched him."

"Ain't you even curious? It's a nice suit."

Hands on Cyril's chest, fingers curling into his pockets—careless of his broken ribs, and whatever was bleeding and bruised inside of him. A thin sound escaped his lungs, and the Ospie snorted.

"Nothing," he said, falling back. "Not a damn thing. In all

those pockets? How come you got so many pockets, huh? Fancy suit like that." He aimed a kick at the soft place between Cyril's hip and the bottom of his ribcage. Bones gave sickeningly, jagged edges sliding beneath his skin and muscles. He gagged and jerked away. The movement didn't get him far, and hurt worse than the blow.

Of course there was nothing in his pockets. He was surprised they'd let him keep his clothes. He'd been through the training; naked prisoners broke faster, robbed of their most basic protection. But then, maybe the Ospies had known from the beginning: Even if they stripped him down, he had nothing left to give.

Some time ago—days?—Rehimov had found the folded square of Ari's note. He read it out loud, or part of it. Then, he'd spat on the floor and torn the paper into pieces. Things went worse for Cyril after that; very much worse.

As his executioners prepared their necessary tools—a cigarette and a pistol, respectively—Cyril let himself hear the words of the letter, not in Rehimov's guttural eastern accent, but first in his own internal monologue and then, more and more, in Ari's tongue-curling central city drawl.

Cyril,

Practiced as we both are in clandestine correspondence, in false-hood and elaborate elisions, I find it difficult now to say precisely what I mean, and say it plainly.

I am leaving Amberlough. That much I may write with ease. It is no longer a city in which people like us—and we are each many things—can live with pride, pleasure, or freedom. And I am leaving on my own. You know as well as I do it's the most efficient way to get things done. But in this instance it feels far from satisfying.

There is a thread which ties my happiness to yours—this is the difficult piece to admit—and I fear that if I go too far, too fast, without you, it will snap and something vital in me will begin unraveling.

Cyril, is there a stitch in your heart as there is in mine? Then come and find me. We can start again. This time we will only tell small lies.

All my love,
Aristide

"Go on," said one of the blackboots. "Get it over with. Tide's going out any minute now."

"Don't rush me," said the other. "Damn thing won't screw in straight."

"Give it here. Look at those hands: shaking like an old drunk. Rotten amateur, you are. Go around the corner, if you can't stand the sight of brains."

"I can't just—"

"I said you can, so you can. I'll finish this, and we'll get on with the day. Shoo."

His footsteps faded away. The hiss of the suppressor's metal threads blended into the distant crashing of the waves against the Spits. Cyril realized he had closed his eyes. Seawater slapped at the pilings of the dock, splashing against his cheek. It was summer-warm, and felt like tears.

Then, as he breathed in, deeply as he could despite his broken bones, he heard a sound. Or felt it, more than heard. A deep rumbling, spreading in waves through the air and the dock beneath him. He opened his eyes, wondering if he'd already been shot.

As he did, he saw something so beautiful it could have been choreographed. The blackboot, all alone now, startled at the noise. He flinched and fumbled his pistol. The suppressor struck the planks and rolled away, but the gun fell straight and landed with a solid *thwack*, an inch from Cyril's left hand.

He had thought all his ties were cut; that his pliancy came from resignation. But when the pistol's steel struck the boards he realized that the strings which held him to his life were only hanging loose. He had not been resigned, but patient.

He was a cleaner shot with his right, but that hardly mattered now. He stretched out, every muscle screaming, and hooked his forefinger behind the trigger guard. The Ospie had his mouth open, about to shout. Cyril half aimed, and fired. The noise echoed off the backs of the warehouses.

It was a bad one, too low: between the ribs and groin. Gutshot. Deadly but not fast. Cyril needed fast. Straining, he lifted his arm and fired again. A lung this time. The man collapsed, blood leaking from his mouth as he struggled to breathe. Cyril rolled onto his side, gasping, and put the pistol to the man's head.

"Hey!"

The other blackboot came pounding down the dock, too late. Cyril pulled the trigger, then turned the gun toward the new arrival. He fired, but missed. The man—so young, almost a boy—skidded to a halt, eyes wide. Cyril tried to steady his shaking hands, sighting woozily down the barrel. If he would just stand still, just for a—

But he turned, and ran, and though Cyril squeezed off one more shot before he disappeared around the corner, it went wide and struck the warehouse bricks.

Well. Now what? He'd bring back others. And where was Cyril going, in this state?

Come and find me, Ari said.

He rolled off the dock. As the filthy water closed over his head, he wondered how far down the docks he'd make it before he drowned or found safe harbor.

———

The blast roared through the city like a tidal wave, rolling between buildings, pushing against Cordelia's body like a sudden, muffling wall.

Joachim—Zelda's man—had taken her up to the top of his building earlier in the evening and pointed out across the river. He had a good view of the theatre district, and she could see the Bee's roof framed between chimney pots. The setting sun turned the brick of the theatre's backside crimson.

Now, a huge cloud of gray dust billowed up and over Temple Street. Below, on the footpath, she heard sudden silence, then confusion. A shout, from a neighboring block of flats where someone hanging laundry on the roof had a good view.

"Mother and sons!" The rooftop door banged open. Cordelia looked over her shoulder and saw a woman scrambling up, followed by two schoolkids. "Is that the Bee?"

"Can't tell," said Cordelia, though her throat was tight. The words came out thick and sounded like a lie.

The woman didn't notice. She stared across the city at the twisting gray cloud of mortar and pulverized brick. The wind began to catch it, pulling trails of powder through the air. "They'd better clear the block." She shaded her eyes with a hand and squinted into the distance. "Big blow like that, there'll be—"

With a sound like ripping fabric, gouts of blue flame tore through the roiling fog.

"—gas," the woman finished, dismayed. She put an arm around one of the children, who had begun to cry. Little ones like that, they always picked up on it when grown folks got upset.

More people trickled up to join them, until a small crowd had gathered to watch the fire grow bright in the dusk. Engines had arrived by then; their bells echoed faintly from across the Heyn.

"What do they think they're doing?" An elderly woman with her hair under a kerchief put her hands to her face. "Somebody they don't like ends up in charge and they think blowing up a play-house will solve the problem?"

"You don't know that's why," said her son, holding her shoulder. "Nobody knows anything yet."

"Of course that's why," snapped a red-faced grandpa, wrangling baby twins away from the edge of the roof. "Bust up the whole city this week, and then start fires."

"Someone's got to do something." A young razor tore her gaze from the flames. "We all know it weren't a fair fight. Acherby's a thief."

"Even if he is," the old man said, "at least the blackboots didn't blow anything sky-high."

The razor snarled and turned away. A few of the other people on the roof shot narrow glances at the grandpa, but a few others nodded. Cordelia's stomach went sour, and she moved off a ways.

Joachim came up, eventually. He was a big bear of a man, bearded and soft around the middle. Jolly-looking, especially now, with a job well done.

"Like a solstice bonfire," he said, softly, so the assembled audi-ence wouldn't hear. "Harder to jump over, though, I'd wager."

Cordelia hunched her shoulders, burying her ruined hands deeper in the pockets of Malcolm's khaki coat. She'd kept it on, the last few days—she didn't have much else to wear. Traces of his cologne haunted the collar.

"You don't look thrilled," he said, taking her elbow to guide her farther from the crowd. "It's what you paid for."

"I know." She'd called in favors all over town to scrape his fee together.

"Regrets?"

She shook her head. "No. Never."

"What, then?"

Breathing deep, drawing in the smell of dry sweat and civet

clinging to Malcolm's coat, she held her old world inside until it seared her lungs.

"It's not enough," she said. It scared her, but it was true. "I wished it had all gone up."

Joachim grinned and tapped his chest. "I think I know somebody who can help."

The corner of her mouth snagged, like a hook had caught it. "I might need it," she said. "I'm starting to feel like I anted in for a long game."

He looked back at the burning hulk of the Bee, orange against the darkening sky. "What are you playing, anyhow? More than just revenge, I'm thinking."

"Tell you the truth," she said, "I don't really know. But I'm mad as a sow and I'm gonna make Acherby hurt."

"So it's politics? Kick out the new batch of scullers?"

She shrugged. "If that's what folk are after. I'm just here to scratch some Ospies."

Joachim nodded thoughtfully, then offered his hand. "Keep in touch, Red. Sounds like we could do some work together."

"Thanks," she said, and didn't shake. "I will."

He looked offended for a moment, when she kept her fists balled in her pockets. Then understanding flashed across his face and he offered his elbow instead. She pulled her sliced hand out and lifted it, knocking her forearm against his.

Frost was on the ground, the morning Aristide walked down to the Akins' shop and saw the papers.

There was a rack of them, at the front of the store. The Farbourgh *Herald* headlined, with the lesser provincial papers arrayed beneath, and papers from the other states in slots below. Nearly ten papers, in all, and every one of them with the same photograph above the fold.

"Oh, perdition," he said, so far gone he forgot to pretend to be northern, and merely fell into it out of shock.

"Terrible thing," said Farah. "Merciful queen, the workmen had the day off. But they're saying at least three people killed, probably a few more buried in the rubble. The whole block is shattered and burned. Anti-Ospie sentiment, they're saying. Rabble-rousers is what I'd call the fiends who did it."

"These papers," he said, ignoring her, "how old are they?"

"We get the *Herald* a bit earlier than the others, but I like to keep them all of a date on the rack. Less confusing that way."

"*How old?*"

"Oh, two or three days. Have a care now, love. Catch your breath. A terrible tragedy, but nothing we can do."

Nothing. He backed up and leaned against the wall. If he had still been there, he could have . . . well, he would have known, at least, before it happened. A professional job like that, there were two, maybe three people in Amberlough City capable enough to . . .

But he wasn't there, and it didn't matter. He was here, and soon he would be gone. Besides, the Bee wasn't Malcolm's anymore; it belonged to the Ospies. Or, no one now. It was a smoking heap of rubble. He wasn't sure if he wanted to laugh, weep, or rage. In the end, he turned and walked out of the shop without buying anything. As he left, Farah called out, "Mr. Sangster, wait!" But he didn't.

Something in him felt like it had been cut, leaving him adrift. Amberlough was a name, a fantastical city that no longer existed. He had said as much in his letter to Cyril, but realized now he hadn't truly believed it. The photograph of the smoking ruin on Temple Street . . . *that* convinced him.

Halfway up the hill, he heard footsteps on the path. Farah was jogging toward him, her sensible boots grinding stones into the mud.

"Mr. Sangster," she panted. "You had a wire."

His heart jumped, searing through the melancholy that had gathered in his chest.

"Thank you," he said, taking the yellow slip of onionskin paper from her outstretched hand. "I'm sorry, about earlier."

"Never you mind." She patted his arm. "These are hard times, and you're upset."

He half nodded, staring at the telegram. *No oranges.*

"I don't mean to pry," she said, "but do you know anyone in Amberlough? The way your face fell, when you saw that photo, I thought . . ."

"No." He had to swallow against a dry throat. Lies came to him easily. The truth was much, much harder. "No, I don't think I do."

He walked into gathering clouds with a curious feeling, like someone had finally drawn out a needle he hadn't felt go in: a pulling, emptying sensation that wasn't entirely unpleasant. There was nothing supernatural about it—he didn't believe in restless spirits or telepathy. He didn't know if the weightless, tugging feeling in his center meant anything beyond his own acquiescence.

It had been two weeks. Some people would wait longer, holding on to shrinking hope. Aristide was not one of those people.

It was not heartlessness. On the contrary, he ached. As he moved around the single room of the cottage, gathering what little there was to take, he pleaded with himself: *Stay, stay.*

But if Cyril was going to come by conventional means, two

weeks was more than enough time. If he was going to arrive via miracle, none of Aristide's actions would hinder him.

As he stuffed the first rolled-up pair of socks into his canvas rucksack, his knuckles brushed the pearls sewn into the lining. He'd never cut them out—there was no place to wear them, though not for the reasons about which Zelda had cautioned him.

He had left this place for something better, once. For furs and footlights, absinthe and artifice. For things he had not even known he wanted. Maybe—it hurt him to hope, but maybe—he could find those things again.

No way to know but try.

ABOUT THE AUTHOR

LARA ELENA DONNELLY is a graduate of the Clarion Writers' Workshop, as well as the Alpha Science Fiction, Fantasy, and Horror Workshop for Young Writers, where she now volunteers as on-site staff and publicity coordinator. In her meager spare time, she cooks, draws, sings, and swing dances. After an idyllic, small-town Ohio childhood, she spent time in Louisville, Kentucky. She currently resides in Harlem, in a tower named after Ella Fitzgerald.